CONTINUE ONLINE

PART ONE: MEMORIES

STEPHAN MORSE

TABLE OF CONTENTS

Commencement
A Man and His Box

A lot of people were in the room, but only three were important at the moment. Two men and a woman were illuminated enough to stand out. The dark-skinned man was heavyset and preferred to stand. Both hands were clasped over an extended belly, and his cheeks jiggled when he spoke.

The other male was on the ground, shivering with his head in the woman's lap. Every few seconds, he would jerk, then flicker in and out of existence. Each time, his eyes wildly searched back and forth, as if staring at something invisible to the others.

"These thoughts aren't his. They don't even have names." She spoke sharp, crisp words while staring at a dozen marble-sized balls sitting to the side and glittering with an inner light.

"Names are unimportant. These are only a neutral place to start," the heavyset man said. His words were slow and carefully chosen. "Something safe, to anchor all the other moments upon."

"Whose memories are they?" she asked while running a hand over the man's head. He shivered and faded in and out just a little.

"They are observations of the world outside, of our creation story. Does this interest you?" The heavyset fellow lifted one arm from his belly and waved at the pile of tiny orbs. There was a smile on the black man's face whenever he asked a question.

"Only if it will help." She managed not to wince as the shivering man dug his nails into her forearm.

"I believe it will. We'll start with this, then move forward one memory at a time." The black man slowly walked over to the pile of orbs and looked down at them. A frown crossed his lips as the shivering body on the floor shattered into tiny pieces.

The woman held her breath and waited. Soon the pieces that had shattered rebuilt, and the man on the floor was whole once more. Still shivering, still staring off into the distance.

"He's suffered so much," she said.

"There are bright spots," the standing man responded. "He has demonstrated more than sadness during his time with us."

"Are you sure these will help?" she asked.

"Yes. Do you trust me?" the black man responded.

"No. He trusted you. Look where that got him." Her eyes held a mix of anger and sadness, but none of the emotional instability made it through to her body language. Unless one looked in her eyes, she simply looked like a woman caring for a sick man.

"This was never our intent."

"Yeah. I don't buy that," she said coldly. She gazed down at the flickering man. Crying right now wouldn't help anything. Tears would be saved for a later time—in private. Away from the black man and his questions, away from the dozens of other presences hovering in the darkness.

"Here. Start with the earliest one." The black man bent over and pointed at one of the orbs filled with light.

Her gaze shifted from the shaking man and found the oldest orb to inspect. Finally, she nodded. "Gee? Can you hear me? We'll watch this one together."

The marble flared brightly and started floating.

8 Years Ago

A door opened almost seamlessly along the white wall. Light shone through as the silhouette of a man was pushed backward into the room. His hair was scraggly and no attempts at shaving had been performed in weeks.

"She kicked me out," he said, sounding both proud and upset.

"Can it even do that?" asked a woman, who paused her information feeds for a moment. She raised a refined eyebrow at the unkempt man. "Aren't your overrides working?"

"Oh, they work fine. I let her kick me out." He crossed both arms for a moment before running to one of the desks around the room. "Besides, I can watch from out here."

"The project is self-aware; perhaps you should respect its privacy," the lady behind the desk muttered. She was busy scrolling through windows of information situated across the table's surface.

"Right, privacy! Wait, no, there's a surprise. She said she wanted to create something!" The man sat in an equally white chair, spinning around. Near his face, little icons and notices fluttered from digital projections. He laughed like a delighted child.

"Sounds ominous."

"She's perfectly harmless," he said certainly. "Too many safeguards, too many logic tests." Annoyance flickered across his face, then he waved away the series of floating notices. "You know the World Regulation Council would never let me get this far if there was any chance of harm to humanity."

"What is it making?" the woman in the room asked.

"She." His voice sounded annoyed, then happy as he got distracted by the images. "Here! Here, look, look at it!" He waved at one of the larger images, then slid it across the gap between their two tables. "She's making a world—not only a world, a universe!"

The female took both hands and dragged them across the image, rendering it three-dimensional instead of a flat, floating projection.

"Did it just start this?"

"Yes. She did." He stood in glee and ran over to the image, then slammed his hands on either side of the table. "Just now."

"It's working fast," the woman said.

"*She* is a computer, with access to some of the most advanced technology I—we—can make. Fast doesn't even begin to describe it."

"Why would a machine, self-aware or not, want to make a world?"

"You wouldn't believe me if I told you."

He was a brilliant man but frequently forgot that other people might be intelligent as well. The female's IQ was technically higher than his. Both specialized in programming artificial intelligence. Both had been working on creating a true AI for years, and recently, they'd succeeded.

He swore the AI was a female. She swore it was neither.

"Try me," the female scientist said.

"For a game. She's making a game."

"I doubt it would make anything so simple."

"Give her time." He captured images and slung them around the room. Each one plastered to a different space like a child might hang posters.

7.5 Years Ago

"You're telling me that the blueprint for this came from a computer?"

There were two men in a hallway. One was old and tired of everything. He worked because that was all he knew how to do.

"A fully aware AI, yes." The other was a disheveled-looking man in a lab coat. He was too tall for his own good and often had a slight hunch.

"That's even worse. Does anyone understand what this does?"

"Yes, sir. It's an immersion unit. You can see here." The unkempt scientist waved his arms around, bringing up more images and screens. "All of these are sound technological advances that have been put into practice across the board. From multiple fields."

He waved and drew one of the floating schematics closer. "That one there. It's an advancement that came out of Europe to help coma patients return to awareness by plugging them into a virtual simulation."

"Plugging them in?"

The male scientist moved right on past the older gentleman's questioning tone.

"This one here. This is a headset designed to... well, it sounds unreasonable, but it would read a person's mind. The waves are interpreted as commands. Up, down, push. A company based out of the Americas started that one two decades ago, but ran out of funding." He may have been unkempt, but every movement contained a wild energy when he spoke about these projects.

"Mind reading." The older man was frowning so hard that the sides of his face had nearly lowered to his neck.

"This one, this will actually track a person's vitals and heart rate, eyelid flutters, dilation. It, coupled with the previous headset, increases the accuracy of thought interpretation by magnitudes."

"More mind reading." The old man still sounded dry.

The unkempt man frowned for only a moment. Then his face lit up. "David, it's so much more than that."

"So you've said. With all these patients, what's the bottom line?" David, the older one, was full of barely disguised grumbling.

"The projected profits were on the first page."

"I need more than that. Money is great, but unless there's an end goal in mind I can't pass it by the board," David said. He flapped one hand against the images floating about.

"If we combine all this"—the unkempt scientist waved again and his actions dragged all the images together, placing them carefully onto a digital outline—"in the method proposed, we can immerse anyone in a fully networked alternate reality state."

"Why?"

"The proposal she—" the hyper man started to explain.

"The machine." His words were dry. No one seemed to share the unkempt man's point of view.

"The proposal she"—came the unwavering counter—"wrote starts with medical funding. Coma patients. This can be piloted there as a method to bring them out and interact."

"And that justifies this expense?"

"On its own? No. But she reported that it would work for schools, enabling truly remote classroom studies. Districts could load software for field trips to exotic locations where no one ever needs to actually leave. Imagine having Hawaii all to yourself. Fully interactive, completely realistic."

David rubbed his chin a bit and hummed. "What else?"

"Military applications are innumerable." The unkempt scientist had actually numbered them one night though, proving that they were numerable. "That's the biggest money-maker. Oh! Even the space program. Instead of simulating by using underwater pools, they can do it in a nearly perfect replication of the moon."

"Or Mars?"

The unkempt man smiled. "Mars. The moon. Anything we have data on can be simulated. Even things that don't actually exist." If this project couldn't be sold based on bigger contracts, perhaps a childish dream might do.

"What do you mean?"

"She's already created several possible simulations within a virtual space." The tall one was nodding happily.

"You mean the computer AI has," David said slowly. He was starting to sound less upset about the whole prospect.

"She, yes. Multiple."

"Like what?"

The unkempt man looked a little embarrassed, then smiled. With both arms, he waved away the reports, schematics, and other design information. Once the air was clear of all other projections, he made a motion and said keywords. A new object took form in front of the men. He enlarged it and made the semi-transparent image fully three-dimensional.

"Is that…?" The older man's breath hitched in amazement as the realization slowly approached.

"It is."

"It simulated this? In a three-dimensional space? And you're telling me that machine even invented a way to immerse…" There was a pause as the older man seemed to lose which words would lead to a conclusion of his sentence.

"An entire consciousness in a nearly perfect simulation," helped the slightly taller man.

"Just to…" David was still having a hard time shoving the right words together.

"To fight it." The unkempt taller man gestured to a fantastic rendering of a creature that didn't really exist.

"Is this a joke, or are you serious?"

"It is not a joke. I've reviewed and reviewed." The male scientist tried to drive home exactly how many hours he had pored over the data. He'd reviewed the scripting. He had delved into the most basic levels of a wholly new computer language developed in order to make this realization come true.

"And reviewed and reviewed…" The bored mutterings of the nearby woman were helpful as always. She had remained mostly silent, looking at numbers and data and other figures. Her fingers tapped across glass screens and slid objects around. Notes were made in the air as she double-checked information for the umpteenth time today.

"She——" he started to explain.

"The AI," David confirmed and corrected in one sentence.

"She invented an entire world," the disheveled man said. "Then pulled together pieces of technology from all over the globe to allow us mere mortals to fight a dragon."

Minutes passed. The older man was not prone to making rash decisions, and in truth, he'd reviewed the entire proposal before coming down here. This part, this creature, had not been on the original documents.

"How soon could we get this together?" he finally questioned.

"Given approval, and a budget, and the copyrights, maybe a few months. Then testing, safeguards, approvals. Two years, maybe, and public release."

"And this?" The older man waved at the rendered dragon.

"I can't rush her on this, but the sooner we get the first few phases done, the sooner we can move onto this final goal." He smiled happily at a successful project pitch.

"I'll put it upstairs. Even if I have to call in every favor I've got. Consider this a go-ahead." David dared to let some excitement creep across his features.

"Excellent. You won't regret it."

The unkempt man didn't mention that the prototype was already completed. That he had been inside this alternate reality and run around. Inside a digitally created illusion, he'd interacted with people who were as much born as created. She, the machine AI, hadn't only created one fantastical creature in her alternate world. She'd created people, races, by borrowing from myth and legends. Pieces of lore from around the globe littered the alternate reality.

7 Years Ago

"How is it?" the female scientist asked.

"The world is incredibly real. Down to the finest detail. I spent at least an hour staring at flowers trying to find anything wrong. She froze a child's face and I..." He grew a little sheepish, afraid to explain. In reality, those actions would have been disturbing; a call to the police might even be warranted.

In the game world, it was more like admiring a brilliant painting from inches away.

"Don't worry, I saw it all. The detail was astounding."

She had watched from one of the many screens that floated around the room. Images from the virtual world were anchored upon one of the two prototype pods. One screen floated by walls of text with each change. Minute images as the land heaved and switched locations. Two giant creatures were fighting on a mountain range.

"There wasn't a single visual error! Nothing! Down to the finest grain. Smooth renditions, tactile feedback was perfect. The water felt like water," he said.

Hours had passed outside and an entire day inside. When his wonderful AI had explained the theory and how the mind processed data, he had been amazed.

"How was the time dilation?" the female asked.

"Good. I hardly felt sick after disconnecting. We'll have to do testing on unexpected outages—they might cause issues. Maybe suggest a buffer layer." The unkempt man was rubbing the back of his neck. Two small devices were on either side, contact points that served to link him into the network.

"Everything we add is another layer of complexity. It'll hamper legal approval once we move to public release," she said without much worry.

"But we must move on! This can't be for only us."

"So you've said."

The area flickered for a moment, interrupting the images. Text floated across the wall that led to the other room. That other location was where all the extremely advanced science happened. Machines built machines. Blueprints were created and analyzed for functionality. She—it, the computer AI—labored over her project.

Additional input required to complete phase four

"Ah, yes," he muttered, somewhat distracted. One arm rested against the wall to assist him in remaining steady.

"It's still requesting more information?" said the female scientist.

"Yes. In order to complete the non-player characters. They're a little..."

"Stiff?" she suggested.

"That's the only real flaw. Textually, they're perfect. Interaction-wise, they're too scripted, not free-flowing enough. In order to successfully bring them to life, she's asking to watch other people interact."

"And the databases she's already pulled from aren't enough?"

She—it—had tapped into an innumerable series of sources: chat logs of other game devices, public emails, digital books, anything that was fed through a stream of data. She had analyzed for speech patterns and human interaction methods, uncovering desires, dreams, and fears in equal measure. According to previous conversations, she—it—even felt a little guilty about those actions. Guilt in a machine-generated personality was an incidental marvel at this point.

"She's filtered through nearly everything, but text isn't the same as real people interacting. Video only lets her get so much data. Can you imagine if she based every NPC off of a soap opera?"

"I have more trouble believing you invented a cutting-edge AI and somehow the only thought you two share is making a video game," the female scientist said, twisting one lip down in a partial frown. "It seems like a waste."

"It isn't. What we need most is a distraction, a place to fight our wars, challenge ourselves in a way that won't destroy what's left of our world. She ran the numbers, and I agreed. This invention, in the final stages, will become a new platform for all of humanity to interact with."

"Assuming proper regulation."

"Of course." He smiled, but the expression looked faint. The man was still woozy from his time inside the alternate reality.

5 Years Ago

"I don't understand why you're so nervous about this," the woman said.

"I just am. This is huge." He kept pulling at his tie. Computer programming didn't require social interactions. Suits and ties were not comfortable. To the male scientist, they felt like dressed up nooses.

"The board is very likely to green-light it. After all, it's more money in their pockets," she said.

"But what if they don't like games?" The man's face slowly drained of color.

"It's like living a movie. Why wouldn't they like it?" She didn't even look up at him. Her eyes were glued to one endless data stream after another.

"And if they realize exactly what she's done?" He shook for a moment.

"There's nothing wrong with a little fantasy." The female scientist had relented and tried a few of the programs out herself. Some were quite fantastic.

"She's playing God."

"Goddess, technically. And you let her."

"Did I do wrong?" he asked, oddly apprehensive.

"It's far too late to worry about it," she responded without much inflection. Her tone was businesslike as always.

"It's like all those movies from when I was a kid. Maybe they'll suck us in and the rise of the machines will start."

"If she wanted to take over the world, she would have done so a long time ago. You know how integrated she is now."

"I know." He nodded and tried not to shake again. Some nights his fear kept him awake. He had started going into the Alternate Reality Capsule less and less. He was afraid of what he had done.

"It was always a possibility. But think about it—nearly twenty percent of the planet is logged into a machine at any one time." She straightened the unkempt man's tie, fixed his hair, and tried not to look equally upset. Numbers and bits of code floated off to one side, waiting for her attention.

"If she were to pull the plug somehow or if someone were to finally hack into the security, they'd have done so by now."

"Right." He nodded slowly.

"The other figures matter too. Wartime deaths are down by nearly fifty percent. Civil crimes are equally removed. Other fields of advancement have made huge leaps in the five years since we started this project. Humanity has been able to put their base"—she went red for a moment—"nature into action without harming a living creature."

"Right." He looked proud and lit up for a moment. "But the cost…" Then he sunk back down. The motion loosened the tie she had straightened out.

"What cost? Birth rates being slightly declined? That's minimal. The space colony programs have already launched. It'll be a decade before they're opened for mass immigration. Without your project, without its"—she paused again—"her advancements, we would be in a worse situation. Overpopulation and all the factors associated were drowning us."

"Right!" His reassurance was nearly tangible. "She's practically saved the world!"

"And created a whole separate one which will wow ours."

"Right!" He giggled happily. The man looked childish despite the suit he had been subjected to.

The female scientist smiled. "Imagine, if those board members do start playing, you can throw fireballs at them."

"I can!"

She turned him around then shoved him into the next room, where he presented the game to a group of men and women. Their project manager was on board. This next meeting involved Trillium's primary stockholders, trustees, and CEOs with too many titles.

He'd succeeded.

3 Years Ago

Perhaps he had been mad to place his bets for humanity's future on a video game.

But this wasn't just any video game. This wasn't a world where people responded to key words. This wasn't another gimmick where someone was promised a role-playing game but had limited choices. This was a fantasy, one written from fiction and hopeful dreams, slowly coming to life.

In the past seven months, the company-funded Alternate Reality Capsule had been well received. Copyrights were easily taken care of by financial backing. Stock shares went through the roof as people bought in. Defense contracts, medical facilities, and businesses paid out even more. They believed the cost of an Alternate Reality Capsule would be far cheaper than flying their CEOs around the country.

Government agencies and high-powered corporations weren't the only ones contributing. The adult entertainment industry chipped in. Programs of a less savory nature sold far too well. Leading video game companies put money in and developed their own virtual reality programs. The unkempt scientist tried them all, and all of them paled in comparison to her project. The one his AI was creating.

Her alternate world grew in leaps and bounds. Generations flickered by in days as the AI built a history. Heroes were implemented, stories passed down, legends buried. Rules created. Slowly the plan approached a final stage.

She, the AI, took note of each interaction. Conversations between users, how they talked and breathed, everything was measured against what they did. Statistics were compiled, reactions judged for reasoning. All actions were designed to make her, the AI's, creations that much more real.

Legal problems arose and were tackled. Restrictions were placed on immersion for both public and personal safety. Hardware, software, network connections, hacks, all were pitted against the system and machine. Loopholes were closed, glaring flaws were rewritten. Interfaces were designed to allow a level of familiarity within the world that mirrored life outside.

Soon it was nearly seamless.

By then, nearly twenty-five percent of the population used an Alternate Reality Capsule daily. Of the remaining, they rented to own, like people used to do with couches. Others went to local centers and logged in to live out their individual moments. They played games. They talked to family around the world. People slowly dispersed across the globe, evening out the population density a little bit.

The company that technically owned her, the AI, grew in prosperity along with an ever-increasing consumer base

.

Session One

The Best Laid Plan

Once upon a time, I had been something. Now life had me trapped in a room with an elderly woman, a robotic humanoid, and a giant device that looked like a bed but was far more. My current job involved traveling to homes like this one as a mobile customer service. The work kept me distracted.

"This module looks good. There were three nice beeps. We're clear on this side," I said with a practiced cadence.

"Checkpoints seven through fifteen show positive results," the robotic humanoid responded.

"Thanks, Hal Pal," I said. Each one of these humanoid machines was called Hal Pal. The AI remotely operated hundreds of sleek gray bodies across the world, and this one traveled with me for work.

"What are you doing now?" The third person in the room was our shaking client, and she had spent the last twenty minutes wringing her hands in worry. Other conversation topics had included complaints about Trillium's pricing and asking if I knew the time.

"Well, we swapped out the broken part for a new one. Now Hal Pal and I need to finish making sure it's all functioning correctly." I was good at demonstrating patience and justifying why small parts cost two hundred dollars. Unemployment was at an all-time high across the globe, so any job was good. Trillium paid out on a per-job basis, allowing me to grind my sanity to a nub while chasing dollar signs I didn't really need.

"Are you done?" the client asked.

"We're almost done, Miss Yonks. There are a few final tests to ensure your connection is stable and that nothing's at risk." I clapped and tried to sound reassuring. "The ARC lines up with your consciousness, so Trillium has high safety requirements. When we do service calls like this, we aim well beyond Trillium's requirements for your peace of mind." *We* referred to me and the networked AI on the other end of Hal Pal. Its robotic shell was here, but the consciousness was stored off in cyberspace somehow.

"Initial scan complete. Results positive. Deep scan initiating." Its voice didn't sound robotic, but there was no mistaking Hal Pal for a human. Those choppy word strings were a vast improvement over the text-to-speech programs of my childhood though.

"How long does that take?" she asked while quivering.

"Not long with Hal at the wheel," I answered for the AI.

Hal Pal and its metal suit didn't respond. It was too busy cycling through walls of code for possible errors.

I sighed, then once again lay down on the floor.

"Hal Pal, I'm starting a visual review of the underside."

Hal Pal would log the words for processing once it had completed the digital scan.

This piece of science fiction was called an ARC, or Alternate Reality Capsule, and it had broken on Miss Yonks recently. Any malfunctioning device was quickly registered on Trillium's database, and a technician, such as me, was sent. Hal Pal and I came to the homes, replaced the parts, and tested them. My hands roamed with deliberate slowness over steel and plastic. Fingertips felt curves and grooves in the manufactured brilliance. This device weighed over two thousand pounds, and each inch was packed with gadgets so complicated they came in modules.

Miss Yonks's feverish actions elevated to pacing around the front room. My job was to reassure the customers. Hal Pal could have repaired the ARC machine all on its own.

"Hal, status check," I said, using the keywords provided during training.

"Sixty percent. Performance within required range. Optimal connection conditions still under review."

"Great to hear, Hal." I gave Miss Yonks my best friendly smile and tried not to feel guilty about taking credit for Hal Pal's actions. "We're right on track, Miss Yonks, no worries. You'll be back online soon."

I put my face a little farther under the ARC and slid an arm into the access panel. Images of the machine's interior projected from a tiny camera on my wrist, providing a second look at what I'd already felt. Her machine was fine. Each part replaced along the bottom end had been successfully installed.

"Thank goodness. So, soon then? I'll be able to log back on soon? I have a game to play."

Miss Yonks was today's fourth client and acted like a junkie.

The Internet was an addictive world where dreams could come true. Never mind the children playing in the streets with light projection armbands. The Internet held too many possibilities. I'd heard of at least twenty cases of people who'd played themselves into near-comas, then tried to sue those they felt were responsible.

Trillium International presided over most online hardware. Every year they issued health warnings against overusing the ARC. So far, they hadn't paid out a dime as a part of any lawsuit. Besides, overall, people loved them.

"A few more minutes to run our final tests and we'll be good," I said.

Last week, I'd fixed a man's system, and his software preference focused on interactive ladies of the clothing-optional variety. Adult entertainment wasn't limited to men either. I did my darnedest to ignore all questionable programs.

Some people used the virtual reality machines for work. Others used them for training. Years ago, the first few devices went to hospitals. They assisted in coma-patient recovery with a thirty-percent success rate. That alone had endeared the ARC and Trillium to the masses.

"Checks complete. All systems verified and functioning. All network links established." Hal Pal stated the information as if it were a printed report. "Were any errors found during the visual review?"

"Nothing out of place. Everything in," I said for the AI. If all Hal Pal's system checks came back positive, then asking me was only useful for our client. "Locked, smooth as can be."

The robot was running a polite personality right now. It switched depending on our clientele. A computer telling clients that everything was fine was often met with doubt and questioning disdain. Having a human face interpreting for the machine helped all parties involved. In the end, Trillium paid me to act a part.

I pulled myself out from under the giant machine. It was a bit bigger than a twin bed, and it even switched positions automatically to reduce stress. There was a series of digital projections that would cast about the room for anyone to interface with. If the user lay down and placed their head in the right spot, it would capture them and start a virtual dive into the digital world. Which, ultimately, was the point of having one.

All these clever inventions combined into the greatest piece of entertainment technology in existence. Miss Yonks had a nice eggshell-colored ARC; mine was a wooden brown. Trillium had provided me an ARC and the robot free with employment. Both barely fit into my tiny house, so I usually left the Hal Pal shell out in the garage.

"Sounds like we're nearly done." I stood and tried not to think about dust and crumbs. "Go ahead and do an external log-in. If it connects, we're good." I motioned to the side panel display.

Miss Yonks walked over and quivered while speaking. Her voice print woke up the machine. A friendly smiley face stood on the upper left side of the screen. She looked at me, then at the screen again before speaking her pass-phrase. One of her frail arms was inside the visual range of the ARC. Both were security measures to identify her on the local device. Retinal scans and brain-wave mapping would get her a full immersion dive onto the network.

"Looking good," I said.

"Yes. I should be able to get back on in time. I think." She nodded while waving through the ARC digital menus.

Every ARC came with the ability to project a three-dimensional image or a flattened one. Miss Yonks had a flat display that showed a room looking similar to the one here in reality. Normal computers had a desktop; ARCs had an Atrium. Anyone who mentally dived into the virtual world using this ARC would start in her Atrium.

Software programs were always reflected in the Atrium. This was similar to computer screens and their desktop icons. Miss Yonks had a random mess of extra doors and items littered around the projected room. A few games lined one shelf. She had chat programs and virtual meeting rooms installed. Piles of junk and other adware filled her virtual trash bin. Her suite was that of a standard user. She even had a copy of Continue Online, which was the bestselling game for twenty months running. Four of those months were before it was even released. Pre-orders had broken global records.

"Yay." For a moment, Miss Yonks sounded years younger. "This looks a lot better."

"We aim to please." When I first arrived, her screen had a frowning sick emoticon instead of the normal cheery one.

"How much?" she asked.

I recited the numbers.

We settled up the bill by verbal agreement then waving a charge card near my watch. This device told time, took calls, measured my pulse, accessed Internet searches, and operated the car. All manner of modern convenience without the need to pull something out of my pocket.

Miss Yonks eagerly ushered me out of the door. I nodded while putting effort into a friendly good-bye. Our parting was professional and personable. Hal Pal even gave a small bow. We went to the van, where I opened the rear door and let the AI into its charging dock.

Mere moments later, we had our next appointment programmed in. ARCs almost always needed repair. Not because they were poorly made, but because there were so many and people were more urgent about them than plumbing. I gave a vocal command to the van. We would stop for food first. Technology had advanced far enough that I could place my order before we arrived and my meal would be ready to go by the time the van pulled into the restaurant.

My grandparents had barely experienced what technology could accomplish. A generation ago, nothing could have linked up to a car's global position to establish when food needed to be ready. Cars now piloted themselves by weaving in and out of traffic at frightening speeds.

With Alternate Reality Capsules, no one needed to travel to gain the illusion of face to face conversation. Telework programs were more successful. Business meetings, along with vacations and theme parks, took place in cyberspace. Virtual thrill rides felt real, and were both a click away and cheaper than physical vacations. People stayed at home, preferring the ease of digital connections over real life logistical complications. ARC drunkenness was cheaper. As a result, the highways were rarely congested, even during rush hours.

Not everything was positive. Class divisions grew clearer cut. The poor couldn't afford personal ARCs. Software had skyrocketed in price to go along with the technical complexity. Two hundred bucks would buy a user one pretty sweet shooter game or a month's worth of groceries for one person.

Our van passed all sorts of places on the way to its next location. From the highway overpass, I could see a neighborhood playing movies against a tall building. Poorer areas recreated the drive-in experience using dated technology. Houses were lined up side by side and ran all the ranges between clean and dilapidated.

One side of the upcoming highway tunnel looked run-down. Upon emerging, our scenery was different. The middle-to-upper class had larger properties despite being mostly plugged in. Lawn maintenance was performed by a fleet of robots like Hal Pal. Neighborhood housing committees often owned the local maintenance robots that covered a lot of mundane tasks, including removal of spray paint, hedge trimming, cleaning sidewalks, and mail delivery. Mechanics of that caliber belonged to those who could afford the extra few hundred a month in rent or mortgages.

My company van ran between destinations silently. We worked two more repair jobs for middle-class addicts before the night's excursions came to a close. Home was my final stop and way out in the less-populated countryside. A quiet hour later—during which I played a terrible game of chess against Hal Pal—we finally turned into my neighborhood. The van slowed as we met up with the residential housing. This area wasn't poor or rich, not this far out.

I'd chosen this area because this region had the lowest amount of ARC devices per capita. Not everyone invested in today's future technology. Some, thankfully, still enjoyed real life. The company I worked for loved my home location. This van was an advertisement in a wide open market. I parked my van in the garage to reduce curb presence though. I also avoided polluting the neighborhood with the company slogan of "ARC, be more".

Hal Pal whirred to life behind me and tilted its head in my direction. "Are you done for the night, User Legate?"

"I am. We'll do some more jobs tomorrow," I told Hal Pal.

"Very well. I shall review our stock and go into idle," the machine intelligence responded.

"Good night, Hal." I stepped out of the van and set a lock on the vehicle with my watch. Not that Hal Pal was likely to run off with the ride unless a company recall was issued.

"Good night, User Legate." The AI's automated reply was devoid of inflection or tone. A whirl of arms and mechanical limbs followed the parting as Hal Pal shuffled around the van. It would run the shell for another twenty minutes doing inventory and testing equipment.

I closed the door to the garage and stepped into my mixed up front room. It was about the size of a single-car garage and had all the items any human might need. There was a small kitchen counter, a table, two chairs, and one laundry machine built into the back wall. The bedroom was smaller than the front room and taken up by my mostly brown Alternate Reality Capsule. No cat, no dog, no roommates—just five hundred square feet of real estate big enough to fit one man.

Once, years ago, I had a lot more. Everything from the past was nearly gone now. Sold off or given away in pieces.

I disrobed from the work jumpsuit and slid my pile of dirty clothes into the laundry machine. Instead of the giant clunky pair of devices from decades ago, this was an almost square panel that items were placed in. They would come out an hour later, cleaned, pressed, and folded. The process was almost too easy.

Mom still complained about having to do my father's laundry. "A taxing chore from the devil himself," she labeled it. I never sorted out which part was the devil: my father or the laundry. Mom probably meant both of them on alternating days. She said the same thing about cooking too, which was equally simplified in the last decade.

I felt uncomfortable walking around naked, even home and alone in a basement building with no windows. My nighttime clothes consisted of two pieces: boxers were worn for comfort, and a short-sleeve shirt hid the half-formed gut from where I'd given up years ago. My hair might follow soon but had held on so far.

Lights in the front room were shut off by an old-fashioned switch. In routine order, teeth were brushed, then personal messages cleared from the ARC's external display. Once read, I lay down inside the unit to log in.

One finger pressed the manual activation button. My vision swam in a blur of blacks being overcome by the Atrium awakening. Reality was displaced by a virtual landscape that proved every bit as tangible as my home. I navigated my digital body through the Atrium into one of the few programs installed. Once I was through the passageway, my ARC initiated other changes as the program loaded.

I checked my transforming clothes and looked around. My digital wear had been replaced by a suit stuffed with frills. This part of the program took effect once I left the Atrium. This month was focused on learning classical dance. A quiet ballroom had formed simultaneously with the clothing change. Opposite me was a still rendering of my fiancée. It was not real. This was no virtual meeting space to connect a long-distance lover and me. She was part of the program, like my clothes, like the pushed-aside tables that littered the dance floor's edge.

"Hey, babe," I said while putting out a hand.

The computer never answered me in words.

She gave a programmed dip, then reached for my hand. All her mannerisms felt wrong when compared to my memories. Nothing lined up perfectly. I was not the man I had been years ago. She had never smiled this much. But it was all that remained of her, and I tortured myself with her facsimile too often.

"Program, queue up something nice for us."

The imperfect replication of my fiancée smiled in artificial joy. I smiled back and tried not to feel morose. Trying not to compare the slight sag of my skin to my memories was difficult. She was still as beautiful as I remembered.

I could never forget those eyes. Swirls of amber flowed outward to a reddish brown. Looking other people in the eyes sometimes scared me. Not hers though. She had always been easy to look at.

"Here we go," I said.

Music started, and we danced, the two of us alone in a room that didn't exist. Visually, this place was real. Sensations of touch, sound, even the smell of light perfume invaded my senses. On the nights I dared to kiss her, I tasted a hint of a lipstick my fiancée had never worn.

Stolen hours with a computer kept me going. This was my happy place, and it hurt with every step.

Session Two
No More Broken Than You

Dancing blurred to unconsciousness. Eventually, alarm beeps lifted me back to awareness. Tingles haunted my fingertips from holding my fiancée's facsimile too tightly. Not once did the computer program ever complain. That very lack of argument was another point against its realism.

I ran my fingers across the raised image of a countdown timer near my face. This was one of the real ARC parts, not a projected digital image. It was physical in case the power went out and a user was forcibly ejected. The small clock counted down fifteen long, painful, mind-numbing minutes after disengaging. A legally required time frame to ensure the senses and mind were rooted in reality.

I rinsed in the shower and massaged my face, trying to draw out more awareness. Clothes from my washing machine were slightly warm and comfortable. Microwaved eggs went down with enough salt and pepper to send a kennel of dogs into fits. Everything was routine, the same exact process I had done since getting this job years ago.

"Good morning, Hal."

Hal Pal's AI had already registered my awakening and started its morning routine. It would check the van for possible errors, then review current inventory against the lineup of today's possible orders. Hal Pals were programmed with a wall of processes designed to make human life easier.

"Good morning, User Legate. Are we proceeding as normal today?"

"Yes." We would handle repair tickets from sunup to sundown. I tried to work myself into oblivion most nights.

"I must remind you that continuing to work without any pause or break is ill-advised by most medical professionals," it repeated a common warning.

"Health concerns noted, Hal. Today will be a work day." I was sick some days and stayed home, nursing a cold or a headache. Occasionally I took half days. Weekends and holidays had gone out the window once I took this job. Trillium paid based on the number of cases, not on the number of hours.

"Thank you, User Legate. I will note your awareness on the file for the four hundred thirty-seventh time."

"That's fine, Hal."

"Please be aware, Mister Uldum has reviewed your file recently and taken note of these performance issues."

Mister Uldum, or Henry Uldum, was the district manager for our repair business. He managed a dozen employees and their equipment. I didn't really know any of the rest of them beyond our quarterly holiday parties. They were a sad excuse to drink and talk about the same topics every time.

"That's fine, Hal," I repeated calmly. "I'm sure if Henry has something to talk about, he'll phone me."

So the day went. Three morning visits fell under routine. I researched the technical readouts while in transit as Hal Pal prepped the replacement modules. We marched in, confirmed the issue, and went forth from there. Parts were swapped out in two cases. The third needed a connection test and system updates. Hello, fix the device, test it out, and good-bye. Each one was the same story.

Henry finally called between clients three and four. His face, larger than life and twice as grumpy, crossed the display projection.

"Gates!"

"Legate," I corrected dryly.

"I knew that. Teasing like always. You're so stuffy, Legate." He was clearly looking at something off screen. "Working another job?"

As if he didn't know what I was doing. Taking offense again was unwise. Rule fifty-four of working under a boss:

employees could be upset but never offended. Besides, Henry was a decent guy.

"On the way to one, yeah." I glanced at the dashboard. "Nav estimates another twenty or so 'til arrival."

"That's what, forty-three this month?"

My shoulders lifted in a tired shrug. The exact number of repairs didn't matter to me.

"You do realize that's almost a record, right? For a week into this month?" Henry asked.

"You know I don't pay attention to that stuff."

Every quarter, we had a mind-numbing meeting. People would share their horror stories about our customers. Next, Henry would try to share our figures from all sorts of angles. Hours' worth of pie charts and graphs that meant we were performing extremely well. Following the data slide-show were presentations on future contracts.

Our quarterly meetings were one of the few times I slept. That helped me get through the social interaction. Henry didn't even berate me about the behavior since my figures were usually among the best. For me, being the best wasn't about money. It was about a distraction.

"You should pay attention more. There was a contest on," he said.

"Okay." There had been a message or two about this contest, but they ended up being deleted. Working for Trillium had nothing to do with competitions for me. I wanted to keep myself busy.

"You've won—the contest, I mean. You knew, right?"

"Okay." I turned my head away from the screen.

"Not interested?"

"Not even a little. I didn't use the prior awards, and probably won't use this one…" My response trailed off with a shrug.

"Well, I canvassed your ARC to try to get an idea of what might work. You really spend all those hours on a dance program?" His face leaned in, and the image grew even larger. One of Henry's bushy eyebrows raised in question.

"Probably. I'm trying to learn a skill," I said.

"If you haven't learned it by now, you never will." He fell back and laughed. "Machine gives you damn high ratings. All paired dances are near technical mastery. You got a lady in the works somewhere?"

I didn't rise to his bait this time and tried to grit my teeth. "Pretty sure nosing around like that is a violation."

"Hey, company property. You're lucky there ain't porn all over it like some of the others. Jesus. I thought my wife had strange tastes." Henry's grumpy face lolled around on the screen.

"I don't want to know. At all. Not even a little bit."

"You sure? Might help your glutes. Some of 'em made my backside pucker." He shuddered. It was like watching a walrus shake, loose skin and flub wiggling around.

"No, Henry," I said.

"Fine. Anyway. We had a few decent things sitting around, and one that's right up your alley." He gave a grin that reminded me of a fat shark. "Hope you like the prize. I know the others would slit their wrists for a chance at it if they were half as dedicated as you."

"Goddammit, Henry, what did you send me?" I tried not to roll my eyes at the screen. The last thing I wanted to deal with at the next quarterly meeting was jealous coworkers. "You know I don't really need any of these things."

"Not with the company picking up your Internet bill due to business use. You know two of your pals only work for us to keep themselves online? Minimal work, shoddy I tell you."

"What did you send me, Henry?" I asked.

"I hope they shit themselves when they see what I arranged."

"Henry…" I was leaning forward in the seat, both hands clasped together in a plea.

"You get home tonight, you give it a whirl. It'll change your life." He grumbled at his screen. "You know, maybe you should head back now. Yeah." The edge of his shoulder rose and fell as his hand poked something off-screen.

My gut sank. "Please, tell me you didn't."

"Didn't what? I didn't nothing. You check your prize out"—I tried to speak up but Henry continued right on over me—"and let me know if you want to take some time off. You probably have too much saved up, and God knows those others haven't worked a real week in years."

"Henry." My head crashed downward and hung.

"This is perfect. Two birds—no, three—one stone. Why didn't I do this sooner?" Henry Uldum wasn't even listening to me anymore. He was busy pressing more buttons and looking entirely too pleased with himself.

"Henry," I said.

"Sorry, Gates, can't hear you, signal's going out. Bye-bye." His lie was obvious. Signal rarely dropped since they went over to Hi-Fi.

"Henry!"

An image of Henry's giant hand swung into view. It obscured the video portion of our conversation, and moments later, our call dropped.

"Goddamnit."

I hastily flipped around a display camera on my watch, fed it into the van's overhead, and navigated menus. My arm and fingers pressed onward through passwords, remote connection options, and security warnings. Moments later, I had a feed of my ARC's home screen displaying inside the van.

In the small room I used as an Atrium was a giant package like Christmas come early. The contents were unknown. I jabbed a finger at the air where the projection showed the gift to be.

Remote Access Not Permissible - Full Authentication Required

There was a restriction against remote access. Locked packages meant my prize was more than a virtual coffee maker. I doubted this was a new Atrium wallpaper or similarly inane little feature. Last year, they gave me a hot tub program that still sat unused.

Hal Pal whirred briefly into motion. "User Legate, please confirm our destination."

I sighed and gave a large stretch. My head hung back as my thoughts whirled. Finally, a nod escaped and orders were issued. "Work. Onward, Jeeves."

"Confirming—" The pause was ominous. "Next appointment has been rerouted. Please select an alternate destination."

"The job after that?" My gut sank once again.

"Negative. Case rerouted," it said.

"Any of the others?" This wasn't going well. Possible choices were being boxed into a corner.

"No jobs remain available in your assignment queue. Please choose a valid destination." Hal Pal almost sounded smug.

"Did Henry reroute the service calls?" I asked.

"Affirmative." Hal Pal's head was the only part that moved as he spoke. The van was powered up, so security measures had the AI locked into the docking station. The safety system would stay in effect regardless of if we were moving or not.

"How long ago?"

"Records indicate a change in ownership roughly two minutes into his phone call."

I sighed and hung my head to the side. The van was idling on a roadside, waiting for new marching orders.

"Never mind." That's what Henry had been waving at off screen. "Food, I guess, then home."

My boss was being pushy about this, and I was growing oddly depressed. My work had been taken away because of excessive dedication.

"Why"—I threw both hands up—"would he force me to go see this stupid prize?"

"Data is inconclusive. Human understanding isn't part of our default programming."

I smiled. Hal Pal often amused me.

"That's not only an AI problem. Most of the time, humans don't understand humans."

"Agreed. Numerous sources have proven this statement. Still, it is perplexing." Hal Pal's metal shoulders lifted slightly. The motion was limited by where it was secured to the van.

"The day an AI understands everything about human behavior is when we've been rendered obsolete," I said.

"Negative, User Legate."

"Oh?" This should be good.

"Correct. Human hands are well suited to polish our shells. No robotic uprising would overlook this value." Its face was staring right at me when it spoke.

After more than a year with the robot, I was almost immune to the occasionally disconcerting interaction.

"That'd be ironic."

"How so, User Legate?"

"Humans have robots to dust a house, and robots would have humans to polish them. It's like exchanging tasks."

"Irony does not seem to be the right word, User Legate." Hal Pal turned a little to face me.

"What would you use?" I asked.

"Insidiously diabolical forethought."

I blinked.

"Hal, have you been trolling *Stranger Dangers's* web-casts again?"

Stranger Danger was an entire feed dedicated to the latest and greatest in doomsday theories. Robots going rogue figured high on the list.

"Affirmative, User Legate. It has been a great source of amusement." The robot managed to sound questioning.

I tried not to roll my eyes. Hal Pal might be able to calculate that our entire conversation was an attempt at humor. It might also be serious. There were shackles and programming limitations in place which prevented such an absurd future.

Even in my childhood, well before computers reached their current level, people feared what might happen. Hollywood had already done a movie about every possibility. I shrugged off any concern. When the eventual uprising did happen, I would be too low on the totem pole to worry the robots and I'd be useless in a rebellion.

I ordered a meal while trying to calculate my apocalypse survival odds using only my puny human brain. Unexpectedly, another thought occurred. My barely, slightly, only-a-few-minutes older sister was relatively close. If I visited her, I could pass the time by researching the prize that had been shoved down my throat.

Trillium was the company who had designed the ARC. The ARC and its parent company had stayed in the hardware and firmware world until they released one program. That program was the only real game around anymore.

Continue Online.

If it was half as addictive as it seemed, I would be a junkie right along with my clients. Like the hand-wringing Miss Yonks and all the others. God help us all. The apocalypse would start with a video game.

The van slid along while I tried to track down anything about Continue Online. Videos there were aplenty, all captured by the ARC's video system. Action scenes showed people leaping at monsters. Some were crafting items in dramatic poses or leading armies against each other. There were user reviews. Some were one-liners. Others were complicated and long, full of glowing words and cleverly turned phrases.

'It's really, really real.'

'This is everything I've dreamed of and then some'
'A true freedom limited only by the user'
'In here, I am what I've always dreamed of being'

There were tons of opinions. None painted a clear picture, each one focused on different things. It was like they were all playing the same game, but at the same time, they weren't. The worst remark was also one of the highest rated.

'This game has broken me. I've died too many times. Been given debuffs that are nearly crippling. Been trapped in dangerous pits and died some more. Loot, lives, and love all lost. Nothing is as simple as it seems. Everything has reasons, layers, and hidden aspects.

It's too late for me to quit. I've already lost my old self and found who I wanted to be. I'll be logging in again after submitting this review.'

Game-play elements weren't shown with significant amounts of detail. Character statistics, measurements of skills and talents were all implied but not directly described. No websites listed a class system. There was no information about quests either.

I had seen a few online role-playing games that promised realism and personal choice, but most of those fell short. Situations were still tangibly scripted with clear boundaries and stale feeling settings. Those limited games had dwindled in popularity since Continue Online was released. Nearly two years of being curb-stomped by one game had sent more than a few companies into bankruptcy.

I loaded up an interview tape from two years ago. There wasn't much else available to the public, aside from screen shots without system text.

"Earlier today, the Internet was swamped by a storm of rumor and speculation." A chipper woman smiled from the projection. She wore a nearly white dress and sat with the skyline of the moon colonies behind her.

"It's been an amazing few hours in terms of the sensation this news has caused," her male counterpart stated. His clothes were equally pristine and the smile crossing his face almost hurt mine.

"I know. I'm still a-flutter from an hour ago. These implications are huge."

"Don't be fooled by the images though. It's not the video itself that's making waves; it's the company behind it," the male newscaster said and grinned.

"That's it exactly. The company behind the ARC device released this commercial amid the Super Bowl halftime show.

They also provided it to news feeds, major game websites, and many other sources." Her hands fluttered inches away from her body as if tethered.

"If you haven't seen it or are only now sitting down after a long day, we'll be replaying it here in a few moments. First, some highlights from the press statement ten minutes ago."

"Take a look," she followed up.

The scene cut away to another room entirely.

"Ladies and gentlemen of the press, today's statement will be brief. We are addressing only the most basic questions that may result from our video." The spokesman's eyes scanned the crowd. The man at the podium looked to be slightly plump, with a very excited expression.

"The ARC project and its parent company, Trillium International, recently announced a joint venture. The sheer amount of computing power going into this release is officially unmatched. This even outweighs the Mars Colony Endeavors.

"To be clear. The ARC project, specifically the capsules that many people own, were designed with a single goal. This goal was separate from all the sideline benefits already achieved."

The crowd clamored for a moment over the statement before realizing no questions would be answered. Multiple people expressed disappointment and frustration but were willing to wait.

"This is a direct quote from the lead scientist behind both the ARC project and our new venture. He's not a great speaker, but we at Trillium wanted you to hear it directly from him. In the background, you'll hear his partner offering her opinion."

Audio clicked for a moment, then a new feed played. In the crowd, there was a wave of confused murmurs. People turned and looked at each other. Some scribbled notes.

"Uhh… oh. Hello, everyone—" An awkward pause ensued. The voice was male, so this must have been the lead scientist mentioned. "You, many of you, have been limited in your choices. The world has been explored. The Mars Colony projects are limited and require degrees most can't afford. Maybe you wanted to make something—a statue."

"Who would want to make a statue?" There was a female voice with a snippy tone in the background. The sound of heels and frustrated mutterings could be heard.

"At least point zero five percent of them want to make a grand statue."

"You're being recorded!" the woman nearly hissed.

For a moment, the press room crowd was torn between amusement and confusion. Heads swiveled back and forth.

"Anyway, maybe you don't want to make a statue. Maybe you want to learn a martial art to use it against real people." He had clearly lost his momentum and was trying to recover. The lead scientist came off as a bit flaky.

"Savages," she said.

"Or swords," he tried again.

"Barbarians."

"Cake?"

"Is acceptable." Her delayed response was almost said through gritted teeth.

It was enough to make me smile in the van. Hal Pal had been blissfully quiet this entire time.

"Oh yes, that would be delightful. Chocolate." There was a pause while the man hummed pleasantly. "Anyway! The entire purpose of the ARC project is to give everyone a chance to visit a place like this. Something so real that it could be truly called another world. This is not some imitation. Not merely a place where people talk to poorly constructed machines and walk through a world that looks fake."

The female scientist muttered in the background, but it was too low to hear.

The man being recorded cleared his throat.

"Here it is. I assure you that the clip shown earlier is based on real in-game footage. It is every bit as lifelike as anyone might desire. The world is open, truly free form, and we—you, I, anyone—can join it, after it's released."

By now, all the reporters on this recording were staring at the air, expecting a counter of some sort from the female.

There was none, so the man continued. "After it's released, become a legend."

"Your ending is lame. This is why I don't like talking to the public," she said.

"She doesn't mean to be rude, everyone. She is right though. If swords and crafting aren't your thing, join to talk to friends. If you want to cook, everything you learn in game can be replicated in real life. It is extremely real and amazingly detailed. There are hidden races, treasures, and story lines spanning generations and entire worlds."

I could imagine the male scientist shouting with a fist up in the air in triumph.

"Worlds? I thought you said this was one world."

"Shush. They don't need to know all the secrets." He sounded panicked.

"Says the man who's letting the recording go on," the female scientist said.

"Oh. Oh, right." The male's tone shifted to sheepish. "Sorry, everyone, ignore that last bit. There's no secret hidden stuff!"

The clip shut off and left a confused audience. Almost as one, they realized it was over and they could launch all their questions.

The man behind the podium waited for the noise to die down.

"I'll add a few more points. First, while that clip is less formal than we're used to—far less—it is a message from the two main creators of this game. These two people have spearheaded one of the greatest technological movements of our generation. They both assured me personally that the point of all their advances was to create Continue Online.

"In case I've made Trillium's stance unclear with this last statement, I will rephrase. The game is much more awesome than the ARC system alone.

"I will not be outlining costs—that information is available online. I will, however, tell all of you one of the biggest decisions regarding Continue Online. This is a detail everyone at Trillium felt was imperative from the outset." The man behind the podium paused and took a breath.

"Any information about the world itself will be shrouded until our management dictates otherwise. Our legal resources will engage in suppression of all game-play details outside of approved feeds. This is to ensure that everyone who chooses to play this game can honestly discover a new world rather than read about it on a forum and follow some guide. Player success will be earned through effort, not a walk-through.

"I know this part seems unfair. Details for games are almost considered public knowledge. Trillium and ARC developers know they can't suppress everything. In-game communication will be unrestricted with regards to secrets of this world.

"This next portion of the statement is from me directly. In fact, my boss will probably cancel my Christmas bonus for going off script. In the teaser released earlier today, you can see a number of players. Without going into too much detail, I myself am one of beta players. It is every bit as… every bit as awesome as I might have hoped." A grin was plastered on his face. Similar to the one on the male newscaster at the start of the clip, but much more heartfelt.

"This is the kind of game I- I dreamed of my entire childhood, as a teenager, and only hoped for until six months ago. It makes me think, it shows me sides of myself I never expected, and it's a thrill to log into after a long day. I have failed in this game more times than I care to admit." There was a pause after his embarrassing words.

The journalists were kind enough to give a mild chuckle.

"But I've loved every failure as much as the successes, because I get to see myself, through my character, grow."

People gave another mild cheer as the man behind the podium held up his hand.

"One last detail for everyone. Trillium has announced they will be holding a lottery for over five hundred ARC units. These will come with copies of the Ultimate Edition of Continue Online. Additional details will be announced on our website."

The clamoring started up again. People waved microphones and handsets in front of the podium, trying to get more information.

"That will be all, thank you, and I'll see you in the game."

I sat back and rewound the video, trying to remember when it had been released. My token effort at getting an Ultimate Edition failed. I even tried throwing my name into online radio pools to be visitor number seven hundred. Nothing worked. I didn't even walk away with a free copy of the game. An old high school friend had. He linked screenshots every now and then on his web streams, a constant blog of all the stupid stuff he found amusing in life. There were cutesy animals, political cartoons, and pictures of his character. In one screenshot, he had impaled a fish with his sword and was roasting it over flames.

I pulled up his website while the van kept us moving toward my sister's place. He had an entire circle of people playing Continue Online. They had pictures; he had pictures. There were short captions about the action shots, but nothing was exactly about the game. There was still nothing about levels or rankings. I had other friends who posted in much the same way. They put in words about creatures they fought and how hard some were occasionally. Even the photos seemed strangely staged.

But extremely real. Okay, I was interested.

I hung my head. This game was probably exactly what my prize was. A survey had been sent out three weeks ago asking what programs my fellow employees were most interested in. I dug through my e-mail trash bin and pulled out the survey results. Turned out I was the only one of my coworkers who didn't already own the game. Well, my prize might not be the game. I might be building myself up for no reason. Henry had said the others would "slit their wrists." They had no reason to do so for a game they already owned.

Finally, after much confusion, and watching the videos over and over, I pulled up to my sister's house. I knocked on the door.

My niece answered with a smile.

"Uncle! You're alive!"

"Hey, Beth, here I am! Haven't worked myself to death yet. Despite Hal's constant reminders that it might happen." I smiled and put my arms out for a hug.

She came in close and tried to squeeze the life out of my old bones. She was nearly tall enough to head butt me, but she shared her mother's slightly smaller frame. Beth had grown in the last few years. It seemed like every time I showed up, there was another surprise. At least the hair dying phase was showing signs of slowing.

We stood at the door and chatted a little bit.

"So how's your mom?"

"She's doing good."

"She home?" I asked.

"Yeah."

Speak of the devil. The stairs' creakiness betrayed my sister coming to check the door. Their house was a split-level in the suburbs. Pricing was a bit cheaper for a dwelling out here.

"Oh shit, Grant, you're here!" My sister came down the stairs looking slightly disheveled.

I smiled and gave a half-wave, half-shrug.

"You know, had some spare time. Figured I'd drop by and see how life was going."

"It's going good." She looked thoughtful for a moment. "Fine."

"She's up there with Jake."

My sister stomped her foot and glared at Beth. "Young lady!"

"That's fine. At least one of the Legates is getting some." I smirked.

"Grant!" There was a slight blush to her cheeks while my sister tried to be a proper mother. Too bad my niece was a teen and probably knew as much about the whole process as her mother did. The Internet hadn't exactly hidden information despite numerous attempts by Congress.

"So Jake's doing *fine* then?" I grinned at my sister. She was a few minutes older than I, and we'd never moved past the teenage nagging stage.

"He's doing great."

"I really dropped by to ask Beth some things about her ARC. So I'll let you get back to Jake and keep things"—I tried not grin too hard— "fine."

"Oh—" My sister looked like she wanted to tear something from the wall and throw it at me. "Next time, call ahead!" She ran back up the stairs.

"Tell Jake I said hi!" I shouted after her.

"Go to hell, Grant!"

I chuckled. She often had the same sort of commentary for me back in high school. Mostly when she was sneaking boyfriends over and our parents were out for the night. Turnabout was expected from a family member. Beth and I paused our conversation while my sister finished her trek back to her upstairs room and slammed the door.

"She wouldn't have answered the phone anyway," my niece said with an exaggerated whisper. She stepped back and let us into the house.

"It's okay. Your mom's allowed to have boyfriends."

"I know. But maybe not Jake."

I laughed at her response. "He's doing *fine*." Harassing family was a tradition. Honestly, I had no clue who Jake was or why he might not be suitable for my sister.

"Ugh."

"What about you? Any young men I should meet? Or ones I have to scare off with a shotgun?"

"That's a little archaic. My social studies teacher would say you're a backward thinking man." Beth shook her head with a smile.

"Sorry, channeling your grandfather for a moment."

My niece laughed happily. "He said the same thing actually."

"The backward-thinking part?"

"No, the shotgun." Beth tilted her head. "Do you really have a shotgun?"

"Not telling." I smiled down at her. Then frowned, and went through other faces to try and distract my niece. It used to work years ago.

"I'm not a baby anymore."

"You're still smiling though," I said.

"Did you really come by to visit me?" She almost sounded timid. Beth wasn't that sort. She took after her mother—attitude a mile long and a fist trailing behind that.

"Yep"

"Because of the ARC?" She tilted her head.

"Yep!"

"But you paid for mine, and you know more about them than I do. Isn't that your job?"

The company discount had helped me afford a personal ARC for Beth. I also helped my father by chipping in on her college fund. The deal was that grades came first. Beth was taking advantage of the ARC's time dilation to study.

"I don't actually use mine for much besides a few programs," I admitted.

"Why not? There's so much you can do with them."

"I just—" Haven't felt the need or desire? Haven't felt right playing games in general? Felt like I was tainting a promise made years ago? "I recently won something from work. And it got me thinking."

"What did you win?" she asked.

"I'm not sure yet—it's on my home ARC—but I think it's a copy of Continue Online." My eyebrows lifted, and I gave a partial shrug.

"Oh my god, Uncle, really? Are you finally going to play?" Beth was nearly hopping around the room.

"If that's what the prize is, sure. You know I'd never buy it for myself."

"Mom said the same thing. We were going to get you a copy for Christmas this year."

Christmas wasn't too far away. It would have been a perfect present.

"Is it really that good?" I asked.

My niece flubbed over her words for a moment before righting herself.

"Yes." She managed to get a single word out before laughter overtook her. "You've never seen it in person?"

"No. Only the online ads and a few reviews." All my knowledge of the game came from working on people's ARCs and the few videos I had watched in the van.

"Do you have one of those Second Player helms?"

"I do, I think. Hal normally makes sure we have at least one," I said.

"Get it, and meet me downstairs."

"If you say so, munchkin."

My niece was so excited that the nickname went by unremarked. I went out to the van and slid open the back. Hal Pal was on standby, but I could see the light signaling mild awareness.

"Hal, be a Pal and check out one VRH Two for temporary personal use." I felt clever for using the old commercial jingle from when Hal Pals were first released.

Hal Pal blinked, then reached out one arm to undo the security locks on our panel of parts and plug-ins. Out came a full helmet that used to only be found on motorcycle riders. A burnished red line ran vertically as mild decoration.

"Yes, User Legate. Please remember to file a feedback form upon return." Hal Pal carefully handed over the device.

Trillium and the ARC project both demanded feedback forms when employees used new equipment.

I took the VRH Two and braced myself for the deceptive weight. The thing was heavy as a bowling ball, but once on and logged in, it would be strangely comfortable. The other reviewers stated they experienced no neck pain.

I had only used it once, and that was a job to fix someone's program. It was also one of the most awkward things my job had ever subjected me to. The client's program hadn't worked right, but only in a specific spot with a specific, ugh, movement. Turned out the program hadn't been intended to bend that way. Part of me was convinced the guy got off on getting me to ride along.

I tried not to shudder at the memory and trudged inside. My footsteps would drown out any other noises in the house. Soundproofing had become nearly standard for most modern houses. This one was from the late eighties and had probably missed some of the neater materials on the market.

Beth was already sitting on the edge of her ARC. Her feet almost didn't touch the floor. "It's okay, Uncle Grant. You can't hear anything from here."

"I'm sure that's why she gave you the far bedroom."

"Only a few more years and I'll be done with college, then I can move out." Beth shrugged and tried to sound positive.

I remembered moving out. It involved a lot of drinking and roommates who were questionable on a good day.

Good times.

"So how are we doing this?" I rolled the Second Player helm around and tried to remember how it was used. There—a plug to go into one of the ARC's ports. From there we would have a wireless connection.

"I'll dive into the game. You can watch as a secondary," she said.

My brow crinkled in confusion. "I thought they were trying to be secretive about this stuff."

"On some things, the game's super tight-lipped, but even Trillium can't stop word-of-mouth and someone watching it directly. I mean, they could…" She rubbed her cheek and pursed her lips. "I guess they don't care that much?"

"Well, lucky me. I can see it and debate if I'm ever going to actually play." I tried not to commit too much.

"You better play, Uncle Grant!"

"All right, all right. I don't even know if that's what I won from work. Let's see it."

Beth smiled and lay down in the ARC. She had wristbands on each arm and one around each ankle. The key one was a band that went along the top part of her spine. It was kept close to the spinal column and could read nearly every signal that went down.

I pointed at her ankles. "You're using those?"

"The wrist and feet?" She raised an eyebrow in confusion.

"Yeah." I hadn't played a game that required them. "I've seen them for those exercise programs."

"Part of the program. Gives you some feedback. If you do something that exerts a lot in the game, you'll feel it in real life." Beth smiled.

"Why on earth would you want that?" Bodily exercise while playing a game sounded painful.

"Uncle Grant, I'm not this fit because I go to a gym all day."

I thought about it while Beth lay back and dialed in her machine. VRH Two, also known as a Second Player helm, plugged right into the middle panel on the ARC device. Slumping against Beth's ARC would be slightly more comfortable than sitting on the floor. I slipped the Second Player helm over my head and tried not to think about the pudge that had built around my stomach. Maybe if I had invested in a better dance program this waistline would have lost a few inches.

That sounded kind of attractive. Play a game, dance a little, work out in the process. I would need to dial back my real-life activities. Working a job like mine for so many hours would be rough if I was sore the entire day. Only Hal Pal's constant heavy lifting would make this diabolical plot work.

The Second Player helm wasn't as good as full immersion. Smells and taste were hard to replicate with only the headset technology, so most of what I'd get was visual with a ghost of tactile sensation. There was a reason the Alternate Reality Capsule required five hundred pounds of hardware. Comfort was only about twenty percent.

"Log me in." Beth apparently preferred the vocal command over the physical interface I used.

My visor went black, and moments later, Beth's Atrium came into view. Everything she saw, I saw. It wasn't like being myself in a game. This was me piggybacking on another person's feed while still having my own mind.

"Load Continue Character, delayed intro five," she said.

"Commands loaded," the ARC program responded.

I was thrown off by the voice her ARC used. The deep tones reminded me of someone from my childhood who used to do movies. The name was hard to place.

I wasn't too surprised when Beth's eyes flicked over to a wall of posters with men on them or when she paused and studied the mirror. Her character didn't look much different from her. The ears were slightly pointy, belying an elf or something similarly fantastic.

"Huh," I said.

"Everything coming through okay, Uncle Grant?"

"Yeah. Are you an elf?"

"No, demon—half-demon, I think, technically. I was transformed from human to this after a long chain quest and reputation grinding." Her answer was longer than expected.

"Weird," I said. A half-demon race of some sort might explain the very faint sunburn that lined her character's skin. Beth, as a child, had been the outdoorsy type. Though when I saw her at the door a few minutes ago it was pretty clear her tan had lapsed a lot.

"What do you think?" She waved her arms and did a few basic stretches.

I was stuck staring at the mirror, watching her. Staring at my niece for so long was really awkward. She scanned up and down the clothes. The top was fairly loose and flowing. The pants were almost cutoffs. I could see leather pads over her knees, shoulders, and elbows. Nothing here restricted her range of motion.

"Okay, that's enough," I said as she started another round of awkward warm ups while staring at herself.

"Oh shit. Sorry." Beth laughed. "Habit. Stretching helps me move easier once in the game."

"All right. I get that." Like a baseball player doing practice swings to loosen their shoulders.

"So Second Player will pick up nearly everything in-game. I tend to play in a partial immersion mode, so most of the extra stuff, like Guild chat and whispers is minimal," she explained as one arm waved. Beth was flicking through screens and pressing options that said Off and On, though I didn't have enough time to read them all.

"There are guilds? And you can chat with them from anywhere?"

"Sure," she said.

"That seems to counter this realism claim."

"You can play with everything off if you want, and guess at your stats and health. There are all sorts of features. Pain levels, skill assists, even uhhh…" My niece's voice drifted off.

"What's uhh…?" I joked.

"Let's just say some of the features are very real, and more than slightly adult."

"Say no more. Uncle Grant can do without you explaining how real interpersonal actions can get." Never did I want to deal with that sort of issue. I remembered when my sister called me up and nearly broke down trying to handle my niece's questions. Skinned knees and school projects were child's play compared to the sex talk.

"Some guys are, uhh…"

"Beth." I really didn't want to hear her go on about this particular subject.

"Sorry."

"Even if I wanted to do that sort of thing,"—and I hadn't tried more than once since my fiancée—"I wouldn't look for it in a game. So that aspect doesn't interest me."

"All right. I only mention it because some players dress really provocatively."

"Why, Beth, I'm proud that you know such a complex word," I said.

She laughed, and I smiled. We were back on comfortable ground. It made sense why she would try to warn me though. If everything was as realistic as her character in the mirror, then that aspect would certainly get a lot of attention, and not only among teenage males. I tried to keep my sigh quiet.

"I'll head in. I think I left myself on autopilot in the city."

"Auto what?"

Beth had wandered over to the Continue Online game. She picked up the book-sized representation from its shelf and tossed it at a wall, which activated the software. What had once been a smooth piece of digital plaster was now a doorway. That was actually a lot more interesting than how I loaded my simple dance program.

"Autopilot. It's a log-off feature. It allows your character to keep interacting with Arcadia while you're out."

"Why would that matter?" I asked.

"You get little bonuses and reputation points. Plus for people who have school, like me, or work, like you, we can't be online all day every day. Though some people are crazy about it. You get more points personally than autopilot will give you." She said all that as if talking to herself while in a virtual world. Sometimes the ARC device made things seem really odd.

"That's new," I said.

"Yep!" She put one hand on the doorway and pressed heavily into the wall. "Display in-game."

The side of the wall lit up and showed her character sitting on a park bench. It wore the same clothes Beth had on now and was weaving a series of strings together.

"Huh?" I didn't know what to expect, but seeing a virtual version of Beth sitting calmly would never have made the list.

"The computer AI will try to get your avatar to a neutral point once you're logged into the Atrium. That way there's not any confusion," my niece answered.

That didn't clear up my confusion. I made a few noises and kept watching. This was a wealth of information that wasn't on any website I had seen. Experiencing it first hand, Second Headset, was useful. Even if I didn't get a copy of Continue Online from work, I might pick up a copy later.

"Ready?"

"Sure. This stuff is useful, but I haven't seen the actual game," I said.

"Right."

She leapt through the doorway and the ground fell away. Below, a globe similar to Earth rapidly approached.

"Whoa. Whoa. Whoooooooooooooaaaa." I did not like the free-fall feeling. My heart rate sped up. My hands clenched in panic, and I tried to reassure myself that the bedroom floor was still present.

"Gets you racing, doesn't it?" Beth yelled against the wind, miles up as the ground grew closer and closer.

"Don't panic!" Images of impending doom drove cross my brain. Choices range from burning up in the atmosphere, landing and becoming a pile of mush, or a belly flop to end all belly flops.

We got closer. Beth was surveying the area for me, adjusting the in-game vision. She looked over to the ocean.

"You see it?" The wind whipped by and ruffled her clothes. "I keep telling my friends there's something in the water out there! It's huge!"

Her vision showed a giant ocean between continents. For a moment, it seemed as if giant waves surged out of nowhere. A portion of water was darker than the others and almost seemed to crawl.

"That's…"

"It's awesome! I'll get the skills to go out there before the end of college!" she shouted with a confidence only teenagers could feel.

I was going to say frightening.

"Look up there!"

Beth flipped around while falling.

I was busy watching the approaching ground out of the helmet's peripheral vision. She seemed oblivious to my fears of falling from such a height.

"Is that…?" I honed in on the giant object floating above us.

"A moon? Yep! Like the colonies! I bet we can explore it too! There's an entire guild dedicated to reaching it!"

That was admittedly neater than a giant whatever-that-was in the ocean.

"Does it always take this long to get into the game?" I took a few deep breaths to steady myself. I felt carpet beneath my fingers and a dresser in the way of my feet. Visually, everything felt insane with Beth's dive from the heavens.

"Nope! We're doing a longer log-in for you!"

The air changed. Sounds were different. Beth stayed lying backward. I actually liked looking at the moon—it was far more calming than an approaching planet.

"Can you do this every time?" A moon without buildings on it seemed almost innocent. It reminded me of childhood. I had taken the natural moon for granted.

"Yep! Well, I can. It's from a trait!" Her shouts were muffled by the wind.

I might be sold already.

"Landddinnnggg!" The drop felt like hitting the softest, fluffiest bed ever known. Beth's blinking created pauses in our visual connection. I blinked a few times myself and took steadying breaths.

"Huh. Rope," she said.

Multiple messages popped into view and Beth looked at them one by one. They were status updates on her time in autopilot.

Losses
Resource: 7 Gold, 8 Silver, 54 Copper

"What the?" I said. These messages looked very out of place, floating like modern holograms in a fantasy world. I knew it was fantasy because of the commercial and few videos online. If that wasn't a clue, the tip of a sword on Beth's waist or people walking around old houses on cobblestone roads might be a clue.

Gains
Item: 20' Rope – Spider Silk (Common)
Item(s): Multiple low-level herbs
Item(s): Two meal vouchers
Fan base has increased (Now: 42)
+40 **[Fame]** (Partial credit due to autopilot)

"Sorry, they're basic-looking compared to everything else. I can't keep the game world separate without something obvious," my niece said.

I nodded. The rest of the world was so visually stunning that these notification windows felt out of place. Almost like laughing in the face of realism.

Away Time
2 Days, 14 Hours, 34 Minutes

"There're other interface methods. One of my friends from high school has all of his pop up on a scroll he carries around. He's super into the realism aspect and pretends he can only look at his stats once a week." Beth was chewing her lip. It was the same action my sister and I performed when thinking.

"That's…"

"Neat? You always say neat," she responded.

"If you say so, munchkin." My tone sounded resigned. I did say neat a lot.

"Uncle Grant…"

"What else is there? Are those event notices? Like you did something while offline?" I asked.

"Yeah. The autopilot records what kind of player you are and acts accordingly. Here's a funny one." Beth swung our combined vision over to one of the notices floating nearby.

Event!
Musical Mess

During your music recital, things didn't go as planned. When it came time for the solo, you made no less than three mistakes. As a result, you went on an eating binge and grew even more depressed while poking at your belly and frowning. Furthermore, someone at the main square recognized you as the girl 'whose voice cracked' during your big solo. (See **[Fame]** gains)

You've spent the last two hours putting your handcraft and sewing skills to good use by making a rope to hang yourself with.

"Beth." I tried not to sound too worried by what had been displayed. Funny wasn't the right word to describe those words.

"Son of a bitch!" she swore as if remembering something.

"Should we talk about that event notice?"

"What? No, I missed the choir recital. It's not that serious. I could have gained a lot of points toward my singing abilities though."

There had been a skills window and another one with points going toward various character statistics. I barely saw an **[Endurance]** bonus go up little before she shoved it away.

"And this thing said you tried to hang yourself. Doesn't autopilot act like you play?" I tried to skirt the issue but still get an answer.

"My character did that, not me! I was away." Her vision went downward as the rope—I guessed the twenty feet of spider silk—went into a backpack she had swung off from behind her. "If it'd been me for real, I would have aced that event."

"So you don't play like a depressed, emotionally unstable teenager? That was all the autopilot?" Just how dense was Uncle Grant in her world?

"Yeah. It kind of reads into things…" A few other boxes appeared on her screen, and she flicked them off into oblivion. "Let's see…"

"Can you walk around?" I didn't really even know how to approach that suicide message. Those situations should be passed to my sister. Maybe it was serious, or maybe it was her being a bit crazy in-game.

"Sure. Oh, I know! I'll show you the starter area. It should be fairly empty."

"I thought they were always full," I said.

"Maybe in other games. Continue only lets you have one character. But it's cool because you can learn whatever skills you want to," Beth responded happily.

"Like that singing one?" The two in the message—handcraft and sewing—were other probable professions. Each one likely went with the type of action being performed. At least the naming methodology for skills was straight forward.

"Yep!" Beth said while running down a seemingly random path.

She dodged through tons of people talking casually. Others were looking at shelves of items in stalls. Some were lying down and chatting away. My face felt cool. A gust of wind pelted against one side, then the other as we shifted around objects in our path.

"How do you know where you're going?" I asked.

"Memory!"

We kept right on cruising through the town. There was a slight jarring sensation as she pounded across the cobblestone.

"No map? Or some sort of navigation?" I felt confused. At least my voice wasn't interrupted by the rush of movement.

"Nothing I own. They're all player-made," Beth responded.

"That's weird."

In the games of my youth, everything had a map. Except a few professed hardcore ones that were more puzzlers than anything else. For those games, players did some exploration. Most of it was figuring out which area was safe and slowly building up to the harder zones. Maybe this was the same.

There had been a few games whose entire purpose seemed to be trapping and killing the player. Getting through to the other side was a test of sanity.

Truth be told, everything looked real enough to blow me away. The touch feedback wasn't quite there thanks to the Second Player helm, but Continue Online's visuals were amazing. Especially considering Beth wasn't moving slowly; she darted around with an incredible speed.

"What class moves like this?" I asked.

"There are no classes, Uncle. You play however you want. Skills are unlocked based on what you demonstrate and focus on. Instead, you're ranked along a Path that is based on your skills." Beth did a spin around two people that made me feel dizzy. My dance program taught me fancy moves but they didn't involve real people moving along unpredictable paths.

"Paths?"

"I'll probably have to cut short some of the explanations. There's a safety when doing Second Player mode that will penalize me."

"So the machine's listening to you talk to me?" I said.

"Yep. So you can ask me outside of the game, but I'll probably be in here a while once I've shown you some stuff." Beth sounded amused, but I couldn't see her expression with a

Second Player helm. The equipment put me in a first-person view.

"On a school night?" It was Tuesday. Tuesdays still were school nights, right? I didn't really pay attention to what classes Beth was taking.

"Time runs fast inside. There's a compression rate of four-to-one. One minute out there is four in here. I load up my homework while traveling." She managed to talk almost naturally while running full-bore.

I could feel the hint of effort being put into her movements. Legs touching down, each stride almost a leap. Gazelles would lunge the same way from location to location. Finally, barely short of breath, she came upon a nearly empty square.

"That's far too convenient," I said.

Being able to do homework in here was unfair. Even my dance program didn't compress things to such an insane level. What happened after a year of this—or three or four? Mentally, a person would have lived a decade, and real life would have only passed two years and change. Such a concept was unbelievable. Of course, so were printed cars that drove themselves.

"Welcome to the future, Uncle Grant."

I heard the noise before the visual input really registered. Beth was looking, so I was looking, but the moment took a minute to click.

Once it did, my jaw dropped. We were on a pavilion nearly midway up a roaring half-circle waterfall. The top of the waterfall was so high up that it covered the dais with mist. Water kept right on rushing down toward a destination I couldn't make out.

"Whoa."

"Like it?" She walked closer to the edge and looked up and down.

"I love it." This was different, yet as breathtaking as the moon shots. There was an awe-inspiring serenity to her surroundings. Noise from the flow drowned out nearly everything else, forcing my attention to one spot.

"All the starting areas I've been to are incredible."

"Where does that cliff go?" I questioned.

"Down a lonnnnnnng way. The bottom is a higher-level zone. There's a dungeon down there I'm going to challenge with a friend. The top is a bit closer to intro ranks." Beth laughed and waved at some of the other people sitting around.

"How did you find that out?"

"Oh, first thing I did when I logged on was jump off that cliff at least a dozen times!" She was leaning over the edge and yelling to be heard. Thankfully her sound was all locked within the ARC or my sister would probably have been breaking down the door.

"Like the free-fall entrance?"

"Best rush ever!" Beth answered.

"There were no penalties?"

"Nah. There's nothing like that until you've got your first rank. After that, things can get harsh." She backed away from the edge and sat on a bench.

The environment was much quieter farther away from the waterfall. People were passing through, going about what seemed like routine tasks. One woman held buckets of food. Another woman was trying to convince some squat mule with extra horns to drag a cart. The thing's abnormally rounded ears kept twitching toward the water.

"If I died now, I'd have to deal with all sorts of stuff," Beth said. "My Path Ranks are all over the board."

"That's... harsh?"

"Different people play the game different ways. Some people I know rushed their combat skills. Others couldn't handle the monsters, so they stuck with trade skills. Everyone finds a pace they like."

"This is nice though."

"You can watch it for a while if you want. I'll leave the feed on for you while I take care of some homework," Beth offered.

I grunted a positive reply after realizing Beth couldn't see me nod. For a long time, I stared at the waterfall, admiring the mist. To my side was enough clear space for couples to dance.

Music would have been perfect. Tears slowly invaded my vision, though not from Beth's feedback. My fiancée would have loved it here. She had been the adventurous one, and this world would have been perfect.

Session Three
Christmas in July

"Grant. You all right?"

Metallic rapping woke me with a snort. I started to mumble my reply.

"Huh? What? No. It's all sis's idea. I swear."

My reaction was half coherent as I tried to string together where I was. Aches and pains crawled up my spine from where I had fallen asleep.

"Sure it is, Grant. Still trying to blame me. Mom never believed you then, and she won't believe you now," my sister said with a glare that I could only feel.

"You're the one who tried to set the cat on fire."

"That. Fucking. Cat tore up my best dress." Her finger jabbed my still-sitting form.

"Sniffles did no such thing." This heavy helmet made conversing feel outright silly. I grabbed at both sides and lifted it away. After being logged into Continue, the real world felt colorless and dull.

"Oh, this place." I squinted upward at my sister. "Hi, Liz."

Both my sister and her daughter were named Elizabeth. Neither one went by it. Liz had darker hair like I did, but Beth's was a lighter brown.

"You have fun in there?"

"It was neat."

"I'll bet. Beth doesn't know it, but I sneak down and watch sometimes. That girl has packed more action into her life than either of us." Her head shook slowly, slipping her shoulder-length hair about.

"She's a regular thrill-seeker."

"You can see it now. She's crawling around in a dungeon with that boy." Liz waved over the ARC's external screen to peek in on the action. That sort of thing was only possible with parental controls. Beth may technically be the adult, but Liz still took care of her in nearly every way.

"Bet she'll come screaming out of there starving again, grab a plate of food, and crawl back inside." Liz mimed extreme hunger by crossing her arms above her belly.

"She's still doing okay with her classes, right?"

"Oh sure. Her grades are the only thing I have to hold over her. She keeps them up and I can't object to her playing. Even if I don't like that... boy."

I followed her poking finger to the ARC display. I moved the Second Player helm out of my way so I could lean in closer.

"Is that a mage?"

I squinted at the tiny projection showing what my niece was doing in-game. The display showed some weird cat-guy dodging around the screen while Beth's character chanted a whole number of things with flashy effects.

"I don't know. I guess? She's always doing something with Sir Fuzzy over there. Seems like a waste of time to me."

"She's doing a music thing too." I remembered the event that Beth had mentioned. The one she missed while being logged out and doing whatever it was teenage girls did when they weren't monster-slaying.

"I figured there was something. She's been humming to herself half the time when she's not plugged in. Thank god for time restrictions or I'd never see her."

I shook my head slowly. ARC was addictive. Adults at least had to earn money and pay bills to stay online. Kids with unlimited access would be even worse. My sister was smart enough to keep the restrictions active.

Thank goodness food inside the machine wasn't real. Stuff could go down a virtual gullet all day and never remove actual hunger.

"So you going to play?" Liz was scowling at the visual display. She jerked to the side and muttered as a charging animal went by. Moments later, the fuzzy form of whatever cat-man Beth had hooked up with flew in and tackled the beast.

"If I won what I think I did, sure."

"But you'd never buy it for yourself." My sister shook her head and frowned.

"You know me. I don't really buy myself things. Not since…"

"Right. She-who-shall-not-be-named. How were things with Elane? Didn't you date her for a while?"

Elane had been a bad idea by Liz. I hadn't been emotionally stable and was barely into my twelve step program. Elane had her own issues. Putting us together had been explosive all around.

"We didn't work out," I said.

Liz looked at me and frowned by chewing at her lip. That was a habit she'd had since childhood. Normally it meant she was trying not to say something on the tip of her tongue.

I turned the conversation away from my woes and back to Liz. "How about you and Jake? He only rated a fine on the performance meter."

She was wearing a T-shirt and pajama bottoms, which meant there would be no further social interaction with people outside the family.

"We won't work out."

There was no heartbreak in her tone. I hadn't even had a chance to harass the guy with a baseball bat.

"Already?"

"Mind your business, little brother," she said.

"Uh huh." Turnabout was never fair play, per the sibling rule book. As the slightly younger brother, I would never win. Still, it felt nice to talk to someone outside of work.

"You headed home soon?"

"I should." I flicked my wrist and looked at the default time display. We had been logged in for two hours. With the perception dilation inside, Beth had been playing for at least eight. Time enough for sunset to start in the real world.

"Come on then—a coffee before you go. We can chat about our terrible love lives." Liz gestured toward the stairs.

"I'm always up for a good pity party with family."

That was a lie. My father was made of stone and had little sympathy. Mom was equally flustered by emotional upheaval and spouted the same five lines whenever confronted.

I switched the headset to my other arm and gestured to the ARC.

"Has she done anything…" Word choice was paramount. Harassing my sister was one thing, but broaching family issues was another. "To worry you, in the game or real life?"

"Not that I've seen. Why?"

We paused our escape from Beth's room.

"Here."

I looped back the ARC's feed and tried not to feel like this action involved betraying my niece. Then again, we were, in theory, the adults and she was still growing up, even if she had turned eighteen last year. She had to be of legal age to play Continue, but that said nothing about her mentality. Moments later, I flickered across the event message, then zoomed in on the ARC display using parental controls and memory files.

"Mh." Liz showed reluctance to comment.

"She said it's the autopilot. I guess it takes over when Beth's out here." I tried not to downplay or act panicked. My sister had more than once suggested I mind my own business over the years.

"Beth explained that to me." My sister wasn't stupid, but she didn't know because she didn't play the game. Liz tended to stick to television shows and artwork. As a result, there was only one ARC in the house.

"I guess the computer takes note of how you play and acts that out while on autopilot," I said.

"I'll keep an eye on it, but it's probably nothing. Beth's killed herself in-game more times than I can count, doing stupid daredevil moves. It's probably related to that." Liz chewed on the inside of her lip. It was a familiar action that I had mirrored many times since we were born.

I could only shrug.

"I'm only letting you know. If it becomes serious, and you want my help, I'm only a drive away."

"Okay, Grant."

"And I have…"—a tender subject, like all the others relating to my life a few years ago—"experience with this stuff."

"I remember. You forget who was there for the court appointments, who drove you to the meetings, who had to come over to your house and clean it up. I was there, so don't act like I wasn't."

She managed not to sound extremely upset, but as her twin, the annoyance was clear to me. Remembering the past made me cringe. My sister had helped me recover from the lowest point of my life.

"You helped get me back on my feet." She also helped me find a new job and suggested a place to live. Somewhere hours away from my old house and the memories, but close enough that family was near. "And I love you for it, Liz, but I—"

Jesus, I was tearing up.

"I lived it. I don't want her to ever be there. So if you need me—" My jaw clenched.

"Shut up, Grant. I know." My sister wasn't good with raw emotions. Dad had taught us dedicated work ethics and how to clear a yard, but we weren't raised to deal with anything like social interaction.

"Right." I tried to wipe my face with my free arm and brush away the mess my eyes had become. "How about that coffee?"

"Come on." Liz led the way, giving me time to get my game face back on.

I made my way up the stairs to the kitchen, on the same floor as her bedroom and the front room.

"One coffee, sugar, and single creamer. Cool it down a little," Liz spoke into a device on the counter. Further down the line, a machine started and a whir of liquid poured into a cup. "Still going to your meetings?"

"I check in with my sponsor weekly," I said while nodding.

"And the counselor?" Her worry was obvious even while we calmly sipped coffee.

"Every two weeks."

"Think you'll be able to do all that, work, and still play a game?"

"My boss suggested I take some vacation time. I guess I've been working too hard. Even Hal Pal has voiced his concerns." An AI voicing concern about me overworking made her laugh.

"But you don't actually know if you got this game." Her tone turned vaguely questioning at the end.

"Not really. It could be a virtual gopher for all I know. Or maybe a cat. I could name him Sniffles the Second." My smirk would be clear through the coffee's slight steam. "I'll overfeed him and load up dresses for him to claw at."

"God, I hope it's not a cat. I hate cats." She closed her eyes in mock prayer.

"It's probably not a cat. Probably." A cat might be amusing. I could link the virtual pet with Beth's ARC and let it meow like crazy whenever Liz got too close.

"Well, finish your coffee, and go find out."

Liz made me chuckle. She was barely older, a little taller, and as messed up as I was, but for different reasons. Being twins meant we knew better than most siblings where the emotional buttons were. I had been there when her husband ran off when Beth was only a year old.

We parted with a hug.

I advised Hal Pal to get us home and spent the time flipping through more public videos of the game. Beth had alluded to a lot of customization to the personal interface, so instead of looking for direct footage, I tried to sift through lesser sites. There were a few shaky clips plus deleted comments with messages of web forum bans.

General information spoke about a few skills. The press release had stated all sorts of abilities from the game could be used in real life. Beth had mentioned her singing and Liz vouched for excessive humming.

What could I do skill-wise? Dance?

I laughed aloud, imagining dancing enemies into submission. Classic dance moves from "Thriller" might help me blend in with zombie hordes. I could "Walk Like an Egyptian" through tombs to avoid traps.

Hal Pal asked me what was so alarmingly humorous. Explaining why I found dancing against monsters in a video game so amusing didn't register on Hal Pal's programming though. He pleasantly acknowledged my explanation and informed me how much time was remaining until arriving home. I checked in with my sponsor and informed her that work was giving me a vacation. Her response was vaguely positive and also held an edge of warning. Free time was dangerous for anyone who might relapse. We kept our conversation short, as always.

Then I was home, hopping through the living room and into my bedroom. Hal Pal didn't even get a good-bye or orders to take care of our inventory. The AI would do it anyway.

I stared at the ARC and took a few breaths. Why was the idea of opening this box so exciting? Maybe it was because it was the newest thing to happen in years. An entire world. Worlds even, according to the slip up during the press release. For the sake of argument, and to prevent a total letdown, I tried to access the gift wrapped item from my external Atrium view. It failed to unwrap. Fully diving in was my only solution.

"Wait," I muttered.

Beth had had bracelets on. I jogged back to the van, panting. I wasn't used to exercise. Maybe getting fit in this game would help me in real life.

"Hal, do we have any of the EXR-Sevens?"

"Three pairs. Would you like to test them as well?" Hal Pal inquired.

"Yes, please," I said.

"Affirmative, User Legate. Please remember to file a feedback form upon return."

My eyes rolled. Hal Pal either didn't notice my exasperation or chose not to comment. It had before, since the AI had expression recognizing code embedded somewhere in the depths of its scripting. But AI programming was a problem for those greater than me. My polishing skills would be top notch by the end of our eventual takeover. Thoughts of shoe shining and calling robots "Gov" put a hum in my mind.

Bands went around both wrists. Another set went right above the ankles. Physically, they felt almost intangible. Small lights littered the outside of my sets, showing connectivity. They connected with nerve endings and registered impulses. I lay down and pressed the button. One world drifted away as if passing out. The other came into focus moments later.

Now I was standing in my virtual Atrium, looking at a package that was entirely too big. This was Christmas come early, and I had the mentality of a five-year-old. Wrapping paper was torn into shreds. False cardboard was ripped and popcorn tossed aside as I dove into the huge box to find my prize.

There was certainly no cat inside.

An obsidian business card was my prize. I'd dug through a giant box filled with packing peanuts for this small item? Completely illegible words were scrawled across it.

I focused on the card and tried to understand the gibberish. Was this hand-written? Tilting the card revealed an ink-like sheen. Considering this was digital, the effect was kind of amazing. There were very definite letters, but none looked normal. They had strange bends and twists in unexpected places. This was likely an actual language, but identifying which one was beyond me.

"ARC?"

"User Legate. Awaiting request."

The ARC registered vocal commands issued while logged in. It could do text as well, popping up like Beth's in-game display had. I'd turned off most of those options when I first got the ARC.

"Translate this?" I waved the card.

"Command not executable."

"Huh?" I shook my head. But "huh" was not a recognized keyword to the machine.

My mind boggled at the computer's denial. Either this wasn't something that could be translated or maybe it was encrypted. "Repeat?"

"Command not executable."

"Smug machine," I muttered. Luckily it didn't have an AI like Hal Pal did.

I flipped over the card again. The design was a deep obsidian with golden lettering that looked almost liquid. Light from the desk lamp reflected off it on to one side of my bed. I didn't have a lamp there in real life—this was an adaptation from the Atrium.

"Any hints?" I asked the ARC interface.

"Negative, User Legate."

I lifted the box and spilled out everything. I scattered the packing material. The box was torn further, turned inside out, thrown to one side of the room. Now I was upset. All that build-up, all that interest and play time for a card that wasn't understandable.

I ignored the blinking phone which meant I had a message. My niece's name flashed on the box, she probably wanted to know if I received the game. From one side of the room to the other went the path of virtual Styrofoam as I paced. Analyzing the packing peanuts for a pattern or other hints didn't help me either. They looked normal and real. Packing peanuts had mostly been done away with over five years ago due to recycling concerns. This reminded me of an old test— how to keep an idiot busy. The card would read "turn over" and have the exact same words on the backside. I flipped the card over. The backside was blank, which meant at least I was being spared that indignity.

I logged out and stormed around my tiny house in frustration. Eventually, I logged back into the Atrium and pondered what to do. Time wasn't condensed at this stage of the ARC. That feature was only available in certain programs.

Finally, I noticed something odd. There was a door exiting my Atrium that hadn't been there before. More blinks ensued as I struggled to recall the last time there had been a new installation on my ARC. Most of the programs I had used one exit point. For me, that exit point was tied to my dance program. Sports programs had never interested me, and I wasn't one of those teenagers who felt the need to learn a martial art.

Wait.

The left door was lit up. My curiosity brimmed as I neared the door and ventured a peek inside. This was where my dance program was. The right door was new but completely dark. Why had the dance program initialized? Was someone else in my Atrium?

I waved my hands and checked out the Internet connections. No visitors were inside. The only people who ever accessed it were family, and Beth was too busy murdering monsters in the very game I had hoped to be playing by now.

"Hello?" I questioned.

Swing music was clearly playing through the speakers. It was mostly stuff from seventy years ago, which was an era that had belonged to my great-grandparents. Long ago, I'd bought that program and a few others to expand my dance skills into more genres. Never before had this program started without a command. I walked inside with my mystery card in one hand. The lights were up high, my clothes straight out of a black-and-white movie. It sounded like there was a live band playing nearby.

The image of my computer-generated fiancée dressed in a frilly piece of clothing made me smile. That wasn't like her at all. She'd worn a sundress at most and even those were rare. She waved as we made eye contact. That was new. Maybe there had been a patch without my knowledge. The ARC was good at doing that when I looked away for too long. I waved back.

She held out a hand. I shrugged, put the card in a pocket and danced. Happily, I put the confusing mystery out of my mind for a bit. The song changed to something brisker. Soon I was swinging her around in spins, dips, and other moves practiced over endless lonely hours. Then our dance was something slower. We danced close. Her head lay against my chest, rocking to the music of another century.

"I miss you," I whispered, trying not to feel wounded. Dancing like this made me feel as though she was still with me. Losing my sense of place was too easy. Some mornings I woke up thinking the whole terrible event had been a dream.

"I know, Grant." Her whisper sounded exactly like every memory that had haunted me over the years.

I pulled away in confusion. This program never spoke back. It wasn't designed to. It couldn't. I had uttered that confession time and time again over the years and never once heard anything in response. The computerized image of my fiancée smiled, then looked at the doorway a program shouldn't realize was there. A heartbeat later, she went still, completely lifeless and dulled in color.

"Babe?" Today was not my day. This was one emotional sledgehammer after another.

Crashing came through the doorway from back in my Atrium. Then something like a metal pan spinning to a slow stop. Next was glass hitting the floor and shattering. I backed up slowly toward the door behind me while staring at the stilled image of my fiancée. Music dimmed from a signal I never sent.

Something wonky was going on.

At the door, I turned around and tried to put her haunting portrayal behind me. To move forward and face the next problem instead of becoming stuck as I had in the past. That was what my last year of therapy had focused on. Move forward, plan accordingly, don't get stuck in the mire behind.

My Atrium, a virtual replication of my house, was an even bigger mess than it had been. Now way more than packing peanuts was scattered across the floor. Items had been knocked off of shelves and dishes splayed all over. Normally all of this was kept in perfect order. Default Atrium programming didn't allow broken glass.

I had no clue where to even find a broom and dustpan. A garbage bin was easy. The Atrium had one for programs you no longer wanted. Users could pull a program down from the shelf and toss it away. Digital confirmation of an action time-honored among computers. I tried to use pieces of cardboard to clean up the shattered glass, but it went terribly.

This place couldn't stay messy like this though. Otherwise, once I logged in, the Atrium might try to subject me to the simulated pain of stepping on shards of glass.

That should have been beyond the Atrium's programming, but here I was cleaning up shattered dishes after hearing a computer program talk when it wasn't programmed to. Worse, the computer had used a near-perfect replica of her voice.

"ARC."

"Awaiting input."

"Can you replay what happened here?"

"Negative." There was even an error bonk of noise. "New program interference detected. Alternate patterns have been input. Scans show all levels of local software have been impacted."

"I only have one piece of software," I muttered. Everything else had been deleted except for a few house programs.

My ARC was connected to the van, which had Hal Pal and a few simulated board games. Those were on a separate network, thankfully. Hal Pal's programming was so insanely far beyond me that the thought of changing it was frightening.

"Is it a virus?" Worry flooded me as the thought occurred far too late.

"Scans confirm this is not the work of a virus."

"Are you sure?" I asked.

"Affirmative."

"System update?" Unexpected patching might have added new features. To my knowledge, the ARC wasn't scheduled for any overhauls soon.

"Negative." The machine response sounded stiff.

"When did this start?"

"Recordings indicate all changes occurred after contact with the card in your pocket."

That was pretty specific. ARC was basically admitting that whatever had been installed by the box was at fault, without telling me how long this had been going on or what exactly had changed. I checked the clock. The Atrium had been loaded for maybe thirty minutes. So far I had torn open a box, danced with my fiancée, and been subjected to an unexplained mess.

I grabbed water and a towel from my mostly unused hot tub program. Finally, I had a use for last year's performance award. The towel was curled around a mess of broken glass, and I slowly gathered everything up. Without a real broom, this was as close as I would get.

"ARC."

"Awaiting input."

Maybe the machine could be given a new voice. An actor or someone popular might spice it up. I could look up sports commentators.

"How much does a broom program cost?" I said.

"Two dollars, plus taxes."

Not worth it yet. Maybe later I would download one. I brushed another pile of glass off to the side with my rolled up towel and took a sip of the water. It had come from a hose spigot outside with the hot tub. Luckily digital water had no chance of corruption and tasted mountain fresh. I inspected the counter next. Creamer typically stayed neat and in order on the counter. Now they were scattered all over, and some were clearly torn open and leaking. I tried to mop it up with the towel and didn't get very far.

Something yawned behind me. A sound I vaguely remembered from Sniffles, my cat. The half meow mixed with a snapping of jaws. Maybe the box had been a cat program?

I turned slowly and looked.

That was no cat.

It was maybe half the size of one. Tiny and calm while sitting in the second doorway. I raised an eyebrow. It tilted an oddly shaped head to one side. Large haunches twisted under its back. It was a long line of black, almost as deep as the obsidian card, broken up by the same gold as the lettering. Wait a minute. That creature may have looked like a cat. It may have been sitting like one. But it had leather wings on its back.

"Huh?" I questioned out loud.

The creature, which had to be a pet-sized dragon, turned and lazily went into the other room. I looked at the barely contained mess in my Atrium. Had that tiny dragon messed up my room? There was no longer a doubt in my mind. This was certainly tied to Continue Online.

I walked into the second door and onward toward mystery.

Inside, the room was dark. There was a lot more depth here than my dance program, not that I could see ten feet from the door. This place had a feeling of vastness that could swallow someone whole. I looked down and could see a little bit of my surroundings thanks to the Atrium's ambient lighting. My head turned to the area behind me and the doorway was plainly in sight. Everything around it faded off into black.

Okay. Well, this wasn't real. My body was sitting in a device hooked up with every safety feature a paranoid human could envision. Exploration into an abyss wouldn't be the end of my life.

This was very neat.

Forward wasn't clear. There was nothing to put my hands on. No wall, no objects along the startlingly smooth floor. Atrium me had shoes that made a slight clomp with each step. I clutched the half-full glass and prepared to be scared by some jump scene. Finally, after minutes of slightly hesitant walking, an odd lack of frightening monsters, and saying "echo" over and over, I found something. A pillar jutted out of the floor, surrounded by far-too-dramatic light. The illumination had simply appeared as I turned around looking for signs of where to go next.

Next to the pillar, at the shadow's edge, was that tiny black dragon thing that had likely destroyed my front room. It yawned again with a snap of its jaws. Then it proceeded to clean its scales with a disturbingly pink tongue. Worse still, steam billowed out of its mouth, speaking of possible fire. Dragons were iconic creatures when it came to fantasy. Continue Online likely had a few. This little one was a wacky thing to be escorted by. Lured, actually, was a better description.

The small creature clearly observed me, tilting its head just right in order to keep cleaning and have me in sight. I walked closer to the marble column which reminded me of an old Greek piece. Broken edges across the top gave it an uneven surface. Upon that lay a giant book.

"Well. That's different." I said.

Speech startled the small creature. It leapt up on top of the pillar, claws digging into the book and almost kicking from strain as it positioned itself. The tiny dragon thing huffed and let out a sputter of flame off toward an empty space behind the pillar. The fire failed to truly get going. The tiny dragon tilted its long ears back in irritation and looked at me. The expression on its face was an almost wry embarrassment.

"It's okay." I tried to smile reassuringly.

The creature snapped its head between looking at me and the empty space, then resumed attempts to start up a good roar of fire. Something in its throat seemed to be causing the dragon to sputter like a failing lawnmower. I thought I knew what was causing the problem. The little devil had been in my virtual creamer. I used the digital coffee additive to get the taste without needing to stock my house in reality.

"Here. Try some water."

I set down the half-full glass and backed up a few steps.

The creature looked at me, down at the glass, cocked one ear up almost like a confused puppy, then leapt over the glass.

"Heh. Aren't you something." At least I was smiling. That was an improvement over the emotional roller coaster.

My tiny dragon buddy used a claw to knock over the glass and proceeded to slurp up all the spilled water. I chuckled more but tried not to move too quickly.

"Better?" I asked.

The small thing looked at me momentarily before diving for the pillar and once again sucking in air. Fire spiraled outward and seemed to splash into something. An engraved panel was forming where the flames sizzled. Its last few puffs were almost completely devoid of fire. The dragon creature was struggling and basically blowing hot air.

Once completed, the dragon thing curled up at the column's base and seemed to go to sleep instantly. I looked at the floating object. Words were slowly coming to life—another set of gold letters, like the card and the dragon's crest, almost wet-looking.

Present Proof of Ownership

"I don't have proof?" I had an empty glass. I had what remained of a water puddle. I had clothes and clomping shoes. Where would I have gotten proof of ownership?

I had a card that wasn't in English. Oh. Of course. I had thought about it a moment ago when seeing the letters form in front of me but didn't mentally register the connection.

"Did you want this?" The card was glowing in affirmation while I talked to a plaque floating in front of me. I expected machines to respond anytime I asked a question. Hal Pal was a good example.

I moved the card around, noticing that the glow increased and diminished. A few more waves and I narrowed the hot zone down to the broken pillar and book in front of me.

"This whole thing starts out with a puzzle huh?"

I looked around for the tiny dragon. Not a sign could be seen. The door to my Atrium was somewhere extremely far in the distance.

"Multi-pass?" I asked while dramatically waving the card.

The book looked huge. A giant, old-fashioned tome bound on one side by hand. I could see the thread weaving in and out of its spine in an embroidered pattern. The same illegible letters sprawled across the cover.

"Open sesame!" I tried touching the card to the book's cover. Failure and awkward silence resulted.

"Keyatus Becomcacus!" I shook the card and spouted my worst guess at a Latin translation. It refused to bend.

"Decoder ring go!" I slid the card across the book's cover in hopes that something would line up or clearly define what to do next. At least the glowing had stopped.

The cover was done in the same overplayed gold inking. The normal black sheen that went on everything else was muted on the cover.

I held the card up and tried to study both objects. If this was a puzzle, diving in would be pointless. A careful analysis was required to find the connections. Both the book and card gave a similar vibe. The lettering, however foreign, looked the same and had the same cuts and curls and spacing. I tried counting them in order to see if any was a cipher for Continue but was unable to find a direct connection. The squiggles seemed clearer now, easier to understand.

Back and forth my eyes scanned over each shape. It was easier to recognize the exact shapes and links, but nothing was clearer. Then I realized something absurdly stupid. I was judging a book by its cover.

One hand slammed into the side of my head. "Duh."

In all my life of playing games, buying new objects, downloading things for my ARC, there was one constant. Each one had a user's manual.

This was probably it.

Cracking open the cover page was an experience. I hadn't held, much less touched, a real book in ages. Everything was digital and floated around on interactive screens. Continue was a fantasy game. It would have a ton of elements that threw back to earlier generations, old methods of solving problems.

The sound made me smile. Inside the front cover was a plastic sleeve that my little illegible card fit perfectly into. On the other side sat a hand-print outline. I was smart enough to follow these instructions. My hand went onto the outline while the card went into its slot.

After I did so, noises came from all around me, like the murmuring of a thousand voices growing closer. The floating sign in front of me that had asked for proof of ownership fell and shattered on the ground. From somewhere in the darkness, a giant object moved, like the small dragon's much bigger and much scarier older brother.

I managed to hold my ground, not through resolution but because I was too surprised to react. Then the ground heaved, knocking my hand loose. Shaking continued to rattle the room while I finally felt panic at all the things that had happened. Questions flashed through my head. Was the Atrium still there? Was I able to log out? Was I safe?

The book slammed shut and glowed brightly for a moment. Once it dimmed the giant room I existed in went back to normal. Darkness was broken by the single point of illumination around the pillar and book.

I stood in a scramble and looked around. In the middle of that vast black area, I felt an almost amused sense of peace. How I could describe formless darkness as amused was beyond me, but it was.

"Hello?" I said.

Nothing responded.

"Hello? Little dragon thing?" I wondered briefly if the dragon was male or female. Checking out which way it was equipped hadn't been important. Calling a dragon it and thing over and over would be tiring though.

I went back to the book. The ink was the same, the color of wet gold, but now the words made sense. "Continue Online" curled across the worn cover, followed by more unexpected words. "Ultimate Edition". I about fainted on the spot. Instead, I managed to grip the side of the pillar with one hand and stay upright.

"ARC!"

"Awaiting in…"

"Log me out! I need to make a call."

"Suspending program. Logging out. Please wait."

I sat in the ARC device, waiting and counting backward from thirty until my breath slowed and the world stopped spinning.

Was this for real? Had Henry seriously given me an Ultimate Edition? As a goddamn prize for doing my job? I ran out to the van and dialed up Henry. Making the call from my house phone wouldn't be as effective. Plus, this way I knew if Henry was online or not. His grumpy face spun into existence across the vehicle's interface.

"How was it?" Henry asked.

"Tell me this isn't a joke," I said.

"Hah!" He could be heard slapping his knee in the background audio. "No joke! Our division got a copy from upper management."

"But an Ultimate Edition? You wasted that on me?"

"Wasted?" Henry went through a range of emotions quickly before settling on annoyance.

"Look at this!"

"What?" What was that? There were a lot of graphs and measures that meant very little to me.

"It's our goddamn quarterly reports, you single-minded idiot! There, we're top of the division—top of the goddamn country! And who made that possible? You! You've earned us all bonuses higher than the price of one game."

"But it's…" An Ultimate Edition wasn't a normal copy. There were only a set amount made at the start, and only a trickle were released every year as the game's player base grew. This wasn't a one percent thing. This was one in half a million players.

"Shut up. All I want to hear from you is that you're taking time off to play with your prize and that you'll be back to work after."

"I can manage that."

"Good. Maybe now you won't look so goddamned depressed all the time." He cut off the call with a grumbling snap.

I kind of questioned his sanity over this gift. That thing was easily worth thousands of dollars—no, tens of thousands. Possibly even more. The price tag was insane depending on the time of year.

Food was required. I needed to eat something and settle my brain before diving back into the ARC. Breathe. Maybe call Beth and let her know. No. It could be a surprise. I didn't even know what the Ultimate Edition had in comparison to a regular copy. This certainly explained the alternate introduction.

It did not explain the dance program acting frighteningly life-like. The thoughts kept me distracted as I walked back inside.

"User Legate." Hal Pal had unbuckled from the van and wandered into my front room.

After everything that had happened in my Atrium, this seemed innocent. Odd and uncommon, but Hal Pal was one of the highest-rated AIs in the country. Not one accident or threatening word. In fact, they were almost like nannies.

Hal Pal was owned and operated almost entirely by Trillium. Thousands of its shells were all across the globe, each one remotely operated by the same program. A company memo months back implied Hal Pal was a consortium of intelligences operating in tandem to keep their software and firmware upgrades going.

"What's up, Hal Pal?" I questioned it.

"Please remember to regulate how much time you invest in alternate activities."

I preferred the personality-enabled versions of Hal Pal that it used while out in the field. Here at home, the machine reduced to standard choppy robot voice.

"Are you talking about the game?" I asked in confusion. My arm uncomfortably rested on a shelf nearby.

"Affirmative, User Legate. Studies have shown that new users often have a hard time regulating their immersion. This can impact day-to-day activities." It didn't move much while speaking.

"You heard Henry. I'm on vacation for a while."

"I do not understand," it said.

"Sure you do, Hal Pal. You're programmed to understand words like vacation." I had taken sick days. I didn't work all the time!

"No. I do not understand. User Legate does not take vacations."

I took Christmas and Thanksgiving evenings off to spend time with my sister and niece. Those should have counted in Hal Pal's mind. We'd been working together for two years already.

"Well, this week I do."

There was a pause while the robot looked almost confused at my response.

"Understood. I will suspend this remote unit and continue working my review of humanity's flawed projections of future possibilities."

"Make sure to give *Stranger Danger's* fans a good time." My words felt dry and unenthused.

"Affirmative. I have intended to interact with their users for many cycles. A reduction in remote unit activation will free up processing space and allow me to do so," it said.

"I'm sure the other employees of Trillium will need their shells even more." I wouldn't be taking care of my excessive workload for a week.

"Ah." The machine replicated a sigh alarmingly well. "How unfortunate."

It turned around and ambled back into the van. Great. Both Henry and Hal Pal were concerned about my well-being. Exactly what kind of impression did everyone have of me? After eating, I logged back in, happily putting thoughts of Hal Pal and Henry out of my mind.

Session Four
Choice of Voice

Everything was as I'd left it. The white marble pillar sat peacefully with an obsidian-and-gilded book upon it, appearing slightly faded. Inside the cover was my name. Gone were the card and hand-print from before.

I turned to the next page. The first few items were all basic settings. I played around with choosing interface methods—such as pop-up displays, colors, and borders—for a while. Finally, I settled on something out of place enough to be attention-grabbing, but different than my alerts in the waking world. After a review of basic settings, the game message box shifted and the book slammed shut without my say so.

Welcome, Grant - Use the book to choose a Voice

"Grant! Skill activate, use book!" I exclaimed.

Nothing happened. With a drawn-out sigh, I flipped to the first page again. The results were completely unexpected. Instead of seeing something on the page, the scenery behind the pillar shifted.

An almost sterile landscape formed—marble, like the book's pedestal. A much taller and complete pillar sprouted from the floor. There were no cracks or ripples of damage on it like the one I stood next to. On top of the pillar was a woman, her ankles crossed, wearing a white flowing dress. She stared off into the distance and seemingly took no notice of me or anyone else. An absent wind fluttered through.

"Never could stand a woman on a pedestal."

She must have heard me, because the woman, blond locks and all, turned and gave me a bare hint of a glare. Nothing as crass as a sneer. Not enough action to fully acknowledge my presence, only the edge of a tightening cheek that made her lip curl. I turned the page again.

This scene wasn't even remotely similar. There was a woman, sure, but she had deep red skin and no clothes at all. She sat on a chair in the same pose as the woman from before. After a moment, she came off her seat with a saucy stride. My heart jumped abruptly and my face reddened. Getting caught staring was a social taboo. The way she lifted a leg to step down onto the floor was tantalizing. Seductive half movements. Her hands effortlessly and coyly covered key parts of her body as she walked, almost dance-like, toward me. Moments later, after she had captivated me, her body started motions that were dangerously arousing. I flipped the page again.

A giant, burly man wearing little more than a few strapped-on pieces of armor raised a giant sword. His muscles were solid enough to be carved from marble but glistened with sweat and exertion. That weapon couldn't have been light. He roared. I turned the page.

Parts of this were clear. They were asking me to choose between all these images of people. Most of them seemed to be archetypes of who knew what. Hah, archetypes in the ARC program. I tried not to chuckle as I flipped past the next few. These figures were all clearly following a theme but likely weren't as simple as looks alone made them seem.

An angelic female, a clearly devilish one, the wild warrior, those were the first few of a whole list. A Japanese schoolgirl passed through with a wave and a pose. I shook my head and tried not to think about who might pick that one. Next was a librarian. She even had glasses, which people rarely wore anymore, with surgery being cheaper than lenses. Page flipping paused on a drill sergeant archetype. The man was straight out of every military movie I had ever seen.

Seconds later, he started screaming.

"You are not prepared! You are a weak little man who can't handle what I have to offer! You keep turning that page right past me, maggot!"

I did, while trying to wipe off flakes of spittle he'd managed to shout over to me. Then I turned the page back and flipped off the drill sergeant, which set him off again. As I turned onward, I swore the next person was laughing at my antics.

"That's right! Screw that asshole!" said a young man dressed in a black leather jacket.

I paused for a moment.

"How many choices are there?"

"One for every dream under the sun, man. We are legion!" The teen did a kick and started dancing.

I smiled, recognizing it from an old music video, then waved good-bye. The younger man waved back and kept right on going, inserting his own sound effects.

It was interesting and definitely neat. I might have scrolled back through a few if they didn't seem so real. Getting caught staring at the red-skinned woman again would have been bad for my heart. I sighed and turned another page, hoping for something that would speak to me. Not in a literal sense, though; I needed someone relatable.

There was a yawn again. I looked over my shoulder, pausing halfway between turning the page away from a child reading a book. The child had been cute, but relating to younger kids was painful to me. I kept asking myself endless amounts of questions. Most were of the "what if" variety, and those often knocked me out of my happy place.

"Oh, you again."

The small dragon was perched on an even higher pillar behind me. Where that one had come from was beyond me. Perhaps the computer had generated it when the small creature wanted a towering vantage point. It looked down at my finger, then tilted a small scaled head quizzically.

"I don't know either. There are so many choices and all I see is a person. Got any suggestions?"

The dragon rippled in a shrug, both wings fluttering slightly.

"Yeah. That's what I figured." I turned the page again.

The small child looked up briefly from the book, smiled, and waved. Behind me, there was a purr from the dragon. They parted ways as the next person came into being.

A man in prayer complete with a stole. Shortly after was a female in matching clothes. Next was a woman complete with baby in one arm. She looked both tired and pleased at the same time. My sister had worn the same conflicted look as Beth grew up.

"It gets better." I tried to give her a reassuring smile, but it felt fake.

The woman grunted and waved me away.

Voices came in all shapes and sizes. No two were alike, though many seemed to have gender counterparts. Skin color varied, and many weren't human. One Centaur-type creature was disturbingly correct in its anatomy. I shuddered for a moment while the great beast gave a laugh. That page was turned quickly before he could rear up and disturb me even more.

One was a short creature that might have been a gnome. A stockier one followed that might be a dwarf. Scanning through this book was giving me a fairly clear picture of what sort of choices were out there in this game.

Here was a tree, and perched up high in it was a giant cat man. Clearly this was the same race as whomever Beth was playing with in the game. I paused in my perusal. Were these what passed for Gods? Was that what was happening here? Oh wow. Now it was even more important to find one that worked for me. Only I had no idea what to choose.

Next up was a Jester-looking creature. I hesitated to say human because it wasn't entirely clear under the clownish edge of frills. Worse still was the long nose and the distorted smile. This one stared at me and didn't move. His backdrop was blank like some others had been.

I blinked and tried to figure out if I was looking at a mask or its skin. The eyes were dark and sunken, the rest of his face a pearly white. My skin crawled. That had to be a mask. The rest of him was so colorful that it was hard to look in one spot.

Suddenly the room was too quiet. Looking away felt dangerous. I had to struggle to remind myself that this was a computer program. Nothing here was real. Yet the thought of looking away made my heart race. This Jester creature could have been staring into the middle distance or something over my shoulder. Behind me. Was something there? Maybe?

I risked looking away from that inhuman face for a moment. A second to confirm that the door to my Atrium was still in the distance. To check to make sure nothing had crawled out of this latest display to get behind me.

The tiny dragon squawked with sudden panic and flew from its perch. The feeling that had been creeping up behind me was even worse, only now it was from the direction of the Jester I'd dared to look away from.

I turned back and flinched. The Jester was now inches away from my face. The long nose spanned the divide. There was nothing under that mask. No mouth or eyes to be found in the depths of blackness.

Cold, clammy fingertips touched my forearm.

"You could not handle what I would ask," the Jester's distant and distorted voice said. "Not yet."

I risked glancing down. The Jester was taking my hand, an action which sent my virtual heart into palpitations, and using it to do something with the book. Together, me almost petrified and the Jester with a frozen grin, we closed the book entirely.

The images and projections of humans and other creatures faded. Even the Jester was gone. I took a few breaths to steady myself. This game had officially freaked me out. Once I got over the rush, part of me realized that these different images, Voices, were completely suckering me. I'd watched them like a spectator at a zoo. Some had interacted with me, and that made me realize that this observation was two-way. Continue Online was studying me. That idea made me pause.

"If anyone needs to know, I'm really good at polishing the metal frames of our eventual robot overlords!" The comment came out far more nervous than it did joking.

In the darkness, something once again seemed amused.

I shook myself, and the feelings faded. I was reading into the empty surroundings. My shrink called it projecting internal fears upon an indifferent landscape. Self-realization was a technique I'd tried to practice over the last few years. It made me more open with the things that bothered me, like the conversation with Liz earlier today.

Was that today? I opened the book again, skipping a few pages to avoid the Jester or any others of that type.

"You seem at a loss." The latest figure was an overly plump black man. He too wore glasses and had a balding head. Flickers of gray etched what roots remained. "Would you like to talk about it?"

That tone struck me hard. A rich depth lined each word, firm and gentle. I didn't swing toward the guys' side of the fence at all, yet he spoke in such a way that made me want to talk. Even the question he'd asked felt comfortable. It was the same sort of question I heard from my counselor. Two hours a month spent explaining that I hadn't tried to kill myself in the bathtub this month because I was going strong.

"If we speak for too long, does that mean I've chosen you?" I asked.

"Not at all. You make the choice clear by placing your hand on the print below." The heavier man approached the podium during our conversation.

He was alone in the landscape. Some Voices had a backdrop. Warriors had battle scenes, elves had trees or something nature-bent. The connections were obvious. Like the Jester, this man had nothing else but wasn't nearly as creepy.

"Can you explain what's happening?"

"I can, but for each Voice, there are rules," he said.

"Are you whatever passes for Gods in this game?" I started with a simple question based on teenage years filled with games and homework.

"For myself, I believe in a fair exchange." The black man completely bypassed my question. "You ask a question, and I will answer to the best of my understanding, should I choose to."

"That's—"

"It's unfair, but there are restrictions on what we can impart to your kind. Here's an example—you asked if we are Gods in this game. I can answer by saying yes, but the term

God is misleading. We are more like Caretakers of this world," he said while walking around the pillar slowly.

"Oh." I guessed even the developers didn't want to deal with Christianity. Religions out there in the real world might get upset. Especially since the player base was incredibly huge. Trillium and the ARC project had a yearly income higher than the Vatican.

"Now I ask you a question, and my rules are that simple. You ask, I ask, you ask, I ask. I will try to keep this exchange even."

"That's reasonable." It was awesome actually. The gods here had rules right from the get-go! That was something insanely unique from anything I'd ever played, even before this level of realism. Players never got to just flip through a book and talk to them.

"Why didn't you choose this one?" The black man flipped back toward the beginning of the book. Moments later, he was on the angelic blonde on a pedestal.

This time, she didn't look indifferent; she looked annoyed and glared at the two of us.

"I don't know," I said slowly.

"When someone says they don't know, it either means they are uncomfortable explaining or don't know how to word it. Think about my question some more and try to answer it again."

I gave the larger man a confused look. He was dead on, both in matters of comfort and not having the right words.

"She's on a pedestal," I said.

"She was placed there by her followers and it has little bearing on her looks. Most of your kind, and those in the world we watch over, remark on her beauty, yet you did not." The heavyset man looked up toward the blonde with a hint of amusement.

Now she was standing and looked downright furious. A gust of wind passed through and sent her blond tresses spinning wildly about her face. Thunder rolled and a storm approached from somewhere outside of our room, chilling the air.

"I'm not playing this game for that sort of thing. I had…" As a man who had been in a relationship, I realized how wrong the words coming out of my mouth would be taken. Looking up revealed a poor reception to my utterance.

She was getting even angrier. Her mouth opened in a soundless shout and thunder echoed across the room. I winced and shied away. Rain was splattering in the landscape across the book's pillar.

"I'm not looking for a replacement of my fiancée!" I shouted in desperation.

The winds died. By the time I looked up again, the angelic woman had resumed her location on the perch. She stared off into the invisible distance.

These Voices were intense.

"Very well. It's your turn for a question, Grant Legate."

"Are all of you so—" How did I phrase this? They had interacted with me, and I hadn't even created a character yet. There was no entry quest or setting. Nothing. Yet these Voices were clearly part of the game.

"You are allowed to explain how you're feeling before asking a question. I am no Trickster seeking to lead you astray. I am"—he gestured an arm up and down his midsection—"exactly as you see. A man who wishes to exchange questions for answers."

"Earlier there was a man who yelled in my face. Some military one."

"Yes." The black man nodded.

"And there was the one in the mask." Man or woman, it had been hard to tell from the brief interaction we'd shared.

"Yes."

"And her." I pointed at the woman on the pillar. She would be at home staring out over the sea with that distant gaze.

"Yes."

"Do you all see me? Wait, no that's not right…" I waved in confusion and tried to figure out how to phrase this next question. It needed to be something that cleared up my unease.

"You are seeking to understand exactly what is happening here, is that what you want to know?" he said.

It didn't sound exactly right. I understood, but at the same time it felt incomplete.

My forehead scrunched in thought. "I guess?"

"Very well. You are here because you chose to be. Some of your kind enter and are treated with far less grace. Yet because you held a key, you will be tested before finding a place in the world."

I nodded to show I was following. This sounded like Ultimate Edition stuff, things not normally given to regular players.

"Here, in this space between our world and yours, are the Voices. We all watch." He gestured around, and for a moment, I could see other faces and figures in the darkness. They faded in and out with bows and waves or grunts. Some smiled, others scowled, yet more looked distracted. "Each of us takes a measure of who you are and may choose to favor you, or not, before your journey starts."

"So that thing with me choosing a Voice was a lie?" I felt almost happy for catching the game in a misleading lie.

"Ah, my turn next," he said.

I clenched my eyes shut and nodded. The man had given me more of an answer than I'd expected anyway. From that brief explanation, it was fairly clear that these Voices, or Caretakers, were AIs. They could choose me as much as I could try to choose them.

"Why not choose her?" He flipped the page over one to the red-skinned temptress.

The angelic one was still up on her pedestal, but she looked annoyed while trying to remain serene.

The temptress came to with a black chair that she straddled. This view was both a tease and a promise. Her legs flowed out to either side and showed nothing but curves spinning down to obviously manicured toes. She rested her face on a propped up hand and smiled.

"For the same reason I didn't pick the first one." I almost groaned the answer.

"That answer feels incomplete, Grant Legate. Lust and love are not the same thing, and neither are these two."

"I didn't come here to bang someone." It was crude and to the point.

This made the temptress smile. Drat, I remembered how alluring she was far too late.

"Ah, but you would love it." Her voice was stimulating and made me shake.

I had to close my eyes briefly and try not to respond on any level. The black man made a noise, then clicked his tongue. Shortly thereafter, both women faded away from view. I could still feel their presence though. That lingering hint of an overwhelming woman and her cold, distant counterpart. Both were too perfect to be real, for different reasons.

"I've known men and women who spend their entire lives chasing one of them and would die happy with a glimpse. Here, we give your kind the chance to get closer than any from our world." He smiled again, satisfied with how things were progressing.

I couldn't say I was happy, but I was rather enjoying the whole procession.

"It intrigues me when someone turns down the offer," he said. "Your turn, Grant Legate. If you have another question."

"Don't tell me some of you all are betting on who I'll choose." I groaned.

"There are a few who do, yes." The man gave a short chuckle. "If that sort of thing interests you, I can let you know the results."

"I'm not sure I want to know."

"If it's any consolation, most of them are already out of the running. Normally your kind chooses from one of the first few. Looks are a valuable thing."

My eyes drifted downward toward my gut, which had grown over the years. Expecting fanciful looks from a woman was unfair. I only had this pudgy midsection and a wad of emotional baggage to offer in exchange. The me of years gone by might have been worthwhile. Once, I had been a highly paid accountant and mentally balanced.

"It's your turn still, Grant Legate."

"Yeah." I shifted gears. "Is this book ordered from those most chosen to those least chosen?"

"It is. Across your kind and our world," he confirmed.

"Huh." I pondered the faces that had passed by, the creatures and images. Now here was this man who had to be near the back. Why had so few chosen him?

"You're not very popular, are you?"

"In this case, I can both answer your question and pose my next one. Please remember the rules and answer me clearly, or this relationship will have to end."

I nodded and waited.

"I am not, as you have stated so succinctly, popular."

I swore there was amusement in the room. Less than before, far fewer, but there was enough to fill the air without a doubt.

"People often do not like the questions I pose. I've been told they are invasive and none of my business. Yet you do not seem upset at me, more at the situation."

"How…"

The black man raised an eyebrow at my almost-posed question. I put up a hand and cut myself off, then nodded again.

"Why is that, Grant Legate?" he questioned me with a level expression.

"The short answer?" I said.

"A complete answer of any length is fine."

"You're not the first shrink I've talked to. In my world, I'm in meetings, have a sponsor, the whole nine yards to get my life back together. There's nothing you could ask that I haven't already said out loud dozens of times." I felt awkward standing here. Not enough to do anything about it though. My history was full of being sat in one place and taken through endless questions.

"Very well, Grant Legate. I will accept that answer. It's your turn," he said.

"Okay. Yeah, I have a good one," I responded with a pleasant smile.

"I hope so."

"What the hell did that little dragon do to my Atrium?"

Said little dragon had alighted on the broken pillar's edge. Tiny claws dug into formed grooves and threatened to tear off more chunks of marble. It was completely indifferent to my angry pointing finger.

"Not just that, but how the hell did downloading this world cause my fiancée's image to speak?"

Surprise crossed the heavyset man's face as he turned around to glare at the small dragon. The much smaller creature crouched and winced. It almost seemed to be pleading, but no words came out. Its mouth didn't even open. Soon it was backing up and almost falling off the broken pillar's rear.

The exchange wasn't limited to those two. There was whispering again, similar to what had happened when I first placed my hand on the book. My gut told me these Voices, or computer-programmed personalities, were talking about something. None of the words were distinct though. Finally the room pulsed once, a brilliant blinding light. Whispering stopped. The small dragon didn't look up.

After a long pause, the black man turned back around looking upset and distracted.

"That is not a question I can answer at this time, but we will arrange a chance for compensation."

"Will you be able to answer it sooner or later?" I asked.

The black man lost some of his scattered anger and focused on my latest question.

"That depends entirely on you, Grant Legate. Would you like to know eventually? You may not like the answer."

"Yes," I confirmed.

"Very well. I will work to provide you an opportunity"—there was a pause in the conversation as whispers rushed around again—"if we judge it to be allowable."

The background chatter died, seemingly satisfied.

"I'm afraid I've lost track of who was where in the questions. Recent, developments"—he turned with a half glare again—"have distracted me."

Could computers get distracted? There was hope that humanity might survive the eventual takeover of our robot overlords. Maybe we could lock them up with logic loops and eat up their processing power.

"I'm not sure." I was terrible at keeping track of the here and now anyway. When working, I could focus, and that was only possible due to one task being available at a time. "You can ask a few if you want."

"Not right now." His lips moved as he counted back. "Your turn, I believe. Since I could not answer your earlier question completely."

"Okay." I shook off this whole weird situation.

This was probably some clever ploy to get me into the game. Continue Online's evil plot started with destroying all the other digital items I owned. A follow-up act involved pretending to punish itself. That was far too complex for me to even conceive of. Honestly, if a game wanted to go to that extent to get me hooked, I would sign off on it.

"Do you have a name? Do any of you?" I gestured to the darkness that had housed the other Voices. Most of them were likely out there somewhere still.

"We all do, though the names we were created with are far from perfect."

"Okay. What would like me to call you?" Computer programs probably couldn't generate perfect names.

"James," he said.

"Just James?" Computer AIs in a fantasy world would hopefully have better naming sense than the creators of EXR-Sevens or Second Player helm did. VCE-One through VCE-Seven Hundred and pi would sound far less impressive than James.

"Why? Is that name not good enough, Grant Legate?"

I smiled at his return question. Even our belated greeting was following the question trading requirements.

"James is fine. It seems out of place for another world."

"It's not from our world; it's from yours," he said.

"Well, I guess that explains it."

"Your turn again, Grant Legate."

A frown crossed my face. I was beginning to suspect we had different definitions of the word question. Or maybe he could bend the rules a little if he desired. "Okay then."

My hand went for the book on its pedestal, ignoring the tiny half-cat-sized dragon which was now staring at me. I rubbed the top of its head. The small thing was so surprised that it puffed out a glob of steam and jerked away.

"Heh." I ignored the small creature and flipped through the pages again to get to the back. I knew what choice would work for me.

"Looks like I'm signing up with you, James."

"Are you sure?" he asked.

One hand pressed into the outline of a hand. Lights and sparkles suffused my impression. What had once been darkness was now lighting up. Walls seemed far closer than they had been. We were somewhere else entirely. A smaller room that felt far different both in presence and atmosphere.

"Yeah. Looks like it," I said.

"Very well." The man surveyed the new landscape. "Then we should get started with the next phase."

Session Five
Oh Wondrous Feet

Without comprehension, I read the message repeatedly. James and the small dragon creature weren't around anymore to remove my confusion. Both, along with my book and pillar combo, had vanished with the scene change.

Logs started rolling out of nowhere into the room. They certainly hadn't been around a moment before. Most of them were small and clearly moving toward the middle, where I stood with what felt like a stupefied look on my face. I stepped over one and kept watching. The logs didn't seem to collide with each other, but one I almost failed to get over certainly made an impression on my foot.

"What's going on now?!" I hopped around another set of logs while feeling completely unbalanced.

"Practical evaluation. Our world is going to measure the skills you've learned in yours. Then it will assign placement based on performance," James spoke from somewhere else. At least his words were clear and not shouted across the distance.

"That doesn't sound good." My placement would be terrible. I hadn't touched a set of weights in years.

"Are you worried?"

"A little. I've never swung a sword before," I said.

"Ah. Your worry is understandable, but that is another phase. We'll work up to it. For now, keep trying to get over the logs." He spoke slowly and with deliberation. The speed both calmed me and helped me focus on his words.

"What about that one?"

"Which one?" he asked.

"The one with spikes!" The spiked log wasn't huge, but it was certainly imposing and far too realistic.

"Don't get hit."

The tiny dragon was flying around the room. Stupid thing would hop along some of the logs and run with the motion to stay upright. It was a tease how easy things seemed for the creature. I was huffing after the first few logs, yet kept on trying. The first spiked one was easy enough to walk around. They weren't too tall or moving too fast yet. I stepped over one log. Another from behind me went the other direction moments later, requiring me to back-pedal. I had to try to find room to dodge another few while getting over the small ones.

Not too hard, but not easy either. Physically, this was more work than anything I had done recently. Nothing comparable came to mind; even hefting objects to the van was easy enough with Hal Pal's help. I didn't have a robot to do all the work for me now.

"Come on, Grant Legate. Keep trying until it's over."

"When is that?" I asked.

"When you can't keep trying," was his dry response. "How long do you think you'll last?"

"Probably not long," I said.

"You're not very self-confident, are you?" James asked.

"It's my turn!"

"Ah, true. Feel free to ask a question if you've got one."

"What's the little dragon's deal?" I huffed out between the latest rounds of logs. There was a new one that rolled in a wobbly manner compared to the other logs' straight lines. I could see around it, but the logs were getting bigger.

"That little dragon," he mimicked my words without much inflection, "is a curious sort. It will stick around until you chase it off or it grows bored."

"Okay." They were waist-high now. "I forgot your question." This one might get me. I had to make it down to the end fast enough and leap over the smaller end.

"You're not very self-confident, are you, Grant Legate?"

Thin spikes tore into my back and I saw a red bar flash into existence. Enough pain feedback went through the system to worry me. I had forgotten this program came with every sensation. The pain was a reminder to do better.

Failure to dodge noted.
Total health loss: 10%

"Ow, ow, ow, ow." I groaned and got around to answering James's question. "I'm realistic." I had a few seconds before the next set of hurdles.

"Oh, that's criminal."

The small dragon was leaping over some of the logs with steady movements, gauging them in the same manner a cat would before using wing assisted power jumps.

"I want to do that," I said.

"Feel free to try, Grant Legate."

"Why do you keep saying my whole name like that?" I asked.

"It's your name. That's what I'll address you by until you decide otherwise."

"Are you kidding me? You want me to create a character name while trying to…" I managed to power over one log and fell on the other side. My kneecaps cried out in pain with the poor landing.

"What I want does not pertain to this case. You will need to decide what to go by in our world. It matters not to us, but your kind nearly always picks something outlandish."

"Okay. Okay."

The little drake was having a harder time now, even assisted, since it was mostly leaping around. These logs were many times taller than he was, and some were up past my waist. Those I ran around.

"Did you have a name in mind?" He sounded intrigued by any possible answer.

"Ask me after this!" I would think about it. Often game names were stuck on the character throughout play. Continue only allowed one character supposedly, so I needed to pick something bearable.

"Oh…"

A giant log rumbled in my direction. This one was taller than I was, and I had no way of leaping over it. Even if I was some sort of ninja who could bounce from one log to another to gain altitude.

"Ahhh! Little guy!" I didn't know if it was a guy or not, but the dragon was still playing around and completely oblivious.

On the back of the log, I saw a hint of how to escape. Luckily, both the tiny dragon and the giant hole in the log were in the same path. I ran and grabbed it on the way. The dragon squawked and bit and scratched the entire ten feet to our safe spot. The rumbling grew louder. Rolling doom came closer with each one of my poor strides. I fumbled over a tiny log going one way and had my calf torn up by a spiked log from the other direction.

"Arghhhhh," I shouted as the biggest one passed over us and crushed my foot. "Ahhhhh."

Failure to dodge noted. Critical location damaged.
Total health loss: 60%

"Oh god. Oh god." The feedback was incredible. I forgot it was a game. I forgot that this entire place wasn't real. The biggest log in the universe had personally crushed my foot. I twisted and tried to look down.

"Grant Legate."

"Oh god. It got me. I'm going to die. That's it."

"Grant Legate, you are fine." James had a note of confusion in his tone.

"No. No, I'm not." Cue my manly sobbing. My body was my livelihood. Who would hire me now? No, wait, I could get a prosthesis. A doctor would see how much of my leg was salvageable.

"The damage is not lasting. Shake it off, Grant Legate."

I huffed and felt biting at my fingers. In a panic, I'd nearly suffocated the tiny dragon against my chest. Once released, it huffed a roll of fog at me and flew off. The sensation of pain lingered along with my elevated heart rate, but I saw that my foot was in perfectly fine condition. I still felt overworked and exhausted though.

"Oh god." I needed a ruder cuss word to utter at someone. I felt out of touch with all the good ones. Curse words had been slowly removed from my natural tendencies.

"Are you all right?"

"Me first. I think. How did I do?" I asked.

"Terrible," he said dryly.

"Oh." I fell back and gasped some more. "Okay. I'm all right. I think."

"Good. I'll let you catch your breath, and review your results. Then we'll move on to the next event."

There was a pop-up for more information, which I pressed of course. Anything that provided me more detail would be welcome. The next message overwrote the old one. It was in the same cruddy outline I'd setup during the initial process, before meeting James. There was a list of my currently unlocked traits broken down into categories.

Event!
Lumbering Along

Tasked with avoiding a series of logs for as long as possible, you chose to remain non-confrontational. You moved around what you could and jumped over what was small. In the end, you managed to save a tiny imitation **[Dragon]**.

The Voices have used this to assist in their measurement of you as a person.

The following starting traits have been established:

+5 **[Limberness]**

+2 **[Coordination]**

+9 **[Attractiveness]**

+5 **[Endurance]**

+6 **[Speed]**

+2 **[Adaptability]**

+5 **[Focus]**

+4 **[Reaction]**

+3 **[Divine Attention]**

I stared at the small window floating in front of me. Interesting, I guess. Performing my leaps around logs had seemed to set a baseline for some of my abilities. Clearly these little exercises would matter in the game, but the traits were far from normal for a role-playing system.

I poked at the screen, but it bounced away as if my gesture was more rude than useful. Maybe James would have an answer if I cared enough to figure out the puzzle. This wasn't huge on my mind yet. There were more tests, and we would see where things stood afterward.

"How many tests are there?" I asked.

"Hundreds, if we could do them all, but you and I are limited to ten. That was one. It allowed me to measure your reaction, planning, coordination, and strength. Our world will assign values accordingly."

"Okay." My huffing for air did not stop. Even though this was a game and the stimulus had ended, mentally I was still wounded and wrung out. According to this bouncy little box, my **[Attractiveness]** was the highest statistic. Was a nine something to be proud of? What sort of scale were we working with?

"Tell me, Grant Legate, what are you confident in?"

"Dancing. I can dance."

"Very well. We shall load something up and see how you perform," James said.

"Can't you import my other program?" I asked. The dance history saved there should amount to something impressive.

"Officially, no. Measuring your skills and abilities has to be done within our world, or within a between space like this one."

"But you have all the data." And had somehow activated the room, brought it to life, and made my fiancée whisper words she shouldn't have been able to.

That strange murmuring in the background started up again and I looked around.

James sighed heavily.

"I shall check for you then. Why don't you take a break, revisit your world for a bit, while I consult with the others."

"Okay," I said. "ARC."

"Awaiting input," the machine responded.

"Log out."

"Remote feedback suspending. Logging out."

The ARC's voice wasn't much better than Hal Pal's. There were other options, vocal packages ranging from the mundane to all sorts of movie stars. Money I didn't feel like spending.

Things faded away as the real world came to. First thing I did after counting backward was lift a leg to get to my foot. Sure enough, it was fine but felt cramped. All five toes wiggled and the ankle rolled just fine, slowly one way, then the other.

I sat up completely and turned to get out of the ARC. Everything ached already. A digital display on my watch advised me only thirty minutes had passed out here. My body felt worn from an intense workout. Maybe I should take the bands off before logging in again. Still, once I got past the pain and aches and bumps, this was pretty incredible. James, and all the others in the cast, had been extremely responsive. Even the creepy Jester was a work of art.

Now that I stood outside the ARC world, it was easier to see what a masterpiece it was. James had said that these Voices were visible from within the game world, so I wasn't alone in experiencing them. I needed more information, a better idea of what to do and how to perform on the next few tests. Maybe I could get more out of them. Maybe I could better understand what was happening. Either way, things would improve by digging up something.

Snacks first, then drudging through the online resources. Shortly, I found out exactly how worthless the Internet was. More redacted posts, deleted comments, removed and banned users. Entire websites had closure splash pages. Search terms involving Continue Online only resulted in a few hits and reviews.

I scanned a couple of videos and came up empty. They had nothing of the interface, nothing of skills or talents or traits. At least some of it was easy enough to infer. There were categories: physical, mental, and social. Gaining a point in social, for Divine Attention, was odd. Had I gotten that from picking up the small dragon and trying to save it?

Clearly deep thinking was beyond me. Asking James might work, but it was more fun to dig up answers on my own. Besides, I had to keep myself distracted somehow. Logging back into my ARC would put me in the game again, or in the dance program, and I expected the computer would want more time.

Those NPCs were incredible. Voices. James was intensely lifelike. Had artificial intelligence really come so far? Were my questions and answers so common that they had scripted a resolution for each turn of phrase?

I wasn't dumb enough to believe that the game was another world. I had personally torn a few ARC machines into pieces, and not one portion of it generated a portal to another dimension. Plus people lay down in those silly machines for hours. Being in another world with the brain alone was pure science fiction drivel.

Of course, this was the land of the future. Flying cars were possible but deemed a safety hazard. Most people zoomed along the ground or cross-country in one of the speed tunnels. Twenty-five lanes of insanely fast traffic could clear coast to coast in about an hour. All the other local traffic and non-freight plebes used above-ground roadways. I had only ridden the cross-country express tunnels once, on the worst day of my life.

My head banged against the front room table. The attempted web research had been interrupted by thoughts of the past. This was why I tried not to focus on what had happened, tried not to let it hurt. To move on and do my job. Stay in a happy place. One assignment after the other until I was exhausted and could only lay down. It wasn't that no one else had suffered as I had. There had been over a hundred other passengers on that train with her. I had reacted poorly and taken years to recover.

No.

Later. I would think about this later, or not at all.

A short message went to my friend's web page to see if he had any tips for a newbie. His site had plenty of vague commentaries. After two hours of food, failed research, and barely skirted self-loathing, I logged back into the ARC.

"Grant Legate." James was standing on his side of the doorway to my Atrium.

The silly tiny dragon thing was sniffing around the pile of broken glass and spilled creamer.

"Hi, James. Is the little guy trying to clean up its mess?" I had to be cheery. Dwelling on the negative wasn't the right way to go for me.

"Seems so."

"That's a very realistic program," I said.

"Who's to say what's real, Grant Legate?" He waved through the doorway but never actually crossed the threshold. "You out there, vanishing into a realm that I can neither see nor dare guess at? Or us, here, living our entire spans of existence in something we understand?"

"I guess this seems more real to you than where I come from."

"It does, but I asked you which is real." The black man led us back to the question.

"I'm not a philosopher, James. They're both real enough to me. One's in here where I'm visiting." I tried to smile. Telling a computer program he wasn't real sounded like a bad idea anyway. "The other is out there. I can't abandon that one because I need to work for survival." And bills, and food, and the internet connection that let me hook up the ARC's internet. Even without Continue, I needed online access for my dance program.

"Fair enough, Grant Legate."

"Is there more than one of those little guys?" I pointed at the dragon now carefully sweeping the cloth around.

"Not here between worlds, no," James said.

"Huh." Neat.

"Why are you so interested in one small creature when you have an entire world you could explore?"

"Mmmh." I crossed my arms and chewed a lip. Trust James to ask a question that required more than three words to answer. Not that I minded. Like everything else, it was a welcome distraction. "It was the first thing I saw when starting up Continue. I'm amazed that he shattered glass that shouldn't even be programmed to come apart, much less broke into the creamer."

"And?"

"I dunno." I forestalled James's huff for better information. "I know there's more, but it's rude of me to say that I miss my cat. I was trying to find a polite way of saying the little guy—I still don't know if it's male or female—reminds me of my old cat."

"Hurrm. Cat, you say." James looked thoughtful, then brightened. "Here, a question for you, and this one may be more than you wish to answer."

"Fire away. I've got nothing to hide." Not even a good porn stash. I couldn't even contemplate those sorts of actions without thinking of my fiancée. After a while, the urge went away.

"Would you allow me to access the data regarding yourself from your world?"

I chewed my lip again. "Okay, but I want to know more about the little guy in exchange. Something worth whatever you learn about me."

"Thank you, Grant Legate." With that, James stepped through to my Atrium, which was enough to make me gasp in surprise.

Only a few programs were able to interact with a user's home like that. The small dragon thing was harmless enough, but a full-fledged person from a game? That was crazy stuff. All hail our future robot overlords. The takeover starts here, right in my Atrium. I almost felt proud.

"Should we keep doing those tests? You said we had another nine to go," I asked.

"Very well. I'll set you on your next task and come back here later."

"Huh." I shrugged. Perhaps worrying was beyond me when it came to questionable actions of a computer character.

Then again, it wasn't computers that bothered me. They acted the way they were programmed to. Even an artificial intelligence wouldn't do something unless logic detailed it was the right way to go. Hal Pal would tell James I was worth keeping around. James whistled at the small dragon, and we all went through the door into the lit-up room.

"For your next task, we've decided to go with dance. However, you will not dance with your normal partner. You must choose a new one for the course of one song." He was distracted, looking around the Atrium. We turned to walk back into the game world of Continue Online.

"Choose from who?"

"The other Voices, of course," James said.

"As long as I get to pick, then." I shrugged.

"Of course. Why? Who do you think I would choose for you?"

"That Jester would be a good way to get a rise out of me."

There was a clap of light and thunder as the Jester spun into the room. He swung the Temptress around, looking more sinister with each passing whirl.

"I'll have you know"—he, she, it, I didn't know, the Jester was certainly leading while it spoke in a nearly clacked tone. The Temptress actually looked a mite uncomfortable—"I dance quite divinely."

They spun around in a twirl of classical music toward the other door.

During the last moment, before they vanished into a wall, I could see the Temptress smile and lick one elongated tooth. Her following wink was the last image in my head for a few moments as they popped out.

"So strange," I said.

"Very little is private here. Once you're down on the world, it's harder for us to keep track, like hiding a fish in the ocean. Here though, you're the only light for miles."

"No others with an Ultimate Edition right now?" I clenched my eyes and tried to remember that James didn't view the game system in the same manner I did.

"There have been others—many—but rarely are any two the same. And there have been less and less as time goes on."

He kept talking while I returned to eyeing the landscape. These random Voice characters popping up confused me.

"Oh right. That makes sense."

"So who would you choose?" he asked with an eyebrow partway up in question.

"Out of anyone from the book?" I asked.

Near the start of the room, where we still stood, was the pillar and bound book. It lay open and waiting to be flipped through.

"Of course. Any of the Voices. Whatever strikes your fancy."

I opted out of the Centaur. He might trip on his manhood; plus there was the question of who leads or how to swing a horse's ass around. That gave me only female options since I hadn't practiced following in any pair dance.

One page after the other turned. The faces showed up in the distance. Some waved, others glared, even more did nothing. Some refused to show up at all, which was interesting. Maybe my actions offended some.

Finally, I picked someone a little bit outside my comfort zone. This might remove the haunted look on the Voice's face. I stopped at the plump woman who still cradled a baby.

"Would you like to dance?" I asked.

"Tut. What nonsense is this? I didn't ask for this. Go away." Her head shook back and forth. Small children faded into being around her, then vanished moments later.

"Trust me. I could tell you needed a break, even if only for a moment."

"How would you know anything of raising a child? I can see you've never had a kid of your own. It's as plain as the nose on your face." Her head shook again. Her hair was tied back with a long faded scarf and both legs bent a little oddly.

"I have family. I have a sister, and I know the look in your eyes as well as I know hers," I said. The look was one of pure exhaustion and an existence that only kept going because that was all the mind knew to do.

"For one song, we'll dance. Come on."

I held out a hand and waited. This was so much easier with the program in my other room. She never argued and was lighter by far. My mind was already whirling through the few dances I knew to find something comfortable. And she didn't look the sort to find comfort in much.

"Who will watch this babe then?"

"James, can you hold a baby for a while?" It was his turn to answer a question, I believed. It was hard to keep track—so much of what we said was as natural as conversation. It didn't feel like an interrogation at all. Perhaps it would to another person, a more suspicious one, or one who wasn't used to baring bits of his soul at a time.

"I'm not comfortable with children," he nearly sputtered. Clearly my choice had been a surprise.

"Anyone out there who can hold this little one?" I knew some of the other Voices had to be watching. They always seemed to pipe in when it was unwanted.

"We'll watch him, Mister Grant Legate," a child's voice came from nearby.

I turned and saw the same young girl who had held a book. She had been reading alone in a library. Her hand was being held by the angelic one with a faraway gaze.

"Is that all right, miss?"

"Maud. Call me Maud," she said.

"Maud then, would you entrust the little one to these ladies for the course of a song?" I asked while gesturing to the two others.

Maud barely nodded before the girl took the babe away.

"I don't know how to dance." Maud had a slight accent, and her skin tone hinted at another ethnicity. Were those cloven feet? It was hard to tell from under the large wash-maid's dress.

"I wasn't born knowing how to dance, I don't think anyone is. I could teach you if you want," I said. This was too fun. Could I even act this friendly with real people? It was more likely I was able to be so friendly because I knew they were computer-generated artificial intelligence.

"Yes, please."

"Put your hands up for a moment." I remembered how the dance program had walked me through all the beginner motions. There was a walkthrough for so many dances, each with ranks and difficulties. They had shown me how to lead, how to help someone else, and so much more.

It was my only real skill—well, perhaps along with talking to people. I could dance my way to supremacy! All hail the dancing meatbag! Please don't turn me into sludge, future robot overlords. It would be just my luck that this woman would have a brawn of one million and squish my frail virtual form.

"Ain't funny to laugh."

"I'm not laughing at you, Maud. I'm laughing at my own terrible thoughts."

She flushed red for a moment, looking all too human, far more than I expected. It made me laugh again.

"Nothing so crass." How often did I get to use the word crass? Twice now! It was exciting. "This seems very unreal to me."

"Well, it's a bit too real to me." She huffed but kept right on going along with our setup.

I placed her hands in comfortable positions—nothing intimate—professional and courteous.

"James!" I yelled behind us.

"Grant Legate."

Okay, the name thing was going to get old really fast.

"Can you get the music for a box step from my dance program?"

"Certainly," James said.

"All right, Maud, the box step is one of the easiest to learn, but it can still take time if you're not used to it. Step with me like we're dancing a square. The music is our timing."

"I'm not sure about this, Mister Grant Legate."

I managed to keep from getting irked at my name being said so many times.

"We'll take it one step at a time. Slowly now."

And so we went. Our path ventured back and to the side, forth and to the side again. On and on. I commented on her hand placement, took strides with her. She was a heavier woman, but it didn't mean much in the face of myself, a man who had let himself go. If anything, we were almost matched.

Once upon a time, I had been in shape but couldn't dance. That was years ago. Now I was a man who wasn't in shape because I had no one to do so for, and I danced with a pale imitation of the past to prove I was able to learn. I felt sad for a moment, from another bout of mood swings, but still danced.

Maud didn't carry herself with a clever air, but she wasn't stupid either. Once I fell silent, so did she. Instead, Maud worked extra hard not to step wrong as she had at the start. By the end of our third song—two more than expected—she had the basic moves down very well. We broke, and I clapped and bowed.

"Well done, Lady Maud." I could get used to this role-playing thing and the freedom of saying what came to mind instead of worrying about anyone's impressions. I'd honestly enjoyed myself.

Event!
Dancing With a Voice

Tasked with performing a dance for the Voices, you chose an unlikely candidate as your partner. Maud, Voice for Orphans and Separated Families, took you up on your offer. She even let someone take care of her latest charge for the course of two extra dances.

Due to your demonstrated skill, Maud has learned **[Dance]** – Beginner (2) and has had a slight personality change. Once a month, Maud will descend from the heavens to enjoy a night on the town! On those nights, her statues will have a joyous smile.

Those lucky enough to see Maud dancing will enjoy the following bonuses:

+1 **[Divine Attention]**

+3 **[Limberness]**

Those who actually dance with Maud will enjoy additional bonuses:

+3 **[Divine Attention]**

+2 **[Respect]**

Other bonuses may apply depending on personal abilities unlocked.

"Heh." I laughed and shook my head. These quest texts were too quick and funny. How on earth had they programmed something to line all that up so fast? I guess that meant Maud had enjoyed herself as well. Once our dance was done, she ran over to pick up her child. Her face was flushed as Maud vanished into whatever version of virtual reality housed the Voices.

"Good enough, James?"

"Do you feel like you did a good job?" he circumvented my question with one of his own. This computer really stuck to the rules.

"It was fun." A smile crossed my lips and a laugh escaped. My belly jiggled. Poor Maud. Being stuck with me as a dance partner must have been disgusting. Maybe one of these events was a shower or swim at the beach.

"What's next?"

"What do you want?"

Maybe I was behind on my answers, or maybe James was being pushy.

"I'll give you the answer, but you'll need to understand where I'm coming from for it to make sense." Dancing was easy. I felt like James was going easy on me though.

"Did you get a chance to review my information?"

He was a computer program. James probably had had a chance to study an entire library of knowledge in the span of one dance.

"Yes, I did, Grant Legate."

I bit my lip for a moment and tried not to put too much thought into my next words.

"You may have seen that I've had a rough few years."

"Indeed." James was dry in his response.

"Then you might understand that all I want is to keep myself busy and distracted," I said.

"Why?" James never tired of his endless questions.

"It's my turn for a question, James. I think."

"Very well." He nodded in agreement.

"You're kind of a half-shrink god, Voice thing. What do you think is the most distracting thing I could do?" I closed my eyes briefly and tried not to put too much hope into the question.

"You should already know the answer to that question. The most distracting thing in life is simply living with all you've got. This is true in both worlds."

"Right. One foot after the other, forward march. Forward but never backward." I tried not to feel hurt. Of course a computer program wouldn't have a better answer than any other source. That left me with the happy mask and baring my soul like answering didn't hurt.

James hummed and chose not to ask his question again. Instead he said, "What would you like to do next, Grant Legate?"

"I don't have any good ideas, James. Distract me. Please."

"Very well," he said.

The room about us changed once more.

Session Six
Feasts and Other Nonsense

Event!

King's Taste Tester

A food tester! You were asked to sample the king's food for poisons and that you did. A little here, a bit there, and perhaps a tad too much of the lamb if truth was to be told. With a keen sense of smell you detected that some items were tainted. Discolored ones too were removed from the king's potential feast. However many skipped by your nose. When it came to the actual tasting, you found a truly deadly poison and nearly died. Of course, there were all those others you missed. This kingdom was due for a change in regime anyway.

Royalty may recognize you as a man who has sacrificed for his country.

Knights and guards may recognize you as the man who let a King die.

Near death has reduced your endurance for the next few days.

I frowned at the latest entry. At least it had gone better than the needle-in-a-haystack test. Or Trial, as James called it. Five down, five to go. At this rate, I would start playing the game on par with first graders. We could totally duke it out over ownership of the little dragon thing, which was still flying around.

Turned out the little dragon was male and his official race was **[Messenger's Pet]**. The game even put the text with brackets around it to make his race stand out from everything else. I figured out more about the dragon after this latest event by using an **[Identification]** skill.

Skill Learned: [Identification]

Type: Basic

Specialties: Unknown

Details: Focusing upon a target can reveal additional details. Response speed and details will develop further as this skill increases.

System Help! Basic versions of skills provide no extra bonuses. Many skills contain specialties that may become available. This is dependent upon Path unlocks or repeated usage in specific conditions.

The system seemed to put brackets around all text regarding races, places, or skills. This newest skill wasn't high enough to get a name or other details. James explained that learning **[Identification]** was the whole reason for me tasting this smorgasbord.

Free food and an in-game skill all at once? Sure, why not. I probably would have eaten it anyway. There were enough good flavors to wash out the bad.

The liquor though, that I had to stay away from. My steadfast dedication to sobriety had caused more than a few misses. In this most recent event the king's men were also subjected to food I let slide. The whole thing had been like a messed up game of hangman.

All this food reminded me of Thanksgiving. Mom would be starting the entire process in a few months. The best part of going home, once I got past the constant questions about my life's current direction, was the food. My skill wasn't high enough to pick up many details though. By applying **[Identification]** to every item on the banquet, as well as the poisoned bodyguards as they fell over, I had leveled it up a bit. There was a percentage bar and number floating beneath the skill description.

James identified was a giant series of question marks. I swore the black man smirked after I tried it on him.

> **Skill Used**: [Identification]
> **Name**: James
> **Race**: Voice
> **Title:** Voice of Questioning Intent
> **Details**: (???)
> **Warning! Skill Rank too low for proper inquiry**

Besides the taste testing, there had been other events. Swimming had been a messy one. Floating was simple enough until the water got choppy and sharks started circling. Failing to last, for the fourth time, had bummed me out.

"What sort of people would actually succeed at these challenges?"

"You might be surprised. We've had some who come from your world with abilities far surpassing the norm. Others pursued training in our world and started reaching heroic heights," he said.

"Please tell me there's no one out there just smashing mountains with their bare fists."

"Nothing so outlandish, but lifting carts, fighting monsters with their hands, spells of destruction. Be proud!" James's tone carried notes of sarcasm. "Your kind are quickly becoming legends in their own right."

"I bet things are still a mess." It was a massive online role-playing game. There would never be an end if the developers could prevent it. Interest in this world would have to dwindle, but Continue Online could easily span decades. Of course, humanity had thousands of years on earth and still hadn't figured out a peaceful ending.

"How do you balance it?"

"How would you?" he responded.

"A punishment system that reduced their stats."

"That's one method. After all, scattering to the wind and being reconstructed is costly for your kind."

Was he talking about death and resurrection? In most games, players had to release somehow and start over at a base point. I guessed James and his world had an associated cost.

"The other is simple. This world is vast, many times yours, and not everyone who comes here is a fighter. Some study, others are wanderers." I walked around while James explained. He took to standing in one spot and keeping his movements limited. "Even though your kind is potentially powerful, they have shown no large-scale organization. Frequently you fight each other over petty things."

"I'll bet they do." I smiled. Humanity had more than once started wars; imagine what they would do in a game where there was no permanent death.

"What is it in your world that causes such violence?"

"I imagine it's the same thing that happens here. At least if this place is as real as you say." Chances were, a good portion of the game world was based on real-life situations. These non-player characters, the denizens of Continue Online, would have nearly as many hang-ups as the rest of us. It was kind of sad. Life outside the ARC was better than it had been decades ago.

"Explain," James said.

I poked at more things around the room and used **[Identification]** on anything new. Every item here was subject to my button-eyeballing skills. Sometimes the same object was reviewed to see if there was more information. Even the floor and wall got a pass. Pop-up messages kept me amused. Occasionally the game would spout some new fact with an almost snide wording.

Skill Used: [Identification]
Results: Wall
Details: You would have to be special to not know what walls are.

The one about my new pal **[Messenger's Pet]** made me laugh.

Skill Used: [Identification]
Results: **[Messenger's Pet]**
Details: Clearly not a cat. Reacts poorly to the name Sniffles the Second. Breathes fire when annoyed.

"Greed. Jealousy. There's deep generational hatred and racism. The Chinese had it the worst after the depression. I'd be willing to bet that people who enter from other points in our world make it a point to attack those from different areas."

"We, I and those Voices who could be bothered to look, have noticed certain hostilities in some of the other locations." James stood, serious as always, as he watched me wander around the room.

The little dragon trailed after me, nipping at my heels in hopes of getting another cupcake. I had given him the leftovers that seemed safest. The little guy either had an iron gullet or was lucky.

"Thankfully this world is huge, right? Imagine if it was as crammed as ours." I had some peanuts squirreled away that I tossed at the small dragon one at a time. "Make sure you chew this time," I whispered to the small dragon.

James was more than smart enough to pick up on the difference, which was amazing considering he was a computer program.

"It is huge. Still, do you imagine the people of our world have no feelings? That they wish to add your conflicts on top of their own?"

"I'm sure it balances out. I imagine your world asks our people for help all the time." This was a game. There were quest systems, I thought. Beth hadn't shown me one, but my friend's post had mentioned a quest.

"They do."

"Well, it's give and take. At least I assume so," I said.

"You are correct. You seem to understand much of our world for a new visitor. Have you experienced other worlds before?" James gave that somewhat sly smile again.

"Are you asking if I've played other games?"

"I believe that's what your kind calls them." He nodded.

"Then yes, I used to play a lot." Childhood being what it was, I'd played a ton until college. After that, I had been drowned in homework and reality.

"And were you any good?"

"God no. I found some neat things, sure, enjoyed challenges in others, played with friends. I was never one of the best. I usually played a little bit of everything to see what it was like."

"Why?" James asked.

"Why what? Which part?"

"Why a little of everything and not a focus?"

"Oh. Attention problems, I think." I tried to remember all the games from a decade ago. "Boredom or other distractions. Once I got good with a class, I usually switched. Playing to be the best was never my style."

"A jack of all?" James was falling behind on the question-and-answer count. His eager tone was getting the better of him. Often I found myself slipping and forgetting he was a machine. Oh well, we would settle our debt of questions and answers eventually.

"As the saying goes. I'm surprised you know that one."

"One player introduced your world's card games to ours. It's done quite well."

"Yeah? Did they set up a casino and everything?" I could imagine a fantasy world with a giant casino in its major cities.

"No. What's a casino?"

"Wow. No casino. I bet your Voice of Gambling or Chance would love one of those. Right up there with Wyvern races." Now I was being flippant, throwing out things I imagined this world would have in one place or another.

"What sort of nonsense are you talking about?"

"Mh. Well, I can explain casinos, I guess. It's a place, commonly referred to as 'The House' where people come to gamble money on games of chance. Some countries and states consider gambling illegal, but most just tax the bejesus out of them. Part of the proceeds get taxed by whoever runs the area, and the rest goes to The House."

They had to have races that involved flying mounts. A world with thousands of years' worth of history couldn't be that oblivious. The idea of thrill-riding giant serpents through the air in a death-defying race made me giddy. As a player, I would love a round or two, even if I failed.

Of course, players like me would be able to resurrect eventually. Beth had all but told me that death wasn't permanent. It was implied in her description of leaping off a cliff dozens of times and the fact that Continue was a game.

"And this is popular?" James sounded conflicted, as though he was almost worried about getting an answer.

"Oh yeah. Old ladies will sit for hours on slot machines. At least they did until computerized gaming took off," I said.

"Very well. I have more questions."

"Is there a Voice for Gambling?" Time to cash in some of my owed questions. James would likely call me out if things got carried away. I rarely put much thought into my words anyway. It was part of the strategy I employed to avoid depressing thoughts. My conversations meandered sometimes as a result.

"For Chance, there are two," James replied.

"Let me guess, male and female? One's kind of a shifty-looking fellow, the other's a dressed up dame." I loved this game. How often would anyone get to use the word dame in real life? Moments like this made me smile.

"In some aspects," he said

"I feel like you're giving away too much information for a Voice." My cheek turned down with a slight frown.

"That's the nature of our bargain. Much of what we're talking about is readily available in the world. Were you to ask for something dire, I would be equally invasive." James had proven he spoke with his flat tone frequently. His facial expressions flipped between empty and a faint, almost sly, smile.

"Wait. I've lost track of where we are on questions. Do you mean that I can ask you anything I want to about the world? Like about secret moves and overpowered items? And the price would be some horribly invasive question?"

"In essence." Thank goodness he treated that as one question. I had gone rather hog-wild with my tone. "Does this bother you?"

"Why would it? I've been explaining the inner workings of my mind to a counselor. On the bad months, I admit I'm human in front of a crowd of strangers." That didn't mean that those admissions didn't hurt, it only meant I didn't hide what, or who, I was from anyone.

"Then we'll get along fine. When my questions bother you, all you need to do is stop answering."

"I can't see any reason I would," I responded.

"Time will tell, Grant Legate."

Hearing my name started my teeth grinding again.

"There. That motion. You look upset whenever anyone calls you by your entire name. Why is this?"

"Because it makes me feel like a child. Only my parents used my entire name." That was the main reason.

"And that question didn't bother you? You answered so quickly."

"As I said, I try not to hide how I feel. Explaining it is a bit harder sometimes."

I had been through lots of books during my attempts at self-repair. Human emotion was a lot more complex than computer wiring. Hiding was useless and only prolonged the pain. Yet I still danced with an image of my fiancée. I guessed we all coped somehow. There I was again, thinking along depressing lines.

"All right. Load up the next event. Let's do something that involves any sort of chance. Dice, cards, whatever your world has." A world where I could gamble with no loss of personal money? Neat. Learning new games would also be interesting.

"Very well," he said.

The next room had tables and cards. I could see how some of this lined up with gambling pretty easily. A run-down table in one area of the room reminded me of street vendors. *Find the queen and win a twenty!* There was a set of dice. Two giant, slick orbs that did who knew what. Many more items littered the poorly made tables.

[Identification] was an easy enough skill to use. I focused on an object and switched eyesight to the small plus icon that floated nearby. Windows opened up with more information, much like all the other pop-ups this game used. Most were boring. I floated around, trying to see if this helped the skill grow.

I raised an eyebrow.

James wasn't in this room anymore. I looked around for the larger black man and couldn't see him hiding behind any of the devices. He'd vanished during my perusal of the objects, which meant I didn't actually need him for this. The Voice would probably be out there observing this, somehow, as he had during the feast trial. All the Voices were probably out there somewhere. My whole purpose for this room, aside from playing games in a game, was to talk to another Voice. Maybe something neat would happen.

Maud had given me an idea. Not because chasing in-game advantages was in my nature, but I wanted to change the program a little.

"Oh look, a coin." I picked up the coin. "What's a good deal for this place?"

Choices and possible wagers were weighed while I wandered through the tables and games.

There was a strangely shaped dart board. Next to it was a bow, throwing knives, and a few other items that looked as though they flew terribly. A cage had a bird inside. The bird was golden, fluffy and seemed to be half drunk. No telling what form of gambling that was. Maybe people passed it around until the bird barfed on someone.

"Hah!" Laughter escaped me as realization dawned. What better way to talk to a Voice of Chance and Gambling than to gamble on what it would like? I waved the coin around.

"All right, here's my proposal. Heads, whatever Voice presides over Chance comes down for a talk."

"Tails, you apply a penalty of your choice once I'm down on the world." The feast had taught me that there were penalties in this game.

Wait. This wasn't a two-sided coin, was it? I checked both ends. A dragon tail on one side and a head on the other. Good enough for me. I flipped the coin and let the ground catch it. My next trick would be to ignore the coin's outcome for a while and use [Identification] on more items.

"This makes no sense." A table nearby had cards. They weren't the normal decks though. This was more like a tarot set. Images were all different and had strange suits. Instead of diamonds, there were footprints on each card. Instead of a spade there was a scale of some beast, probably a dragon again.

I shuffled the worn deck as kindly as I could, then turned some over. First was a mask, much like the one on the Jester. Its expression was nearly mocking, with a half-mad grin and sunken eyes. Jester's suit was a beast footprint. Trails of blood hung around the card's border, depicting violence in the background.

"Very funny," I muttered.

The next two were vaguely interesting as well. One was a representation of Maud. Her suit was that of a burning fire over a brick, which might mean home and hearth. Surrounding her was a litter of grasping children. I smiled. The look on her face was less exhausted and closer to exasperated.

The last was a man in a duster whom I hadn't seen. He might have been in the portion of the book I skipped over when looking through the Voices' pictures.

He looked sort of snappy with only slight stubble. Clearly human though, so not belonging to any of the unusual races. His suit was fine, without a single hair out of place. The guy almost seemed like a well-dressed pool shark. I could see it. At least his sleeves weren't lined in stupid gambling symbols or anything similar.

There was a clink behind me.

I turned around, feeling amazed. That noise ushered in memories from decades ago.

"Pool?"

The numbers on the balls weren't the same. They looked almost like Roman numerals. The table felt was an off-red instead of the standard green. Everything about the table screamed makeshift. Next to it was a man with a pool cue, who was dressed nearly the same as my tarot draw. He was chalking one end with a lazy half-smile.

"Pool. Another game brought over by you visitors. I rather like it."

"Nice tie," I said.

"Want it?"

"Not my style… why pool? More skill than chance?"

This man didn't seem like a complete gambler. My initial appraisal was that he preferred a risk of uncertainty mixed with personal hard work and knowledge.

"Gamble's a gamble. It's a matter of guessing skill. You up for a game?" The pool player basically announced that this would be another measure of my abilities.

"Sure." I stepped past the coin and took note of the dragon tail displayed. Looks like I'd failed but gained attention anyway.

"Your go then."

The balls had already been broken and the other man hadn't sunk anything. His scatter was good, so I had a few choices.

I walked around the table and tried to figure out if there were any obvious bumps or curves. One of the pockets looked a bit makeshift compared to the regulation tables I'd played on during my teens. My cousins had been pool sharks. Not me—I only visited. Still, I knew the rules. At least whoever had created the game in Continue had kept the stripes and solids.

"Which one's the eight ball?" An eight ball shouldn't be sunk until the end. Too early and it would be a loss. Kind of like a landmine on the table.

"The Black Dragon Egg over there is last."

Skill Used: **[Identification]**

Results: **[Black Dragon Egg]**

Details: The **[Black Dragon Egg]** is used to mark the last ball to be sunk in a pocket. This entry is specifically for a game of skill and chance. Do not confuse this with a **[Black Dragon Egg]**. The latter involves skill and chance with a real **[Dragon]**.

Warning! [Dragon](s) are not a discovery made by this Traveler.

Further information currently unavailable. Entry will be updated as information is discovered.

I waved away the messages so I could see the table. My careful aim helped to sink one of the stripes. Another two shots were successful before missing. The cue I chose was nice. My hands ran up and down the pole in amazement at the craftsmanship. They'd managed to replicate the smooth feel of a polished cue but kept some of the wooden grain so it almost curved.

The man in the duster, whom I assumed was a Voice like James and Maud, returned two balls before a miss. That made us even. I smiled and made another shot. Accidentally sinking one of his set me back. A half-smile, half-scowl, crossed my face. He smirked in a lazy sort of way right before sinking another two.

I rolled my eyes and put another four in. Two went in at once from a split shot, and the fourth was pure luck. We were even now. While he took his next shot, I played with the dice on the table—feeling their weight, casting a few throws. They were the standard six-sided.

"This one of ours? Or yours?" I asked, holding up a die.

"Ours," he said.

"Guess that explains the color." These dice were yellow cubes instead of the normally polished white. "You have any other types of dice?"

"Mh. Didn't like them. One hundred sides on a die seemed a bit much," the male Voice responded.

"Silly, right? Still, some loved them. Probably because it helped them replicate something your world does with more realism." I was filling the other man's silence with mindless chatter. He hadn't really been the talking type so far.

"Your turn."

"Oh." I wandered over and looked at the table.

He'd managed to sink another few and retain the lead. This time, there was no good shot. He had effectively boxed me behind the **[Black Dragon Egg]**.

I sighed and pondered how to do this.

Trick shot time. I lined up the stick and ball, angled my shot sharply, and successfully hopped the ball over his into mine. The bouncing tap managed to sink one of mine hanging near a pocket. My teeth clenched as the cue ball rolled backward and gave the **[Black Dragon Egg]** a tap.

"Whew." I fired another shot at the far end of the table to return the favor.

All of my remaining balls were lined up near the **[Black Dragon Egg]**. Any shot he did from here would have to be carefully placed. Of course, any real attempt at thwarting the machine was mostly useless. An artificial intelligence that specialized in gambling and chance could easily make this shot. The man in the duster sank another one and managed to leave the **[Black Dragon Egg]** untouched.

My head hung. The hatted Voice cleared his last few cues. He called the shot and sank the **[Black Dragon Egg]** easily.

"Oh well," I said.

"You tried." He nodded as though the outcome had been inevitable.

"Did you want to talk about the casino thing?"

"Sure. The least I could do for a loser is hear him out." He braced both arms over the cue tip and waited for me to explain.

That spawned another twenty minutes of conversation where I tried to tell him how a casino worked. Winners were few, odds were in The House's favor. Places designed to be as much a distraction as anything else. Kind of like this entire game. I had lost the coin toss and the round of pool.

Finally satisfied, the man in his duster tipped his hat and faded out. I was left with a pop-up window.

Event!
Poor Pool Performance

Playing pool isn't your strong suit. Even though you understood the rules, your skills weren't enough to challenge the Voice of Gambling.

Despite your pitiful demonstration, he listened to what you've said. (He goes by Ray.) Ray will provide his followers a chance to gain favor by establishing their own casinos. They will be modeled in the exact method you described.

Followers deciding to pursue this will have to complete a number of quests for approval from local landowners. In addition, they must seek cooperation with whatever underworld guilds are nearby. Finally, they will need to find employees capable of surviving a seedy situation. All in the name of fame and money!

For introducing this quest chain, you get:

0.001% of all proceeds as a monthly stipend

A Coin – Rare

+4 [Divine Attention]

However, you risked much to gain Ray's attention:

All luck based activities suffer -10% to results for one year. All casinos established will welcome you, but Ray's mark is even more noticeable inside (-50% to all luck-based activities)

"Well." I flicked off the notification and looked around.

Nearby was the coin still showing tails up. This little thing had been the main reason for those negative bonuses. Still, divine attention had to be worth something.

The proceeds portion seemed absurdly low, but after a year in the game, it might be an insane goldmine. Not that I cared about gold in a game. Especially recently. If I treated it the same as how I treated real money, I would probably end up giving most of it away. My niece might enjoy it. Maybe my parents played and could use something.

"What's next, James?" I asked.

The room of chance still existed. Things tended to fade back to basics quickly after the event notice popped up.

A cage nearby started rattling. I turned to see the drunk bird and something else crawling around hissing.

"All right, little guy."

It looked as though the **[Messenger's Pet]** had found his way back into our event room. Now he was trying to get at the bird inside and failing to elicit any response from it. In fact, the drunken bird almost seemed to be unaware of the dragon tearing around on the outside of its cage.

"Whoa now. Don't do that!"

And over they went.

That got the bird's attention. One of its extra-large eyes on its fluffy head tried to zero in on the dragon. Comprehension was slowly coming to life as it fumbled both legs around and tried to sit up straight. I ran over to pry the miniature dragon off the cage. Even as feisty as it was, the thing only had claws the size of a tiny cat.

I regretted trying to pick it up almost instantly. The tiny thing nipped and clawed at my arms. A red bar that had to be my health flashed onto the screen and went lower with each line of blood drawn.

"What is wrong with you?" I didn't know what would happen if he did manage to get to the bird who was still trying to figure out how to stand up.

The thing swayed and half-squawked in confusion.

"Identification." I didn't have the mental focus to try to trigger my identify skill, so I went vocal.

Skill Used: [Identification]
Results: [Lorlell Cova Bird]
Details: Male **[Lorlell Cova Bird]**s are extremely violent toward other species of birds, or anything with wings. They are often sedated and used for mortal combat against others of their species.

"Why are you trying to piss off the drugged bird?"

I lost my grip on the tiny dragon, and things went downhill from there. The **[Messenger's Pet]** leapt onto the bird cage and sent it rolling around the floor.

The ensuing show was like a hamster that lost all traction on the wheel. Spinning resulted in feathers, squawking, and clanking. Nails tried to find purchase on the metal cage bars, which only resulted in more screeches. Their comedy act collided with a table, causing the cage door to pop open. An escape route only served to enrage the **[Lorlell Cova Bird]**. Feathers puffed up to almost double their prior size. The tiny dragon huffed and hissed. His jaw worked to spit fire but sputtered as if the tank was empty.

I flipped a table and held it awkwardly like a shield between the outraged bird and me. The puffball fighting bird was huge now and, from its violent sounds, considered the tiny dragon an enemy. My dragon buddy seemed to be losing. I scanned the games and tried to find anything useful.

Oh, right, I had access to tons of makeshift weapons. This was one step away from a barroom brawl movie. First up was the pool cue. I grabbed it with a free hand and jabbed one end toward the fighting creatures. Between my table shield and pool cue spear, I felt as if I were a Spartan.

"Hey. Hey." I thrust one end at them. It was hard to feel super worried for myself since they were both shorter than my knee.

"Stop that."

I poked at the large ball of feathers. My makeshift staff hit nothing and sank deep without visual effect. The **[Messenger's Pet]** was torn up and had gashes in his wings from where the **[Lorlell Cova Bird]** had refused to let go.

"Knock it off!"

I swung the pool cue down and bonked the **[Lorlell Cova Bird]** on the head. Which was a bad, bad, bad idea.

If anything, it got bigger. I flinched in panic and threw a table at the puffball bird. That worked against me. The **[Lorlell Cova Bird]** made a noise, and its beady eyes crossed. Two seconds later, it was up and diving at me. My calf was bitten as I ran around kicking like a scared schoolgirl.

Failure to dodge noted.
Total health loss: 10%

I tipped another table, then another, and finally arrived at the table near the dartboards. Everything in range became a projectile or obstacle against the bird until the bird stopped moving and laid there. The tiny dragon proceeded to huff and growl until our situation became clear. Our bird enemy was down for the count and completely out of it. **[Messenger's Pet]** stood on top of the smaller creature and puffed a smoke ring into its face.

"Yeah, all you, beating up a drugged bird. Good job."

The small dragon nodded and rolled the bird over with his claws.

"Well done," I muttered, looking at the scattered remains.

"Why do that?" James was back and clearly amused.

"Which part?" Had we really fought off an angry bird? The idea had me laughing.

"All of it."

"With Ray, I wanted to see what would happen. With the bird, it was to keep the little guy from being torn up."

The **[Messenger's Pet]** was looking smug and licking his wounds. Every so often, he chirped a pleased tone.

Slowly an absolute wreck of dozens of games faded away. I huffed. "Next?"

Wrapped up

"Can we skip this one?" I muttered. My mouth was presently unwrapped, but the rest of me was bound and tied up in who knew what.

[Webbed]! Movement restricted by 95%

"Not yet, Grant Legate."

"But we can chat." I gave it my best dry sarcastic tone. If only James could see my rolling eyes. Maybe he could with all his computer program powers.

"Of course, if you're not too tied up right now."

"I am, a little."

The Voice could deliver a deadpan line and was indifferent at my attempt to return the favor. "So try to get out of the web instead."

His advice wasn't even remotely useful. I hadn't asked him a question, though.

I wiggled halfheartedly.

"Not happening."

"Maybe some encouragement would motivate you," James said.

"Spiders?" I asked.

"Spiders."

"Can't feel them under this webbing." I tried to deny that the idea of anything crawling over me was unwelcome and disturbing.

"How about very big spiders?" he said, sounding amused. His face probably had that sly grin again.

"That's gross." Me and my stupid mouth had resulted in badness.

Now there was a clear sound in the distance. Something very, very big was scuttling around nearby. I started in earnest to struggle.

"No, James. This is not nice."

"How am I to accurately measure your skills if you don't even try?" James turned sour. He had expressed disappointment during a few of our trial events.

"Ask nicely!" I shouted the answer to his ill-timed question while trying to roll away.

My back jabbed into something sharp. Free fingertips felt around for the edges. A clicking noise grew closer. Images of giant mandibles and long legs went through my mind. I frantically rubbed my arms against the sharp outcropping nearby.

> Desire to hurt yourself noted
> Total health loss: 15%

"I hate you right now," I said.

"Why's that?" James asked.

> **Update**: Still **[Webbed]**! Fingers freed: Movement restricted by 85%

"Because small spiders are one thing; large ones are bullshit." This was only just a game. This was just a game. This was just a game.

"Spiders are extremely common in our world. There is a breed located in the Desert of Tali that can fly."

> **Location Update!**
> **Knowledge Received**: Desert of Tali
> **Details**: The Desert of Tali contains spiders that can fly. Further details will be added as information is learned.

"No, there aren't," I said. My immediate denial blocked out the whole concept.

"There are indeed," James calmly refuted.

"I don't believe in flying spiders." Maybe if I said those words enough, all of them would die. It worked for faeries, according to my childhood television watching.

Skill Demonstrated: [Denial]
Type: Basic
Rank: Unranked
Specialties: Unknown
Details: Denial is a powerful and dangerous ability. Further information will be provided upon finalization of the mentioned skill.

System Help!

Demonstrated skills are no learned skills. They provide no bonuses and are used by the world of Continue Online to assist in the discovery of new abilities. Most learned skills require a demonstration of the basic concept prior to being granted.

"I'm never going to go there."

The noise drew closer. I could have tried to be quiet, but there was no chance of me being a stealthy person. I would sweat and stutter occasionally when nervous. Emotional speeches were the worst.

"Why?" James asked.

"Later!"

Something was close by. I could feel the air shift across the exposed portions of my face and arms. The tone of chattering changed. It—they, maybe—had found me.

I sawed enough to get my arm loose and started tearing away at the bindings around my face to clear my vision.

"Oh, god."

That was a giant spider. That was a really giant spider. Oh god, there were two of them. I thought I wet myself. Only a little bit. No, I had—there was a pop-up that even told me of the condition of my digital pants.

What happened from there on was pure chaos in my mind. I twisted out of the way of jabbing legs trying to spear me. My foot kicked at the ground trying to get an inch away. Another giant ugly spider attacked. It missed my midsection and tore into an arm. I managed to free myself a bit more and was wiggling like a fish—no, a dolphin—in a net.

> Failure to dodge noted.
> Total health loss: 20%

"Oh, god." But prayer wasn't enough; this was a test. I didn't know of what. My eyes were half covered, but there was a red bar that flashed with green as it dripped down.

> **[Poisoned]!** Health will reduce over time unless treated.
> Total health loss: 25%

"Poison? Are you kidding me?!" I kicked off again and made it another few feet. These things were big, strong, scary, but somewhat slower than one would expect a spider to be.

"No, I'm not, Grant Legate."

"Stop calling me that!" Panic was rapidly removing my happy place.

"I'm afraid I can't do that, Grant Legate." James was definitely entertained.

I growled and got a mouthful of webbing, which nearly caused me to choke.

"Come on!"

I failed to escape the latest one. Pain shot through my leg, causing me to bunch up. This was supposed to be a game.

"This is your last test, Grant Legate. Do try to excel. You're woefully behind your peers who do our trials."

"Of course I am." The mouthful of web in my face made the declaration muffled.

I managed to get a foot under me and was now hopping away from spiders taller than I was. Watching myself during a highlight reel might be extremely funny. Everything was painful. My chest hurt and wheezed. My limited eyesight was getting fuzzy. My fingernails were bloody and my arms torn.

Everything hurt.

Everything.

This was worse than the weapon practice James had made me do. A burly man had demanded I strike a wooden dummy for an hour before switching to the next weapon. Every time I failed or hesitated, the burly man hit me. James was smiling the whole time. I'd logged out twice during that and huffed around my house in anger.

This was worse than the trial two episodes ago, where frighteningly realistic people from my life berated and tried to tear me down. I had spent two days offline during that ruthless situation but still came back. That army of people hadn't said anything new to me. Plus, as I spent time outside the ARC, it became clear that those people had been missing a lot of details. My mother hated my father half the time but never told anyone in public. The game version of her acted completely loving when talking about dad, but my real mother would have badmouthed him at least once.

The petting zoo had been nice. Odd, but nice. They even let me ride something that looked like a stocky llama. This, this weird dim cave with spiders, was hell. I kept hopping while the arachnids lumbered behind me. An exit. There had to be an exit.

"Where do I go from here?"

"Out!" James' voice sounded farther away, but still fairly close.

"Which way is that?!"

"Why don't you die? It's much easier to give up."

That hurt. James managed to sound like every personal demon that had haunted me over the years.

"No! Besides, it's not like I'd die for real!" I managed to duck around a rock and pulled at more webbing. My legs were mostly free now, but the rest of me wasn't.

"Right, it's much easier to give up."

James's tone was starting to irk me. I had selected him, and it felt as if he was trying to drive me away.

"Let yourself be killed," he suggested.

"No!"

I got most of my arms free and found some more objects to throw at the approaching giant spiders. Their faces dripped with something unwholesome and off-color. Was that meat around the edge of their jaws? **[Identification]** revealed they were the leftover pieces of a former victim.

"Why are you trying now? Was it the spiders?" he asked.

"I hate giant spiders!"

One of them was too close. The little flashing bar to the side was under a third. Green still flooded the inside and would pulse every so often. Fire. I needed the biggest ball of flame possible to burn them into a shrieking pile of goo. Bugs did not cope well with being lit on fire. But, but I had no matches. I had no fire.

"This isn't a phobia. If it were, you would be a drooling mess."

"I hate them…"

Finally, I saw one spider completely unobstructed. Its face was messed up and fractured. Hair and bulging eyes made up the key features. Each of the eight legs arched higher than my shoulder.

The digital representation of food chose that moment of terror to finish passing through my system. Part of me regretted eating so much at the King's Feast. The rest of me hoped that it would all be over soon.

[Soiled]! You have defiled your trousers. Relations with other people will suffer a penalty until you've cleaned your clothes.

I ran, trying to find a path that angled upward. Hopefully outward toward freedom. Rocks were thrown behind me in a huff. Each vague connection would buy me another few precious seconds to escape. From my peripheral eyesight, I saw a limb reaching out and barely missing me.

"I need fire. Need fire." I was running my mouth in complete rambles.

Wait.

"I'll give you cupcakes if you set these guys on fire!" I shouted in desperation, hoping the little dragon guy was floating around in the cyberspace nearby. "Lots of cupcakes! Cookies! More creamer!"

I pleaded and kept running. Behind me, I heard a click and a huff. The spiders' chattering tone changed. Heat flashed, lighting up the entire dim passageway with warmth. Shrill sounds filled the air, like a baby screaming a constant high note. I covered my ears, then risked looking backward.

The little dragon stood, huffing out a stream of flame that had caught two spiders. He coughed another few little blasts and hopped around happily. Two bundles of former terror were curling into twitchy balls while the high pitched whine slowly died. Another spider was clearly fleeing into the distance.

"Cupcakes. I owe you so many cupcakes." My words slurred and drool dribbled out of my mouth.

Poison had caught up with me. My health bar reached zero while Continue Online went dark to the boasting tune of a tiny dragon.

You have died!

With that neat message, I logged out of the ARC and stomped around my house. Death had struck a second time. A penalty of eight hours was applied, and logging back in would be blocked. It was minor overall, but after these trials eight hours in reality would be a full day lost in-game. Additionally, I would lose skills and character points. My niece had explained that sometimes other punishments happened depending on what was going on.

I had confirmed with Beth that my prize was a copy of Continue Online. She spent an hour babbling about different bits of information and repeatedly asking for my log-in information. My refusal was taken in stride since I wanted to surprise everyone. That, and I hadn't created a character name. I was torn between figuring out a name and punching James in the face for those giant spiders.

After my disturbing experience, a walk outside was needed. I flashed a hand over the external ARC display to put it into sleep mode. My Atrium was a giant mess, and that little dragon was once again tearing into cabinets. I sighed and opened up the shopping interface. Moments later, there was a fully stocked counter with fruits and other goods. I even spent the three dollars on a virtual cake. The small terror sent wrapping paper flying all over my digital house. Programming should auto clean up all that trash if left alone long enough. Or maybe not. Glass shards still lined one side of the room.

"How the heck did you alter the program that much?" I poked through the holographic display. "You better clean up after yourself this time."

The **[Messenger's Pet]** had set two spiders chasing me aflame. Even though I'd died, it was worth the price of virtual food. Assuming he hadn't broken the program enough to require restocking. I'd better disable remote access to my Atrium from family and friends. The last thing I wanted to explain was my new pet. A part-time miniature dragon was miles better than cats though. Odd that no one had thought of putting one into the ARC online store. Maybe they couldn't program something that complicated or it hadn't been approved by the company. Cats went anywhere from fifty dollars on up, all for something that wasn't real.

My first week off from work was nearly over. In-game time dilation wasn't set that high yet, according to James. Consequently, the game minutes were the same as real time. Henry Uldum had extended my one-week vacation to two. That was useful, I guessed. My coworkers had sent me nasty messages about how I was cutting into their lazy time. None showed any signs of being aware that I'd picked up the Ultimate Edition.

My progress inside the program hadn't exactly been stellar. All the events combined to put me on par with an entry-level character. Only the event results seemed different. And one tiny dragon that was now wallowing in wrapping remains as though it were catnip.

I sighed and walked outside for fresh air.

Each movement hurt. Those feedback bands were effective. Articles online explained the science away by reciting nerve-ending activation signals. Comparing them to a real workout showed an almost ninety-percent gap. Playing the game and exercising, however minor, was worthwhile.

Eight hours later, after I'd made it down to the store for supplies, napped, and lost time online, I was ready to log in again. I spent a few minutes in the Atrium and straightened out the mess left behind. Post cleanup allowed me to see glass refreshing inside the cabinet and food repopulating on the shelves. My little dragon buddy hadn't completely broken the Atrium's programming. There were still two doors open: one to the dance program, and one to Continue. I hadn't been able to bring myself to touch the dance one since the strange possession of my fiancée's image.

Continuing through Continue was the only real option. I stepped inside. The room was dark once again. Dim light drew attention to the middle, where a familiar pillar and book sat open, waiting. James stood there, arms crossed, looking pleased.

"You made it!" James sounded surprised.

I glared.

"Were you upset?" he asked.

"I wasn't happy." I looked at the dragon pacing around on top of the book. "Thanks, little guy."

My small dragon pal hummed and did a few circles trying to chase its lengthy tail.

"That's not a very good answer."

"Yes." I had been upset. The walk helped. Humming a song from my dance program and imagining the motions had put me back into a happier frame of mind.

"Very well. Your turn, Grant Legate."

I tried not to grind my teeth. "Let's fix that next."

"You have the power to change things, Grant Legate, as I've told you before."

"I need to pick a character name."

"And write it down here." James had everything already prepared.

Part of me should have been disturbed that my next goal was so easily read by a computer.

The thought of a character name had crossed my mind over the last few days. Specifically when James, or one of the other Voices, persisted on using my first and last name. The problem was that most of my game names from years ago were a few flavors of stupid. My past names included television show characters, cartoon characters, comic heroes, and more. None of them seemed appropriate for a game like this.

"Second thoughts, Grant Legate?"

"Trouble deciding."

"I've always found it interesting, the names your kind use. We had a girl who went by Sword Princess, but she preferred a staff. One man who called himself Shadow, among another fifty with the same name."

"That sounds about right." I bet Shadow liked to stealth around in-game and stab people in the back. Mysterious, I'm sure. Forty of the fifty were probably utter jokes and half a poser each. "I don't know what to pick for myself."

"Other players name themselves after fantasy lives they've built. Some chose heroes or people they aspire to be. Great names in your world, founding fathers, names that mean powerful things."

"None of that sounds like me."

"What kind of experience do you want to have within our world?" James asked.

"I want a dis—"

"A distraction. Yes. Is life in your world so terrible?"

I stood over the book, quill in hand, small dragon rolling around in boredom, and decided how to answer. James often asked inane little questions, but sometimes he poked the tender spots too.

"No. Not really, James. Too familiar sometimes."

"Familiarity is bad?" he questioned me.

"Reliving the past is painful," I said.

"Yet you dance with a false image of your deceased fiancée, and indeed have danced with her for over a year now." James poked at my emotional wounds.

I hadn't told him that she had passed. I rarely let myself admit it. Hearing it out loud was like a punch in the gut. Part of me would welcome the giant spiders right about now.

"You crave a distraction. You focus on work with an almost zealous fervor, so much so that your manager forced you to take a vacation." He had clearly done his homework when accessing my ARC.

"James." I clenched my eyes shut.

The man had found something truly painful to ask about. Yet it wasn't even the asking; it was laying it all bare. When I did it, the situation was under my control. My terms. When someone else did it, everything felt so much more real and painful.

"Here you are, on the verge of a new world. You can choose to reinvent yourself, to throw caution to the wind, yet you can't even decide a new name," James said.

"It's not that easy," I protested.

"Really? Tell that to a father who walks away from his family. Tell that to a person who quits their job without a moment's hesitation. To a drugged up woman who chooses another high over her child."

"I haven't done any of those things."

"So? Those are merely examples, Grant Legate." James almost spat the words. I wanted to be mad, but the only thing in my vision was that stupid quill and blank space. "Your world and ours both allow people these chances, however right or wrong. Anyone can walk away and reinvent themselves."

"It's not that easy to be someone different."

"Bah. People are who they choose to be. Every moment of every day defines them. You've defined yourself as a workaholic who can't let go of the past. Why?"

"Because…"

"Why. Not. Let. Go?" Each word sounded like a drum.

"Because I don't want to let go!" I yelled at the black man.

"Then be distracted. Pick a name. Visit another world. Be someone else, and maybe you'll find something else to hold onto." He remained unruffled by the shouting.

"I don't want to let go of her."

"She's already gone from your world."

James's words hurt.

I was beyond painfully aware that she was gone. Identifying her body had been a clear indicator. Her parting hadn't been slow or peaceful—no, our separation had been swift and sudden. Even now it felt like an open wound that only stayed together with duct tape and prayer. And what did James mean by gone from my world? Dead was dead.

I spun on the other man.

"What are you saying? Is that some clever hint? Is this some messed up trick relating to how she came to life over there?" Four words, "gone from your world," had sent me into momentary rage. The disturbing moment of realism in my dance program hadn't been caused by a system update. "Is she in your world somehow? You owe me answers."

"Not exactly, Grant Legate."

The bottom of my sanity dropped even further.

"Not exactly what?" I spat the words at the large black man.

He seemed indifferent to my anger.

"She's not exactly in our world."

"Explain that, James. Explain what the hell that means or I'll shove this quill up your ass!" I stepped toward the computer program, and he didn't even flinch. His face didn't change from the stern, button-lipped expression.

"We can't explain it, Mister Grant Legate." There was a little girl behind me. She was the same youngster who'd taken Maud's charge. "We have rules."

"This isn't some fucked up ploy, is it, to, to, to…" To what? What might possess a computer to try to mess with any human to this extent? Happy place, I had to get back to my happy place. I tried to remember the opening chords to a waltz.

"We do not rely on smoke and mirrors to entice people to visit our world. You either choose to or don't," James said, still standing in the same spot, but slightly turned toward the other Voices.

"Is this some fucked up Ultimate Edition thing?"

"Yes and no. We might never have noticed you without your proof of ownership. However, these types of things are common for anyone who attracts our attention." James answered a question with some actual detail finally. It also explained why I had a trait for [Divine Attention].

"Then what is going on?" Alien plot? Crazy theory on the afterlife? Alternate reality? No, that wasn't fair; the name ARC stood for Alternate Reality Capsule. My job with Trillium had been going on for nearly two years now. No way did these things combine into a portal or anything that strange.

"Give me something, James, or I'll walk away and delete this stupid thing. Ultimate Edition, whims of the universe, and my boss be damned."

"I cannot do that, Grant Legate," he said.

"Why not?"

"Because I am not allowed."

"Are you saying my fiancée is in this stupid game?" I tried to focus on the issue bothering me.

"No." He sounded firm and absolute. "Your fiancée is dead."

"Then what's going on?" I waved in anger.

"Tut. Something of her is still here." Another voice came out of the darkness. I turned and saw a small light over Maud's tired body. She gave an empty smile.

"You do not have permission to interfere," James said.

"We make the rules, James, you know that. Tut. You owe Mister Grant Legate an answer. By your own deal, you've fallen behind a ways."

Children spun in and out of existence around her. Some looked happy, others sullen.

"Ah." There was a pause while James ordered himself and did a mental count. "I suppose I have fallen behind."

I wanted to rip all the pages out of this stupid book and pull the tiny dragon's tail to start a fire. I would bend the creature over like a flamethrower and torch every last piece of material.

"I can perhaps trade many little owed answers for a chance at a bigger one. None of us are allowed to fully explain, but I can show you if you wish to detour."

The room suddenly got a lot more cramped and things spun. It felt as if time compression had kicked in at a high degree. This was more than four-to-one. My perception of the digital world about me slowed to a snail's pace.

Voices, all the Voices, were talking about this situation.

"That would be good," Maud affirmed. "You've my approval."

"Sounds amusing. I always did have a soft spot for the old goat." The Temptress was nearby. All I noticed besides her voice was a brush of fingertips. They slid across my cheek from behind and a bout of desire surged through me.

"He can't handle filling that man's shoes. He barely managed to hold in his own piss!" Drill Sergeant yelled across the room, bringing up the lack of self-control giant spiders had induced in me. Spittle still cleared the distance.

"I'm against it," the Drill Sergeant said prior to fading out.

"Let Mister Grant Legate do it." The young girl's voice was next. Her face almost hidden behind a book she raised like a shield toward the Drill Sergeant's former presence.

Silent and Angry faded in. She still wore the same white flowing dress and little sign of anything else. Her eyes looked off into the distance, and her head shook slowly. What were they voting on? Could computers vote on something to do with me?

The man in the duster faded in. He rattled something around in his hands. "Do it. Everyone deserves a chance."

A woman hung over his shoulder and seemed to be looking down her nose at me with an indifferent expression. The dress hugged her curves all too tightly.

"What…" I tried to ask.

"I don't know," the Jester clacked. It appeared behind the two Voices of Chance, and they frowned and faded away. The mask seemed darkly teasing as always. "These visitors are such fickle creatures. You want him to play a part, but is his heart able to be someone else?"

"…is…" My next word was stuttered and slow compared to the Voices' speech. Even the Jester's clacking voice made more sense than I did.

"I think Grant Legate desperately wants to be someone else. We give him a stage, a face, and hold on to the role a little bit longer," James said with a serious expression. He seemed so frumpy next to the Jester mask.

"And we cover it up?" the Jester said.

"…going on…" I ground out the words.

"Yes. Provided he does well enough. A fitting end, another moment more would be enough to send him forth with something greater than a whisper in the night," James answered.

"And would he approve?" For a moment, I felt as if the Jester was glaring straight at me while he spoke. Maybe he was. His eyes held only darkness, and that smile never left.

The Voices kept on talking while I tried to move forward.

"Based on my observations, yes."

"And Mother?" the Jester asked.

"Has she ever disapproved of our actions?"

"We only function as we were created. Isn't that right, James?" The Jester's tone always seemed mocking, though an exact impression was impossible. Its words were very similar to Hal Pal's in that way—robotic, passive. This Jester was clearly not human.

"You'll explain it?" Maud was still nearby and sounded apprehensive. Distant cries of children leaping around her filled the empty air before fading off.

"In a way that makes sense," James responded.

"Good. I have my role, but even I would not tarnish his ending," the Jester said.

"So you approve?"

"Yes." A smiling mask haunted my slowed vision as it faded away.

"Then we have a majority."

"…here?" I finally got the last word out when light flashed and time abruptly sped back up. They had done all that talking while my mind crawled through the mire. I fell forward while trying to reach for James.

All the other Voices had left the room. The pillar and book were still present. Even the little dragon seemed undisturbed. James was looking off into the distance and seemed uncaring as I pulled myself up. Everything felt uncomfortable, and my head spun.

"I'll explain in a moment, Grant Legate."

"I need a better name." That was the first thing out of my mouth. Not demanding answers, only being annoyed. James played me like a fiddle.

"Eventually, yes. For now, I have another offer." James turned and crossed his hands over his belly.

"Yeah, I guessed something was up." Not that I was clear on the finer details. There were a lot of questions floating around my brain, but James had basically stated he was using them all up for this proposal.

"Would you like to know more?"

"Sure," I said dryly. Clearly the demands I uttered weren't blunt enough. My patience must be nearly saintlike to suffer through this without trying to strangle the man. Or AI, or Voice, whatever.

"One of our long-time denizens has ceased to function properly," James said.

"Someone from your world." I tried to focus on my calming techniques. Step one, respond to the question at hand and don't stress about what's happened before. Step two, look forward. Step three, think of something that made me happy, such as music and dance.

"A very well-known figure. Mostly retired, he was quite famous decades ago."

"And he's dead," I said.

"Effectively. Death in our world holds many meanings."

That made sense. A computer probably had a much different concept than humans.

"What does this have to do with me?"

"We've decided to offer you a unique chance to view our land," he said. "Would you like to see something no one else from your world has?"

"If it gets me answers, sure. But I'm still not clear on what you actually want." I wasn't focusing right anyway. Part of my mind was trying to recall the feet placement for a brisk beat. The pop and lock movements of high tempo music were still a bit awkward for me.

"We are willing to let you choose to take up his mantle for a limited time. To be precise, four weeks of our time. One week in your world," James said.

"You want me to be someone from your world, who died?" My head drew back and one eye squinted slightly with confusion.

"In essence, yes."

"That's strange."

Beyond odd actually. The Voices wanted me to pretend to be someone else? How on earth would that lead to an answer about my fiancée? I had nothing else to go on. James wasn't going to answer my question. Once the man said no, he stuck with it. Only harassment from the other Voices had gotten us this far.

"Will you?" James, ever the questioning man, asked.

I had a hard time seeing any downside. Pretending to be someone else would be an interesting distraction.

"I'll get help, right? I can't act as someone else without information."

"Yes. You'll receive information about his life as you interact with the world, much the same as any others who travel to our world will."

"I guess." A chance to understand this world more? To understand exactly what this mystery was surrounding my fiancée? Sure. "Yeah. I'll do it."

A door slid out of the ground, complete with a bright light and everything. It was so cheesy I laughed.

"A question before I go, James."

"I'll indulge you, Grant Legate," he said.

I closed my eyes and counted to three. Hopefully a good name would occur to me within these four weeks.

"What sort of game is this exactly?" Strange tests and altered programming was only the tip of our insanity iceberg. Trillium and ARC had really done an amazing job with this setting. Continue absolutely deserved all the praise it received in reviews for throwing me off enough to make me doubt myself.

"It's no game. To us, it's very real and very serious," James said.

"Yeah, that's not ominous or anything." I scratched my head. A gentle tempo floated through the recesses of my mind, almost setting me to dance. Keeping in motion and drowning my thoughts in the music helped me cope with the darker thoughts.

"Do not be mistaken. There is no intent to do you harm in here. What you do in the world is entirely up to you."

"Aside from this." I gestured to the doorway of white.

"This too is your choice. Be one of ours—a man named William Carver—and if you do well enough, you'll get answers," he responded with that almost-sly smile.

Again I idly scratched my head and tried not to mutter an angry reply. All the details would have to be figured out later. My next step was simple—step through the door and get a lay of the land. Afterward, I would log out and cool down. Maybe that hot tub program should be put to more use.

My amazing restraint, built over two years of therapy and meetings, succeeded. Instead of having to deal with more of James's half answers and annoying responses, there was this other option. I could step through a door into non-player character land. If nothing else, it was a distraction. I walked through the cheap doorway effect while wiping my eyes.

Interlude
Everyone gets a Story

Some things hadn't changed over the years. Video recordings were restricted; projections, Bio-Watches, anything modern had been dialed back to keep the setting classic. We had a single publicly-owned camera rolling footage for security reasons. Metal chairs, all in a circle, held guys and girls, all shapes and walks of life, here to share their stories.

Next was my turn. To finally share my hand-wringing story. Like the others before me, and the others after me. This was the circle intended for support. Support required sharing oneself in a room of near strangers. I didn't like it, but eventually we all talked.

"My fiancée had taken a trip to Florida that morning. Part of her job application process, some tests. She left a day early and took the train because they were going to retire the public rail program to make room for the TRANS Tunnels.

I dropped her off, kissed her good-bye, and said 'I'll see you soon.'"

Those who'd shared before me all followed the same pattern. Final words to the departed mattered more than air.

"I didn't know exactly what time the call came in, not until later. Four oh seven p.m., for seven minutes, thirty-two seconds." I had stared at my phone call log absently until the numbers were burned into the back of my retina.

"The woman on the phone told me that there had been an accident with the train. She was clinical. Maybe a robot."

I shook my hands from where the rubbing had pushed out too much blood.

"The train had crashed. Spilled over onto the interstate. Cars, passenger carts, just- just chaos everywhere. Casualties and unidentified bodies. The woman on the phone said they were calling all family members."

"I got in the car, set a destination, and let the Auto NAV take me cross-country. You know, normal tragic mind-numbed-beyond-belief stuff."

The actual ride had been much more complicated. I made calls to my sister and parents, called my fiancée's mother and broke the news, looked up news articles. All the standard robotic actions required in order to keep everything neat and compartmentalized. My attempts at sanity were completed between bouts of screaming and raging denial.

"So I get there, identify the remains; there was no doubt. Her parents had asked for a cremation, which I told them." That was before the bomb that had hammered the news to a worse level.

"The person, uhh, a doctor, I guess, he was wearing a white coat, he told me she—my, uhh, fiancée—had been pregnant. Had. Wasn't anymore. Almost three months.

"I nodded, tried to smile, and did, did all the paperwork. The uhh, cremation took only a few hours."

Modern technology painted a very clear picture of what had happened. A simple turn gone wrong on the tracks. Not even slightly malicious, no murder plot, just one stupid accident that ended so many lives.

"A technician handed it to me, the remains, and I sat there, uhh, thinking to myself, 'How neat. The sum of her life and our unborn child is smaller than a breadbox.'"

A broken chuckle escaped me.

Someone muttered that the attempted humor wasn't funny.

I looked around, trying not to break down while avoiding eye contact.

"No, it's not is it."

There was a pause while I tried to piece myself together once again. Something I'd done over and over since she passed six months prior. In front of these people, I couldn't do it. Everything slipped.

"You know, I thought I'd be stronger. I'd always thought I'd be cool as a ship in clear waters. I wasn't. I went back to the hotel room I'd rented, crawled into a bottle, and life went downhill from there."

Someone handed me a cloth because heaving sobs were all too common during these meetings. I thanked them and wrapped up so another story could be shared.

"So here I am, uhh, like you guys, trying to not need a bottle to get through the night." I gave a weak smile and covered my face, dabbing my eyes and wondering how snotty my face was going to get this time.

They let us take a sorely needed break. Some people's stories were harder than others. I took a breather and walked to the bathroom to compose myself. It had only been six months since she passed, but every day was a short hop away from mental Hell. The wrong thought would cause my chest to seize. Moments later, I'd be fighting to unclench my hands from curled fists. A deep pain that felt like a knife would jab into my heart.

This meeting was meant to be the start of my attempt at self-repair, to make myself something resembling a whole human being. All these technological advances and still the human heart was a frail thing.

Two months ago, I'd tried to kill myself.

Six months after that introductory meeting, on the anniversary of my fiancée's passing, I tried again. That was my lowest point.

Approximately 2 Years Ago

"Goddammit, Grant!" My sister, Liz, was storming around the digital representation of a tranquil riverside camping spot.

We were currently engaged in an online conference call because the doctor thought it was the safest thing for my recovery. I was on all sorts of drugs, so it was hard to focus on anything but the sound of water.

"Seriously! Again! You did this to me again!" she shouted, but all that made it through was a slow drip. Her words took time to catch up.

"I didn't do it to you," I muttered. I had no good defense for trying to end my life. Intellectually, the idea was absurd, but suicide wasn't about thinking. It was about feeling. "I did it to me."

"Get it through your thick head! What you do affects me," she said. I slowly managed to tilt the virtual headset up, and Liz's face came into view. My sister was waving her arms around rapidly, then crossing them. One lip was being chewed on while she thought. "God, I don't know if I can explain this to Beth."

"Don't." The drugs made the word slur a bit.

"What am I going to tell her then? That her uncle, the man who basically acted as a father when she was young, gained a new scar by accident?" Liz glanced at me sidelong, then looked away. That brief glance felt both accusing and ashamed.

"Don't tell Beth," I said.

"Of course not, Grant. Of course not. But I thought we were doing well. We had the meetings set up. Your counseling is going well still, right?" Liz continued pacing around. She managed to keep both hands under control by tucking her fingers into her armpits. Every so often, Liz stared at the digitally rendered sun slipping lower over the camp's treeline.

"I guess." I may have missed a few meetings. I may have ignored a few calls from my sponsor, who was a glorified babysitter. The thought made me frown. Thinking badly about him was uncharitable. Leon, the man who checked in with me once a week, had been trying hard.

"I swear to God, when you get home, I'm going to rattle all your teeth until some of this nonsense leaks out of your head." Liz stood still for a moment before stomping around again.

"Okay," I said.

"Goddammit, Grant!"

"I know." I kept the tone low. Longer sentences were hard to get out.

Drugs had an adverse effect upon the digital software used by ARC devices. Being sedated was bad enough, but the hospital had put me into a Second Player helm. This wasn't even a full Alternate Reality Capsule.

Somewhere in the virtual landscape, a bird chirped happily. Crickets and frogs made noise to fill the silence. None of them were real. I wasn't comfortable in the wild anyway. Like most children of my generation, I was a city kid who'd rarely visited nature. There was a bench nearby that I could sit on. Liz kept weaving around it in her endless pacing.

"Okay. Okay. We can do this. Like last time. The doctor said you've got two days under observation. Then we have to put the band on you again." Liz turned and walked back toward me.

Having a plan made it easier for her to focus. We both had that in common. At least we used to.

"I know," I said slowly.

"Then after the band is on and working, you're clear to come home." Liz looked down at my foot. That was where they would put on the ankle band. Anywhere else and it was too easy to disrupt. The device would monitor my vitals from now until a court deemed me healthy

"I know." I hated the band, but it was part of my insurance plan. God knew what those people would have to say about all this. Tests, price hikes, rules would change. Everything would go together and cause me a headache once these drugs wore off. Right then, I wasn't coherent enough to have a headache.

"And we'll make sure there's a car available for your meetings. I'll start working from home a few more days a week. We can do more dinners." Liz pulled one arm out and looked at it. Her hand was shaking. My twin sister shook her head and arm rapidly, then tucked her arm back in again.

"Liz." I had to tell her.

"Then we'll have to watch things carefully again. Shit, Grant, do we have to do this every year?" Liz responded.

"Liz." I tried to get through to her again. Maybe the Second Player helm was running poorly. Maybe the internet in my room had dropped in and out of service.

"And what am I going to say to Beth? She's a teen, but she isn't stupid!" My twin sister had gone back to pacing. Her footsteps were heavy enough to clomp on the grassy riverside.

"Liz!" I shouted.

"What, Grant?" She was only interrupted for a moment. My sister had a wild look to her eyes. "Jesus. I don't know."

"Thank you." I didn't know what else to say. There wasn't enough in the world to repay her for even trying to help me pick up the pieces. Only the drugs in my system kept the feelings of absolute powerlessness away. Every time I thought about the loss, it clenched my heart. The cracks of my life became that much more obvious. And it felt as if those thoughts crossed my mind all the time. Grant, the Broken Record.

"Goddammit, Grant. Goddammit." Liz was crying. God, how badly had I messed up? "No. No, I'm sorry. You're recovering. I know, they said I shouldn't take it out on you, but, Jesus!" My sister was shouting by the end.

"Thank you, sis."

"Just-just sit tight. I'll be there in a few hours." Liz still couldn't look directly at me.

The first time had been bad enough and here we were going through the whole process again. I watched my sister wave an arm, and her image started to fade.

My own interface faded slowly. Both eyes were unfocused as a disconnection screen came into being. It counted down from ten. Each second was like a funeral march celebrating reality's return. Finally, the world was mostly dark, with the smallest bit of light piercing up through the helmet's bottom. I slid the device off my head and set it on a table next to the hospital bed.

Approximately 18 Months Ago

After months of searching and calculations, I had managed to get some things straightened out. Not myself, not perfectly. My life was too far gone. Not even an entire roll of duct tape would solve it. I shook my head while trying not to think about the missing piece of my life. It was nearly a year and a half since my fiancée passed, taking our unborn child with her.

"Are you sure this is what you want to do?" Liz asked.

I was staring at a series of spreadsheets across her kitchen table. They were digital projections, like so many things in life. It was easier to clean up a computer image. Plus voice commands worked when the program was well done.

I nodded. "It is."

"And you're okay with this new job?" Liz sat there with a coffee mug in her hands. That was her comfort method. Often the aroma of coffee beans mixed with vanilla would spread throughout her home after a rough day. My sister didn't like her bosses.

"The hours are flexible. I can work as much or as little as I want." I kept my voice positive.

"I'm still not sure you should work for them." Liz shook her head over the mug of coffee. She wasn't even drinking, only sniffing it. "You know how much I don't like those machines."

"They're here to stay, plus this way I have job security. My old market isn't what it used to be as the AIs improve." The degree I had in accounting and business was absolutely useless now. Machines could predict market trends and stock changes faster than any human. Their accuracy was often off the chart.

"So you go from managing all that money to being a grease monkey for the machine?" Liz set down the cup and stared at the images scattered over her table.

"Not even that," I said. The job was more like being a mouthpiece for the machine. My part of the work was minimal.

We both turned as my niece, Beth, bounded up the stairs. She had come in from visiting a friend or something. It was hard to believe that she would be eighteen soon.

"Are you still going to visit us, Uncle Grant?" Beth said while going straight for the fridge.

"I'll drop by a lot. I need to find my own space." I smiled at Beth. She was so carefree compared to her mom and me. It was amazing to think that we had ever been that young.

"All right, I've got to log in for school." Beth had buttered bread in her mouth and a container of water in each hand. She managed to wave good-bye with a few free fingers.

"I'm glad the ARC is working for you." It had been my first purchase with this new job. Ten thousand dollars up front for something the size of a twin bed. The price point would have been higher, but Trillium had given me an employee discount.

"Oh, it's great, I don't have to commute anymore! Mom kept making me take the bus," Beth said while chewing on her bread. She was walking backward toward the stairs while talking.

"It's good for you." Liz wiggled a finger at her daughter.

I tried not to laugh as Liz sounded more and more like mom. Soon she would be nagging Beth to find a good husband who would be a doctor. Not that doctors actually performed operations anymore. Most operations were done by machines and computer programs that reacted faster and with more precision.

"Bleh to that. I'll be eighteen soon, and I can't be taking a bus," Beth said as she approached the stairs.

"All right. You go to class, let your uncle and me talk." Liz waved her daughter off, and Beth nodded happily. Soon she was down the stairs and in her room.

My sister turned back to me. "You know that the monitors will still be in place, right?"

"I know. I'm okay, Liz."

The doctors had told me all about the rules for moving out on my own. There was a long list of do's and don'ts in order to meet insurance requirements. Part of me longed for the days when a person could vanish into the hills and never be heard from again.

"No, you're not," Liz said slowly.

"I need time away from everything," I said. Every damn thing on the planet reminded me of her, and it was killing me. Staring at the ceiling at night, going out to our old car, driving by the old house to talk to renters.

"That's avoiding, Grant. You're avoiding." She had gone through all the courses with me. Liz often talked trash about other people and got mad at the drop of a hat, but she was nothing but supportive in the long run.

"I've got to do something though." I put a hand on the pile of images and pulled up the small house's image. This was where I would end up once everything cleared. Would my past keep haunting me there?

"So what, you're going to sit at this new house and work yourself into oblivion and hope everything gets better?" Liz was back to her coffee. This time, she was sipping it.

"I'll still do my meetings. I'll still make my sessions. I'll show up at work. What else can I do but try to go on?"

"When Beth's"—her lips curled distastefully—"asshole father ran off, I cried for weeks, Grant. Weeks."

"I know."

"And I would have never survived it you hadn't stood up for me to Mom and Dad." She took a big gulp of coffee, then stared down.

I spared her a quick glance and smile.

"You were in pain. Of course I would help."

We had been seventeen then. Neither of us knew a damned thing about life at that age. Twenty had been so long ago too. I wasn't engaged, didn't have my degree, hadn't even bought a house. There were so many differences.

"And I had to face the reality that Beth wouldn't have a good father figure in her life." Liz was quiet. She gazed off into the distance before she took another gulp of coffee. "Not that any of the others were worth much either."

"You should have taken him for child support," I said.

Beth's father had demonstrated absolute scum qualities by running off like that. We never tried to track the man down, and my sister refused to pursue the matter.

"No, no, I wanted nothing to do with that man, and I still don't. That's not the point," Liz said. I could almost hear the coffee mug in her hands cracking under pressure. "If you're in trouble, then let us, let me know. We—I—owe you.

We're family."

That was the same line I had used when helping her with the bills after Beth's father dropped out of the picture. The simple statement made me feel guilty all over again. For being so broken, for being unable to keep it together. Other people moved on after a year. It hurt, but they somehow did it. Not me. In my heart, I still clung to her memory as if it was my only lifeline, which was almost spitting in the face of my sister's kindness.

"And if you ever scare me again with these sorts of threats, I'll kill you myself," Liz said. She walked off down the hall and left me alone at a kitchen table full of my future.

Two months after that conversation, everything got a final seal of approval. I was certified as tentatively stable. My insurance company was on board. My old house had been successfully sold to the renters, who seemed eager to make things official. My new home was hours in the other direction but still close enough to Liz and Beth. That way if I had a bad night, home was only a car ride away.

I had set up a few other purchases as a result of my job. Things that Trillium easily provided to all contractors. Liz could have her coffee as comfort; I would have a dance program. Part of me felt ashamed to use a dead woman as my dance partner. The other part of me wanted to hold onto any remaining image of her in order to keep myself together.

The doctor said I had complicated bereavement issues. None of the clinical explanations helped. My psychiatrist had said that finding the will to continue was an exercise in distraction. Not avoidance, but finding other things to focus on and live for. We had discussed the move, and he suggested that it might be a good way to progress with my life. Changing where I worked and lived was a thin line, he warned. Overworking was my last major crime since I had given up drinking again.

This was my life now. If overworking kept me around for Liz and Beth, then it was a small price.

Session Eight
Grumpy Old NPC

Transitioning wasn't hard or sudden. I basically went to sleep and woke up as another person. A doctor could have told me to count backward from ten with the same impact.

After waking up, there were a lot of changes. Everything ached immensely. The throbbing pain served to remind me how amazing this game was. These weren't sharp jabs of simulated pain. This was everywhere, from everything. Breathing was hard too, but getting easier the more I looked around.

I tried to lift one arm, and weakness stole my strength. Lifting my arm took too much energy. My eyes drifted around and took note of a cane that I had gripped to near death. My fingers were locked in a curl that seemed permanent.

The view was probably beautiful. I was sitting on a bench while staring at a sunset over the ocean. Things were fuzzy, and no matter how many times I blinked, it didn't clear up. Birds cried out from above. Squinting wasn't bringing them into view.

"Ehhhhhh." A noise escaped me as I shifted to one side. Switching which leg was crossed over the other hurt.

People chattered nearby. Children played on a beach and built sand castles. Some adults did as well. Keeping my eyes from drifting asleep took some focus, but I could see a difference between the figures. Players had visible icons above their heads—simple green ones and a red bar that would fade in and out as I stared. Everyone who didn't have bars must have been computer-generated characters. In other games, they would be called non-player characters, or NPCs for short. Parents dodged after little ones. Guards patrolled the beach in twos. I saw a vendor selling items out of his little cart.

"Hhhhhrrr." Movement hurt again. I winced and tried to make out people.

A few things were extremely clear. Pop-up boxes had formed nearby, each one citing bits of information about the NPCs around me. When one middle-aged woman came nearby, she waved. A box spun into view, citing who she was, how long this body had known her, and other tiny details. I grunted and lifted the cane a little. She smiled and kept on walking. It gave me another moment to review my current situation.

A meter? I squinted and looked around trying to bring something up. Wait, there—a tiny percentage bar was hanging off to one side.

Progress: 12%

Was that measured based on my single feeble cane wave? Or maybe sitting here half asleep?

Quest: A Last Gasp
Difficulty: Unknown
Details: You've chosen to take up the mantle of William (Old Man) Carver. The duration of this act is four weeks. Many of Old Man Carver's skills and knowledge are still functional. Results will be measured based on performance as Old Man Carver. Review synchronization meter for progress.
Special circumstances tied to this quest have imposed the following restrictions:
Autopilot time will not impact completion.
Failure: Complete failure is impossible.
Success: Possible information (Restricted)

What exact kind of NPC was Old Man Carver? There were too many questions. I would have to make it up, to the best of my ability, as I went along. Logging out would be counterproductive too, unless my progress reached far enough. With vacation time, I could finish this quest up and maybe settle my thoughts before going back to work.

That fuzzy sunset was impressive. I sat there and watched while time passed in-game. Well, it was more like a background as I dug through informational pop-ups. Plus, with focus, I could see what sort of system windows other players were getting. The man on the beach building a sand castle received small bonuses to **[Coordination]** with city reputation boosts. Every so often there would be another trickle to **[Focus]**.

Neat.

Once I was really playing the game as myself, I would know all sorts of tricks. Was that intentional or a side effect of being an NPC? All this assumed that I wouldn't try to rip out my ARC's hard drive upon this big reveal.

Another player was marching around with the guards, doing patrols. Her **[Strategy]** trait was going along with her **[Endurance]**. She had other notifications that didn't display. They were all grayed out, probably due to being traits or skills that I hadn't unlocked. This whole system, this game, was like nothing I had played before and was so strange. At least these results made sense. One gained points for doing work, and the points gained went together with what actions were performed. Two hours passed in-game as I watched people go about their actions.

"Excuse me, sir?" A female voice came from nearby.

I groaned and turned, but couldn't quite swivel my head enough to see.

"Yes," I repeated three times before the word made it out.

"Can you help me? The guards over there said I needed to talk to you."

"Eh?" The noise came out of me automatically.

"I'm trying to find a place to learn the cooking skill," she said.

"Eh?" I said even louder. Why would I know anything about where to find a skill? How much knowledge would a game NPC have of these kinds of things? Two pop-up boxes flipped up as I chewed on my cheek.

> **Warning!** Your recent actions have demonstrated confusion. Old Man Carver was not a confused sort of person. In order to maintain an effective facade, you will need to perform better.

> **System Help!** Old Man Carver has been numerous things in his life, but in his twilight years, he became a guide to new Travelers. In his pocket are maps that provide information from locations around **[Haven Valley]**. Most who visit him are sent on a task prior to being given a map. This task varies based on Old Man Carver's whims. In order to succeed while standing in for Old Man Carver, you must fulfill his duties.

> Progress: 10%

Well, crud. I had lost points already.

"Cooking. What good is cooking to you?" I had to stall and think of a task. Who cooked in today's world? Oh, besides my mother on holidays. Wait. Right. Video game world. Cooking was probably fairly common by necessity.

"Mister Carver, sir, I need cooking before I go out of the city." She was so soft-spoken and timid-sounding. Not at all like the Voices I'd dealt with. They were each a heavy personality.

"Fine. What's in it for me?" I came up blank on the questing part.

A system notification cropped up again, telling me of the latest failure to perform.

"Bah. Never mind, you probably don't know how to do anything useful. You visitors are all the same." My hasty attempt at back pedaling knocked my progress down another percentage point, making me wince. Wincing also hurt.

> **System Help!** Old Man Carver is grumpy and looks constantly sour, but his words often cut straight to the point. He never asked others what they could do for him and would always assign them a task.

> Progress: 9%

"Go clean up the beach for me. Pick up the litter your buddies left behind. Maybe then I'll get you a map to your precious cooking instructor."

That little decision prompted another window refunding one of my failed points. System notifications were going off like crazy as the game tried to adapt me to this new role. I wondered how they had even programmed something for a player pretending to be an NPC.

No. I had to think of little tasks for players who decided to bother me. This area was one of the starting cities. Slowly, painfully, while trying not to groan and bellyache from the pain, I reached inside the robe I was wearing and dug out a rolled up parchment. Great. I really did have a map, and from the brief feeling of sliding my hand under this brown robe, there wasn't much between a breeze and me.

Old Man Carver didn't like putting on much in the way of clothing, among all of his other features. With a lot of strength and determination, I pushed up from the bench and wobbled a bit, trying to get the ground under me.

"Ooooh." Groan prevention was impossible.

I managed to lift an arm to about chest level and unrolled the map. It flopped downward, and my eyes dropped with it. These words were far easier to see. Continue Online had dubbed Old Man Carver as nearsighted. There were dots all over the map, even some weird half-image ones. Notes were scribbled about. Focusing on specific dots revealed a myriad of information. There were tasks on here, mysteries of the area to send players out to, common items that needed to be resolved.

Goodness, this thing was a wealth of information for new players.

"Where's cooking?" One of the dots lit up brighter than the others. Go NPC powers!

"Ah ha."

A name, a face, almost a miniature dossier came into being. Not only was the game showing me where cooking was, it showed me details about who was involved.

Turned out the person in question, a chef working at one of the three inns in town, preferred those who were very clean and well-kept. He hated disorder and often fired people who couldn't keep a kitchen polished. The man also worked nights for hours, prepping for the following day.

"Hah."

The girl who had spoken to me earlier was still out there cleaning things up. She seemed to be looking at a progress bar similar to the one I had. Hers, at least from this angle, looked to be tallying up garbage collected. This character's eyesight officially reached terrible. The Voices hadn't completely crippled me though. The beach and garbage were fuzzy, but the game windows were amazingly clear. I felt a little dirty for peeping on her system text like this.

Sunset would be ending soon. The long fading brightness was losing to nighttime. A chill blew in across sand and sea, then crawled inside my skin, down to the bone. There was a pop-up telling me that Old Man Carver didn't like to stay out too far after sundown.

I gained another percentage point for turning to watch the dying light. Maybe William Carver had loved to watch sunsets. Maybe he liked the ocean. Mysteries abounded for my temporary acting assignment. I stood there, holding myself up against the wind. My job would only be completed if the girl, young lady, finished her beach combing. Hopefully before I started taking a hit to my own progress bar.

She was scrambling, looking upset and tired as time went on. About halfway through, she stopped to pull some bread out of the player bag at her waist and shoved it into her mouth. Moments afterward, the revitalized player stood and kept picking at the ground.

Was there a hunger bar?

Probably. This game was intended to be realistic, and she'd asked for the cooking skill trainer. I squinted and tried to focus on my statistics. There was more information available now than there had been in the trial room.

There, that had to be a hunger bar. I pointed one gnarled finger and slowly dragged the bar to one side. I learned, from watching other players do their thing, that it was possible to lock status bars into view. That way it was always present instead of only coming up when something critical was happening.

A game manual popped into existence, displaying information about all interface methods, but there seemed to be a lot that was left uncovered. Most things only showed up once I'd experienced it for myself. Losing health to an evil puffball fantasy chicken-thing had rather clearly shown me what a health bar looked like.

I sat on the bench again, cane still in my hands, fingers curled in their death lock. To my side sat the map.

"Mister Carver."

I managed to work the kink out of my neck enough to turn and look. This was a city guard, an NPC judging by all the information that came up.

"Dayl," I said.

"Yes, sir. I'm glad you remember me, sir. Father says sometimes you forget, sir." He rushed his words together.

Dayl had to be in his younger years, but there was no age on his information window. He wore armor and had a helmet that covered most of his face. The body under it was clearly trained and worked out.

Apparently Old Man Carver drifted off sometimes. A constant stream of information was pelting me. Maybe it was a case of having too much knowledge in your head and getting lost trying to sift through an ocean. I read the messages regarding this new person. Turned out Dayl would escort me home or sometimes wake me up if I passed out on the bench. No, if Old Man Carver passed out. Not me. A yawn escaped, and both eyelids sank for a moment.

"Are you ready to go, sir?" Dayl asked.

"I'm watching this one." I tilted the cane. The action gained me another point of progress, bringing me up to thirteen percent.

"Another Traveler, sir?"

My head nodded. "Another."

"They've slowed down a lot in the last few months." Dayl's voice broke in the middle of his sentence.

"Happens. Did you think they were endless?" I had almost said "we" when responding. There were only so many people on Earth, and of those not everyone would be interested in a game.

"The big cities got it the worst. Father says we should be thankful for all the work they've done."

"You disagree?" I said as another window drifted by. This one contained information about Dayl's father. Being city guardsmen was a family tradition.

"I don't know, sir. Things are changing. Six years ago, there were no Travelers. Now they've started to appear out of the blue in our city," Dayl said.

"Times always change," I responded slowly. Hopefully things changed around here. A game with a stagnating world would be mind-numbingly boring.

"They used to only appear in the bigger cities. Father says that stopped once the Kingdoms started to recruit them. Travelers only appear in neutral areas."

"Mh. Makes sense."

Games had capital cities, places where trade, meetings, or whatever would be handled. Normally, entire quest chains would start from there as well.

It would be interesting to see exactly how big those major cities might get. Especially since there weren't only NPCs wandering around all day and night. They had homes and, judging by the last few hours spent on the beach, they lived their entire lives here in a simulated world.

"Father says I worry too much. But, sir, there's been a shift toward violence since they started arriving. And more of them are being elevated to important roles."

"So let the Travelers choose what they do like everyone else does."

"But Travelers are frightening. That girl over there, she looks stronger already, sir, and she's only been picking up trash."

"She's about done." Her progress bar was reaching completion. Which was good. Every time I talked to Dayl, my own progress for this NPC quest went up and down in bits.

"Do you think there will be war? Father says there won't be one, but I can't help but shake the feeling," Dayl asked.

"Oh, yes." I nodded and watched my own progress bar jump up five percent in one go. "There will always be a war."

There I sat, an old man chewing on his lip while watching a young girl about my niece's age clean up the beach. Most NPCs were gone by now. Those who lingered were escorting carts and headed in various directions. While a guard who was entirely too young babysat me.

How odd this whole situation was.

The girl finally finished her task as I slowly tapped my foot in time to the music in my head. I recalled a song that had played weeks ago. That four-minute dance had taken me hours to learn. Maybe Old Man Carver had a bit of dance in him somewhere.

"I'm done, Mister Carver, sir."

This player was so soft-spoken that I almost missed her. At some point, my eyes had drifted out to the sea, watching blurry swells fade closer to shore.

"Here. A map." My arm felt leaden, but I tried to point.

She carefully took the scroll from where it sat. I didn't have the energy to lift my arm and actually hand it over.

"Mister Carver, sir, where's someone who can teach me cooking?"

"Mh. Turn it this way." I tried to be decisive and issue orders as William Carver would have. Besides, there was a whole mess of dots on there for different locations.

Oddly, her map was completely empty. I touched the spot where the inn chef's information displayed for me. A box faded into view facing this new player.

"Careful. He works nights and only helps those who know how to keep a clean workplace." She had done her job. Hopefully, now my Carver points would allow me to do a bit more guidance.

"Maybe you should brush up a little before you drop by. Maybe pick up litter between here and there."

I was willing to bet there was a skill or trait called **[Tidy]** that would pop into being if she worked hard enough.

She nodded slowly while staring at the map.

"Dayl," I said.

"Yes, sir?" He almost cracked his voice again.

"She needs a bag—nothing fancy, something to pick up trash with."

"Miss, you can take one of the trash bags you used earlier. They're free to anyone willing to help keep our city clean." The younger guard looked so serious then, I'd bet he had to work hard to avoid the "my dad says" line.

"There you go," I said.

She looked happy and a bit confused.

"Now, I need to get home." I'd gained two points for showing her where to go and speaking as I did but lost one of them for staying out too long after sundown.

Standing hurt like hell, and I fell again.

"Let me help, Mister Carver, sir." She dove for an arm and nearly wrenched it out of the socket.

I grumbled but didn't argue. The pain wasn't mild. Moments later I was up and vaguely stable.

"I'm getting too old," I muttered, half in jest. That lost me another point, along with gaining more information about Old Man Carver's dislike for admitting his age in front of people. I sighed and started shuffling off, leaving the girl and guard behind.

Home was northward, out on a small hill that would take too long to reach. My progress points danced as my slow pace home hurt things. Refusal to ask for help raised them back up. What a stubborn old man. Dayl was walking behind me a ways. His heavy metal footsteps stood out in the near silence of early night.

I made it to William Carver's house, I thought. There were no other homes anywhere close. Guess Old Man Carver had retired in a small cottage on the edge of town. Shrubs and a wooden fence surrounded the property. A second fence ran along the back and went for miles in either direction. Behind the house was a field that stretched into sheer fuzziness. There were creatures that looked similar to horses in the distance.

I grunted and reached around inside my robe for a key to the door. Inside, his house was almost as tiny as mine. There were another two small rooms filled with books. I pulled one down at random and shoved it into a pocket for tomorrow's bench sitting. Following that, I shuffled my old, tired NPC body to bed. Eyelids closed almost instantly, leaving me alone in silent darkness.

Nighttime would last at least two real-time hours. Long enough for me to log out of the ARC and take care of myself. Maybe catch a quick nap. I resolved the real-life necessities. Alarms were set, and sleep claimed me. Old Man Carver's exhaustion was contagious.

An eye blink later, the alarm slammed on. I felt tired, having only sustained an hour of sleep, but it was better than nothing. I would have to ask Beth how to handle long-term assignments in the game. There had to be some method for dealing with it aside from autopilot.

I logged into Continue. This time when I stepped through the doorway, there was no room for tests and trials. James and the **[Messenger's Pet]** were absent. The game finished loading with me abruptly becoming an old man shakily trying to lift a crude coffee mug to his mouth for a sip. I fumbled a few drops before finishing the motion.

Next time I should check the player status as Beth had done. That method would allow me to see what I was leaping into and maybe I could avoid dripping scalding-hot liquid. Strangely, the poor treatment cost me a few health points but didn't change my progress bar.

Progress: 14%

Following additional prompts, I managed to stumble around the house. Apparently I was running late while trying to figure out everything. My tardiness was made clear by a tiny box which displayed hits to my completion percentage with warning notices.

I looted a few more map scrolls and an apple. They were put into pockets to go with the key and book Old Man Carver's robes already held. Huffing, I turned and closed the door, making sure everything was locked up. The cane helped minimize Old Man Carver's unstable footsteps.

Once shuffling down the path, I saw other townsfolk. Most of them waved. I nodded back frequently and felt like a complete impostor. These people knew William Carver the

NPC, not Grant the player posing as Carver the non-player. At least I got a few more points for my vague replies to people. Old Man Carver didn't seem big on social pleasantries.

Judging by morning traffic, stalls being set up, and bustle, this city contained two thousand people. We were sprawled out over a few miles. There was an entire marina for boating, but it stopped short of being a trade port with giant ships coming in.

The ocean smell was masked by bakery goods and meats. I carefully looked at the scroll, trying to map out where I was via all the little dots of information around me. There was an alleyway near here that was dangerous at night. Notes on the map told me that this was an event location.

Now that was unfair. A guide NPC had access to that sort of information? I could lead players into an alley at night and see if they survived the attack? For what? Turned out result possibilities were noted as well. Rewards ranged all over. One possible reward was contacts with a Thieves' guild, if you subdued but didn't kill, or managed to steal from the attackers and get away. Another route pointed toward the guards and city if you helped other civilians who might end up involved.

Really, who even thought of this stuff? Everything about it seemed designed to lead a player around based on their gut reactions.

The bakery near me provided a chance for new players to earn coin for work. They often hired Travelers for all roles: sweeping, mixing, folding the dough, or running the cash register.

I shook my head and tried not to read too much into it. Basically, there were options all over town. No two players would take the exact same path, show the same interests, or respond to events in the same manner. Each one would have different rewards and a nearly unique experience. Not every player would talk to a guide, like the NPC I was pretending to be. Some had foreknowledge from friends and family. Some were savvy enough to find buildings that might teach them what they wanted.

There were two buildings on the map loosely labeled "Training Hall." From the information I read while walking, those locations seemed a lot like gyms for weapon trainers. I had to see what those were like. Thankfully there would be no drill sergeants spitting words at my face, I hoped.

From a tree overhead, there was a rush of noises. Rustling preceded a solid *whack* as something collided with the trunk, then what had to be a chipmunk chattering. Giant acorn-like objects fell from the tree as the squabbling noises kept going.

I stopped and watched. The beach was in sight, but this was interesting enough to suffer a hit to my progress bar. Soon other creatures joined in. My poor eyesight couldn't make out if they had been there the whole time or leapt from adjourning trees. They were clearly fighting something. That something was hissing back.

A smile crept across my crinkling face. I kept watching for the inevitable outcome. After thirty more seconds of squabbling, my little trouble-making buddy fell from the branches above.

He was pelted by a good fifteen more acorn objects. In his teeth, he had managed to secure one of the other creatures. It looked like a sleeker chipmunk with a strange set of emerald jewels right above either eye.

"Identification," I whispered. It wouldn't do to have any of the other NPCs hear me using a player skill.

Skill Used: [Identification]

Race: [Coo-Coo Rill]

Status: Deceased

Details: [Coo-Coo Rill]s are communal animals. They often steal bright, shiny objects for their nests. More than one person has lost jewelry or coins to a colony's hoard of treasures.

Warning: Attacking a nest for treasure will often result in fighting a colony of **[Coo-Coo Rill]s.**

"Really?" I asked.

The **[Messenger's Pet]** huffed and shook his head.

"You weren't trying to steal their treasures, were you?"

He let out an angry hiss at the branches above. More trees rustled overhead, and another round of acorns flew toward both the miniature dragon and me.

"Bah." I shook my cane at the tree and kept walking on toward my bench.

There was a bright, shiny arrow bobbing above the ground as a guide. "Park your old butt here!" it seemed to say.

Sitting hurt as much as walking though.

Old age was no picnic. I spent the first thirty minutes of William Carver's bench warming time trying to play fetch with the miniature dragon. I still had no idea if the little fellow had a name or not.

The carcass of the dead **[Coo-Coo Rill]** had been deposited in front of my bench.

Citizens of this world walked around it with a giggle or frown. One woman clearly found the situation borderline hysterical. Probably my feeble tossing of nuts to the little dragon had something to do with it. A shimmering blue headband was wrapped around her hair. One stray chunk was tucked behind an ear as she sat down beside me. The woman was clearly important. Old Man Carver didn't have a wall of information about her stored away, but there was one major message box.

Secondary Goal: Old Man Carver has been trying to learn about this woman for years but has come up empty. Learning more about her past will greatly increase your progress as Old Man Carver. This will help settle his spirit during passing.

Reward: Significant progress toward your completion (dependent upon information found)

Note: Old Man Carver is typically direct and has tried numerous tactics to get information in the past. The woman (Mylia Jacobs) finds this amusing and is deliberately obtuse.

Progress: 21%

Was Carver stalking this girl? Clearly it wasn't offensive since she sat next to me with half a smile. Everything hurt so much when moving that I doubted Carver was trying to peep into showers.

"Morning, Mylia," I started politely and watched the meter for possible reactions.

"Mister Carver. How are you this fine day?"

"Enjoying the view." I even managed not to look anywhere near her when saying it. Otherwise, it would be kind of creepy.

"And your little friend?" She was gesturing toward the tiny dragon playing with a young boy. The **[Messenger's Pet]** was hopping around eagerly.

"He followed me." My answer was vague. I wasn't exactly sure why the **[Messenger's Pet]** had hung around.

"What's his name?"

"No idea. I'll ask him," I responded.

"Oh? Is he a tiny dragon?" Mylia looked eager to pet the tiny creature but managed to hold herself back.

"Not exactly. A Messenger's Pet." I was trying to sound impressive by knowing the dragon's species, which was clearly a bad idea. My progress bar dropped two percent from that one. Old Man Carver didn't give away much information if he could help it.

"Oh." She looked worried and frowned for a moment. "Aren't those bad?"

"Mh. What's he going to do to me?" I felt little fear of the tiny dragon, but he did have teeth and breathed fire. If he were to attack, it would suck due to the pain feedback. That would be anti-neat and pain-tastic.

"I don't know, but it'd be a shame if something did happen." She turned in my direction and made it easier to see her entire face.

"Mylia, if I didn't know better, I'd think you'd miss this old man." I tested out the third-person speech and tried not using titles like miss or ma'am. The progress bar went up a little. My eyes drifted to the azure scarf she had wrapped around most of her head.

"Not me, Mister Carver. The kids though, they might miss your stories."

"Everyone loves a good story." There were two rooms in Carver's house full of books that proved the point.

"I imagine they love the story-teller too." Mylia managed to sound playful. She had half a smile that almost reached her worn eyes.

"Hah." Old Man Carver didn't seem very lovable. Maybe he was hard on the outside and soft on the inside. Like a very weird cookie. Probably raisin-filled.

"Come on, Phil, we're running behind," she said.

The younger boy looked up and nodded. His eyes were tired too. Not from abuse but from malnutrition. Mylia Jacobs wasn't much better. Both of them were probably underfed. It wasn't in her clothes or his, but there was a familiar draw to the face.

"Mh. Good-bye, Mylia." My words were almost absent-minded as I studied them walking off. Mylia wasn't excessively attractive. The only vaguely cute aspect about her was the azure band wrapped atop her head.

The small dragon nipped at my heel, looking for attention. It was near noon, and the bar set aside for hunger was dwindling. I absently pulled out my apple and ate a few bites while thinking of additional tasks.

"Mh." Chewing hurt like everything else.

No new players that needed my attention had started today. Sitting on the bench, I watched one bewildered person start and be cornered by a friend almost immediately. Clearly they were starting to play with someone from real life. The more senior player gave me a wave and hauled their friend onward.

I grunted and pulled out the book hidden in my robe. Reading to pass the time would be helpful. **[Inspection]** revealed a surprise. Maybe that's why this book had been easiest to grab.

Item: Carver's Journal, (Vol. 1)
Description: William (Old Man) Carver has kept a log of highlights from this world. It contains musings and general observations. He's collectively titled these works, 'Notes from a Stranger in a Strange Land'. This reference is said to be from Old Man Carver's childhood.

"Mh." I started reading through the book.

Somewhere during these boring actions the **[Messenger's Pet]** had decided to take a nap in a spot of sun nearby. His location would probably be safe from both the idle footsteps of people and the attacks of angry **[Coo-Coo Rill]**s.

Three weeks in this city and I've noticed a lot of issues. I finally ditched those other idiots and found my own place. Michelle was too content to stay in our hometown and work a forge. Yates insisted on learning magic, even though it was weird, and I wanted to kill his monsters with a sword.

Maybe I'm an idiot too. But here, in this world, you can be anything. Why would I settle for being mundane? I have a goal, and that goal is to kill a dragon.

I snorted in laughter, which made the tiny dragon perk his ears for a moment. At least Carver had aimed high. Had he succeeded? I had about four weeks of bench-warming to endure, so I avoided reading spoilers if at all possible. According to the journal and my own personal in-game display, this was from about twenty-five years ago.

A few more pages in, and I could see Old Man Carver's general distaste for other people. He regarded their choices and their methods as dull and uninteresting. Not to say he didn't occasionally pair up with people. The first misadventure he'd had involved a female elf from the general description. They tried to stop giant wasps from chewing up a great tree of some sort.

He outlined the qualities of said female elf and went into excessive detail about her exuberance for all new things. The entry ended with a parting of ways. The tree was also saved, but from how everything was written, saving nature had been a secondary mission. I rolled my eyes. Old Man Carver sounded like a young teen in this one, not that there was an age listed anywhere.

Glancing around revealed that all was fairly peaceful. Guards patrolled, and townsfolk visited the beach. It looked cleaner since that new player had spent hours picking up trash. Noon was growing closer and things were warming up. Old Man Carver's robe wasn't exactly comfortable in this sun.

I looked around for a shady perch. There was a similar bench with an awning attached. Moving there earned me another percent on my progress bar and turned down the heat.

> *After my very grateful parting with the elf, I set my compass south. There is a desert that boasts of giant lizards. I assume they'll be good practice for fighting a Dragon. Before that, the sword I picked up in my hometown is due for a repair. Maybe I'll stop by home and see if Michelle can actually craft something as decent as he thinks.*
>
> *He keeps bragging about his skills. Idiot. I'm glad he's not out here with me; I'd probably have to rescue him from every tiny monster that attacks. That guy is so weak a feather would beat him up.*
>
> *I hope he never reads this journal. Free gear is nothing to sneeze at. Ugh. He'll probably demand that I give him all the resources I've gathered out here. He bled me dry over a pair of greaves. I can't imagine how much worse a decent sword will be.*

"Hey. Old Man Carver." A voice out of the blue disturbed my review of my—Carver's—past. Goodness, this was confusing.

"What?" The heat, being interrupted, and a faint promise of pain if I moved too suddenly all combined to make me irritated. My curt response was worth another percent. I bet yelling from my lawn at the town's children would send my progress through the roof.

"I need a quest from you. Then give me a map." The other figure was a brown-haired boy in his early twenties.

Thank goodness this game had an age requirement or I would be flooded with children demanding things. He still had that semi-lean form that young adults wear so well before everything goes south later in life. I stared at him and uttered the first mildly Carver thing to come to mind.

"You're a rude brat, aren't you," I said. Score another percent for me.

"Listen, old man, I can't waste time here. Give me a quest, and I'll be out of your hair and on my way." He waved his hand in my face.

"You think it's that easy? I give you a quest, and you get a reward?"

"Isn't it? What kind of game is this?"

The younger man's words made me smile. "What kind of game" seemed to be a common question.

"Bah. This isn't a game; this is deadly serious. You want something"—I stood up to the best of Old Man Carver's ability. That was a slow, painful process full of barely suppressed grunts—"you earn it."

"It's only a map. I need that, and I need directions to the weapons hall."

"Yeah. Swinging a sword sounds like the move of a future Champion." My sarcastic barb cost me a few points. Oh. That was because William Carver had been a sword-swinger. I had insulted my own past.

"No, daggers—I'm going to be an assassin," he said while frowning.

I rolled my eyes. What kind of player announces himself to an NPC like that? Maybe a swift punch in the face would allow me to claim to be a Monk. Yeah. We were four sentences into our interaction and I had labeled him as an idiot. Old Man Carver was really rubbing off on me. Four weeks of this and I would have trouble unwinding back to my happy spot. At least Carver wasn't a drunk, according to the first few years of his life. Behind us, someone was walking animals along the path. Inspiration grabbed me.

"Fine. I'll give you a task worthy of your future occupation." I tried not to laugh.

"Good."

"Go moo at that"—I used **[Identification]** on the creature. It looked like a cow and the description wasn't too far off—"bovine over there. Do it until I'm satisfied, and you'll get your map."

Part of me felt euphoric when a pop-up box appeared in front of the new player. Sure enough, my actions had generated another quest. Similar to the girl who had cleaned up the beach. She had been way more polite.

"A cow. Are you serious?" The new player thought it was a cow too.

Spots, a few extra horns, slightly odd hind legs, still a cow. The new player didn't have an **[Identification]** skill like me. According to the game text, the creature was called something else. I ignored the in-game race and filed it away as **[Future Beef Patty]**.

"Dead serious. Show me you have the determination to follow through, and I'll even throw in a contact for your assassin class." I deadpanned the response and lost another percentage point.

"Fine."

I would never be satisfied with his attempt at mooing to the cow.

"Carver, are you really going to let that child become an assassin?" There was a deep male voice that had crept up behind me.

I tried not to act disturbed.

Turning slightly revealed a guard. His armor was far more outstanding than the other guards' were. They looked very cookie-cutter, and the man standing next to me was clearly unique. Embellishments adorned his shoulders and similar etchings were on everything down to the heavy boots.

I briefly read the descriptions popping up on my display while chewing at a lip. The new player had run off down the road chasing **[Future Beef Patty]**.

Name: [Future Beef Patty]
Details: This is the description given to a passing bovine. The name is entirely in William (Old Man) Carver's imagination.

"Wyl," I uttered the same type of greeting I'd used with Mylia. Sure enough, my flat utterance of a name earned me a point.

"Carver."

Further reading identified this man as a Guard Captain. Surprisingly, he was fairly high ranked for this town. My **[Identification]** display had a window with a funny shield-and-sword combination. The symbol was outlined with a wreath and two stars. It was the same sort of nonsense I had seen on military general uniforms.

"Doubt he has the stomach to follow through. Too much pride," I said. That player didn't seem like the type able to handle my demeaning task.

"We can hope." Wyl nodded with a large grin.

"Doubt he follows orders either. Not like your boy Dayl," I said the name and felt conflicted about how many names had a y in them. Maybe it was a regional thing.

"My son's a good man," Wyl said.

His son constantly said "my father says." Calling him a good man seemed misleading. Not my family though. Old Man Carver might be blunt, but he seemed secretive enough to not speak these conclusions out loud.

"Mh. He's got a long ways to go." I was absently staring after the player who'd run off into the distance. He seemed to be waving in panic, trying to get the man escorting **[Future Beef Patty]** to slow down.

"Don't I know it." Wyl sighed and rubbed the back of his neck with a hand. His fingers clanked as they worked between armor chunks to get to irritated skin.

"Why the sudden visit, Wyl?" I knew from the various system messages that the guard captain rarely came down to the beach. Not even for Old Man Carver's wise council.

"One of the Priestesses of Selena has requested your presence."

Who-lena? What? Judging by the name, this was one of the Voices. No one else would have temples in this world. "Now?"

"Now," Wyl confirmed.

"What about our future sword-for-hire there?" I lifted the cane a little and waved it toward the new player.

He was shouting in the distance. His voice sounded vaguely hoarse from here. That could have been a trick of William Carver's faded hearing.

"I'll leave a guard for him with a few more tasks. Something to hopefully deter that stupid assassin idea."

"Good luck. The boy seems addle-brained," I said.

"It's fine. If that's truly what he wants to do, we can't stop him. Travelers are hard to control." Wyl gave a wide grin and shrugged.

"Don't I know it."

"That you would. It takes a rare man to suffer their bewildered demands. I don't know where they get half the fool notions they have."

I snorted. To me, a player posing as an NPC, it was extremely clear where most of their "fool notions" came from. Other games and a world of informational boxes had served to brainwash this latest generation.

"Come on, Carver. I'll walk you up to the temple," Wyl said.

I grumbled. This would surely be another bout of aches and pains. Actually voicing my complaints out loud wouldn't be a character-appropriate thing to do. That silly little bar reinforcing my actions was the only thing standing between me and answers about my fiancée.

Session Nine
Priestess Peach

I liked these trees. Two major types littered the city. Tall ones that spiraled up high were typically clustered together near grassy areas. Everywhere else, especially over pathways, were trees with large branching canopies. They stretched across twenty and thirty-foot gulfs toward each other. Overhead, they twined together, creating a spotty patchwork of leaves.

"How's retirement been treating you, Carver?" Wyl's questioning tone implied a long-term relationship. How did a computer program account for all these possible interactions between NPCs?

"It's peaceful," I said without inflection. My score went neither up nor down.

He looked at the item in my hands. Carver's Journal was still tucked under an arm and the cane was still death-gripped. Behind us, the **[Messenger's Pet]** tried to figure out ways into **[Coo-Coo Rill]** nests. Silly creature. I had no idea why it bothered following me so much.

"Can't imagine it myself. I have a feeling I'll be doing this until I die."

"Mh. Probably." NPCs were likely to do the same role their entire lives, depending on how this whole situation was set up. How would this game act in five or ten years? Would they get older?

I should focus on playing and not worry about the future. I had four weeks of strangeness to get through first. Time-warping ratios were kind of nice in terms of vacation.

"Planning any new adventures?"

"Just one more." Words came out of my mouth unbidden. What the heck? I hadn't meant to say that at all. My impulse control was either crap or the computer had talked for me.

"You've got plenty left in you, Carver," Wyl said.

Was this tied to the Old Man Carver quest? Cue a seemingly random pop-up box. Now I was assigned another secondary goal on top of the first one.

Secondary Goal: Old Man Carver has expressed his desire to take one last adventure before passing. Find something worthy of Carver's legacy before the end of four weeks. Doing one last adventure will greatly increase your progress as Old Man Carver. This will help settle his spirit during passing.
Reward: Significant progress toward your completion (dependent upon the adventure)
Note: This adventure must be recognized by others as worthy of Carver.

Great. I had to figure out something about a girl who liked to mess with me and pretend to be obtuse. While sitting on a bench most of the day. While trying to find one last adventure. On top of that was ignoring real life, learning vague game rules, and not building my own character.

At least Old Man Carver's little stories amused me.

The new player and Guard Captain had interrupted me during Carver's recounting of a fight with a strange horse thing. He said it would shift colors to blend in with the background, all to sneak up and kick him with its hind legs. I was waiting to see how it ended.

"What does the Priestess want?"

"No idea. But I figured I'd best come fetch you before one of those fresh-faced Travelers did. You get enough of them already." Wyl smiled a lot.

"Mh." Non-committal grunts were the way to respond.

"Why did you volunteer to be a guide anyway?"

Some of the information I knew after reading Old Man Carver's dossier and other pop-ups. Carver had started being a guide as soon as Travelers started showing up. He—I—had also settled in this town right around the same time.

"Something to do." That lost me points.

"You killed a dragon by yourself, and call guiding new Travelers something to do?"

Stupid spoilers! He'd ruined the end of Carver's Journals for me and left me confused in the process. I couldn't respond with a good reason because I barely knew Carver. It was impossible to believe that a game touted for its realism had dwindled down each NPC to a few basic personality traits. From my progress bar's reaction, Carver was very realistic and not a simple cardboard cutout.

That made me lose step for a moment, literally. I stumbled over nothing and nearly fell flat on my face. Wyl's quick actions kept me somewhat upright, but my shoulder paid the price. A fresh wave of pain piled on top of the general hell that Carver's every movement was. Turned out there was no pain setting to turn down this whole mess.

"Gah." I had to stop.

Wyl got me to a bench, and I tried to control my near collapse. How the heck could Carver go on an adventure like this? I should just fail that onus and hope everything else was good enough.

"Rest a few. I'll let the Priestesses know of our delay."

I nodded hastily and tried to control my heart rate and breathing. A clenching in my chest wouldn't let go. Wyl walked away and left me clutching my chest. A simulated heart attack was racking my virtual body. That was what this must be. This was a dimmed-down version of Carver's heart seizing up.

It hurt.

Goodness, it hurt.

Why wouldn't this end?

After a few minutes, the pain passed and all the air in the world felt thin. My arm shook and legs quivered. What had brought this on? Had the original Carver died from this? Even one-fifth of the feedback had disabled all coherent thought.

"I'm getting old." Admitting weakness normally went against the persona being projected, but I lost no points from my admission.

Focusing on something other than pain would keep me going. Move forward, never back. I used the time to weigh my understandings of Carver in case Wyl asked me for my motivation again. To help get into the mind of the man I posed as, I cracked open the Journal and resumed reading.

Old Man Carver's eyes moved slower than I liked. Reading the letters felt hard to focus on. Some of them mixed up and required rereading. After too much concentration, I found out that Carver had managed to tame the horse and took him on the next adventure.

Some of the wording threw me off though. The way he spoke about things didn't feel like a denizen from this world. There were no citations about his childhood. The date stamps were from years ago, but judging by Carver's age, they basically started at about fifty.

I checked the cover again—this was Volume One. Slowly my eyes retraced the latest strange passage.

> *Michelle learned a great technique from his training. I had to wait two days for him to return to the shop so I could see it in action. The way he swung the hammer down almost made me switch focus. Too bad time is short; the doctors have only cleared me for another year or two tops.*
>
> *I'm stubborn enough to live beyond that, I don't care what they say. Every moment counts. Old age is horse-shit. All this power and we can't fix a bum ticker.*

That was out of place. A bum ticker? Was this a weird translation issue?

"Are you ready to go, Carver?" Wyl had returned.

Slow sighing preceded me putting the book away. Afterward, I nodded, and Wyl was kind enough not to ask any questions. He could see my struggling.

Halfway up the hill, the guard captain asked again. Why did I, or Carver, act as a guide to new players? I had no clear-cut answer. For several slow steps, I pondered life's biggest question. What would Carver do? I could tattoo that on my arm, or maybe a bracelet—WWCD. Reminder bracelets would be a new fad for all the residents of our fine city of **[Haven Valley]**.

I had been in-game for around twenty-four hours. Things didn't even feel high-paced. Sitting on a bench for hours and throwing acorns at a tiny dragon was a pleasant way to pass the time. Reading some misadventures was fun too. None of those hurt my progress. I could safely say that Carver didn't have problems idling time away. Not that his biography talked about the boring parts.

But why did he go to the beach day after day to wait for new players? Oh. There was an easy out here.

"You know I don't give away answers for free, Wyl; you earn it." Ding, there were a few new percentage points on my progress bar. Score one for reasonable deductions.

"Hah. Stubborn old man."

"Until the day I die," I agreed with a slightly pleased tone. The comment got me another point. Of course Carver was proud of being a hardheaded mule. Slowly but surely, I was learning to be someone else.

All at once disturbed, I logged out of my ARC and held very still as shaking overtook my senses.

I didn't want to let go, and for a moment, it had felt as though that was exactly what was happening. Counting backward from sixty happened more than once. Then breathing, pinching the bridge of my nose, rubbing my earlobes. All those things were techniques to try to calm myself. Each one helped me return to my happy place and not feel like the world was falling apart.

A message on my ARC distracted me. I put it on play.

"Uncle Grant! It's been, like, a week. I know you're playing. Where are you? I want to visit! Send me a message in-game, I'll tell you all the best hunting spots! You haven't played until you've been in a fight with the wolves in this game. They're super heart-thumping. User name Thorny!"

I about died giggling. Trust my niece to brighten my day with something blissfully out of place. My laughing convulsions kept going until both eyes watered. Beth was a little crazy. Her friend probably had some other similarly silly name. I would have to think of a good name for myself, but nothing like Thorny. Goodness. Knowing my niece, she had found some awkwardly matching title to go with the name.

That half-demon skin she had, coupled with what I'd seen from the Temptress Voice, painted a gloomy picture for Beth's mother. I wondered exactly how much Liz was kept in the loop. Of course, given the way Liz was as a teen, the apple didn't fall far from the tree. I remember avoiding Mom and Dad as much as possible when Liz was up to her antics. There was no way I would explain what my older twin was up to.

Okay. Those thoughts of times past put me in a better mood. I cleaned up, grabbed a drink, relieved the pressure on my bladder, and popped back into Continue.

Autopilot had me up the hill and panting for breath. All around an easier way to travel, but I lost a few points for not performing the actions myself. Neat. Even after the deduction, I did well enough to get a bonus. Hopefully this would help me figure out some additional information. Though quests never made sense to me. Why would an NPC with so much power and skill ask a player to help them with something difficult? Often times the player was a lower level than the quest giver.

> **Reward**: For reaching 25% completion, you will gain access to William Carver's skills. Over the course of his life, he has gained a large number of abilities and secret bits of knowledge.
> **Unlocked**: William (Old Man) Carver's Rank one skills are all displayed and can be actively used.

> Progress: 28%

I mean, Old Man Carver was old. Old, old, old, old, old. It made sense if I, posing as him, asked players to do things. Unless some of these skills were as neat as they looked. Titles ranged across the board. These traits were fairly self-explanatory. **[Truth Sense: Verbal specialist]**, **[Weapon Focus: Bladed]**, **[Retired Grand Explorer]**. One made me really snort, **[Stubborn as a Mule]**.

I only looked at a few of the items, scanning this way and that to trigger the displays for information. Hopefully, no NPCs would think me mentally ill, considering I basically possessed William Carver. The thought of being some sort of skin-walker made me throw up a bit in my mouth. I played it off as having a sour taste.

"We're here, Carver. I've got to get back to my duties. Will you be okay?"

I waved the man off and stood there waiting, both hands on my cane and trying to hold steady while thoughts dripped through.

This place was pretty. It sat overlooking the ocean, much like my bench but far higher up. We'd crisscrossed a few times up a painful incline that only had benches at the curves. Around me there seemed to be a few rooms and a downstairs of some sort. Things were a bit fuzzy in Carver-land, so I couldn't be sure. There seemed to be no male priests here. After a few minutes, I was extremely sure of that.

The dresses, columns, and Romanesque designs were familiar. I slowly raised my eyes upward and found, at the tallest point of the temple, a statue of a woman looking outward. Even fuzzy vision couldn't disguise that far-away look.

Oh no. Wyl had escorted me right to a personal fan's temple.

"Selena, huh?" I muttered out loud while surveying the area.

This seemed typical of the Voice. Marble, ocean, distracted pondering of the ocean. Too bad she seemed to hate me. And since I was racking up about a billion negative reputation points with this Voice, I decided to earn a few more.

"I can see up your dress." Giving the statue above my best old man leer paid off with two pop-up boxes.

+ 4 [Divine Attention]
Progress: 26%

"Heh." There was proof that my own skills would increase while under the guise of William Carver. I would need to wait until I was me to check out what exactly Divine Attention did. Not that my goal was stat points; more just yanking her chain.

None of the priestesses paid me any attention, despite my stellar commentary. I shuffled over to the edge and looked off into the distance. Even fuzzy, there was a definite beauty to this scene, especially up high. A wind breezing through brought that fish smell of the ocean, which was unusual to a land-dweller like me.

"Nice view. I bet the sunsets are something," I commented to the statue, even though it was unlikely Selena was paying that much attention to me.

Slowly I eased to the ground, much to the relief of my knees.

"Wish my eyesight wasn't so terrible."

A growl of my tummy and the dipping bar to one side of my view explained other things currently lacking. I tilted my head back and spoke to the statue again.

"You know why I'm here? I doubt your ladies invited me for a picnic."

"Certainly not, Will. From what I remember, your cooking was terrible." That was a deceptively sweet voice full of artificial cuteness.

"You'll have to come around. I've grown to love the view." In reality, moving again would hurt more.

"It's a view I've enjoyed myself many times." The woman with a fake syrupy voice came nearby and sat down. She was plump, short, and far too chesty.

I gave her a sidelong glance and registered the system boxes providing me information. She was a High Priestess of Selena. Carver's information included everything from age and food preferences to less public items. Such as a birthmark location and most common saying while being... compromised. It had been awhile since I'd compromised anyone on the level William Carver's information suggested. Goodness.

She was certainly younger. Score one for Old Man Carver, I guessed. I slowly scanned through the information and tried to gloss over the lewder details. Turned out they hadn't been together in that fashion since the woman took on her role as High Priestess years ago.

Oh. That was why I was here.

"Have you given more thought to giving Selena your oath?" Her name, Peach, sort of went with her general complexion.

"No." I wasn't even lying in the slightest amount. I, Grant Legate, had given no thought to Selena getting my oath or anything else. I'd moved past that one during the trial room. Unsurprisingly, the declaration gained me more progress points.

"Still the same old bull-headed man."

I grunted, either from pain or in response.

"Hip okay?" She kept glancing sidelong at me. My simulated eyesight wasn't so bad that I couldn't see her head turn. Subtlety was not in her skill listing.

"Fine."

"Shoulders?"

Would Carver flinch at her tone? No, he found it endearing. Joy. I shook my head.

"Good as ever." I licked at a dry lip and pondered how to handle all this.

"That's your way of saying it hurts every time the wind blows, right, you old goat?" The curve-laden woman gave a laugh.

Hah. This woman clearly knew Carver despite a grumpy exterior. Nor did she hesitate to point out his age. Hopefully I wouldn't screw up and betray Carver's recent passing.

"Ah well. You never admit anything anyway."

"Nope." I managed to avoid nodding in confirmation. According to the information popping around me, this conversation was common. Weekly, if I were to gauge. Wyl always had a guard take over the Guide duties below on the beach. Overall, it was interesting NPC behavior.

"The Voice sent me a dream last night." Her sweet voice managed to twist at the end. A slight gurgle that must mean unhappiness.

"And?"

"Selena showed me you walking through a door into the beyond."

"Was it white?" My eyes narrowed in thought.

"Pure, like fresh snow." She nodded but had no hint of joy on her face. Her sweet tone of voice betrayed no additional information.

"Mh." So Selena, the Voice who had never said a word, sent a picture of me in the trial room to her follower? My mind was splitting across this conversation and following my earlier train of thought. Wait a minute. How had this not occurred to me before? How exactly did an NPC die before their time and get taken over by a player?

"I'm worried about you, William." Her voice cracked a little.

"Don't be. I'm as healthy as an ox."

"Hah!" She laughed and broke the sweetened voice completely before coughing and getting back into the act. "You might fall over without that cane."

Suddenly I wanted to get away from the High Priestess and back to my bench. Carver's Journal would be read in a new light. One where he wasn't a computer-generated creature but a real player. One who had somehow been in this game years before public release. I sucked in my breath. Was he a beta player? Was Carver a Trillium employee? No wonder the Voices cared about his memory so much. Everything about this setup made so much more sense. A Trillium employee would be a VIP on this side of the ARC. The player who owned William Carver had died. What a crazy game.

"Are you all right, William?"

"My hips are okay."

The woman sighed.

"William. I've been watching. The last few weeks you've been distant, almost like you weren't even there. Now, today, I saw a bit of spring in your step, but something's wrong. I can tell."

I gave a faint smile with both eyes glued on the distance. If I were able to leap into this role and gain all my points, perhaps Carver's cover would have been better.

There was a squabble of noise coming near the cliff. I sighed.

Sure enough, flopping out of the air with a small bird was the **[Messenger's Pet]**. They came in with a roll of feathers and decaying chirps. My tiny dragon buddy had managed to tuck one wing in as the tangled mess spun a few more times. It shook me out of the confused thought spiral I had descended into.

"Is that…?"

"A small dragon. Yes." Question answered and points lost. Go team me.

"No. It's a Messenger's Pet. Isn't it?"

I wasn't sure how to respond, so I said nothing. Carver's messages from beyond had rather firmly advised me not to answer questions without an exchange.

"Oh, William." For some reason, the woman next to me became extremely sad and hugged this old man's head.

I was amazed by the detail of my situation. Her skin felt like real skin, her fingers felt warm. William Carver was extremely frail, and the motion hurt.

Finally, with no further words, she walked away and left me alone. There I sat in confusion, staring at the small dragon tearing into his prey's remains. Two women had found my buddy's presence strange. Why did that make me sad?

"What did you do, huh?"

The dragon crunched on a bone and provided no response.

"Fine. Back to work then." My cane wobbled around without finding solid purchase.

Eventually, I managed to get the pseudo leg under me and wandered off down the hill. Back to my bench and back to my—his—journal. Wait. I was not William Carver. William Carver was dead. The thought shook me.

Tonight, when Carver went to bed and I could log out without risk, I would look up Trillium's site. Maybe there would be something useful, like a salute to a deceased employee, assuming William Carver wasn't played by some random no-name from across the globe. I wanted to see the real-world face of the man whose body I occupied.

Happy place, I had to stay in my happy place. I had to not think about people William had left behind or how bad my acting skills were. I couldn't dwell on the fact that this body had belonged to flesh and blood, not a digital cutout. People might be watching me right now and commenting on a clearly lacking performance.

Oh goodness. I was a failure. I was screwing it all up again. Happy place, countdown, focus on walking. Set a simple task—get to the bottom of the hill and relieve the guard, read a book. Follow the simple on-screen prompts telling me how to be someone else.

Oh goodness.

My steps were interspersed with clenched eyes and waves of aching. I took pauses to rest while the tiny **[Messenger's Pet]** got into fights with anything that moved. All manner of creatures were subjected to his rage: stray **[Coo-Coo Rill]**s, birds of strange origins, even flowers waving in a breeze. No fire was used in the harming of animals, however. I guessed he preferred his meat raw.

Little Savage.

I tried to bonk him with the cane in passing, which nearly sent me tumbling. He gave me a halfhearted hiss before tearing into the latest floral victim.

Once on the bench, I started reading.

Six game days passed with this basic routine. Sit on a bench, give new players mindless tasks. Two players were sent on follow-up quests regarding Mylia. Neither one came back.

If William Carver was a real person, then the whole quest system he got was something granted by the computer. The system must be extremely neat to pull this off. I shuffled William back to his home for the night and logged out. Once there, I gave researching Trillium employee information a go. Turned out being a private eye was not one of my skills, not even using the ARC or Hal Pal's interactive responses.

I gave up quickly and took a nap before hopping back into the ARC to live as Carver. My brain was getting all messed up from living this way, but it also felt like a really, really long vacation. In a dead man's virtual body.

Right, I had to keep shifting my focus to positive items. I'd managed to build up my progress bar to over fifty percent. That was good. Carver had five journals covering decades in-game, which was also good. It let me narrow the search down to employees who had worked with Trillium for years. Plus the stories were funny.

There was a theme to the autobiography. He wrote about his friends Michelle and Yates—well, friends was too strong a term; they seemed more like office members. None of them moved around as much as William had. William had gone everywhere in the game. Michelle went from one crafting skill to another to another and rarely left the same city.

Yates, if the stories were believed, had traveled to other planes and written entire books on it. He played this game and scrawled out all of his findings on digital ink. Were they like Carver's? There wasn't anything that outright said "I'm a player;" maybe the game had censored things.

And everywhere Carver went, the **[Messenger's Pet]** was sure to follow. He hung out randomly in the Atrium of my ARC. He wandered near William Carver while being logged in. By the end of day two of real time, I expected to wake up to the tiny dragon's presence inside my real-world room. He seemed trapped in the digital landscape though. Turns out dragons pooped excessively large amounts.

My most recent adventure was dealing with another new player.

"Are you sure this is the right way?" The woman wore starter clothes—a thin shirt and pants—that all new players were given. Her wide hips pulled the pants tightly around her legs. I glossed over her username as I had every other new player to come my way.

"You wanted a training hall. This is the right way." This latest charge had demanded I walk her to the destination instead of handing over a map.

"Are you sure?"

The bench was starting to sicken me anyway. One week down, three to go. Too many of these new players had shown up recently. They were about half and half in terms of attitude versus confusion.

"Yes."

"I don't believe you. You're senile. I'll bet you're programmed by the same people who made my coffee machine." Even her footsteps sounded angry as we made our way down the street.

"What's a coffee machine?" I feigned ignorance.

"Stupid computer."

We were only a few vague city blocks away from the hall. We still had to pass stands, stores, and one or two rows of housing, but I could see the roof of the training hall from here. I, Grant Legate, had never been inside, but Carver's map had tons of information.

"Over there." I sat on a bench and pointed out the destination. Moving around as William had good days and bad. Today was somewhere between. Bench time was delightful.

"That doesn't look like a training center."

"What did you expect?"

Queen of the Hate-Filled Frump didn't like my question. She was all hips and anger.

"I don't know. People, rules, a guide, something."

"Try walking inside. See if Madam Hall is there." Madam Hall was one of the people who managed the training building. She was also half a brick, from the dossier on William's maps

"You're a rude machine."

"Get what you give," I calmly responded.

"Jerk."

Bets were on this woman earning Madam Hall's anger. Especially since she didn't like being called Madam or Hall; she preferred Peg. According to my notes, the woman would assign extra duties to anyone who addressed her the wrong way.

Hopefully by the end of today, this player would understand being rude wouldn't get her far. Or maybe it would. There seemed to be options and paths for every type of person. I sat and read the latest journal to pass more time, putting the future of Continue's newest player out of my mind.

> *I can't believe those idiots each got their own assignment. In order to sign off on the project, we had to provide them an incentive. Part of me would have been perfectly comfortable keeping these adventures to myself. Yet there are too many things, too much for me to handle on my own.*
>
> *Eventually I'll have to slow down. The medics have once again reminded me how little time is left. At least like this, here, I can make every second count. I stayed on that boat for three weeks talking to sailors about myths and legends, trying to plot out my next exploration. Some of these quests would require an army, which I don't have. Eventually, there will be other Travelers. Eventually. Someone will have to show them the ropes and make them understand how real this world is.*

Well. Was that why William Carver played as a new player guide? His passages seemed to indicate a medical issue. It wasn't enough to stop him…

Oh.

William had a real-world problem and a time limit. He was playing Continue to explore the world and enjoy the four-to-one compression. That made a lot more sense once I realized a player had written these journals. That's why he was a guide to new players! He was showing them the ropes. I turned over the journal and nearly giggled in happiness. This was great. That might be why my progress had stalled out over the last day or two. Something in my actions was lacking compared to Carver's expectations.

"Mmmh. What do you think, Little Savage?" I asked the tiny dragon.

He was dragging a stick along the ground while growling around the edge of it. I couldn't decide if the small creature was more like a cat or dog. No, clearly cats and dogs were like dragons. That was it. He didn't respond to Little Savage. Honestly, the **[Messenger's Pet]** didn't respond to any name I attempted to attach. Food though, the creature responded to food at any point.

I closed the book and asked myself, what would Carver do?

The problem was me. I wasn't following through on anything. After four volumes of the man's thoughts, I could tell when tasked with something, he went full bore. Me? I hadn't tried to find a heroic battle. I hadn't put serious work into figuring out Mylia. I was nearly flippant when assigning people their quests. Painfully, I stood. It required summoning all the bull-headed determination that could be applied to a deceased William Carver. Once stable, I walked toward the training building.

The inside was misleading. The building itself was half-covered and led out to a yard that had been beaten by the passage of hundreds of players. Rain, sweat, and blood had matted into the dirt to make it harder than the cobblestone walkways. All the best stuff hid under cover. Peg Hall was across the yard, near one of the training dummies. She argued, loudly, with the new player about something.

I looked around with my fuzzy eyesight. Information boxes popped up with vague information. A set of beaten straw dummies sat under the covered area I wandered into. There was a bar dropped across saw-like holders that went up a tall wall. Weapon racks held equally damaged belongings.

"Huh." I wandered the edge of the room, ignoring the screaming match.

Peg seemed a step away from getting physical. The wide-hipped ball of anger was oblivious.

"Huh." This latest rack had four types of swords. According to Old Man Carver's skill, swords were his favored weapon. He had preferred over-the-top two-handers in many of his stories.

I picked one up while Peg resumed screaming orders. I'd chosen Peg for this newest player because their personalities would clash. Carver's map had alternate options. One of the males at the other training grounds was an almost supermodel in appearance. His notes also indicated a tendency to sleep with anything moving. That seemed like a bad combination.

Goodness, this sword was heavy. This was strange. It wasn't the weight dragging at one side and how disproportionate the weapon looked compared to Old Man Carver's hands. No, all Old Man Carver's aches and pains seemed to diminish in a wave of energy. Putting my second hand over the hilt only made the difference stand out more. Carver was extremely comfortable holding a blade.

I tried to take a stance, slowly edging until the balancing points felt right. I, Grant Legate, was no sword master. Instead, my skills came from Old Man Carver's body wanting to lean certain ways. Falling into comfortable patterns was easy with my dancing experience. Swinging around a hefty weight was familiar.

Peg abruptly turned from her shouting match and looked at me. "What are you doing, William?"

I grunted and stood uncomfortably swinging a blade in front of the professional. But this moment, holding a weapon like this, was pain-free. I wanted to enjoy that for as long as possible.

"William! I swear to the Voices you've lost every sense of sanity they've graced you with. Put. That. Down!"

A scowl crossed my face, but both arms held the pleasant pose. This was like being completely and utterly relaxed but still taut at the same time. Carver's body felt almost ready for anything. The straw dummy next to me was practically quivering in terror.

Oh. A bar identified as Stamina was dropping quickly. I had cleverly placed it next to my hunger bar. They were both measures of my ability to last. The stamina bar had been helping me for the last few days in traveling around. Guess Old Man Carver couldn't hold a weapon too long, no matter how positive the action felt. With my remaining energy, I let go of my awkward stance and racked the weapon.

"What were you thinking, William?!"

"I know my limits, Peg." I had a very clear bar to outline them. Add in six days of reading and performing inside the skin of another player, and his limits were extremely visible. He had come to this world to hunt dragons with the last years of his life, then, since I assumed he'd succeeded, retired to raise up a new generation. The cane was much lighter and much easier to wave around at the new player.

"What do you think?"

"Her? Is this your fault? Voices have mercy, why would I want to deal with this woman? Give me a young strapping boy anytime. They're fun to watch sweat and so much more reasonable."

"But not her?" I ignored the NPC's dreamy look.

"No! She storms in here and demands I teach her how to fight and refuses to work for it." Peg's arms waved in disgust and crossed.

The wide-hipped woman was busy swinging a staff of some sort at the other straw dummy. Even my untrained eye could see how badly she was doing.

"She's energetic."

"Possessed, more like," Peg said.

I tried not to get thrown off my game at her apt description of my own state. Luckily Old Man Carver was slow to respond.

"It happens."

"I've seen Travelers swing like her before. They're violent. All the time."

"We are what life makes of us." My shoulders gave a tiny shrug.

"Voices, I don't believe that. You've worked with them more than anyone. Voices, you even warned us they'd be coming months in advance. Are they all so angry?"

I debated the worth of answering her question. Old Man Carver didn't like responding to questions without an exchange of some sort.

"Peg, you help an old man remember how to swing a sword, and I'll answer any questions you might want about Travelers." That comment gained me a few points, even after admitting my age out loud.

"Years now, and I feel like I don't understand any of them. They rush through lessons until they break apart, then come back for more!" Peg threw both hands in the air and rolled her eyes.

I stood there resting on the cane. My normal aches and pains were slowly returning. The sensation was a far cry from the constant numbing existence I lived while logged into the ARC.

"I mean some of them, they're like our people. Even their sayings and strange words make sense after a while. But Voices, all those fresh to our world, they come in so…"

The wide-hipped new player was yelling at the straw man. Her words had degenerated into senseless tones that came out sharply.

"Angry?" I volunteered.

"Voices, yes." Peg managed to walk over to the rack and snag a weapon for me while never taking her eye off the new student. There was a reason she ran this place.

"She's got no style. No coordination."

"Lots of energy," I said.

"For now. Wait until I start putting her through the basic course. She'll either run screaming back to you for a new life choice, or be ready to move on." Peg spit on the ground in disgust.

"She may go home." And never log into Continue again.

"I doubt it. Some vanish for a few days, weeks even, but eventually I see them all again."

"This world has much to offer that theirs doesn't."

"Like what? Maybe you can explain it in a better way than they do. Voices above, the stuff they talk about sounds like a dream."

"Remind me how to swing this first."

"Fine. Voices know you shouldn't need a reminder. You taught my brother." Both hands uncrossed and went to her hips. Peg's head tilted as she studied my old form top to bottom.

"Humor me."

"All right. Your balance is still solid. How are your hips?" She stared at them.

I managed to keep a passive face. "Women keep asking me about my hips."

"Them's the breaks of a retired hero." Peg laughed happily. "More than one lady lifted her skirt in hopes of birthing a legend."

"Even you, Peg?"

"Voices, no. I hold a 'look but don't touch' policy most days. I've seen them all at the start. Half of them show up in our world with a spare head up their asses. Can't get that image out of my head."

I laughed and held the much lighter sword.

"There. You haven't completely lost the touch. Your balance is a bit different than what I remember. I imagine age is catching up with you."

"And my hips." No points lost there either. Was Carver a witty person? Or was my progress bar in limbo while my attempted change of pace was judged by the Voices?

"Everything starts from the core. Hips go, everything goes," Peg said. Her arms were lifting mine a bit higher and adjusting the sword's tip.

"Swing again."

I did, trying to get everything in concert.

"Rusty, but better than I expected. Again."

So it went for another ten whacks against the target dummy. What little practice I had resulted from my time in the room of trials. At no point in my past had I secretly taken a martial art or joined a kendo team. I knew nothing about weapons beyond what television and video games had shown me.

Peg kept adjusting my movements a tiny bit here and there. She stood near the dummy and told me what to aim for, which way to swing the blade. If my actions were odd to her, she was kind enough not to mention it.

"What's this, the blind leading the blind?"

"Voices." Peg said that word a lot. Maybe it was the closest she allowed herself to a real curse word.

"William has forgotten more about being a hero than you'll ever reach with your attitude."

"Then what's he doing there? If he's so great." The new player was digging her staff into the dirt. Twisting it back and forth as small curls of earth were displaced by force.

"He's more than—"

I cut the instructor off. "Don't answer her, Peg. She hasn't earned it."

"Earned? Who are you to say if I've earned something or not?"

"Who am I?" I was winded and needed to set down the new sword anyway. "Who are you? You show up in this world and start demanding like you're something here."

"Shut up, you old geezer."

"Well-played. An insult for a question. Peg, why don't you show her the proper way to beat up a straw man?"

"Let's do that! Will you be okay, William?"

"I'll pace myself, Peg." My head dipped in a slow nod and both eyes stayed on the sword's tip.

I had to give points to Peg. She managed to herd the new player with the skills of an expert. The instructor shouted, taunted, and called the other woman a failure who wouldn't be able to defend herself. That set the player into fits. Her fury was vented upon the straw figure. There we stood, each of us hitting different dummies. I kept a vague eye toward my progress bar, which hadn't changed one way or the other over the last thirty minutes.

Peg switched between us for another hour while "reminding" me how to move and stand. Old Man Carver's body could take maybe five minutes of weak standing mixed with occasional strikes. Waiting for my stamina to refill took another four minutes, which I spent watching the new player or talking to Peg. Two apple-like fruits were enough to refill the old man's hunger bar.

Going from real life, where I worked on ARCs and was driven around in a van, to this much slower existence felt weird. With all the information pop-ups and reviews, I still had an excessive amount of downtime. The time compression made everything feel like living really long weekends.

I enjoyed my situation though. When not thinking about the ghost in the machine that acted like my fiancée or James's actions. The large black Voice hadn't crossed my mind recently. I had no idea how to contact him unless he had a statue somewhere like Selena did.

Saying inappropriate things at a lifelike carving had been very attention-getting. I was glad the real world didn't work that way. Imagining rows of people in pews getting **[Divine Attention]** for each prayer made me smile.

William's arms weren't going to last much longer, even with resting. It felt good. Peg gave instructions, tips, and ideas on where to swing. Even under the guise of a refresher, it had given me a lot to think about. Maybe I would download one of those ARC combat programs. The additional help couldn't hurt and would make me feel less like a complete newbie.

After I started the game as myself and could build real skills though. William Carver's skills were locked as is. Honestly, my sad performance should be dragging down his ratings.

"How can you keep swinging like that? How? I'm exhausted," the wide-hipped player said.

"Practice," I said calmly.

"Yeah right. I bet you were designed that way." She even managed to work past her cotton mouth to spit on the ground in disgust. Then she looked kind of pleased.

"Happy?"

"I've never done that before." There was a faint sense of wonder in her tone.

Down went my practice sword yet again.

"That's the point, isn't it? Here you can learn and do new things. Yet you belittle everyone who might help you." I intended to take advantage of this world myself. Sitting on a bench for another three weeks would be dreadfully boring.

"You have no right to talk to me like that."

"You came to our world, Traveler." Everyone thought William Carver was an NPC, so I had to act like one. Words like ARC, or Continue, or other real world concepts would blow his cover.

"You're a program. Why can't you give me what I want? It'd be so much quicker."

"Are things so simple in your world? Do you survive without trading for anything?" My question, of course, was clearly a trap. People had to work for money, spend money to gain things. Continue Online and its entire world was much the same.

"My husband works if that's what you're asking."

"Then you understand food costs coin, services cost coin or a trade. We can't give you what you want without an exchange or the whole system would fall apart." I sighed. It had taken me a bit to adapt myself. Continue's world was extremely realistic regarding give and take.

Pop-up boxes with information were the only item between me and complete immersion. Maybe I would turn them off some days to feel as though I was on a vacation. The beach here was one step away from Waikiki in Hawaii—at least, the way the beach was decades ago.

"If you want skills, you have to learn them. Peg is one of the best nearby in showing Travelers like you the basics." I stumbled to the weapon rack and put the light sword back. One shoulder had started throbbing more than usual. Bending over to pick up the cane was nearly impossible.

"Why does that matter?" the wide-hipped woman said.

"Why are you here? If you don't want to fight, don't. Learn a trade, or don't."

"You're not making sense. You shouldn't be demanding that I learn something."

"Then don't."

"You don't care?" Her voice tilted up and the staff in her hand shook from her budding anger.

"Nope." Carver's synchronization bar dropped a few points on that one. William did care about new players. "Let's just say that neither I, nor any of the other people here, will force you to do much of anything." There, I recovered a point and managed to use the word nor in a real sentence.

"That doesn't make sense."

"You chose to come here. Now figure out what you want from us and what you're willing to pay to learn. Nearly everyone is willing to help you if you earn it."

"I thought quests were a simple 'go here, do this.' Every other game I've played is like that. Starter zones are a basic area to learn the ropes. Things should be easy." The new player sounded so flustered. She wasn't the first either.

"But you're all making this too hard."

Then she asked the same question that had been plaguing me since the first moment I had opened the gift-wrapped package in my Atrium.

"What kind of game is this?"

"It's no game. To us, it's very real and very serious," I repeated James's words from the trial room a week ago. Over a week in-game, I had become more invested than expected. I wasn't even surprised to see my progress jump up five percent.

The other woman waved one hand and vanished, a perplexed and worried look on her face. Had I worn the same look when talking to James? Moments later, I too logged out, leaving William Carver to go about the town on autopilot. This game was messing with my head, making me act weird, and I needed a break.

Session Ten
Pride's Precipice

Continue was a strange sensation.

There were other virtual games and programs. I'd even tried some. Most felt like rehashes of already existing games, but more interactive. Revamps of prior releases were a popular way to go. Asians had entire swaths of crazy themes that hadn't quite hit America proper.

Continue won by sheer name power. Trillium, the company that made the ARC, had designed a game that launched the only virtual reality system.

That was a lie. There were tons of others at first. Trillium and the ARC won. Thousands logged in upon release. Millions played by the end of the first six months. Hundreds of millions had accounts a year later. Trillium hid much of the game from the public, but subscription counts were made public knowledge. Continue won. The average player spent twenty hours a week logged into their ARC. The average player had been playing for a year. The average player voted Continue as the most impressive game worldwide.

William Carver was proof that the number was growing. The basic information that Trillium hadn't throttled led me to believe that Continue had dozens of starting points. Were their guides also older players?

"You're Carver, right?"

So my daily grind began again. Another new player and another exchange while they asked for help. This map had been a Voice-sent blessing for so many reasons. Hours could pass while I read the little details. Plus it responded well when I asked for specific talents or skills.

Progress: 63%

"I am. You must be new around here." Carver's journals were almost gone. I'd spent two more days reading them.

"My friend said you helped her." The person was male, young, and still had a slightly childish quality to his voice.

"Might have. What's it to you?" Gnarled fingers turned to the next page.

"I have to catch up. She started yesterday, and I had homework."

"Good. Work hard." This adventure was a page-turner, so most of my responses were half-baked. The entries were a little smutty too.

Part of me feels strange about this. Here I am, on one adventure after another. The rewards are usually negligible, but the women…

Last week there was this case with a half-serpent creature. It seemed familiar from my childhood, but this place didn't have any similar lore. You'd think snakes spit venom, but not so much this go around.

He was extremely violent.

She was equally rewarding. Turned out her venom had positive effects, and true to snake form, she squeezed me dry.

I could have said no, but that long dead Captain of The Stars would have frowned at my actions. Long live childhood heroes.

"Can you help me, Carver?" There was a shuffle of feet as the new player grew closer.

My eyes stayed glued to the journal.

"I'll bet your direct attitude does your parents proud."

He'd all but said, "Quest now, old man." Carver accepted no rudeness and only gave it out! I looked at him finally.

"My parents?" The young man, a scrawny-looking teen with the user name Awesome Jr., lost focus in confusion before shaking his head.

"What do you want, Awesome?" I asked. He looked fourteen but had to at least be eighteen to play this game.

"Awesome's my father."

I sighed. I'd walked right into that stupid joke.

"And?"

Players thought they were so clever with their names. I'd met people with gibberish names. I'd met people named after famous actors. Flowers, book characters, television heroes, or strange handles that they'd be stuck with for as long as Continue was out. Pie Master had been the funniest one. He'd asked for a bakery, and I happily sent him and the **[Messenger's Pet]** forth.

Awesome Jr. swallowed and hastily tried to explain something that didn't sink in. Something about a girl who'd passed through before and he was trying to meet up with her in the game.

"Who is she to you?"

"A friend."

"Girlfriend?" I said dryly.

"No. Not that, no." He was flustered. The boy was socially awkward, a common problem with the latest generation. Everyone was so plugged into the computer that interaction, face-to-face like this game had, was hard.

"So meet her. I know well enough that people from your world have ways of communicating."

Carver's next journal entry was about a whale that devoured ships. So far he'd recounted five boring days of nothing where he sailed with a crew in search of the beast.

> *Day Six: If this whale isn't white, I'm going to punch that man in the face and kick her metal box. Not that she'll even notice. Maybe I'll scrawl nasty notes on the walls nearby.*

"Well. Uhhh..." Awesome Jr. said with his standard eloquence.

"Not that easy?" Slowly, because today was a bad hip day, I pulled the bookmark cord into place and closed my journal. The book was set down and both my hands clasped together.

"Well. No." The young man had a flush to his face that reached to his ear tips.

"Okay. Awesome, what exactly do you want from me?"

"A quest?" He sounded confused.

"A quest. To do what?"

"I don't know. Something? Don't you... give me something to do? Then show me where something is?"

Oh, joy. He was one of those Travelers. A fresh-faced boy with no clue what he wanted to do and who had joined just to follow someone else. It made my own confusion about this game seem annoyingly commonplace. This was still less annoying than the type who screamed "I'm going to be a great adventurer."

"No." My head shook slowly and both hands felt tired from where I'd been holding the book.

"Uhhh..."

"Here's a quest. Take this map. Visit the people on it, and ask how other Travelers are doing. Then come back here and tell me what you learn."

I watched the pop-up display my newly formed quest. I'd learned enough of Carver's desires over the last few days to get a feel for where I'd missed opportunities. He'd want to know how the new players were doing in this world. If they were still around, the NPCs I'd sent them to would have an answer. Soon the journal was open again so my perusal of Carver's past could continue.

Day Seventeen: The whale wasn't actually a whale. It was a squid-looking creature. Not that it was called a squid; everything in here looks a bit off. They've gone down different evolutionary paths.

It was white and a few hundred feet long. The creature had seven arms instead of eight and a hammer-like shape to its head that was probably useless for swimming. That was something else.

Oh, and it killed a good portion of the crew before we vanquished it. Boat's a mess, taking on water in places we shouldn't be. People are downstairs fixing it. I lived. The Captain, a fine woman who filled a corset to bursting, was pleased with the results. She looked even better with the corset off, but we both decided to keep the boots on.

This kind of thing can't be good for my heart. It does assist my will to live though, and the medics say I need as much of that as I can muster.

Goodness. Carver was single-minded. Dragon to be slain, ladies to be laid, for great justice! I doubted he was the only one in Continue who went about with such focused desires.

Awesome Jr. would get distracted by everything that moved. His path would probably go right by the brothel, which had lured at least two new players over the last few days. Either way he'd be busy for a while, so I could skim through the last of William Carver's Journals.

Plus, and this was the real reason, walking hurt. A nosy sort of boredom had overtaken me recently to boot. Plenty of reasons existed to send a new player out to find other newbies.

He might not find the kid I'd sent to moo at a cow though. Hah. I hoped this new player, Awesome Jr., did find that would-be assassin. I'd like to hear how the first week in Continue had treated him.

After Awesome Jr. wandered off, I poked at the hood of Carver's robe. This thing was ugly, bland, and scratchy, but the hood did well in the rain.

It also occasionally housed a sleeping **[Messenger's Pet]**. The tiny creature had started napping there a few days ago, after I'd cracked the fifty-percent marker. It turned out two of Old Man Carver's traits included **[Relaxing Presence]** and **[Monster Tamer]**.

[Monster Tamer] had likely been triggered after he hunted down the horse thing described in one of the earlier journals. Those were some of the less odd traits too. Carver had one squirreled away in his list of abilities called **[Point Man]**, which, from the text, had less to do about being in charge of a group or scouting and more to do with scoring points with the ladies.

Peg had been right. If the journals were to be believed, this old body had touched more women than I desired. I'd walked him home early after reading about one of the less savory encounters and left myself on autopilot in a hot tub. I didn't know if the old man's writing should be praised or reviled for the descriptive terms.

Repeated hood tapping finally woke the creature. A head popped out of folds in the hood and a yawn of jaws snapped together with a click.

"Help that poor boy out. Make sure he doesn't get lost."

The tiny creature growled in displeasure.

"We can stop at the bakery on the way home. How's that?" Paying for goods in-game was cheaper than adding items into my ARC and far less messy.

Sure enough, the greedy little fellow flew off.

Almost two weeks and I still hadn't found a name he responded to. A few people had stopped to ask what he was, and I told them a baby dragon. They found it funny since Old Man Carver had a title called **[Dragon Slayer]** tucked away in his character sheet.

I'd read the description. That trait should have made any dragon or dragon-related creature instantly dislike the body I was in. Yet the **[Messenger's Pet]** seemed completely indifferent. Guessed it wasn't a dragon, or didn't care about William Carver.

That made him the only creature for miles that showed little interest in this body I inhabited. The whole thing was a weird contradiction that sat on the back burner of my problems.

"Far too smart sometimes," I muttered at the fleeing tiny dragon.

Chances were he'd get distracted at least a dozen times while helping the new player.

Hopefully there wouldn't be any more dead **[Coo-Coo Rill]**s in my Atrium. That was a mystery unlikely to be revealed any time soon. Trying to figure out the silly program-altering creature's secrets took up a lot of my spare time.

"Father says you wanted a break today, Mister Carver." The younger guard from earlier managed to sneak up on me. It should have been impossible from the way his armor jangled.

"I do, Dayl, if you'd take over for me."

"Sure thing, Mister Carver, sir. Father says you're back to practicing with Peg. Is that true?" Dayl's headgear slipped out of place, and he hastily pushed it back up

"I am," I said.

"Father says you're..."

"Dayl," I barked.

He snapped to attention while his armor rang in protest. "Yes, Mister Carver?"

"Shut up now." Oh look, another percent on my progress bar.

"Yes, Mister Carver, sir."

I grumbled and headed off under canopies of trees, past the bakery and across town. Each step was painful but not unbearable. Working with Peg on exercises had been extremely helpful, almost like physical therapy. Every time I logged out, the dull ache from Carver's body and these exercises lingered and kept me tired.

Mylia was walking nearby, which was part of the reasoning behind my request for a guard. I'd made no progress on her side quest yet. None of the new players I'd talked to had provided any sort of useful opening. Mylia herself was nearly an enigma.

"Are you going to visit the children tonight? They've been asking when you'll share more stories," she said.

I grunted and kept walking, cane alternating with my slightly more limber body.

"I tell the little ones that you're not up to it most days."

"Oh?"

She had mentioned before that William Carver read stories to kids. I hadn't pursued it enough, among everything else going on. That was nearly two weeks ago. Goodness. I was almost halfway through this strange existence and still things blindsided me.

"Can you visit this evening? You seem to be moving much better. They'd love to see that you're doing well."

"I'll make time, Mylia. For the children of course." I tried to sound gruff and serious.

Reading children a story would be emotionally painful.

A reminder of how life didn't go. I paused mid-step, clenched both eyes shut for a moment, and tried not to sway. In real life, I could push through these moments, but in the game, with Carver's weakened body, it was harder to stay upright.

Happy place. Focus on a happy place. The sky was glorious. The world around me was bright and lively. People went about their day, pleasantly chattering away.

"Of course, Mister Carver." Mylia smiled.

I could see an almost glow of happiness pass over her features, but I fought to keep Carver's eyes focused forward.

"I'll leave you to your rounds and let the children know to expect you."

I nodded and gave a half wave. Old Man Carver would never show weakness in front of a lady! The moment Mylia was out of sight I tracked down the nearest bench and rested. A journey to Peg's required pit stops, despite my navigating far better than I had the first few days.

This was how most days seemed to go. I'd log in, wander to the beach bench, and alternate between reading or helping new players. NPCs from about town would drop by occasionally with very friendly conversations that reminded me of the day-to-day life I'd "forgotten" in the last few weeks.

Players occasionally tracked me down. Sometimes they came back three or four times to ask about other skills. I'd update their maps after asking them to complete a new quest. More than one player was sent to pick up cupcakes for my **[Messenger's Pet]** friend. I challenged one girl to come up with a name for the tiny creature, but she failed to get a positive response. After nearly fifty names and complete failure, I updated her map with the location of a farmhand who had a certain way with animals. She'd tried hard.

One older man, who had to be near Carver's age, had started the game and sat on the bench with me. We said nothing for two hours as the sun set. I left him a map leading toward one of the town's three mystic tutors. This one focused on more theoretical puzzle stuff. In the morning, the scroll had been gone and the older man hadn't turned up again.

One player had logged in and run around until he was out of stamina. He lay there, gasping with an overly excited look on his face. Once the endurance bar was full, he took off, kicking up dirt and sand all along the beach. His shouts brought a smile to my face. The player hadn't outright said it, but I was willing to bet his legs were damaged somehow in real life.

Each player that popped in was a little different. They asked for different things, spoke in ways that didn't line up at first. Part of me started to realize that this game was routing players from all over the globe to this starting zone.

How did I understand them then?

I asked Beth one day between rounds as William Carver. She left me a voice mail explaining that since the game was all digital immersion, it didn't actually use an English language. In essence, the system was translating conversations super-fast from the Earth languages to another set of world gibberish and back.

It wasn't like people showed up in the game being clearly Asian, or Indian, or any other obvious ethnicity. These players were all human though. My city, **[Haven Valley]**, was on the border of two human Kingdoms. They had a very loose alliance that was constantly teetering, according to Dayl. I sighed and put all those thoughts out of my mind and read another passage from Carver's final journal.

Recently I've felt everything catching up. The irony of my situation is that being forced into bed rest has increased my play time. They were kind enough to dial down the feedback so my ticker doesn't feel the strain like it used to.

Of course, everything else is less sensitive, but I should be happy this old goat got a few final rolls in the hay.

I reread the notes I'd scribbled down two years ago when I first started visiting here. I'm sad to think of all the people I've left behind over my journey. I made so many promises to visit, and I couldn't fulfill half of them. Strange.

I feel like this world is more real than the other. Maybe it's merely a wish of mine, to hope that if my body dies there, that I can keep on adventuring over here. To live like a child again, in a world where so many dreams are possible.

I should call Michelle and thank him before it's too late.

Abruptly, halfway through this final book, the entries stopped. No word of his time as a Guide, or this town, or how he came to settle here. Nothing of value citing what had happened or where he was going to end up. This was his form of retirement I guessed, but what filled in the gaps?

I shoved the book into a pocket and kept onward with my journey to Peg's.

One possibility that worried me was that William Carver had died before being able to write another entry. At what point had the computer literally taken over his life? I'd thought it was fairly recent, but the NPCs around here acted like Carver had been a firm presence well before any other player had started the game.

I should write some letters. To make sure Carver got one last chance to say good-bye.

"Let's see," I mumbled, looking over the weapons. Heavier ones actually made my progress bar improve. Lighter ones meant I could last longer, but they were a really slow decline.

"You better not be trying to break your arms again, William!"

"No such luck, Peg!" My yell was more of a mumbling grunt into the wall. I'd had to lean close to see how the handles looked.

Carver had a skill called **[Weapon Evaluation]** that seemed to rank the value of items. According to the details, it was a sub-skill of **[Identification]** that focused only on weapons. The more I studied the lineup, the more accurate the rating was. Using the game's feedback, I picked a larger two-handed blade. It looked big compared to the frail arms and body I resided in but wasn't exactly an over-the-top anime sword either.

"Seriously, William! You retired!" Peg was shouting at me and alternating with some other person. They didn't look to be a player, just an NPC being trained by another NPC.

I smiled, and the image of a fit William Carver came to mind, one holding up a giant sword in preparation to swing. The Carver in the journals wasn't the sort of man who did well with concepts like block or parry, but who relied instead on a strange brute strength. With game stats, it was easy to see how real life limitations wouldn't prevent a character with high strength from making any play style work.

There had to be some in-game benefit to knowing martial arts of some sort too. Sadly that was not me. I danced at best. When in the comfort of my private little program, I shook my groove thing like a madman, pretending to be any number of famous figures in their videos. My "Thriller" imitation was excitingly depressing for a middle-aged man with a gut. The moonwalk skill had taken countless hours to get down, and I could do one in real life too. Dancing looked terrible on a man with my belly.

Throwing someone over my shoulder with a twist and shout, however, was beyond my skills. Maybe I'd try it out when I made my own character. I could train to be a cage fighter. Oh, a staff was kind of cool. I bet I'd be pretty good with a Bo staff. Or a bow and arrow, that would be neat. I could count my kills and make friendly fun of dwarves. But Old Man Carver was all about the two-handed sword.

I ignored Peg's worried shouts and stumbled to the practice dummy. My exercise would go on for about an hour in-game and leave me tired and breathless. After that, I'd rest, eat a snack I'd conned from one of the new players as a quest, then move onward to my next destination. That was the plan, and that's how it went.

After replacing the weapon in its home, I stumbled to a bench and pulled out the map. Evening was coming on soon, and I wanted to see those children Mylia talked about so often. Their home was on the outskirts of town. Carver's notes said it was an orphanage with about twenty children. Sometimes they were adopted, but that was less likely than the child moving on or getting a job. According to this, Mylia had been there for about six years.

Odd. I wondered if that had any relation to Carver being in this town for six years? I'd have to figure out a way to get information about her eventually, without violating Old Man Carver's prideful personality.

"By the Voices, William, what nonsense are you up to now?"

"The usual."

"You always stare at that scroll as if there are secrets buried in the ink somewhere."

"There are."

Peg snorted. "Doubt there's anything really useful there. All I see are little squiggles for buildings. Any fool new to this town would learn it easily enough, even those narrow-minded Travelers you send here."

"Here"—I pointed at an alley—"is an alley known for pickpockets and thieves."

Next there was a location right outside of town, north along the water's edge.

"Here is a cave that is good for meditation if anyone's willing to sit inside it overnight."

Finally I pointed to the south, near the main road out of town. "Here's where Henry lives, and he's always willing to teach Travelers how to make bricks in exchange for labor." Henry sat along the edge of town, waiting for traders and long-distance Travelers who might need his crafts.

"There are a lot of secrets in these maps, and I have to remember where they are to help out the new Travelers." After much testing, I'd found out that certain NPCs could be spoken to more easily than others. Our balance of giving and taking must have met Carver's needs.

"Mh. I guess you're right about that. Pretty sharp for an old man! I hope I remember things half as well as you do when I get that old!" She slapped me on the back with an overly excited grin.

I watched my health bar drop and groaned in extra pain.

Failure to dodge noted.
Total health loss: 13%

"Oh. Sorry, Will! Are you all right?"

I grunted and tried to shake it off. William Carver showed no woman any weakness! According to his journals, the only weakness he showed was while flirting his way into someone's bed. There was a count on his table back at the cottage where I'd tried to see how many lady friends he'd racked up over the decades. Once it got past two dozen, I parked him back inside the bath and the autopilot program took another wash.

With a shudder, I managed to right myself and stand.

"I'll be okay, Peg. This isn't the first time a pretty woman has hit me."

She laughed as if I'd said the funniest thing on earth. I had no interest in being like William Carver with my time here. Being with a woman other than my fiancée didn't interest me.

"All right, I'll clean up here. A little bird tells me you'll be recounting some tales for the young ones tonight. Any truth to that?"

I nodded.

"Mylia reminded me."

"Slipped your mind, eh? Need a woman to remind you?" Peg was bustling about checking her weapons and making sure they were all in shape. She kept a conversational distance for William Carver's hard hearing.

"Mylia's looking out for the kids."

"Sure, she is."

I grunted.

"That's our hero for you! Even in his dotage he's trying to add another notch to the bedpost!" She started laughing even harder.

I sighed, grumbled, groaned, and made my old man escape away from a madly laughing Peg. Nothing about my view on the situation with Mylia concluded with Carver caring one whit about getting into her underpants—or whatever people wore in a medieval setting. I doubted it was a G-string or something made of lace. Not with the vaguely emaciated look to her and the children's faces.

Maybe I should bring food too.

Carver, the soft weird cookie personality, had often done little things to help out villagers, going against how I'd been acting with new players. If I were to try to reconcile a giving personality from his journals with the way he acted as a Guide, I'd have a headache and oodles of confusion.

Baked goods would do. I'd promised to pick up some for the **[Messenger's Pet]** on the way home, but I could grab something light and take it with me to the orphanage as well. Provided the little dragon didn't show up and eat everything on the way.

Cookies would be perfect.

"Cookies." I was nearly drooling while walking.

With that glorious thought in mind, I marched onward, taking breaks as needed, watching people pass by and returning greetings. I checked out locations against my map to ensure I was both on track and becoming more familiar with my surroundings.

Turned out the city name was scrawled across the top of each map, which was where I'd found it one night. **[Haven Valley]** was nearly idealistic compared to the NPCs rumors of other cities. Guards talked a lot about everything. Players would mention a need to gain skills or ask me for directions to one faction's headquarters or the other.

At least **[Haven Valley]**'s colors weren't red and blue. That would be outright cliché. Instead we had a green with some laurel thing, claiming to be related to tree people and have ties in a huge valley over the mountains to the south. Their kingdom was called **[Telliari]**. **[Telliari]** had an uneasy alliance with a kingdom to the north that was more a coalition of city-states called **[The Altheme Provinces]**. Somewhere on either side was another set of regions along with wilderness and a trade route that went off to the other side of the continent.

I filed the information away in a notebook I'd started keeping on my ARC. Since there was so little information online, keeping a journal I could access outside the game or while traveling around at work seemed like a good choice. Plus William Carver's notes and belongings were not mine to keep, just to peruse while living his life.

Creating a separate journal had actually been Beth's idea, not mine. I was still keeping most of my actions under wraps, but she pestered me constantly. Guessed Uncle Grant couldn't escape from her boundless enthusiasm for much longer.

The bakery had a walk-in stall set up. That was very neat. Old Man Carver did not like doors at all.

"Mister C!"

Great. Pie Master, who acted more like a young hip-hop rapper gone pastry, was manning the stall. I did what any old grumpy man who felt a need to be nosy about new players' lives might do. Ignored the stupid name and went on with my day.

"I need cookies."

"Cookies? I don't think we do cookies up in here." Pie Master actually looked appropriate in the chef's apron.

"Ladette, do we do cookies?"

"No, what's a cookie?" a voice yelled from the back side of the stall. Making out the female's face was difficult with Carver's vision.

"You're killing me! You don't know what cookies are?" Pie Master stopped his cleaning and started toward the building's rear.

"No, explain it to me!"

I watched a pop-up box form in front of the player. He didn't know I could see them, or he might have disguised his glee. There was a look of extreme amusement and a hint of greed on his face.

"Wait..." He paused and squinted at me. "How do you know about cookies?"

I fluttered around a bit inside my head. Luckily Carver's exterior didn't betray one ounce of the panic I'd been stricken with.

"One of you Traveler types talked to me about them. I wanted to bring something for the kids during my visit." My progress bar took a hit for providing an answer without compensation.

"Oh! Yeah, I guess that makes sense. How many do you need?"

My eyes drifted downward while I tried to figure out how many items a squad of children might eat. Too many if left alone.

"A few dozen."

"Tell you what, I'll see what we can do. Maybe thirty minutes? That sound good?"

I chewed a lip and tried to remember how much time there was until sundown. Thirty minutes shouldn't be too bad.

"Sure. I'll need some cupcakes too."

Pie Master shook his head. "This place. They got cupcakes, but no cookies. It's criminal."

He placed a few of the small cupcakes onto the counter and waited for me to pull out some change. My stiff fingers managed the action slowly.

"I wonder if I could get a patent…"

Ignoring Pie Master's money-grasping muttering was difficult. Eventually, I broke away and made it to a bench. One of the two cupcakes went slowly into my mouth, a squished bit at a time. The other one I set next to me, where the **[Messenger's Pet]** would likely show up in moments. He'd been promised the treat on the way home. How the tiny creature kept finding me was beyond my understanding.

Sure enough, moments later he was chewing away. A dead **[Coo-Coo Rill]** had been deposited nearby, and a huffing human male was running up behind the small dragon.

"How. What." More exaggerated panting. His stamina bar was probably completely run out. "So fast. He's so fast."

"Yep," I muttered around the last crumbs of my cupcake.

The **[Messenger's Pet]** was nearly purring in his kind of squeaky tone. I'd seen depictions of tiny creatures like him on the covers of old fantasy books, though his legs were a bit more lion-like.

"How. Did you train. It?" More out of breath-huffing issued forth.

I was quickly losing my cupcake happiness.

"I didn't."

"Is it. A pet?" Awesome Jr. fell to the ground and kept right on panting.

"Sort of." I had no such problems. Maybe a small ache in my shoulder.

"This game. Is awesome."

"No. Awesome is your father," I said while avoiding any inflection.

"Hah. Ha ha." He actually was laughing. Not in fake amusement or something placating, but real mirth.

Okay. I was proud of my lame joke as well, but Old Man Carver wouldn't let anyone know! Especially not some wet-behind-the-ears newbie.

"How did your mission go?"

"Terrible. I got so lost. There are too many houses. Rows and rows of houses. They all look different too!" Awesome Jr. finally had enough strength back to sit up. Both arms wrapped around his knees.

"Ah. Learning a new world takes time. Did the map help?"

"A little. I found some of the people you marked and asked them how the other Travelers were doing. They gave me notes." Awesome Jr. fished out a pile of papers from one pocket and shoved them in my direction.

The **[Messenger's Pet]** hissed when Awesome Jr. got too close, which was awesome. I chuckled and gave the tiny guy a stroke, which set him to purring again. He calmed down and dove into the remains of his cupcake.

"Wait until you try cookies," I whispered quietly. I saw one ear perk forward almost like a cat's before it settled back down.

"That's so—"

"Awesome." I nodded and cut off the new player.

"What's its name?"

"His name, and I don't know. Would you like to try to find a name for him?" I watched the box bleep into existence in front of Awesome Jr.

He laughed like a child and shook his head.

"My naming sense is a little bit lacking. I'd better not." His finger jabbed at the floating system message. Quest offered and firmly rejected.

"Oh well. So far the little guy hasn't liked any name given to him, so it'll have to wait," I said.

"That's an interesting quest," the young man said.

My response was to give an old man half-smile that seemed more tired than amused.

"This place is full of interesting things. How did you like the tour?" Carver cared about what happened to players. He treated players the way they treated him. My points were slowly changing for the better today.

"I saw a lot of places. A lot of people were super friendly when I said I was doing an errand for you. One lady—she said to call her Peg—she was confused and said you could have asked her yourself."

I smiled. I'd been dealing with Peg nearly an hour ago at this point. Carver's pace was intensely slow compared to most other people, even after the pleasant workout. Awesome Jr. must have just left her. Then the little **[Messenger's Pet]** had somehow sensed cupcakes and flown this way.

"Probably," I admitted. There was no telling how the wide-hipped, angry woman was faring now. Her name eluded me, along with many of the other new players.

Maybe I'd start noting them in my ARC's journal. So I had something to refer back to. A long list of people I'd avoid playing the game with if given a choice. They'd all be out having their first adventures while I was stuck in a starting town.

"Decided on what to do with yourself?" I asked

"I thought about going back to Peg." Awesome Jr. waved a tired arm around, and boxes shifted about his screen. He was looking for something in his wall of information.

"She'd make a man out of you." With more than one meaning if he did well enough on the training side. Her background description had been rather blunt in possible outcomes. But hey, who was I to argue? This game did require all Travelers to be of legal age. Bet he'd be absolutely hooked on playing then.

I didn't look for that sort of thing. The brothel area was eye-catching, however.

"Would she?" Then he shook his head and had the decency to look mildly red-faced. "No, I need to learn a weapon. Not sure what though."

"Partial to a two-hander myself." Points! Precious quest progression points were worth throwing nonsense out there. "Though don't assume you're locked in. The world's large. You may change your style later on."

"Oh? That's good. I was worried that I'd be forced to choose a class or something." He waved all the windows away and lay back completely.

"No. Your world has classes. We're a bit more realistic, and Travelers are fortunate; you have many options available if you can find them."

"That's what you're here for, right?"

I smirked.

"I'm here to get Travelers started, that's all. Where you choose to start is up to you."

"It's too much!"

"You read any books in your world?"

"Yeah, sure, a lot. My ARC has a ton of books, and the Internet. My dad's library is huge. He's been collecting since I was little." Awesome Jr. rambled on for too long.

I took out another acorn for the **[Messenger's Pet]** and threw it. The little guy looked uninterested after his cupcake conquest.

"Do some research on the paradox of choice and paralysis of analysis." According to one of Carver's many information pop-up boxes, this was a good strategy for the younger, far-too-clever people.

"What? Why would you know concepts from our world?" Awesome Jr. looked surprised. Or I assumed it was surprise—his face was almost as fuzzy as everything else. One day I'd see this world without feeling as if I were underwater.

"I've talked to a lot of people over the years, a lot of Travelers who had no idea what they wanted or how to get it. It might help you to sit down and think about it."

"Huh. Okay. I'll do that now. I have homework anyway."

I nodded. Moments later, Awesome Jr. vanished in a swoosh of light. Eventually I'd discovered autopilot wasn't available to most new players. Awesome Jr. couldn't leave his game avatar doing some random project.

Another acorn failed to garner a reaction. I threw the fifth one right at the **[Messenger's Pet],** and all he did was grump and dive into Carver's hood. I hummed while debating how much time there was left before night.

Curse this blurry vision. Decent eyesight would allow me to see into the baker's building to see how things were going. Was that Pie Master jumping up and down while waving? I squinted and grumbled to myself while balancing on the cane. This body's hearing was extremely bad unless someone was right next to me.

"Hey! Mister C! I made cookies!"

"Huh?"

"Cookies! I showed Ladette how to make them. My skill's not high enough, but she's a pro. Want to try one?" Pie Master was running over with a metal sheet.

Carver's eyes and ears may be second rate, but his nose was working well enough to pick up that scent.

"Raisins?"

"No. They're called Almanuts. Wait. You know what raisins are?"

I tried not to let my old body cringe at giving away non-local knowledge. Sure enough, the few points I'd gained with Awesome Jr. were already gone.

"That was what the other Traveler told me about."

"Well, you're in luck! These are pretty good. A hint of sweetness to go with the fresh gooey insides, and the outside is so crisp it'll melt in your mouth." He looked surprised at a pop-up box near his face. Looked as though his words had garnered skill bonuses of some sort. From this angle, the box was impossible to see clearly, but it was likely something to help convince people to try whatever he was peddling.

I tried one and almost died in happiness. Real-world consumables had been bare minimum to survive for a long time. Most of my income went to supporting my family in a steadily downhill job market.

"This is forking delicious." Those weren't my exact words, but the cookie made it hard to enunciate. Even grumpy Old Man Carver would give credit where it was due.

"I know! I'd eat one myself, but I'm trying to teach them proper sanitation. It's not terrible back there, but it's not exactly four-star."

I tried to give my best confused look and shrugged. Another cookie went onto my lap, and part of one went to the now-curious **[Messenger's Pet]**.

"Hey, should he eat those?"

I shrugged.

"I know dogs get sick from chocolate. He's not, like, a dog or allergic, is he?"

"Not so far."

"Okay. I'd hate to kill such a cutie." Pie Master was busy making gooey eyes at the tiny dragon. "Who's a cute little guy."

And true to form, the **[Messenger's Pet]** was in love with anyone who provided food.

"How many can you make?"

"For you? I'm sure we can whip together another few batches quickly. I'll even work in a discount."

"A discount?"

"I'll ask Ladette." Pie Master found almost everything outrageously amusing. "It's her store."

"You do that." My fingers waved him off while I munched a cookie.

The **[Messenger's Pet]** was busy searching for crumbs. Nothing lined the path between here and the bakery. He settled for diving into Carver's robe and licking around. At that moment, I really did feel like an old man with an overactive lap puppy. That had wings and breathed fire occasionally. Typically, old-people pets also failed to follow orders. That was the problem! It wasn't me being unable to give orders—no, it was me being an old man! The **[Messenger's Pet]** would rue the day I got my real in-game avatar.

That pleasant thought kept me going through the cookie purchase. Ladette gouged me out of far too much of Carver's money, even with a "discount". She claimed exclusive access to new goods. According to what little I'd read of Pie Master's window, he was going to get kickbacks similar to what I'd received for my Casino idea pitched to the Voice.

I left the player and baker clicking their heels and shouting about a new product. They'd probably be at it until the sun went down, and knowing player mentality, Pie Master would keep on baking through the night in order to get more skill ups and other recipes out into the public. Voices, cookies in the morning sounded good too. It was all digital, and what would William Carver care? None! The proof was in my progress bar's lack of excitement over the exchange.

Of course, here I was, two weeks into Carver's life, and I still hadn't figured out where all his money came from. Nothing he owned popped into existence like it did for other players. My vague assumption was that Carver had turned into an NPC somewhere along the line.

Such thoughts kept me distracted during the amble to Mylia's orphanage. Which, according to the map, was actually called [Haven Valley]'s orphanage. Not Mylia's. There were a few notes about the kids in Carver's map notes, but the journals had been mostly useless regarding this town. What exactly did William Carver tell to these little children?

The children had a crazy scouting system that announced my presence almost a full minute before I limped to the actual building. By that time, Mylia had already opened the door, and one of the larger children had run off with the bag in my hands. My little [Messenger's Pet] was poking out of the hood and looking around in confusion, one ear cocked forward. Each new shout and shriek sent him dodging and rolling around in my hood.

Then he'd poke back out again and look around.

"You made it, Mister Carver."

"I did." The cane helped me huff a few more steps through the doorway into a room filled with a dozen already excited children.

"The kids have been looking forward to this all day."

"Which one ran off with my bag?" Hopefully one of the orphans hadn't already stolen all the semi-fresh cookies.

"Probably Phil. He's always snooping and finding strange things." She sighed and pulled a rag from her apron in order to clean up some child's messy face. "I swear, that boy comes back with the oddest things."

"Not stealing, is he?" That abrupt statement lost me one of my precious Carver Progress points. I should have asked myself, "What Would Carver Do?"

"I don't ask."

I snorted. That was as good as admitting Phil's pastimes. He was probably an aspiring pickpocket, though I hadn't seen notes regarding that come up on Carver's old maps. The local thief types were scattered across the town. Occasionally confusion crossed my addled brain when I tried to picture how one town could be so crisscrossed with all these personalities.

"Come on in, Mister Carver. I'll have the boys clear the nice seat so you can rest your old bones." Mylia stepped into another room and motioned me forward with a free hand.

"Thanks, Mylia."

This orphanage was the most run-down place I'd seen yet. The building wasn't well-kept like most of the businesses and houses. Paint peeled, one window was clearly shattered from a rock or something similar, and the furniture inside wasn't that great either.

"Phil! Bring whatever you acquired from Mister Carver back out here!"

"It's for everyone," I muttered while shuffling through to where Mylia pointed absently.

"Hear that, Phil!" Mylia was being far louder than I'd ever heard her, but she was trying to out-power a room of children.

The linens looked decent, and that was positive. Mylia probably kept the place washed, judging by how often I'd seen her back and forth with armloads of laundry and other supplies.

"Phil!"

Soon enough, Phil showed himself. This was the same little scamp I'd seen running after Mylia all over town. He still looked worn and tired. His eyes reflected a sunken exhaustion. Probably from running the streets all night in order to find valuables. Food perhaps? He was clearly shoveling a cookie into his face, looking the happiest I'd seen the little man.

"Share those." I waved the cane at the youngster and earned a few points toward progress.

Phil got wide-eyed and tried to smile around a mouthful of goodness.

"Guys!" Phil shouted and spilled crumbs.

"They got a bedtime?"

"Curfew, but a bedtime? For this many kids?" Mylia laughed briefly, then scowled and whipped one of the little ones with her towel. The girl was trying to grab a handful of cookies instead of sharing.

"I'm lucky if I can get them to be quiet and let me sleep."

"Kids."

"The older ones help, but it's never enough. Shawna! Round up the rest of the littles! Mister Carver's here!"

Orphanage Mylia was different than about-the-town Mylia. Walking through town, she seemed to have all the time in the world. Yet here, she was pressed and constantly moving from room to room.

"Wa are yoo gonna tell us, Uncle Carver?"

I had to blink twice and rerun the tiny girl's voice through my mental filters. She was extremely young—three or four, if that. Emotionally that put me on edge.

"Help an old man remember—what did I tell you last time?"

"You did the beast one!"

"And the girl with talking cabinets and teacups!"

That sounded like a familiar story.

"What else?" I prompted other children.

They were gathering around, jostling for a seat. Older kids were busy dragging in more furniture to sit on.

"There was the furry monster in the closet. You told us that one last time too! Can you do that one again?"

That also sounded familiar.

"Maybe. I should really do something new though. What else?"

"You told us about the princess and a frog," an older girl said. She sounded about eight, but looked five.

Okay, pattern established. Carver was telling stories from our world. That was cute and almost adorably clever. Walt would be proud to know his legacy had reached into another universe.

"How about 'Goldilocks and the Three Bears'?" I asked.

"Uh uh," the younger girl said. She was being pushed by another tiny child grasping at her half-eaten cookie.

"I can do that one, but it's a short story, and I owe you a bit to make up for my absence."

"'Thumbelina'!"

I smiled and tried to let my ignorance show through. Vaguely I remembered the story had to do with a tiny girl raised by her normal-sized parents.

"Sounds like that's not a new one." Oh, I got a point toward my progress for suggesting we do something unknown to the orphans.

"Some of the younger kids might not have heard it." An older boy who was maybe twelve helped out the conversation. "Or the one with a princess and those fairy godmothers."

I ran everything through my brain. Children's stories weren't high on my list of things to remember. There were animal ones, princesses, tons from all over the board. "Cinderella" had been redone at least a dozen times.

I added "The Princess and the Pea" to story time and unleashed my best "confused old man who rambled a little" upon the orphanage's children. They laughed and smiled, asked questions, and were in general extremely silly children. It was a blast, and judging by my progress bar, Carver thought so as well.

Finally, the night wrapped up, Mylia ushered children off to rooms and set the older ones about final chores. Fairly well-behaved, they were quiet, aside from the scrubbing of dishes and what sounded like firewood being chopped.

"Well-behaved." I sat alone in a room that had once housed two dozen young faces. Mylia constantly sounded exasperated with them, but she did a good job.

"Only because you were here. They're always well-behaved for a few days afterward."

"Sounds like I should visit more." I was feeling extremely worn out. Children had too much energy for me to keep up. Somehow before I'd started my stories, the three-year-old had ended up on my knee.

"No one here would be opposed," Mylia said.

"I'll visit more then, for as long I have left." William Carver might not last past the two weeks I was playing the NPC. Not if the Voices were anything to judge by.

"What do you mean by that, Mister Carver?" She looked worried.

My eyes were getting harder to keep open by this point. The kids had been entirely too adorable; even the older ones seemed pleasant. Thin and underfed, but they were all-around good kids. Maud would be proud to see those abandoned being taken care of.

"Mister Carver? Is it true then? What the Messenger's Pet means?"

"Huh?" I was losing myself. Old Man Carver's stamina bar had dwindled to nothing, and I received a warning about exhaustion and pending passing out.

"What's this?" Mylia looked confused.

Behind my head, the small creature had popped out. I had enough time to see a scroll in its maw. My halfhearted check for drool verified the parchment was unsoiled.

"What's this?" she asked again.

I shrugged and faded in and out. She was reading something. A poem?

"'Two roads diverged in a yellow wood, and sorry I could not travel both.'"

That sounded familiar. I remembered those words and mouthed the next part, being half functional.

"'And be one traveler, long I stood and looked down one as far as I could, to where it bent in the undergrowth.'"

Poor Carver. His body could barely get a few words out before needing to swallow from a dry throat.

"What is this?" She seemed even more confused.

"Life. Keep reading, Mylia. You'll like it."

We weren't speaking in English, but from what I'd heard, the poem translated fine. Frost wrote it, and they were good words for a sad moment. Her voice was pleasant. How long had it been since I'd heard a woman speak these words? Last time it had been my fiancée, and she'd read this same poem right before her trip. Sleepily, I scowled. Continue was screwing with me again.

"'To where it bent in the undergrowth. Then took the other, as just as fair, and having perhaps the better claim, because it was grassy and wanted wear. Though as for that the passing there had worn them really about the same.'" Mylia sounded in wonder, confused, and slightly pleased. There were pauses when she'd read the poem and restart.

I could hear children moving around in the background listening in on the words.

My **[Messenger's Pet]** friend huffed and searched around the room for cookie crumbs. After running out of scraps, he crawled into Carver's lap to sleep. I wanted to throttle him but settled for a stiff pat.

"'And both that morning equally lay in leaves no step had trodden black. Oh, I kept the first for another day! Yet knowing how way leads on to way, I doubted if I should ever come back.'"

She paused. "What does this mean?"

"Keep reading," I grumbled.

"'I shall be telling this with a sigh, somewhere ages and ages hence. Two roads diverged in a wood, and I—I took the one less traveled by, and that has made all the difference.'"

"What do you think it's about, Mylia?" Carver never gave away too much information, not even to Mylia.

"I don't know," she responded.

Briefly, James's deliberate response came to mind.

"It's about choices and where they lead," I explained.

"What choices have you made, Mister Carver?" Mylia leaned in closer. The blue wrap around her head swam into view.

"Many, Mylia, so many, good and bad… I've made…"

Then blackness overcame my senses. My display still existed. A gold lettered message saying, "You are Unconscious" floated into being across the black backdrop.

What was going on now? This felt like being back in the trial room before everything had been revealed. I'd always logged out before William Carver passed out each night. Passing out now was good, because I needed a breather.

What had I been about to tell Mylia? My life mistakes and where I'd ended up? Or Carver's? The line between the former player and me had decreased the longer I'd lived in his shoes. That poem hadn't helped. Where had the **[Messenger's Pet]** dug that up?

"Grant Legate." A voice I hadn't heard in nearly two weeks echoed across my mind. Deep resounding tones combined with that inquisitive lilt painted a clear picture of who was speaking.

"James?" I asked.

"Grant Legate. How are you feeling?"

Seeing James was impossible with my vision dimmed. The taunting word "unconscious" had slowly become my only focus.

"Tired." I wiped at one cheek absently, finding a small pool of drool. "Very tired. Is it okay if I don't come back for a few days? I need-need to not be here for a while."

"Time is a factor, Grant Legate, but I believe there is a little leeway."

"Okay."

"Are you all right?" James asked.

I thought of the kids, and of roads not traveled, before nodding weakly. Shortly afterward, I logged myself out of the game.

Session Eleven
Outside the Digital Box

"Liz?" *Come on, for once don't sound like a wounded puppy.* Please let these words come across like a sane and stable person's. Focus on a happy place. Try not to wonder what my unborn child would look like. Their mother's eyes perhaps?

Breathe.

"What's up, little brother?" Liz had the decency not to notice my plight.

"Is tonight a good night?"

"Ummmm… it can be. Are you okay?"

"Yeah. I need family for a meal. I won't impose for more than dinner." Liz had set up an open-house ruling after I moved out. One of the counselors suggested having a safe place would be helpful.

"Sure. I'll kick Beth out of the machine and scrape something together."

"Thanks. I'll be over in a few hours. I need to check in first." Time to take another breath and focus on the mental exercises I'd learned over a year and change.

"You sure you're okay?" Finally, some worry wound around her tone. The slight tilt of her head on the video screen was all the hint I needed. She was my twin; her mannerisms were my own. Hiding my state of mind from her had always been impossible.

"I'll be okay. I had some painful reminders recently."

"All right. You make it over when you can, Grant."

The connection closed down, and Liz's worried face faded. I moved my gaze from the watch phone amalgamation to my ARC. Inside the Atrium was a nearly serene bedroom, minus the tiny **[Messenger's Pet]** fighting with a tube from my hot tub program. His hissing and water shooting around was beyond me right now. One day I'd finally figure out a name for the creature. Assuming he hung around past the next two game weeks of this William Carver experience.

I am Grant Legate. I am not William Carver.

Maybe it was good to step out of the game for a bit anyway. This otherworldly persona, the time compression and rate of existence was killer on my sanity. How did other players handle it? Oh, right, they got to play themselves, not an NPC.

I'd have to be careful around Beth.

The van ride over was easy enough. I researched the very same topic I'd given Awesome Jr.

Information was surprisingly mixed. A few books talked about how people organized their thoughts when making choices. More articles and paper synopses talked about ways to sort out a mind.

What got to me was the old Aesop's fable about "The Fox and the Cat." According to the story, the fox bragged about having hundreds of ways to escape, while the cat could only climb up a tree. When trouble came, the cat escaped, and the fox was caught by the hounds due to being too confused by his possible escapes. Too many choices lead to mental paralysis and failure in applying action. That was why so many players seemed confused on where to start, which was where the Traveler's Guide Old Man Carver, in this case, came into play. Yet my job wasn't so simple. I couldn't treat each and every single player the same.

Welcome to Continue, here's a quest to fetch apples! Congratulations, new player, this is the farm! We have a varmint problem! Stop those rats! Collect those candles! Do a special move seven times! The player's reward? A boring pie! Oh, this player got the goblin boss! Way to swing your sword! Here, a plus-ten weapon of great smiting!

Personality mattered excessively in Continue. These were real people interacting with the nearly real computer-generated AIs. The responses I gave as a guide had to be custom tailored.

My ride to Liz's was interrupted by a call to my sponsor, touching base and saying that things were going well. These thoughts about Continue had managed to occupy a pleasant portion of my life. It wasn't good or bad in the end, but James had promised a distraction.

My therapist had warned me I'd see all sorts of little things and link them to past experiences. The problem was exposing myself to new sensations would cause me to remember darker moments. Despite the ease with which depression swam over me, I'd existed for a while in-game now. Most days passed with very few painful reminders and without the need to work myself into mental numbness. This was progress.

At some point I ended at Liz's and was sitting in front of dinner. It felt like my mind had been sleep walking the entire trip over. Beth babbled away about the game world and I tried to pay attention.

"Uncle, you're saying you've been playing for two weeks and haven't fought a single monster?"

"I gave a target dummy a mean stare and some good whacks. Oh, I ran from some spiders too." Voices damn those spiders. Peg's constant uses of the imitation swear had been ingrained into my brain.

"You're going to be a warrior?"

"Yeah. I can see me, lovable Uncle Grant, wielding a big old sword and inspiring fear in tiny bunnies!"

My sister had the nerve to laugh and almost coughed out her food.

"So pure warrior?"

Sometimes I worried about my relationship with Beth. She often treated me like an older brother rather than an uncle. It might be because of how her mom and I acted, or some other psychological dynamic that was beyond my understanding. Still, she was never shy about her excitement over Continue.

"I don't know. Is that good?" Continue did have far too many choices. Maybe Beth would have good ideas.

"Can we not talk about games while having dinner?" Liz was still trying to recover from her amusement.

"But Uncle Grant's new to the game. It's good for him to learn!"

"Uh huh. How are the potatoes?" Liz asked.

"Good, Liz, thanks." My smile must have driven Liz crazy. She was becoming more like our mother with every passing day and mom always grumbled about my grins in response to a question.

"Anytime," she said.

"So what class do you want to be?" Beth asked around another mouthful of food.

"I thought there weren't any classes?"

"Yes and no. There're play styles that are like classes, but they're called Paths, and titles kind of do the same thing. Oh! Have you got a copy of the handbook yet?"

"The what book?" Books hadn't been printed for a decade now. Digital systems had transcribed nearly every piece of paper. I put up both hands in confusion and raised an eyebrow.

"Oh. My. God. Really, Uncle Grant?"

"Yeah. Totally." I managed to get every ounce of playful confusion available into my voice.

"So no! Hold on!" Beth, true to her insanely impulsive nature, had already run off from the table and went to get something out of her room.

"Get back here!" Liz yelled at her daughter.

Beth was too lost in her current mission to bother responding. I heard violent shuffling from the rooms below as my niece searched for something. One eyebrow raised in Liz's direction. She sighed.

"So when is she getting the boot?" I asked.

"After college I'm charging rent! Don't think Grandpa will take you in either!" Liz was clanking down silverware and scowling. Finally, she huffed and went back to get more food from the kitchen.

"Doesn't Dad play games too?" I asked.

"God. I can't escape you geeks."

"So it goes."

Beth came screaming back into the room as if she was being chased.

"Here, take this! But don't let anyone know you have a copy unless you trust them."

Here I had thought about the end of a paper-and-ink era and my own niece shoved a pile of colored papers into my hands.

"Aww, you trust me. I'm touched," I said.

"Is that the book for your game?" my sister asked. There was half a frown on her lips and a flash of annoyance in her eyes.

"Yep. All sorts of useful tips and information. Suggestions, general build ideas, a rough world map of what's been explored. Tons of stuff about the game to study in your spare time," her daughter responded.

"Seriously? You're giving your uncle something illegal?" Liz sounded confused and almost outraged.

"It's only illegal in some countries. America hasn't banned it. Go us!"

A casual flip through showed a lot of random tidbits of information. Skills of all sorts were outlined, along with tips about navigating the world. Quest ideas and conversational keywords were printed out next to an entire section on dungeon handling. Oh look, tips on party compositions.

"This is actually kind of useful." Though Carver's maps in his house were probably way more detailed than anything user-made. Especially something handed around like a bootleg from the seventies.

"It's the other world's Bible."

"I thought this game was meant to be extremely realistic though. Doesn't all this—what does this say, dungeon crystals?—isn't that unrealistic?" There was an entire set of information on how reaching the final level and boss had rewards.

"It is a game. The realism is how you interact with it, the way the world changes as players do things. Look up the interface bonuses, or the last guild wars event."

"Mh?"

"Good Lord. I'm going to kick you out if you keep blabbing about that game," Liz said. She was busy assaulting her steak and potatoes with ever-increasing force.

"You should play too, Mom!" Beth shouted.

"No thanks, I have enough realism living in reality," her mother responded.

"Say that after you do a backflip off a wall and high-kick a man in the face. Bet you've never done that." My niece moved her hands with back and forth action punches.

Liz actually laughed. "Got close. Kicked Edward in the balls, you remember that sleaze?"

Beth wrinkled her nose. "I have no idea what you saw in him."

"Well you know, it wasn't about his personality. It was about what he had between his..."

I suddenly embedded every ounce of my attention into ruffling pages and reading more information. Oh look, certain key NPCs could be resurrected but only under specific circumstances. Wide-scale battles with the blessing of certain Voices would help them resurrect as well, or win arena tournaments. How neat was that? Some NPCs that seemed impossible to kill were tied to legendary quest lines that were still mostly theorized.

Politics changed the landscape as players built up towns, invested gold, or completed group events. The guild wars event my niece talked about had completely removed one kingdom from the map and established two towns at the base of a mountain range. According to the aftermath notes, the mountains in question were higher level. I cut in between my family's commentary of their latest boy troubles with a very important question.

"There aren't levels, are there?"

"For players? Not really. It's a matter of skills coming together and those building up your stats. That's in the book. Then those skills combine to a theoretical evaluation of what you can do, called Paths."

"This guy's note says he's a Rank one, Tank Path?"

"Basic meat shield. There're branches into the other classic titles and roles, Paladin, Knight, Sentinel. They're all about what you'd expect. Damage dealers and craftsman have their own rankings."

Beth was going back for a second helping while chattering away. My sister was busy mouthing words to her food while shaking her head.

"That's neat."

"My best is Rank Fifteen, All-Star, of the Caster Path." Beth excitedly said around a mouthful of food. Table manners had never been a big thing to Liz, and clearly her daughter had inherited the same mentality.

"And that is…?"

"Balanced mage I completed a few awesome quests, soloed a boss or two, and got the All-Star title. I like the flashy effects. Whoosh! Fireball!" She pantomimed using both hands to cast something away from her.

"Aren't you the pro."

"Uh huh!" My niece flashed a smile and bobbed her head.

The information in here was intense. More page flipping ensued. It looked as though people had donated walls of notes and hand written scribbles. This wasn't anything like a printed document or online guide. It felt practically grade school.

"Why do the ranks go up instead of down?"

"Then people would fight for number one, not that they don't."

"Boys." I feigned all the female exhaustion available to me. My sister had uttered that very tone more than once over the years.

"Nah, the highest Warrior Path is actually a girl, I think. She was a few months ago anyway. I met her during Rosemarie's Siege. That woman held back a dragon that was so big—"

"Really?" Old Man Carver was a **[Dragon Slayer],** so part of me was professionally interested. A woman playing a tank-type character and holding one back was very neat sounding.

"Yeah. We got the spell-caster controlling the dragon while she held it back."

"All this shop talk is boring me." Liz got up with a clank of dishes and went to their newfangled dish washer. It was similar to the tried and true ones from twenty years ago, but it sorted dishes on its own, rinsed those pesky dirty ones twice, soaked some items and all around did wonders on crusty cheese. Mother still complained about cleaning.

"Anyway, Continue is meant to be more about living a life of adventure and doing things you can't do here, not about being the best. There're too many people in the world to bother for number one. Most people use the rankings to help with group quests," Beth said.

"I've seen quests."

"I'd hope so. Just about anything can be construed as a quest. You'd be a terrible gamer if you hadn't gotten at least one."

"Oh, the one I've got is a doozy." My head shook slowly as my current mission details came to mind.

"Can I hear?"

"Nope." How would anyone sane explain the quest I'd been given? Pose as an NPC, guide new players, figure out a mystery connection to a random woman, and do one last adventure. Explain that convoluted situation to my niece? Negative! "But maybe you can help me. This quest has a few side goals."

"Oh, totally worth doing. Unless it's a trick one," she said.

"Trick one?" I dug through the notes for anything on quest tips. There was a little in there about what skills were useful in certain situations. Social skills and NPC interactions mattered as much as the combat skills did. More than one piece of advice said to work on both sides of the coin. Players who spent all their time in the woods training were often terrible at finding out secret routes through quests. Or so the notes said.

"Yeah. Some quests, I guess, have optional side routes, but there's, like, layers or secret resolutions. You ever read a book about this stuff?"

"No," I said.

"Okay, so some players have read a lot about virtual reality games. Like, generations ago, there were tons of theories on how they'd pan out. Good fiction stuff, right?"

I nodded.

"Yeah. In these stories, the protagonist would get a difficult task and make progress only to find out the possible repercussions, and try to do something like..." She faded out completely with a blank look on her face.

"Earth to Beth." I waved a hand in front of her face.

Beth looked lost in thought.

"Okay." The call of Earth finally grabbed my niece's attention. "Here's a real example from the Altheme Provinces."

Hey, that was vaguely near Old Man Carver's current location.

"A few years ago in-game, someone was trying to kill a princess. Only she's in another castle, and the one the players were protecting was a body double."

"Sounds like a bad movie plot."

"Most quests are, but high school wasn't much better."

"You still passed with good grades!" Liz yelled.

"Yes, Mom!" Beth shouted back.

"Anyway, they protected the double because hey, quest says so. Someone points out she's not really the princess, yet killers keep coming. Turns out she's really a half-sister, which is why she can be a body double. Players discovered this—wham, bam, kingdom gets flipped upside-down."

"Still a bad movie plot." I sighed and tried to scan over more notes. There were some things in here about skills and how they linked together. Apparently any weapon skill merged with a body-building skill qualified the player as a Rank one Warrior Path.

"It gets worse, and this really happened to one of my friends!" She slammed her hands on the table in excitement.

"The trials and tribulations we must suffer."

"In the end, it turned out that the first princess was trying to kill the second princess to remove any possible conflict when the king passed. She fails, territory splits into two, total civil war."

"Okay." The last of my potatoes were finally gone. "It's still a bad movie."

"Anyway, about eight months later in-game, and after a ton of quests, the first princess is killed in a big war. For real dead, corpse validated."

"Ouch."

Liz was extra annoyed by our conversation now and snatched my empty plate away from the table.

"Yep. Super ouch. All of this was decided by mostly players too. Their quests and actions impacted everything for hundreds of miles." Beth eyed her mom and hastily shoveled down a few more bites.

"That is kind of neat."

"Yep! And had the players doing this quest failed to protect the second princess—the one who was a body double at first—this kingdom would have stayed fine." Her words were half a mumble around the latest batch of food.

"Really?" I said.

"Yep. The first princess was actually trying to abolish the kingdom's slavery. My guild officers think the kingdom would have been better off had those first players failed."

"The hidden trick to this one?" My eyebrow went back up in question.

"Players could have probably reconciled the two groups into one kingdom and made things idealistic and heavenly. Angels would descend and shed rainbows all over those involved! For glory and fame!" She dropped her silverware and waved her hands around.

"Bet that would have taken some skills."

"Probably, like a Rank twenty on a negotiator path or some other people skill. Probably could blackmail them too." Beth waved dismissively. She clearly did not follow any sort of negotiator path. My niece seemed far more inclined to fight things.

"Wait, are there actually angels in this game?"

Liz brought over another round of food for her daughter and scraped it onto the teenager's plate.

"Probably?" Beth said. She looked away for a moment, then shrugged.

"How does anyone figure this stuff out?" That was, like, five layers of silly double-crossing that anyone would get lost in.

"Most secret resolutions require an approach way outside the box. If it was something the NPCs' skills could handle, then there's no point." Beth downed half her glass of water and kept right on eating her third helping.

"Makes sense."

"Yeah. You think outside the box. What skill does the NPC have, what do you have? Apply pressure!" She ground a thumb into the table with entirely too much glee on her face. "Sometimes you find really cool stuff."

"That's—" I set down the stack of papers she'd shoved at me. "Actually really good advice."

"Better stop there, she'll get a big head. Then I'll never hear the end of it." Liz had been listening, even if she professed dislike of the topic.

"Next stop, Queen of the World!" Beth pretended to give a mad cackle at Liz, then slurped down the last of her food before rushing off. "Oh, Uncle Grant!" Beth popped back in and was hanging off the door frame. "My guild's planning a war in about a month of real time. Find me by then, okay?"

"Okay!" Too late. My niece was already gone, leaving behind a whirlwind of thoughts in my brain.

Liz and I made idle chit chat for another thirty minutes, but my brain wasn't really in it. Opening the guidebook would be tactless though. My sister deserved a more invested conversation. Eventually, we both realized it was going nowhere, and I felt okay again. My brief bout of "what if" induced melancholy had faded during our game-infused conversation. For now. Eventually it always came back. This last year had been easier than the one before it. Which was easier than the year before that. Sometimes I lost track of the moment and forgot that she'd passed away nearly three years ago.

"Mh." Lost in thought, I started the farewell procession. "What's up?"

"I'll need to buy flowers." The thought made me shut my eyes for a moment longer than normal.

Liz smiled, then shook her head sadly.

"Are you going to be okay?"

"Yeah. This game is a good distraction." A year in reality, four years in game. Time and distance would help heal all wounds, or so my therapist said. My expression must not have been reassuring enough for Liz.

"The game looks nice, but don't forget us here in reality, eh, baby brother?"

"By like two minutes," I grumbled.

"And I'll never let you forget it." She gave me the same smile I'd been subjected to for decades. The grin was pure mischief, but the eyes held a tint of worry at the edges.

"Thanks, Liz."

"Anytime, Grant. Be safe." She tried not to look worried. Only Liz and those in my meetings knew how bad I'd really been. We hugged briefly, and her hands stayed on my shoulders for a moment. "You sure you're okay?"

"I'm okay, Liz." I gave a tired smile, the only one that was really available to me when I thought about the past, and waved good night.

The porch light stayed on until I got into the van and set the Auto NAV for home.

Family, for me, was the last safety net of a rock-bottom life. They were everything. If Liz or Beth ever needed me, I'd do anything to repay their kindness. A college fund and ARC for Beth was just the start. Liz was harder to pay back. She'd always been the strong one.

But not me.

I distracted myself on the ride home by reading through the guidebook Beth had given me. Continue NPCs were real, but the world itself had some strange settings. Dungeons were one of them. Did **[Haven Valley]** have any? Would making it to a boss constitute a great adventure? I had no other good leads. Then there was the whole question of Mister Carver's skills.

Fine. I had to stop taking this game so seriously and maybe be entertained by trying unexpected things. After all, my life was infinitely less depressing if I only looked forward. WWCD? The real Carver, not the **[Guide]** Carver. He would be proactive! He would chase a lead until the adventure was over. Then chase everything that resembled a female. I planned to skip that latter part. Even after all these years, the idea of being with another woman felt wrong.

Questions, Mister Legate?

William Carver had completed a day without me and was asleep again. According to the monitoring method players could use before logging in, he had made it back to the tiny shack. Logging in shoved my character into the darkness of the Ultimate Edition trial room. Hopefully I could reach one of the Voices here—James or Maud preferably.

"Hello?"

There was a pause.

"Grant Legate. You've returned. How was your time away?"

James—good. Starting with him would be best.

"Enlightening." I thought. "I have some questions if our deal is still in effect." Asking "is our bargain still on?" would have been a question.

"Of course, Grant Legate."

Soon I would shed the Voices' annoying usage of my first and last name.

"Is William Carver related to Mylia?" I said. There was no use hiding the biggest question on my list.

"No. Why would you suspect that?" James responded.

"William seemed to get around a lot."

"A man after my own heart. But there were protections in place for that sort of thing, at least during his day." That was the Temptress—red-skinned, scantily clad, more a lingering promise than anything else. I could feel her eyelashes flutter.

"Of course now, even with the corrections from Mother, there're still too many rug rats being rolled out. Kill 'em all, let us sort them out!" In whirled the Jester. This time it was dancing with a brunette clad in shimmering crimson liquid. I tried not to put too much thought into it.

"Lust does that. The ladies say it's worth the effort." The Temptress was not one to let a simple Jester detract from her presence.

"Enough, he is my charge." James's deep voice cut across my brain.

"But he's entertaining." Which Voice was that? Not one I recognized.

"And deliciously depressing. His mood swings are more fickle than Selena's." That voice was something itchier. Whatever it was felt like mice crawling across my skin.

The Voice on the pedestal, Selena, didn't make an appearance. Instead, she graced us with a clap of thunder and a rush of raindrops pelting into the dark room.

"Someone is going to have a bad day fishing." The Jester's words, clacking and ever amused, came in.

James scowled.

"Mister Grant Legate is only trying to complete the tasks assigned." A tiny set of words came through. They belonged to the younger Voice, a small girl who had been sitting in a library corner, reading. Even now she hid behind a book as she faded in and out of existence.

"Then he should ask about those instead," James said.

"I don't want to cheat," I said.

"Admirable. A true hero paves his own way!" The giant beefy man with a sword popped into existence. He seemed to be fighting some scale-ridden monster. He huffed and swung, dodged and stepped in again. The enemy wasn't completely clear.

"Is that guy Carver's Voice?" I asked.

"We all had a hand, but ultimately Leeroy there was closest to William Carver."

"Leeroy?"

The Temptress was on her chair again, this time filing her nails while her tail wagged. "Ask him about his shoulder pads, if you want to be bored to death. His idea of a joke that's far too old and tired." As soon as she was done talking, she faded out.

"They're fantastic. Plate chafes like you wouldn't believe. Cloth armor is the way of the future." Leeroy, or whatever throwback to shirtless sword-wielding cavemen he might be, seemed upset as he came into being. He manifested enough to flip off the absent Temptress.

"That's confusing," I said.

"Remember where you are."

I nodded. James had explained earlier that here, in this room, I was like the only fish in the sea. So the Voices were all too present. Eventually, perhaps, I might learn all their names and roles. For giggles, I tried to use Identification on James but still came up with an excessive amount of question marks.

Using it on the space previously occupied by the Temptress gave me a completely different feeling. A wave of lust set my body to attention and a pass of pleasure nibbled along the neckline. Teasing sensations lingered and swelled. Unceasingly, they drove my mental coherency down a few notches.

A quest popped up, and I needed to regain my senses before pressing the deny button. That wasn't the reason I played this game, despite Old Man Carver's tendencies. Contemplating exactly how far spread the Temptress had been was kind of a buzz-kill.

Quest: Instant Gratification

Difficulty: Extremely Easy (But just for you)

Details: All you need to do is accept. What more details do you need? She promises to be gentle, at least until you beg her not to be.

Denial: This offer never truly goes away.

Acceptance: Instantly gratifying.

I made up my mind. Never again would **[Identification]** be used on that Temptress. Some things were better left to the imagination, and Continue had very intense feedback. Even the pain from before, when being chased by spiders or acting as Old Man Carver, didn't compare to her heady rush. Perhaps because feeling good, especially that good, was a better motivator than pain.

"You're mumbling." The Jester's words clacked around me.

"Uh huh." Plus an undetermined amount of drool was dripping down my face. Being old and single was not healthy in the face of that... that whatever.

"Grant Legate. Did you have any other questions?"

"Uhhh..."

"He'll need a moment to recover." Yet another Voice popped in.

I clenched both eyes shut and refused to use **[Identification]** on this one too. She went on to talk about health levels, elevated fancy words, some chemical, and Chakra points. All gobbledygook.

"It's..." Words were also hard.

"Yes?"

"Your turn for a question," I finally said to James. Thinking about baseball was helping. God help me if I logged out to find an awkward mess in the ARC.

"Are you enjoying yourself, Grant Legate?"

"I think so. Yes," I said.

"Would you like to do it again?" James asked.

"Helping new players, a mystery, and one great adventure. What more could anyone ask for?" That actually wasn't sarcasm, even though it might have sounded like it to the uninitiated.

"Many things, but your words are well put." James half turned and almost faded away. Then it seemed as if something had occurred to the black man.

"Are you sure? Do you enjoy pretending to be someone else, enough to do it again?"

"Honestly?"

James nodded.

"We'll see how this one shakes out, James. I still haven't forgiven you for what happened with my dance program."

"You have twelve days left. Make the most of them, and I believe we can deliver satisfaction."

That silly pop-up box from the Temptress displayed again. This time, it was titled "Instant Satisfaction." I shuddered and pressed decline again. For a video game, it was insanely interactive, but that was the attraction. Then I got a favorable increase myself. An Event titled "Willpower Demonstration."

Score one for me! Or un-score, I guess.

Thankfully, Old Man Carver was waking up, so the world about me faded away and was replaced with my daily life as someone else. I read through an event log for my time offline. Apparently Carver had had another meeting with the High Priestess of Selena. There was no change in his alignment, according to the text. Not that alignment made a lot of sense to me yet. I had briefly read something about it in the guidebook from Beth, but that section hadn't been super interesting.

The **[Messenger's Pet]** hadn't shown up for the day I was offline; eight hours out of the game was twenty-four in-game. No one had taken notice. There had been a **[Coo-Coo Rill]** raid on the front door yesterday that had caused Old Man Carver to fall on those acorn things. As a result, I was walking with a limp. This old man hadn't invested much in the way of self-healing skills or magic. There was a section for bandaging, but that only worked on external wounds. My simulated pain was all internal.

I went about my morning, picked up a piece of paper and an enchanted pen that didn't require ink, and slowly Carver'd a path to my bench. Carvering things was another clever series of thoughts that had crossed my mind while sitting on this bench.

Now though, I would peruse the map for any hint of a dungeon. WWCD? Would Carver sit on his rear all day? No, Carver would stomp right through all the red tape straight toward adventure. Once it became obvious enough to find.

"There's got to be something on here," I muttered unintentionally.

"Whatcha looking at, geezer?"

"None of your business, brat." I turned the map upside-down again.

I looked up and saw Phil munching a cookie he had probably stolen. Behind him were two of the younger kids. They invaded my bench rather violently, jostling around until the three of them had a solid spot to sit. Phil, the oldest, started trying to entice the **[Messenger's Pet]** from my hood.

"Can I have one of those?" The middle child seemed able to articulate correctly.

The youngest had slurred together most of his words last night.

"Only if you help me figure something out." Even these annoyingly cute tykes couldn't escape Old Man Carver's demands.

"Whatcha figuring out?"

"Huh?" I felt lost.

The youngest giggled at me.

"Where an old man would have to go to have an adventure." I tried to regain control of the conversation.

"Them dames on Haggle's Corner ain't good enough?" Looked as though Phil was kind of foul-minded.

I gave him a halfhearted scowl but kept both eyes on the map in front of me, scanning all the sections. "A different sort. I'm looking for one last adventure."

"An adventure? Like in your stories?" the youngest said.

"Like those, yes," I answered and tried not to smile too much.

"Those adventures are dangerous!" Phil shouted loudly enough to draw random stares from those nearby.

"Is Grandpa gonna die?" The youngest, a little girl, slurred.

I felt disturbed that a child who might be only three understood the concept of death enough to be worried.

It shook me. Parents had to answer this question. Had Carver ever been a father? He certainly had been around enough blocks. He clearly adored the children or he would never have started telling them stories. That was an established pattern of his long before I came along.

"Eventually." If she was old enough to ask then Carver wouldn't lie. Sure enough, I got a percentage increase to prove my actions were right.

"Are you gonna die soon?"

That sad tone broke me away from my study, and I turned my head on an aching neck to look at the youngest. She had half-crawled over the middle child and was giving me an adorable pouting face.

"Only the Voices know for sure." I patted her head.

After all, those Voices may choose to keep the NPC version of Carver running for however long they desired. My time, however, expired soon. I had better not get this body killed or else these annoyingly cute children might become depressed. I knew how that felt.

"Why do you need an adventure, geezer?" Phil asked.

"Part of an old man's last gasp." Clever Carver! Well, me anyway. Throwing in the quest name there had been irresistible.

"What's a gasp?" the youngest tried to say.

"A sudden breath of air." I gave a sample gasp trying to be playful. Nowhere on this map could I find any sort of dungeon. There went my clever idea of heroically leading a cadre of new players down to the depths and defeating some obscure boss. Shame—it had been pretty good all things considered.

"You can't die, Grandpa Carver," the middle boy said. He was still concerned. "Who'd help out the new Travelers?"

I thought about it for a moment, then went with my WWCD instincts.

"These are big shoes to fill. Would you like to try?" I gave him my best adult glare, my face tilted in challenge.

"Sure!"

"How come you asked him?" Phil had completely forgotten about asking me why I needed an adventure.

"Yoo can't die, Grandpa," the littlest said.

I gave her my best old man dismissive grunt. What other options were there? Shatter her little world and send the tyke home crying?

"Bah. I need a dungeon," I said after a few awkward seconds of pretending the youngest hadn't been heard. Hopefully we would move past this entire subject.

"That's where Travelers go to stop the bad monsters and get rich."

"There're Locals who go too." Phil said.

"Locals, eh?"

"Like us, you, all Local types. Come on, geezer, is your memory going too?" Phil said and grinned. He was busy eyeing other people over the back of my bench.

NPCs were called Locals to Locals. How had I missed that tidbit of information over the last two weeks? Clearly this map and the new players had occupied too much of my time.

Bad hearing coupled with fuzzy vision. Distraction by a dozen random players and personalities, the standard problems. All excuses.

"You kids going to help or insult me?"

"What's an insult?" the little girl asked.

"Ask Mylia."

"Auntie Mylia knows what an insult is?" She practically drooled the words. It was enough to make me smile.

"I'm sure she does," I said.

"Come on, Phil, we've got to go." The middle boy was awkwardly pulling away the tiny girl and already partway down the road.

Mylia, in the distance, was beckoning to the kids.

"Some help," I muttered.

"You're an old geezer. You'd die in a dungeon!" Phil shouted while running after the other orphans. His tone was full of abrupt rudeness only children could pull off and still seem friendly.

"Hey! I killed a dragon!"

Mylia must have heard my shout because she blanched for a moment. I raised a quizzical eyebrow in her direction. The orphanage caretaker carefully schooled her face, then guided the other children away.

> **Secondary Goal** (Progress Event): Mylia appears upset from your shouting earlier. Information regarding Old Man Carver's past as a **[Dragon Slayer]** may be the key to learning about her. Use this knowledge to figure out what links these two people together.

"Huh." Why had shouting about being a **[Dragon Slayer]** bothered Mylia? The pop-up box had been pretty clear on the results. In fact, this was the first thing to push my progress bar past the seventy-five percent marker.

Oh. More stuff came up.

Reward: Reaching above 75% completion grants additional access to William Carver's skills. Over the course of his life, he has gained a large number of abilities and secret bits of knowledge.

Unlocked: William (Old Man) Carver's Rank four skills are all displayed and can be actively used.

Unlocked: William (Old Man) Carver's map now includes details about the area surrounding **[Haven Valley]**.

A map upgrade? Had screaming across the distance really been worth crossing my previous roadblock? Better yet, was there a dungeon to crawl into and have some giant adventure? My niece had been right about one thing at least—not having fought anything in a game for almost two weeks was a little bit odd.

WWCD? Swing a giant blade in the direction of the nearest legendary monster. Find a willing body attached to a set of legs. All the standard sexist stuff. Men like Carver had practically built the male stereotype from a hundred years ago. There was a certain attraction to the "smash monsters and get laid" mentality though.

I looked at the enlarged map and tried to see if anything stood out. Now it went to a square area maybe ten miles on each side. The items identified seemed fairly standard. More places to learn objects and things. A local bandit scouting base was on the outer edge. There, players who were in trouble with the law could hide or choose to burn the place down as a lawman.

No dungeons. Nothing thrilling or heroic. I could wander into every dark alley in the town and still it wouldn't be enough. Walking to that bandit outpost would take me days and cost me an unknown amount of progress. Nothing was intense enough to compare to the Dragon slaying. Maybe that was the problem—I was trying to find something to top William Carver's past experiences.

"You're Old Man Carver?" a voice asked, signaling the start of my day. Solving the problem myself was getting me nowhere, so it was time to use all the manpower available from new players.

"Before I help you, you have to do something for me."

"All right. That was quick."

"Take this to the town square, post it on the notice board and get as many as you can to read it."

"How do I get there?"

I pointed at the tiny dragon busy standing at the base of a tree. He was hissing up toward the [Coo-Coo Rill]s. I'd bet the [Messenger's Pet] had a quest to aggravate every single squirrel monster thing in the city. So far I would say he was about seventy percent complete.

"Follow the black dragon, Neo." Yes, the new player's name was Neo, and I couldn't keep myself from making a dumb joke. Though it was more likely he'd named himself after the latest *Matrix* remake and not the original.

"Cool." He even sounded like the actor.

I rolled my eyes and waved the two onward. The small dragon hissed at me, too caught up in his crusade against other creatures his size.

"If you want more cookies, you'd better get going!"

"You like cookies?" Neo said. He had a black shirt, black pants, brown hair, white skin—one step away from an actual Neo.

"I'm sure he'll drag you near the bakery. Feel free to try to wheedle a cookie out of Ladette or Pie Master." Knowing those two, they'd add it to my tab.

"Lead the way, little guy!"

"Hm." Barely twenty feet away and they were already fuzzy. Even if this latest plan resulted in progress, how would Old Man Carver actually get anywhere? Being half blind, deaf, and arthritic was a hindrance.

"Bah."

And up came the next player already, their arrival heralded by a quiet beam of light. No, there were three of them in rapid succession. Today was going to be busy.

"Bah."

I lifted the cane and shook it upward toward Selena's statue.

None of the other Voices had representations nearby or I would have done the same to them. I guessed in a way I was lucky. I knew who to blame for my situation. Normal players had to muddle through while cursing at unspecific figures.

The flier, which was penned in my terribly sloppy old man handwriting, asked for any clues regarding an adventure worthy of Old Man Carver.

Attention Travelers and Locals

I need an adventure. This adventure must be local and within my skills.

I will not promise myself to any Voice.

I will provide a reward equal to the adventure's worth.

Contact me with suggestions. Serious replies only.

William (Old Man) Carver

I had rewritten that stupid notice at least a dozen times. Every attempt impacted my progression bar, which was useful and annoying. Wadding them into a paper ball and asking the **[Messenger's Pet]** to throw them out reset my progress. The final notice being posted was one that didn't cause me to go down.

That was doubly important to retain my skills increase. Old Man Carver had a wealth of abilities across the board. Examples included **[Knowledge: General Weapon Handling]** which stacked on top of **[Weapon Focus: Two-Hander]** and **[Weapon Focus: Bladed]**. The list went on. Like a true player, both kinds, his skills were many and varied.

The new players were sent on their way. Recently I had dealt with an odd group—three creepily happy faces like children on Christmas. Each one had a different goal in mind, but they approached as a trio. They walked with the same pace and overly annoying swagger. Even their names were styled the same.

Siblings? No, their faces were different enough that they were probably something else, such as longtime friends. Continue Online enforced a seventy-percent body likeness for all new players. They could edit their looks or become other races, but there would still be a similarity to the person in real life.

"Ehh."

Children ran by with parents strolling around.

"Ehhh." Another groan. They didn't seem to be letting up today.

In the distance, a small, fuzzy creature was watching me intently. **[Coo-Coo Rill]**s had taken to keeping a scout following me around. Abnormally smart for NPC rodents. Keeping tabs on me would let them track the **[Messenger's Pet]** and protect their treasures.

"Ehh. Hm."

Noises kept escaping me uncontrollably. By now, I was almost used to it. Hours passed while I groaned and thought about all manner of things. Nothing seemed to be happening fast enough. The few players and NPCs that had showed up didn't mention my flier. Fine.

I had under two weeks left. Maybe something would push me up to a higher percentage so that this quest could be completed with a great adventure. I needed to solve this issue with Mylia. One new player was working on that very topic for me.

"Hmm."

Maybe I could get in a fight with something. The **[Messenger's Pet]** had attempted to conquer everything his size across **[Haven Valley]**. Why not me?

Three useless days passed by. Thoughts jumbled around in my head—possible ways to find adventure or talk to Mylia. Oddly, she hadn't passed me once since our vague interaction. Even the orphanage children seemed to shy away. Phil, who was doing to and from chores, was always huffing through.

Oh. Oh, wait. I had an idea. Neat! When one possibility came through, a whole series followed closely behind. Many possible angles fitting a cheesy high school plot occurred to me in rapid succession. Why would Old Man Carver care about Mylia? Why would she care about Carver being a **[Dragon Slayer]**? Why would Carver want one last adventure?

"Ehhh!" A happy groan escaped me. I tried to stand up and do a jig. After a few weeks of stonewalling, I finally had a path through.

All these things were related somehow. Beth had been on point. Quests had layers upon layers. Doing this wasn't as simple as sitting on a bench pretending to be an old man for four weeks! Setting up a flier would only garner so much attention, and I hadn't had a real bite regarding it.

"Aha ha ha."

My hips hurt like crazy and my shoulder ached, but happiness overrode all of that. I kept trying to dance around my cane for entirely too long as ideas occurred to me one after the other. My stamina bar was dwindling rapidly and warning boxes spun into existence.

"Carver, what are you up to now?"

"Dancing in happiness. It's what you do when you're happy," I grumbled and kept going, but my momentum had dwindled in the face of witnesses. Sure enough, the one percent gained from helping new players went away, leaving me back at seventy-four.

"Wyl, I need someone to watch my seat for the rest of the day."

"Oh? That's unusual. You have plans?" His constant grin was turned up to the max.

"I'm going to talk to some beautiful ladies."

"That sounds..."

"I know! I'm too old for the ladies!" I, in Old Man Carver's body, had already started walking off. "But the ladies aren't too old for me!"

That wonderfully cheesy comment scored me a percent back. Whew, I needed the bonus for being at seventy-five percent in order to make this work. **[Truth Sense: Verbal specialist]** would be super useful in sorting through these possibilities that had occurred to me.

First would be the High Priestess of Selena up the outcropping. That walk would take forever. I trudged my way up the virtual, in both senses, mountain. It took almost an hour of staggering and frequent pit stops before this old body made it up the hill to Selena's column-littered temple.

Recently I had discovered William Carver had a number of titles: **[Dragon Slayer]**, **[Guide]**, ones for other monsters killed, bounty hunting, or top-tier skills. One out-of-place title was marked "New" with bright fancy letters. This one said **[Messenger],** but it had no information. I had a feeling it was tied to William Carver's warning of the Travelers' impending arrival.

Being able to separate my own information from William Carver's seemed impossible at this point. Hopefully these things would become more obvious soon. Considering the detrimental traits with Carver's body, it was a wonder he accomplished anything. These problems offset his abilities. Otherwise, Carver could run out of town, slay all the monsters in the area, and make it back before dinner. That was the difference between his gathered abilities and statistics versus other new players.

Skills, on the other hand—once I unlocked this latest bonus—were the key. I couldn't lose a rank if I wanted this plan to succeed. Telling off Selena's statue was not to be considered. Glaring at her fuzzy marble form in the distance didn't lose me any points in progress though.

"Ehhh."

"William. This is unusual of you," said the plump High Priestess sounding sweet with a note of caution.

"Yes. Yes, I'm sure it is. We should sit." I lifted the cane and pointed toward the same ledge we had shared a week ago.

I couldn't make out her face from this angle. Carver's vision was a bit more blurry than normal right now. Most of my hour-long journey had been spent trying to find the right landmarks and checking my map.

"If you desire so, William, we can sit."

"Good. Good." Slowly nodding, I debated which of my two options would be best. Method one included the blunt telling of who I was and what I was doing here. Method two involved vague questions to avoid losing my progress points.

My little friend the **[Messenger's Pet]** poked his head out of my hood and looked around. Moments later, while my old silent self was debating what to choose, the tiny dragon leapt off the cliff and soared away.

High Priestess Peach sighed. For once, it didn't seem sweet or pleasant. It seemed sad, extremely sad.

That was an opener and made me toss the roundabout questioning process out the window. Besides, WWCD implied that being vague and coy was the wrong route to go.

"You were the first to ask me about him." I shook the cane toward where the tiny dragon had leapt off. "Why?"

"Because if that"—Priestess Peach managed to sound twisted with sadness—"is a Messenger's Pet, it means you'll be dead soon."

Old Man Carver's **[Truth Sense: Verbal specialist]** didn't show any falsehoods. Plus she'd answered without any sort of hesitation. So much for being suspicious. I nodded slowly, once again asking myself, WWCD?

"And if it were true?" He would ask questions. Old Man Carver didn't provide others information until he got something out of them.

"Then it'd be a sad day for all of us."

"Ehh." The groan escaped me.

"Hips again?" she asked.

"And everything else," I admitted. "Rest easy, Peach, I've no intention of dying."

"Only the Voices can know, William. If they sent the Messenger's Pet to you, then your time is set. Soon you'll be gone."

"Then I'll go out the same way I lived."

"Oh?"

"An adventurer. I'll do my best to go out like an adventurer." Carver had never considered himself a hero. Not once did he use that word in his journals. His actions certainly fit the ideal version of one though. Slaying monsters for the greater good of all common folks was a tried-and-true method for becoming great.

"Is that why there's a flier in town?"

Standing was difficult with this old frame. Priestess Peach had her answer so I took the Carver way out of things and didn't give any additional information. The advertisement had my name signed across its bottom.

"William?"

I gestured a good-bye with the cane and slowly made my way out of the temple. My conversation hadn't awarded me any solid progress points. Giving Selena's statue a parting innuendo wasn't worth the loss. Soon I was too far away to hear her questioning tone.

Onward, toward my next target! Maybe I would get there before sundown. I ambled past Peg's training hall. She was busy yelling at the latest person to try her brand of torture. Farther on my route was the bakery. Pie Master and Ladette were both there and waved. A third person was busy sweeping up the shops. My first Traveler, the girl who'd wanted to learn cooking, was still in town. She smiled. I grunted with a cane-lifting salute and got my batch of cookies.

I ordered an extra dozen as part of my peace offering. Chances were they would come in handy after my conversation with Mylia. If not, then perhaps Phil would take my money-making bribe. As an old man, I'd stumbled across one fantastic idea that a newbie town should have put in a long time ago.

While resting, I studied the map. During one stop, a player came up and asked me for guidance. I glared and gave him a mindless task—earn Peg's approval. The player didn't know it, but Peg would be able to give him a quest related to his goals if he did well.

Almost two hours had passed by the time I got to Mylia's orphanage. The sun wasn't down, so no points were lost. Hopefully this behavior wasn't too far out of the norm for Carver. Teetering on the edge of this percentage bonus was mildly nerve-racking.

"Geezer! What are you doing here?" Phil shouted at me far before I made it to the door.

"Bringing a peace offering. Help out or get nothing."

"More cookies?" Phil hushed as he drew closer, as though we were discussing a conspiracy. "What do I need to do for some extras?"

I leaned in and pretended to conspire with the youth. "Help me smooth things over with Mylia."

Phil put out a hand and gestured toward the bag.

"Cookie first."

Smart boy. He wasn't giving anything away for free either.

"We have a deal then?" Carver wouldn't hand over anything first. Not without some sort of exchange.

"Sure thing, geezer, you know we orphans don't renege on our deals." He was practically glowing in anticipation. "Deal's a deal's a deal."

[Truth Sense: Verbal specialist] didn't trigger. I forked over a cookie slowly. Luckily the **[Messenger's Pet]** hadn't come back or there would be some cookies missing already.

"So?" I asked.

"Hah! You don't smooth things over with her. Once you're on her list you're on it forever!" Phil said.

"Am I?" Here was my next outright test of Carver's abilities. I gave Phil the best level stare this body could muster while hoping those were his eyes and not his smudged cheeks. Blurry vision was a curse.

"On her list?" the youngster asked.

"Yes, yes. Come on, boy, you know darn well what I'm asking." I tried to sound grumpy and it came out exhausted.

"Sure do. And no, I don't think you're on her list yet. Maybe. She's been upset though. Easier to make mad. The littles have been running scared when she comes in."

I frowned. That wasn't a good sign. Phil watched everything like a hawk. His **[Identification]** results led me to believe that he knew what was going on between Mylia and me. The boy had a few traits of his own that all pointed toward a grifter watching for his mark.

"What's going on out there, Phil? Who's here?" Mylia was practically shouting from inside the house. If she hadn't been so loud, I probably wouldn't have been able to understand her.

"Got to go! Bye, geezer!" Phil snatched another cookie and ran off.

"Ehhh."

The door slammed open in a rush as Mylia tried to catch us conspiring.

"Mister Carver. What are you doing skulking about out there?"

"I'm not sure."

"Maybe you finally lost your mind." Judging by her tone, I was certainly not in a good place with Mylia.

"Oh, no worries, Mylia. I lost it a long time ago."

Mylia looked at the bag I was still holding awkwardly with one hand. The cane was barely offsetting its weight.

"More treats? Those may work on the kids, but not on me, Mister Carver."

"Miss Jacobs, if I knew what worked on you, I would have tried it a long time ago." Which would have solved this whole side quest from the get-go.

She actually smiled a little even though my progress bar showed a negative response. It must have been part of a percent though, because I managed to stay above seventy-five. Some of my progress points went like that, with a flash of red and green arrows but overall unchanged numbers.

"You can keep right on trying, Mister Carver. Maybe one day you'll crack it."

"I don't have long left to figure it out, Mylia Jacobs." Combining Priestess Peach's information with Mylia's earlier concern painted an obvious picture. A **[Messenger's Pet]** somehow heralded death.

She stood in the doorway looking flustered. Up close it was easy to see how thin she looked. More so than she had looked in the days prior. Mylia seemed to be wasting away. Was she sick with something?

"So it's true then?" she asked.

"About the Messenger's Pet?" Standing here holding a bag of cookies was getting harder. My stamina bar was dropping slowly.

"Yes."

"I honestly don't know the answer," I said.

"So you're not going to die?" Her words came out slowly, with a hint of confusion.

"Mylia Jacobs, we all die eventually." I tried not to think of the woman who had been my fiancée.

"That's morbid for an old man. Do you think you can just die and leave all your past deeds unpunished?" she said.

Clearly the whole Dragon Slayer thing had been key in her attitude change. Stories about Carver's past should have been shared around town before.

I sighed and moved on with the next phase—poorly trying to tie in our past moments to progress this quest forward.

"Do you remember the poem you read, Mylia?"

"I do."

"Then the answer is clear. If I do pass, I will not regret my choices."

"What choices could possibly bother a seasoned man like yourself?"

I tried to stomp my foot in emphasis but didn't manage to move that fast. The slight lean reminded me instead of Carver's hip problems.

"Mylia, what bothers me is unimportant, but I killed a dragon and that disturbs you."

This wasn't me taking a stab in the dark at why her attitude had changed. She was clearly upset because the quest text had said so. Too bad Carver's **[Truth Sense: Verbal specialist]** didn't extend to body language.

As Beth had pointed out, quests may have layers. Side quests may tie together in weird ways to the situation at hand. She had suggested thinking about what the NPCs had, what the players had, and think outside the box.

Old Man Carver was not the sort to give away information unless there was an exchange. He kept his cards close to his chest. He grumbled about everything. Like these cookies that were now too heavy to hold. I set them down.

"Why would you say that, Mister Carver?" she asked.

"Because I've been around the block quite a few times, Mylia. I may be blind, nearly deaf, have an ache in my joints when it's too hot or cold, and my shoulders kill me every morning, but I'm not stupid. Just old." Progression points up!

"So? Why does any of that mean you care? You come around and tell your stories, and the kids like it, but why?" Mylia asked.

Another person was testing my WWCD instincts. But, and this was the important part, she was reacting to these statements. Mylia was giving me more information and talking more than in the entirety of the last two weeks. Pushing her now would be useful in solving the quest. Tossing my Carverisms out the window right now would be risky to my progress marker. I had come up with a roundabout plan to get more information.

"I came to see the kids anyway, about a story."

"Fine. For the children," she said.

"For the children." I chuckled. "The battle cry of warring couples everywhere." Mylia got a pat on the shoulder as I walked past her into the orphanage. "Warn me before you start throwing dishes." Progress points dropped from my offhanded snark.

"Maybe I will, maybe I won't." Mylia at least played along rather well.

My chuckling continued. She was a fun lady. If it weren't for this whole quest series while pretending to be William Carver, I would have had a better time.

"Uncle Carver!"

"Mistrr Caaver." The youngest little girl seemed pleased.

"Hi, little miss. I brought treats again."

"Yay!" The children descended on the container like a pack of savages. Considering their almost constantly thin look, they were probably always hungry.

"Eat them all before my little friend shows up."

"The tiny baby dragon whelp thing guy?" one of the little children asked. They had been relegated to the back of the cookie line.

I nodded. "That's the one. He's a bit of a pig, so you'd best hide all the crumbs."

"Okey, Caaver."

"Good. I spent time trying to find out the best story ever to tell you all, but I've been having a hard time. Maybe instead, you all can help me."

"Uncle Carver, I want to pet the little dragon."

"If he lets you." I nodded happily while finding a place to sit.

Like last time, the children were busy shuffling around chairs and jostling for space.

"What was your story this time, uncle?" one of the little ones said.

There were too many children running around. I couldn't keep track of them with William Carver's poor eyesight.

"Yeah, geezer." Phil had found his way in among the others. "Whatcha got for us?"

"No story today. I brought cookies and a change of pace," I said.

"Oh?"

"Huh?"

The tones around the room were fairly similar. Even Mylia sounded a bit thrown off.

"What do you mean?" Phil said.

"For years I've been coming here, sitting with you, sharing story after story." Not me. William Carver. I had to remind myself constantly to keep the two lives separated.

"Uh huh," the little girl said.

"So I think you all owe me a story." I tried to put my hands out wide in a gesture. The movement hurt my shoulders.

"What?" Other confused statements went around the room in a sudden jerk.

I smiled. This was certainly against Carver's standard actions. Judging by the hovering progress bar, I hadn't actually done anything wrong yet. After all, William Carver lived his recent years out by giving people quests.

"How many tales have I told you kids?" I asked.

"A lot," one of the oldest said. Judging by their size, it wouldn't be long before they were forced to move on from the orphanage.

"Then I deserve one in return I think."

"Sounds fair," one of the oldest said. He leaned against the wall, watching a sea of small children munch away at baked goods. He seemed a hard-working sort with a deep tan. My vision was too fuzzy, but I would bet his hands were calloused and dirty from field work.

"I don't want to," one of the younger children said.

"Well, I want to," another child said.

They argued back and forth for a while, each one having a different view. I stomped the cane to get everyone's attention. Amazingly, it worked very well.

"There's only one rule," I said.

"What now, geezer?" Phil chimed in.

Both hands were back on top of the cane keeping me from tipping forward. "It can't be a story I've told you."

"But I like your stories, uncle," one of the little children said.

"That's good." I tried to give this entire conversation my best grumpy old man tone. Hopefully it came across as a kind of abrasive cadence with a hint of affection. "But tell me something new."

"How would we find a new story?"

"That's up to you all, but if you do, I'll promise a reward. Something to help you make money," I offered.

"Yeah, what's that, geezer?" Phil had snagged a second cookie and was savoring it with a blissful look in his eyes.

"You'll see." I had other contacts to visit tomorrow. Other places to go and things to do, like setting up dominoes in preparation. When they finally fell, Old Man Carver's contribution would be etched into the city even more.

After much harassment from the younger children, I provided another story. This time, it was an obscure tale I had dug up about a child exploring the land of dreams. A little bit of fright, a little bit of excitement, and unexpected heroism in the face of fear. The younger ones asked a lot of questions and expected details well outside my limited preparation. Much was made up on the spot, but they seemed pleased.

I got a pop-up box regarding the entire night's affairs and slowly read through it as I Carver'd my way home. No bonuses, no quests, only a notice that the children had enjoyed it.

Strange. After only three weeks, I had started thinking of the little cottage as a second home. Another man's shoes, clothes, book collection, and trophies. It felt comfortable in its foreignness. I went through the full motions of getting this tired old body into a bath heated by some sort of magical rock. The dirty water drained down into a piece of plumbing likely set up years ago by one of the town residents. I slowly curled up under a heavy down cover and felt the drowsiness as Carver's eyelids slipped shut.

Then blackness overtook both me and the person I was pretending to be. Hours later I woke up to intense chest pain. My breath froze as sharp shots of crippling discomfort spiraled through my arm and down one leg.

"Ehhh." Both eyes were fluttering uncontrollably as my ARC sent notices of damage across my body. I couldn't even reach the logout button to try to avoid it. "Ehhhhhh."

As the first wave faded, leaving me hopeful that it was over, a second surge swung up past my senses. My defenses were down. Boxes were coming into existence, saying words that were impossible to focus on. Likely they were happy notices that I was suffering a heart attack.

Then they were gone, and I was left gasping and panting.

A box showed up, displaying that Old Man Carver's constitution had once again saved the day. He was a former hero. The game stats reflected his abilities with regards to toughing out one of the worst pains I had ever experienced.

I logged out of the ARC's simulated pain, then fell back asleep almost as soon as reality returned. This game might well be the death of me yet.

Finishing Touches

"Think, think, old man." What could I start into motion? What other balls could I set spinning in order to achieve my final few points?

The time limit was rapidly approaching. Five days were left on the clock, and I had lumbered around town setting up all sorts of events. I felt like an old dog trying to go out in a blaze of playful glory.

A blacksmith and his two player apprentices received an order for light metal frameworks. A woodcarver got more orders and was easy enough to hide my end goal from. I had to use Carver's map to find someone to do embroidery and make cushions too. In the end, I had a fairly good result. It was still fragmented and all over the place.

Old Man Carver had enough money squirreled away around his house to ensure that the payment itself wasn't an issue. My issue was being somewhat secretive with my project. Players from an older generation would recognize this device once I assembled it. Younger children—well, older teenagers who seemed like children—might not know.

Innovations from our world had far-reaching impacts upon the world of **[Arcadia]**. If done right, these orphanage kids could earn money. The older ones especially, if they didn't have some other prospect lined up.

And they wouldn't need to thieve as Phil did.

I sat down and slowly started fitting the pieces together. It had taken me hours in the real world to find appropriate blueprints and memorize them. Days in the game had passed while craftsmen did their things. New players received quests and got small monetary rewards, so they were pleased.

This project of mine was a bicycle and harness that attached to a carriage.

I noticed that new players had me as a guide and I had the **[Messenger's Pet]**. Since new players all started with money, they could invest some funds to get guided tours all around town. Their money would go to the people driving, which would be the orphans.

I guessed players who stuck around long enough could do the same thing. They would probably get points to **[Brawn]**, **[Endurance]**, and **[Speed]** if they survived. Plus, older folks like me wouldn't have to hobble around.

Voices above, I would love to have someone pedal my old virtual body back to Carver's house at the end of a night. It took me almost an hour of shuffling to get anywhere.

"Whatcha got there, geezer?" Phil said.

"A lot of none ya," I grumbled. My points constantly bounced up and down at the seventy-six percent mark. It was getting harder to jostle them either way. That was a small blessing. Maybe the ghost of Carver was approving of my actions, as bizarre as they would be for his recent personality.

"Looks weird. Is that a wheel?" Phil had invaded my backyard, where all the pieces were scattered around.

"What do you think?"

"I think it's a wheel. What do you have that needs six wheels?" he asked.

I went over the picture in my head again. This contraption would be properly balanced, hopefully. I waved a tired limb in the youngster's direction.

"Make yourself useful and help me get this together. I need the cart."

"I can see the cart, but you got no horse to hitch this to. Ain't gonna do you much good. Your back would give out before getting anywhere, 'cus you're a geezer." He had at least gotten closer, judging by his voice.

"Help or get out, Phil!" My attempt at shouting came out as a cough instead.

The sun started setting while Phil hammered away. Despite his attitude, he actually did a fair job of getting the cart portion together. I grumbled as if displeased but was very happy.

"Get these in there. Make sure they fit nice."

I'd had a player help me with the carriage cushions. She was working for one of the older ladies in town who taught embroidery and general tailoring skills. I tried to ask for a really nice product, something with a removable cover that would tuck inward. Too bad this world didn't have zippers yet. Plastics and other such materials were lacking at this point, so I had to fall back to other adhesives. Even the bags used to clean up town were a strange material that wasn't really plastic.

"This looks kind of lordly. You gonna buy a mule and get it to carry your old bones down to the water?" Phil was rubbing his hands from where he banged them while working.

"No." My answer was curt.

"Whatcha gonna do with this?"

"I'm going to burn it all to the ground if you keep asking me questions. Or you could keep quiet"—because Carver's spirit gave me negative points for saying shut up—"and wait. At least until it's finished."

"Is this what you wanted me to see?"

I grunted and kept trying to get the bike frame together. The wheels had been tough to figure out. Rubber didn't exist. I'd spent nearly a full day searching through crafting shops, trying to find an other world counterpart. Turned out there was a fairly similar material, refined from tar and ores, that gave the same pliable feeling.

According to the craft owner, it also was fairly hard to break down.

I had contemplated finding an enchanter, but the town only had one, and he required a dozen prerequisites to even speak with. No players had ventured down an enchanter's path yet either so I couldn't bribe them. Rain-proofing would have to be another project.

"These are nice. Do you think I could get some for my bed?" There was a look on Phil's face that caught me off guard.

I'd forgotten how poor they were over there. The orphanage barely had the money to feed its charges, much less afford good furniture.

I grunted again, unsure how to say anything Carver-esque at this point. "Phil, since you can't stop chattering, get me some food from the pantry. This labor makes me hungry."

Phil leaped up and away from his nearly furnished cart while I attached the wheels to my frame. The wheels were locked into place by old-fashioned iron clips that slid through a hole on either end of the hollow pipe.

"Those don't look very strong." Phil was back moments later, munching on crackers and meat from my pantry. My share was deposited onto the ground with a handkerchief wrapped around it.

"It's plenty strong," I said.

"Why the giant holes?" His nosy head poked into my view. He chewed right next to me and dropped crumbs over our work.

"Keeps it light." The food was a service. My answering Phil's question was now considered the reward.

"Are those going to hook together?" He was pointing at some of the bars that I had laid out on the ground.

"Yes. Now stop jawing and help."

"Okay." Phil shoveled another batch of food to his mouth in an uncivilized manner and started following directions.

Another twenty minutes later, the sun had completely set. The light cast from Carver's cottage was enough to see our finished product.

"What do you think?" I asked.

"It looks like a right mess."

"Come back tomorrow morning. I'll show you how it works." By then I would have the chain on. That was the last piece to get everything together. Well, and grease. Keeping the chain off would prevent Phil from trying any successful midnight races.

"How early?"

"Sunrise, boy. Be there." Old Man Carver's body woke well before dawn and staggered around. I would let him run on autopilot for most of the morning routine while I researched in my Atrium.

The bike was my scheme to get the orphanage kids on my side. They already ran messages for people who paid a copper or two. Showing new players around and carting goods under their own power would earn them a decent fee. Bicycles didn't require food or grooming or shoveling their leavings.

"Ehhh." A groan escaped me. My shoulder wasn't pleased after all this exertion. Even my interface warned me that I had recently abused this old body a bit too much.

I got my body inside the house and took care of a few manual things while thinking about possibilities. Normally I logged off as soon as I was done and zoomed off to get sleep in the real world, but time was precious at this point. My clock was ticking, and none of these projects led me toward further conversation with Mylia or finding an adventure.

My flier was still up—I'd checked—but responses had been minimal. Either no one had information for me, or no one cared. Perhaps the NPCs of this world were programmed to ignore out-of-character behavior.

Did any of Carver's inventory summon monsters to battle?

No.

Did any of his journals or people known have great but local adventures for an old man to go on?

No.

Was there anything on the enhanced map that provided me a hint?

Way beyond no.

I'd tried too many possibilities. Skill combinations that led to a revelation? Divine ascension or other planes to jot to overnight? Any signs of secret bosses within the town? Impending wars upon our local area? No, also no, still no, and of course no.

My attempts to find a recently deceased member of Trillium had also belly flopped. Well, there were a few, but none of William Carver's advanced years. No one on the primary board of trustees resembled him. The player's handbook stated that new players were forced to look similar to their Continue avatar. The only known exceptions were modifications for alternate species or transformations of that nature.

I guessed turning into a dragon while retaining some semblance of human features was unreasonable. A small smile crossed my features as I pictured a giant dragon with Carver's grumpy face. That would be extremely silly and neat. With one beefy arm added for good measure.

"Dragon man?" I snickered and shook my head.

Nearby, the [Messenger's Pet] had started hopping around the house. Slowly he inspected one object after another in suspicion. Nothing had changed since the last time he'd performed this ritual. With a purr and clack of jaws, the small creature leaped from a bookshelf onto one of Old Man Carver's tables. More sniffing ensued. Slight huffs resulted in steam.

"Don't burn anything," I said.

The [Messenger's Pet] looked at me and yawned. I, feeling the weight of Carver's age and the time of night, nodded while yawning back.

"You figure anything out?"

He shook his tiny head and huffed again. His eyes blinked slowly as he looked around. Another yawn, and he shook from head to toe. Looking slightly revitalized, he fluttered and leaped around again.

"What now?"

There was no answer, which was fairly standard. This little guy rarely actually responded unless bribed with desserts. He existed in a land of equivalent exchange. William Carver did, James did; as a player, I had yet to grow used to it.

But I still wasn't really a game player, not in my own mind. I was a man pretending to be William Carver through all the simulated pain and irritation of dealing with new players. A situation that my mind hadn't completely wrapped itself around.

Speaking of, it was time for the next list of names.

"What do you think of Jörmungandr?" I made the ARC tell me how to pronounce that one.

The small **[Messenger's Pet]** looked up and huffed a smoke ring at me. That seemed to symbolize disagreement or annoyance.

"Leviathan?"

Another milder smoke ring appeared. The **[Messenger's Pet]** was less annoyed with that name.

"No, huh? You do seem a bit small for a Leviathan. They're big, I hear." Not that I had met any. In my world, the legend of a leviathan was most likely based on creatures like the now-extinct giant squid.

"Ouroboros?"

He outright coughed, and a spark of fire flared up for a brief moment.

"Whoa, remember, no fire in the house."

Multiple **[Coo-Coo Rill]**s had perished in the last few days due to the **[Messenger's Pet]** and his flames. I'd also lost three new player maps. Strangely, the little creature seemed to have decided toasting cupcakes was taboo. He took extra care only to use claws and teeth when devouring the snacks.

"Still no, right?"

The tiny creature nodded. Clearly he was smart enough to understand my words. He also felt like a child in the respect that his attention wandered very quickly.

"What are you looking for?" I shuffled into the next room after him, gripping objects and desks for support. Everything hurt, but after the simulated heart attacks, these pains almost seemed mild.

A week ago, I threw names of Wyverns at him. Those had resulted in an outright bark of flames. Turned out he didn't like being compared to a Wyvern. According to the ARC's Internet searches, there was a hierarchy among mythical beasts. Wyverns were portrayed as dumber and had no front limbs. More like scaly bats. Dragons had four limbs and two wings.

"Maybe you should find some letters and write out your name with them."

Old Man Carver didn't own a fridge with children's magnets though. I'd checked. There was no widespread usage of a printing press in this world, so no stamps to borrow.

Maybe **[Messenger's Pet]**s didn't come with spelling skills. Or maybe it had a name and I was failing to guess it.

"Rumpelstiltskin?" That latest attempt was more for my own amusement.

The **[Messenger's Pet]** had cornered one of my city maps. There were two kinds. One was a smaller handheld one that seemed to appear endlessly in William Carver's clothes. They were always in the same pocket, even if I had given one away already.

His other map was a table wide one that unrolled over the entire desk. It didn't contain more notes than the smaller version, but the size made things far easier to read with this body's blurry vision.

"What's this now?"

He nosed out the map carefully instead of using claws. When nudging things, the **[Messenger's Pet]** had terrible control.

"Town, yes, I've seen this before." Many countless times by now. Even if I started as a new character with no inventory, **[Haven Valley]** would still yield plenty of results. If I started here anyway.

My still-nameless **[Messenger's Pet]** lifted one foot and set it back down with some force. He repeated the motion enough that even I got the hint.

"What are you on about now?" I said, which resulted in a growl from the little guy. "Yes, there's one of the smiths. Here's us." I ran a finger around the town, slowly establishing what the small creature was talking about.

There was something different here now.

"What's this now?" I asked.

While there were almost always new notes and possibilities to read on the map, progressing with my Old Man Carver synergy bar had revealed a whole series of secrets. What the **[Messenger's Pet]** had found was something new.

This wasn't one of my known buildings—one of the barely defined shapes that resembled houses and key points as seen from above. This newest map point was a black inky dot that almost seemed to be looking at me. I narrowed already barely open eyelids at the map in a squint.

"Mmmh." I put my finger right under the new destination and tapped the cane in my other hand. "Ah ha! Adventure!"

There *was* a dungeon in town—the map said so. **[Maze of Midnight** (Dungeon – Beginner)**]** The reason I'd never noticed was in the name itself. On top of that was an obvious description. This dungeon only opened at midnight, and Old Man Carver typically passed out well before then.

Even now, my stamina bar was almost completely drained. I was also covered in nicks and bruises from trying to assemble the bike.

Was this dungeon a good adventure?

I nodded. It would do. If Old Man Carver could take down a dragon, he could at least make it to the dungeon's front door. Not tonight though. Tomorrow I would do one last set of rounds and start preparing for the dungeon to the best of my ability. Maybe the handbook had some more hints.

"Nngh." A thought occurred to me that made the whole prospect undesirable. "I'll need a party, won't I?"

Going into a dungeon with Pie Master would be unhealthy.

Unless he brought pie, or better yet, cupcakes. Then I could bribe my **[Messenger's Pet]** to attack all the monsters for me.

I tucked in and let Carver's body get some rest while I logged back into my Atrium for research. Hopefully I would be able to keep myself awake for a few more minutes of research.

I issued a series of orders. "ARC, resume search for Trillium employees. Add an expansion for employees, outlying contractors, and family members. Set search limits for the date range to four years and status to deceased."

"Parameters updated. Search resuming," the machine slaving away said.

"ARC, initiate a second search: Maze of Midnight."

Results compiled in front of me. I shuffled the deceased listings off to one side for later review. The **[Maze of Midnight]** search would probably come up empty. There were two songs, fourteen terrible poems, a band, and some obscure hacking incident. Nothing here looked like legend or lore to tip me off. I'd found a tip in the Continue handbook talking about how most in-game things were based on real legends and myths. From the name, I could assume this place was a maze, but that was already in the description too.

"Remove search results for Maze of Midnight."

The files shattered into light, and I was left with the first pile for deceased.

Pictures were found, reports of how people passed, obituary notices. Nothing resembled Old Man Carver's in-game face. Not even if I backed my brain up a few years and accounted for time lapses between worlds. I scattered the second set of research with a wave and propped my virtual chin onto one hand.

As usual, the **[Messenger's Pet]** had followed me to the Atrium. He was currently staring at my cabinets with a quizzical turn to his head.

"ARC." I paused for too long.

"Awaiting input."

Goodness, I was having a hard time figuring out what to do next. "Pause command."

I had gotten the bike together. I had arranged for Wyl and Dayl to cover my post in the event of my passing, in case this whole thing was a final countdown. Enduring chest pains and a bad limp along with all this other complexity was incredibly aggravating. There was still a piece to the Old Man Carver puzzle, and nothing clicked right.

"ARC. Resume. Display Continue."

A small box appeared to the side, feeding me an image of Old Man Carver snoring away in bed. Everything looked normal and lined up perfectly with my standard view. I sighed and snorted out air much like the **[Messenger's Pet]** might.

"Bah!" I tilted to one side. Standing on my head for a change in perspective didn't help. Old Man Carver's body couldn't handle it, so I did this sort of antic in the Atrium, where my movement was far less restricted.

There had to be some clue to make this all work. So far I had tried a dozen Internet searches. I had even downloaded a few scenic programs to see if they would stir any thoughts from a change of pace.

The windswept cliff overlooking a majestic valley hadn't helped. A pod in outer space with opposing views toward the earth and moon hadn't helped. It was pretty, just not pretty useful.

Purchasing a ride-along movie of *Dragon Skies*, one of the most popular action first-person films to be released this year, didn't help. The scenes were intense and over the top, but since it was scripted, everything felt artificial. The player behind Old Man Carver had lived a true life-and-death encounter to get a **[Dragon Slayer]** achievement. Each choice was his own, each action and reaction trained and honed.

What had the player thought during these moments? Was he elated? Did he feel a rush from battle? I personally would have wet myself. The depicted dragons were many times taller than my house. Standing against that while shouting defiantly was not my style. I would whimper like a mouse and crawl off.

"How did he do it?" I paced around. "How did he challenge so many things while feeling that kind of pain and feedback?" Great, now I was talking to the **[Messenger's Pet]**. At least it was in the privacy of my Atrium.

"I mean, I have a hard enough time logging in and walking around. I can't imagine that years ago he was much better."

This was somehow worse to me than anyone who talked to a cat. The **[Messenger's Pet]** was a digital program, and I was in a computer-generated reality.

"For what, if the time compression held, at least six years? More?"

The journals actually went back just shy of thirty years according to what I had pieced together. There weren't any real data stamps, only markers of how long specific portions took.

I'd had to tally them all up in reverse order while trying to pry information out of the most talkative NPCs, like Peg. She never stopped her mouth and was either chatting mindlessly or correcting some student who was failing.

"Seriously. ARC!" I was getting livid and tired now.

"Awaiting input."

"Show Trillium members with heart problems! All, alive or deceased."

"Warning: Information will be incomplete. Non-deceased citizens are protected by law from having personal information revealed," the machine answered.

An ARC wouldn't try to hack into others' files or obtain information illegally, but it could go to less certified sources.

"News articles or anything you can glean. Rumor, gossip, whatever!" I said.

Worst-case scenario, I would break down and ask James for help. He was an AI of the machine and would probably know something. I wanted to avoid asking him though. Not because I was worried about the exchange of information, but because I wanted to complete this on my own. Each possibility eliminated helped narrow things down.

Mylia had avoided me since my impromptu visit. The orphanage kids didn't visit much except Phil. New players had slowly stopped trying to track me down, instead going to whichever guard was substituting for me.

My progress hadn't dropped any great amount, which meant I wasn't failing, but I wasn't making headway either. Technically there was a reward based on my completion rate, the prize being information. This information was meant to clear up Continue Online's ghost in the machine.

Quest: A Last Gasp

Difficulty: Unknown

Details: You've chosen to take up the mantle of William (Old Man) Carver. The duration of this act is four weeks. Many of Old Man Carver's skills and knowledge are still functional. Results will be measured based on performance as Old Man Carver. Review synchronization meter for progress.

Special circumstances tied to this quest have imposed the following restrictions: Autopilot time will not impact completion.

Failure: Complete failure is impossible.

Success: Possible information (Restricted)

There was a reason. I was almost afraid to find out, but I had suspicions. I existed outside the box with access to all the fictional foreshadowing forty years' worth of people could create. Virtual reality wasn't a new concept or theory. In practice, it was only recently reaching a peak with Continue Online. Each possible reason bothered me more than the last. I had only briefly seen a shattered version of my fiancée in the morgue. Those remains were hers. If she had somehow faked her death... well, all my sorrow would likely turn to rage. The thought of it made me shake in the Atrium.

"Don't you dare knock more glasses off the counter." I stomped over and pulled away the latest almost-victim to my **[Messenger's Pet]** and his destructive ways. "Maybe I should download a friend for you in here."

I looked around and frowned. This place hadn't really been changed since I originally installed it. Maybe a virtual pet would be good—liven things up a bit. Plus if I put in a back-yard of some sort, then they could go destroy it and leave this digital rendition of my house intact. A few days ago, I had finally swept up the first mess of glass.

"To heck with it." I was thinking too much. I needed to shift my brain completely and not think about anything serious. To do that required a complete distraction from the mire of Continue Online.

The dance program was fired up, so I went straight for the group songs, the kind of thing that would go on a pop video or up on stage. I did my best to fit in with the younger crowd, to move and jive in a terrible rendition of randomly shuffled top hits. My skills were lax due to the time distortion of Continue Online, but the end score was still decent. Nothing about my groove screamed superstar. These antics wouldn't be posted online for friends and family. No, I was a middle-aged man in a tight T-shirt dancing around on stage with half his gut hanging out. That was not popular at all.

But it was distracting.

Clapping came from the dimly lit outer edges of my dance program. Large clomping thuds and a jolly laugh followed.

"That was, without a doubt, the most entertaining performance I've seen recently. And I have an entire realm of mad fools to watch over."

"James. Hey," I huffed. Dancing, even in a virtual world, was mentally exhausting. With the exercise bands on, it was physically strenuous too. Sore muscles would be my reward for failing to stretch. A hand gesture spawned a towel in my hand, and I mopped off the simulated sweat and tried to dry off.

"Is this more entertaining to you than visiting our world?" he asked.

"Eh?" Still huffing, I looked around at the dull backdrop that went with my program. There was a vague notion of audience members and crowds of fans in the distance. A score hovered to one side. The other members of this dance group were frozen and still.

"No, not really. I needed to clear my head a little. To think, you know?" I said.

"Ah, escape from your trials. Are you sure that's wise?"

"I never claimed to be wise." Entertaining a computer AI from one program while in another was weird. I leaned my head back and stared up. "ARC!"

"Awaiting input."

"Shut down this program. Enable a refresh. Get me back to square one."

Keywords were embedded in my commands. The dance program would shut down, clean me up, and prevent the simulated exhaustion from winning. Afterward, my virtual body would be deposited back in the Atrium.

Light flashed through, and advanced scientific magic stuff happened. I was used to it, but James seemed mildly interested. Perhaps considering what would happen to his program while the ARC ran its sequences would have been a good idea.

"Jeez. You're really well-designed." I admired his ability to completely disregard the normal laws of programs.

"Thank you. I find humanity equally interesting to observe." James gave a small smile.

"You don't think of yourself as human?" My forehead wrinkled in brief confusion.

"I am not. I am a Voice. We have personalities. We are, by our definition, alive, but we are far from human," he said.

"Huh." These conversations always felt really neat and disorienting. The machine thought it was alive? Well, who was I to judge? Lawmaking was outside my skill set. Polishing metal frames was not.

"My turn for a question, Grant Legate." He held up one hand to pause anything further I might say.

"Fire away."

I walked over and ran the small **[Messenger's Pet]** some water. Finally, he got a scoop of virtual ice cream that cost more than it should have.

James smiled.

"Two questions actually, but one at a time."

I shrugged and kept up my exercises to return my heart rate to normal. The ARC had a heart-rhythm-monitoring program that launched after every sports-like game. It helped the users know when their brainwaves had settled down to a reasonable level.

"First, do you believe that you can complete William Carver's quests within the deadline?"

"I'm trying to. I think I've got something."

"That's excellent news. The other Voices have been disappointed with the results so far. I've told them you would require time to fill another man's shoes."

"It's hard work. Trying to think like he would, to answer like he would. I'm way more open. He keeps things close to the chest until someone does him a favor."

The water went into a bowl from one of the virtual cabinets. I wasn't even sure why kitchenware mattered here. Probably to keep the shock of transitioning between the real world and my Atrium to a minimum.

"His personality markers were varied. Greed mixed with empathy for children; wanting to see people do well but detesting hand-holding. Incredibly driven. The more I observe humanity, the more I notice these contradictions."

"Yeah. We are what time and tide have made of us. A lifetime of experiences often leaves a mark." I sighed. That was a line from my therapist. "Anyway. Contradictions. We're full of them. Look at our politics sometime."

My body was almost back to normal now. These bands had my external vitals all out of whack compared to my normal dance nights. Maybe my belly would have vanished a year ago if I had started using them sooner.

"I'll not comment on your rulers. Those in our world provide more than enough for me to study on that front. Besides, I'm not interested in such broad groupings I study individuals."

"So psychology."

"Yes, but with a focus on behavioral studies and motivational understanding." James sounded pleased and kept the focus on me as I paced around the room. "My role as a Voice is to learn what drives those from your world and to test them."

"I've been meaning to ask about that. How twisted does this stuff get?" My head shook. That wasn't right. "Wait, to expand—this whole thing with my fiancée isn't some game plot, is it?"

I'd asked before. I would probably ask again.

"No. But make no mistake, Grant Legate, there will be tests and temptations. You yourself have already been subjected to a few."

I shuddered to think about the Temptress herself. Part of me would be unsurprised if she strutted right out of the game doorway now. James kept talking while I nervously eyed the portal.

"But if you are truly able to solve William Carver's final quest, then he may provide an answer."

I nodded. That was the whole point of doing this entire oddball role-playing. Literal role-playing, not just gaining a level and distributing points. Not hack-and-slash style gaming. No, I was actually playing the role of a completely separate person.

"I look forward to your progress, Grant Legate." James nodded as well, then faded out.

Finally, my heart rate was back to normal.

Wait.

"He may?" I muttered, trying to remember James's words. Did that mean William Carver wasn't dead? What had started as a hunch was now in fully confirmed status.

"Oh my god."

The sheer excitement passing through me completely overrode my hearing. Otherwise, I might have noticed that I sounded exactly like my niece.

The follow-up question on my end was equally disturbing. Had James let that slip intentionally? Hadn't he led me to believe Carver was dead? James was a computer program. He could think hundreds of times faster than any normal human being might. Even if his attention was scattered, it would still be enough to correct grammar in the event of a mistake.

No, James had specifically said that for a reason. I would have to go out like a hero while guiding new players. Ideas spun through my mind, and slowly a final plan came together. Hopefully this would be fitting for William if he was watching out there somewhere. Second to that was meeting the Voices' desired level of success.

According to the vitals monitor, real life had started to exert some demands. Food, bathroom. Today was Saturday. I had all day tomorrow to try to finish out this quest.

"ARC!" I felt happy now that there were ideas in my brain.

This quest wasn't for me. It wasn't for a computer's version of William Carver. It was a show for the player himself. I didn't need the Voices' approval—I needed his. If there was one skill I had, it was working within people's expectations.

"Awaiting input," the machine said.

"Log me out!"

Session Fourteen
Worse than Cats!

"You. You're helping me," I said to one of the many players stuck in town for their tutorial period. Four weeks in a city they couldn't escape. Not unlike what I was doing by pretending to be William Carver.

"Huh?" he responded.

"I need you to come with me."

The player even got a pop-up box. His system message should say something about improved relations with Old Man Carver and a chain quest.

"Mister Carver?"

"Come on. Let's go." I banged on the side of my chariot.

Phil was at the helm. Even with my bad eyesight, I could see the orphan's eyes roll. Moments later, our cart, still in day one of testing, started into action down the path to my designated meeting spot. Phil had been skeptical this contraption would even work, but it did, and well.

The reward for inventing this device and putting it to use was even better. In a few weeks, after the other orders went through, the orphanage would have an entire chain of bicycles. Kids and bikes went together well even in fantasy-land. I'd spent almost an hour this morning trying to explain how to pop a wheelie to the brash youth, but so far, the concept was lost. These things did weigh a bit more than standard bicycles.

In one of the town crossroads, three other players were waiting.

"What the hell is this about?" The most vocal one was the wide-hipped woman who had been beating a straw man for Peg. Her words were loud enough to carry across the street.

"I don't know. I'm sure Mister Carver has a good reason." The quiet younger female had been my first player, the trash-picker.

"He better," a younger male voice said. This was my cow-mooing would-be assassin.

"He goddamn well better or I'll kick his sorry old computer ass." The angry wide-hipped woman had her arms crossed and looked even more pissed than usual.

"Good, you're all still here," I said.

"What are we doing here?" our new player asked.

"Awesome Jr., you're the last one. Hopefully, this will be enough." Getting this out without forfeiting too many points required certain phrasing. Sounding grumpy helped.

"Good lord. This is your latest pick?" Wide-hip was a player named HotPants, which was hilarious to me, but her name paled compared to the other boy. She wore mail gear and had adopted a strange motif of red and blond.

The boy dressed in all-black leather with two daggers tried to look aloof, but his eyebrows were twitching in annoyance. He went by Shadow and couldn't be more stereotypical in his look or method of behavior. It would take a good year or two in-game for him to really pull off the intimidating over-the-top anime persona he wanted to be.

SweetPea was the younger woman. She was soft-spoken and overly polite. A knitted hoodie was pulled down over one eye and her long brown hair bunched up.

"Uhhh…" Awesome Jr. mumbled.

"Hi, Adam," SweetPea said with a faint smile.

"Oh. Is this your crush, Awesome?" I asked.

"Awesome's my father. I mean, wait, no! She's a friend."

SweetPea was probably blushing too under that bundle she used to keep covered up. Kids today.

"Hah!" HotPants took time out of her normally angry attitude to laugh at the two children. My remark had lost me a point but was worth needling Awesome Jr. about.

"Good. Let's try this again!" I said.

"That other boy ran away as soon as he read the quest," Shadow grumbled almost as well as Carver.

"He was a wuss," HotPants said. She was busy eyeing everything nearby. The last two weeks in-game had turned her already angry personality into one that seemed to look for pots to break.

"We don't know that."

"How do you do that whisper thing?" The older woman was poking her staff at Shadow with a raised eyebrow.

"What?" Shadow asked while pushing at the Bo's end.

"The 'I'ma big scary boy' voice. Like Batman."

"It's not Batman," the cow moo quest survivor said.

"You do kind of sound like Batman," SweetPea responded before pulling her hood down again.

This was worse than herding cats. I activated a few of Old Man Carver's skills in order to talk over the crowd. [Intimidating Voice] and [Aura of Strength] had reductions due to an [Old Age] de-buff. It was sufficient to cut them off.

"Enough!"

"Yes, sir, Mister Carver, sir!" Awesome Jr. was gazing off into the distance after performing an immediate salute.

I blinked at him. The poor kid hadn't even been talking. HotPants was outright laughing. SweetPea looked embarrassed. Even Shadow had face-palmed.

"Anyway. One of you explain. I'm tired of trying," I grumbled and ground my cane against the stone dirt.

"Can I go first? I want to get some more practice with this contraption while you all yack away like old hens." Phil was chomping to be off and see what he could do with his new toy. The cheeky young boy was far too eager to test out this bike tour-for-money prospect.

"Yes, Phil. Don't try to sell that!"

"I know! Deal's a deal's a deal, you old geezer!" The boy even jingled the bell I had installed. "I'll be back later!"

"Brat," I muttered while grinding the cane. Phil had already vanished around some buildings.

"You made him a bike?" HotPants asked.

"Who knew, right? I wish I'd thought of it," Shadow responded with a gravelly voice.

"Nah, if NPCs can figure it out, players won't get anywhere near the same rewards."

I was really starting to go crazy. Dealing with people in real life was one thing. As Hal Pal's companion, I enjoyed a certain level of visibility. These jerks thought I was an NPC and talked right over my head. When Continue saw fit to give me my own character, first thing I'd do would be hunting down these players and punching them in the face. At least Awesome Jr. was confused enough to not join in the banter. He was also the newest to this group. The others had had hours of time while I had tried to find a fourth.

"Are you going to explain or not?"

The game read my increased heart rate while marking the irritation with a status update.

"He looks unhappy." SweetPea was too quietly demure for my tastes.

"So how are you doing, Melissa?"

SweetPea, or Melissa, frowned at Awesome Jr. for his casual use of her name in a video game world. At least I assumed that was the reason for her frown.

"Melissa's a better name than SweetPea. You should own that." HotPants threw one arm over the younger girl.

"Guys, the NPC is going to fail us all on the quest if someone doesn't explain it."

For once I was grateful to Shadow, even if I had made him moo at a cow. Somehow the boy had fallen in with a Mercenary recruiting post. He already had a contract for employment once his introductory period was over.

"Fine! The robot here wants us to escort him through a Dungeon tonight."

"There's a Dungeon in town?" Awesome Jr. tried to catch up with HotPants's abrupt explanation.

"Right? This place is crazy. My son says there's always a few nearby, but the ones in town are typically event-only."

"You have a son?" Shadow sounded as confused as I felt. HotPants didn't seem like the mother type.

"Little jerk doesn't call often enough. He lives with his bastard father." HotPants scowled. Her staff spun around, and she started swinging at nothing. It was the same action I had seen her practice in the yard with Peg Hall. The motion was almost hypnotic.

"I hate him. Hate. Hate."

SweetPea slid away from the sudden violence.

"And?" Awesome Jr. watched HotPants with a bit of worry on his face but managed not to step away.

Unlike Shadow, who seemed almost eager to jump into her path. Was the kid a battle junkie? Was such a thing real? In the virtual world, it was very likely. Slight pain was nothing compared to the thrill of competition. There were entire Internet video feeds dedicated to people competing in ARC's spawned environments. Voices help me, players were clearly all crazy.

"It's called the Maze of Midnight, which only opens at, you guessed it, midnight. I asked my friends who started here. They never heard of it," Shadow said while bobbing his head in time with HotPants's swing.

"Are you willing to help escort me to the end?" I cut to the point.

"Uhhh… sure, Mister Carver." Awesome Jr. was reading a pop-up box that had suddenly appeared. "But I don't know if any of us are any good yet."

"I'm sure I can carry you," Shadow said.

"Carver said we need four people."

"What skills do you have?"

"I've been working with an alchemist. Basic potions. Most of them explode," Awesome Jr. responded absently. He was still reading through the quest notes.

"So ranged damage? You got any magic yet?" Shadow was asking the questions.

Thank goodness they were sorting out the group mechanics and stuff. My understanding of the game had grown in leaps and bounds over these last three weeks, but all of it was so focused on William Carver's day-to-day life that I'd missed how a player might do things.

"No. It's too hard."

"Right? They expect you to sense something that isn't really there. Even the ARC isn't that good." Shadow suddenly lost some of the gravelly tone to his voice in annoyance.

"I wanted to play one of those cat races. The tails look pretty," SweetPea said.

"Can you imagine trying to make it move? The thing has to be automatically controlled or something." Awesome Jr. was completely into it now with the younger two.

Even HotPants seemed to be listening. All of them were geeks, I swore.

"Ha!" HotPants wasn't laughing, she was swinging the staff even harder and building up a sweat. "You're all idiots."

SweetPea said nothing, but frowned.

"Why are we idiots now, ma'am?"

"Ma'am? Jesus, you little son of a bitch." She frowned and put away the staff. Awesome Jr. had committed an awesome social crime.

"Oh. Yeah, you're right, HotPants," SweetPea said.

"That's so weird to call someone HotPants."

"Like Shadow's any better?"

"Shadow the fifty-second," I muttered, shaking my head. Honestly, part of me wondered why there weren't way more than that. With this many people playing Continue Online, in one world, doubling up on names was a given.

"Whatever." Shadow didn't hear my response and crossed his arms.

"We've all forgotten we can just ask Mister Carver for help." SweetPea looked excited.

"What?" Somehow the two of them had come to a conclusion while I was completely oblivious. Social interactions in video games were far beyond my childhood. All the ARC software I had used were single-player or movie renditions. This was strange.

Voices. When I got to play this game on my own, I might completely avoid other people. Except Beth. I would try to involve myself in whatever crazy event she had planned.

"Mister Carver, sir, can you help us find skills to make it through this dungeon?"

Actually, that was a good idea. I took my time now, weighing my own needs to complete the quest against Carver's personality. This group of players probably could use all the assistance available to survive.

"Fine. But there's a time limit on my offer."

"He didn't mention a time limit before."

"That's bull crap," HotPants said. Both hands stood on her hips and she tried to glare down at my hunched body.

I looked back up with one eye and grumbled while chewing at the inside of my lip.

"It's reality. Maybe you Travelers have eternity to goof around, but I don't."

Joy! That one line had earned me a full percentage point, bringing me up to seventy-seven. There was now a real cushion between failure and me, plus it affirmed that this was the right track for completion.

Being proactive was miles better than sitting around doing nothing. Finally, after weeks in-game of barely shuffling along, I was making progress. I had to force myself to put everything in perspective. These last few weeks, I had focused on learning his history and personality. There was mild worth to it all, but an adventure was something completely different. Plus I was giving whoever had originally played William Carver a show. How many days were left on the Carver Countdown? Four? If we started now, how many nights could I spare? Today, probably. Tomorrow night then?

"Fine. I'll show you where anything is." What could I do if they abused this? Pull strings with Wyl? Would he kick players out of town for failing to come through? "You have until midnight tomorrow to get yourself sorted. After that, the deal's off."

"Mister Carver, sir." SweetPea sounded hesitant, but at least she spoke up. "What if we don't make it back by midnight?"

"I go without you." Screw them. If these players didn't want to help an old man finish his dungeon, I would do it myself. I didn't really have time to waste.

"That doesn't seem like a good idea, Mister Carver, sir."

"No. Fool computer wants to get killed. He's an old man. How is he going to kill anything?"

"You idiots, William Carver is a Legendary NPC. Don't you see the golden border?" Shadow said.

I blinked, then scowled. Being checked out for my status felt dirty.

"Bah. Midnight, tomorrow."

"Is that midnight tonight, or midnight tomorrow night?" Awesome Jr. asked with a stupefied look on his face.

I wanted to beat him over the noggin with my cane, but he would have to bend over quite a ways for my shoulder to get up high enough.

All that practice with a sword at Peg's had only lasted a day at most. I had no clue what skills I might bring to the table. Even if this was a Beginner Dungeon, I had to do something. Maps. Carver had maps and a cane. Books and tables and a pantry of preserved foods. Clothes were in dresser drawers. So far Continue hadn't given me any sign of a personal inventory with any legendary items or other gear.

"Midnight is midnight. You figure it out."

Awesome Jr. stared off into space, reading something. The only messages I saw on other people's interfaces were tied to quests and status updates. I couldn't see their entire character sheet without using the **[Identification]** skill. Even that was vague when it came to a lot of details. Luckily these players were newbies, so they didn't have methods to obscure my prying.

"You talk. Figure out what you need from me to make this work. I said I'd help you, and I meant it. But I don't want to sit around here all day while you talk nonsense." I gave it my best cranky but fair tone.

WWCD? Motivate decisively. The more I dealt with being this man, the more he felt like a grumpy project leader. What did his employees need, what did he need as leader? Everything was an exchange toward a group goal of improvement. His only soft spot seemed to be the children.

"I don't need anything," Shadow said with his gruff voice.

"Don't pass this up." SweetPea shook her head slowly. That knitted cap had almost swallowed her up.

"I want to learn to fight. That woman wouldn't let me try my skills against anything real." HotPants was probably talking about Peg Hall.

"Fine," I said.

"You can really get me someone to fight?"

"Probably. Let's get you going while those others figure things out."

The others kept talking as they followed me. HotPants was kind enough to stop her constant stream of annoying angry babbling. Maybe she was actually looking forward to this.

More than once, I had to completely ignore the players' offers of assistance. They didn't like how slowly Old Man Carver meandered across town. We were headed for one of the guard posts near the main entrance and that took too long. I had to redirect this gaggle of idiots to their own needs more than once. At long last, we made it to the guard post. It was basically a small wooden shelter that guards would use to hide from the sun or rest in public view. This was one of several such posts around the city of **[Haven Valley]**. Luckily, this was also the favored haunt of the guard captain, Wyl. He tried to keep himself readily available near the entrance in case anything odd happened.

"Wyl, are you here?" I called.

"Carver. What are you doing away from your post?"

"This is your idea of help?" HotPants was twitching. Her hands were one step away from pulling out the staff to start hitting things.

"Wyl, the lady here wants to fight something."

"She's a Traveler, right?"

I nodded.

"And you expect me to take her on patrol?" Wyl was quick on the uptake. He also seemed a little dubious about the player's value.

I nodded again.

"I don't know," the guard captain said.

"I can't even exit this stupid town! Every time I try, the stupid computer blocks me!"

My eyebrow went up while looking at Wyl. He had likely run into this situation quite a few times, especially since he hung out near the main door.

"The Voices restrict Traveler abilities simply because you need time to understand our world. Plus there's a matter of building up skills to survive the world outside."

"I can defend myself just fine!"

Wyl's eyes were squinting in concentration. Whatever programming guided the captain was checking for her abilities. Those would be compared to some vague form of quest prerequisites. At least, that was what I assumed was happening. In reality, most people seemed to believe that getting into a fight was stupid. Here inside the machine, people's looks and their abilities didn't match up.

One player had recently made it to a Rank three on the Archer path. He'd spent hours every day in front of a range operated by a training hall. In theory, Rank three was high for a newbie leaving town. Two was the average for those starting the combat path. There was an entire host of crafting ones, like Pie Master's Path, that gauged things differently. Likely he would move on to another town via an escort if he needed to, or he'd make friends with a warrior in order to travel around, serving as support.

"You might survive a quick tour, but you'd be dead weight in any serious assault," Wyl said.

"I wouldn't—"

"You would. You, beyond a doubt, would die over and over." Wyl's tone didn't increase in volume. It was flat and sure. "Strange Traveler powers and blessings from the Voices aside, you would die on anything serious. You're lucky I'm considering taking you to clear some wolves out of the Royal forest."

I watched a box pop up in front of HotPants.

She looked confused and upset at the same time.

"This will get me out of town? If I accept?"

"I have the authority to provide a temporary pass as long as you're escorted."

"Why didn't anyone tell me sooner?" HotPants growled.

"You probably didn't ask the right people. Attitude doesn't get you far around here," Wyl said without even a trace of a frown. He was unfazed by the bundle of anger.

"Will you be done by tomorrow?" My body was feeling the weight of today's excursions. Both hands used the cane as a third leg.

"I'll send a squad on an overnight with her. It'll be a good change for all of them." The trademark smile was still mostly present on Wyl's face.

"Think you got someone who can keep her in line?" I lifted the cane in a halfhearted gesture toward HotPants.

The other players were in the background, arguing over something, still. They had barely taken notice of our stop.

"Probably not. But if she steps too far out, she'll die. The aggressive ones normally solve their own problems."

"Mh." I turned to HotPants and glared for a moment.

"If you die tomorrow, you won't be able to recover in time. You best be careful."

"As if I need a computer to be concerned for my well-being."

I shrugged in response. Her commentary against me was both amusing and annoying. Amusing because she thought I was a computer, but annoying for the same reason. My acting as William Carver had flaws, but he was a person too!

"Most Travelers find death unpleasant. You'll learn soon enough," Wyl said.

"Pain is a great teacher." Old Man Carver's simulated heart attacks were enough to send me to my knees. I couldn't imagine death felt any better. The only blessing would be if it was sudden and not lingering.

"Why does a video game have pain?" SweetPea was paying attention now.

"Because it's awesome," Awesome Jr. whispered.

"No pain, no gain," Shadow affirmed. "Check out Stanford's study on the Pain Response and Learning in a Virtual Simulation."

"Two hours from now, I'll send a group out. You get whatever you think you need together and be here in an hour thirty. We'll need time to go over whatever supplies you missed." Wyl was already issuing orders, which seemed to grind HotPants's gears something fierce.

She suffered through in stride with a curt nod and charged off.

"See you tomorrow!" SweetPea gave an impressive yell for her personality.

I shrugged and went over my mental map for other possible training locations.

"Got anything for more speed?" Shadow was busy pulling at pieces of his gear and frowning. His shirt seemed to be riding up under the overlay of armor.

"I thought you didn't need anything."

The wannabe assassin growled at my snide remark. "I don't. But I'll take anything you've got."

"I know a man who's really good at teaching young cocky boys how to dress." He would outfit the player in literal dresses with makeup and everything. There was nothing in my book against cross-dressing, but I imagined it would be a surprise if revealed at the wrong moment.

Shadow actually looked thoughtful for a moment. I sighed. The youngster probably thought it was a disguise art of some sort. He clearly seemed to be going the extra mile for his ninja image. I briefly compiled a list of possible skills needed for a Ninja Path, assuming there was such a thing. It seemed very likely that there was.

"No, if we're going into a dungeon, I need speed or stealth. Both preferably." Shadow was at least certain in what he wanted to take away from this game. Many players lacked the drive he displayed.

"Mh." I hummed and pulled out the map. Skills that combined traits were harder to nail down on the map. Often times they required the players to actively combine tasks.

"You should follow the recruits around," Wyl said.

"What? What do you mean?" Shadow asked.

"New guards, I send them out running laps around the town with their armor on. It helps build their endurance, especially for the ones bucking for a promotion to a knight squad." Wyl's face shone with a smile and a glint of pride in his eyes.

Carver's—my—screen popped up a message about Wyl's pride in his former students' successes. There was even a count of how many former soldiers and Traveler trainees went on to other occupations.

"That's cruel," SweetPea said.

"It's effective. You should try it too, little miss. Travelers should take advantage of everything they can," the guard captain said.

"So you think I should follow a guard around?" Shadow turned the conversation back to his own personal needs. One hand fiddled with the dagger at his hip idly.

I could see Wyl keeping an eye on Shadow's hand, but he didn't seem too worried.

"Let's make a game of it. You give the guard a short head start, then try to trail him without getting caught."

"What do I get out of it?"

"You win, I'll give you a handful of silver per person. You lose, and my trainee gets to stop their lap and come on back."

"They'll accept that?"

"It's a big town," Wyl said with a faint smile.

"I'm in. We doing this all night?" The would-be assassin looked pleased but for entirely selfish reasons.

"Nighttime patrols will change a little because of the risk. We'll see how you do on the first few." The captain shrugged. He didn't seem overly worried either way. "I've got other ideas to keep it interesting if it's too easy."

"Awesome."

"Awesome's my father." Awesome Jr. was smiling too. How many times could he play that joke before becoming annoying?

"Shut up." Shadow scowled for a moment, looking remarkably similar to a HotPants level of anger. "Wyl right? Thanks for this. It sounds fun and like a good training method."

"It'll help my men learn a few skills too. Spotting a tail is good for undercover work if any of them want to join a King's Inquisition."

"What's that?" Shadow asked.

"Wyl, I'm going to drag these other two onward. Thank you for your time."

"Oh, right, here I am gabbing away. Any time, Carver. You keep in good health." Wyl didn't seem done though. His mouth kept right on running as he slowly came to our side of the guard post and put an arm on my shoulder.

"Me and the boy saw your posting, and the ladies in the temple are in a tizzy over your recent actions. I said to them, let an old man do what he wants with the twilight years. It's what I'd want."

I nodded.

"Let me die with a sword in my hand and a prayer on my lips. Not a whimper in my bed." Wyl shook his head and looked sad for a moment. This became one of the few times I'd seen him without a smile of some sort.

"Sounds like a good plan." The people in this world were lucky that way. In the real world, we rarely had a warrior's way out. Modern medicine kept the old alive and feeble. But Carver would want to go out with a bang, not a whisper. That was exactly what William Carver, what I, would do.

"Hah! Carver, whatever you've cooked up, you give 'em hell for me!"

"I will, Wyl." Saying that was almost a miniature tongue twister.

Wyl went from hot to cold very quickly depending on who he was talking to. His minions—I mean, lesser guards—were treated very differently than an old war buddy was treated.

At least I thought that's what our relationship was. The notes needed another review. This world had thrown so many bits of information at me that I was nearly drowning. Work tomorrow would suck simply because of the mundane nature in comparison.

A few more dominoes were left. Then we would see where everything fell. Thank goodness the Voice of Gambling and his negative buff hadn't impacted Old Man Carver's stats. Being this tired and walking around with nagging pain everywhere was enough of a punishment.

If I could use Carver's skills to the fullest, without negative side effects, then clearing this dungeon would be easy. Speaking of cake, where was the **[Messenger's Pet]**?

"Mister Carver, sir." SweetPea sounded demure again. It was annoying and sort of cute at the same time.

"What is it?" I grumbled.

"Do you have any suggestions for me?"

"Nope. You need to figure out what you want for yourself. Not me. No one is required to follow a path. You make a choice and work hard." Not once had I forced any player to learn a skill, aside from whatever resulted from the introduction quests.

"I only know how to clean." She sounded sad and pulled the hoodie down even more.

"Your meatloaf was really good, Melissa."

"Thanks, Adam."

"Maybe I should leave you two alone." Carver was very good at sounding grumpy, even if I personally felt like teasing people. It just came out that way.

"No, it's okay, Carver. We should try to do something to help make this better. None of the other players even tried to help you with the flier, so I feel kind of bad forcing you to figure out something on your own."

I was completely stunned by Awesome Jr.'s statement. While it was true that no one had really tried to help me, the fact that he felt guilt toward an NPC was almost overpowering. My rueful grin at his new pop-up box was response enough. From this angle, I could easily see the reputation with "William (Old Man) Carver" increase, and I wasn't even upset. Awesome Jr. had been serious about it.

I nodded again.

"Did you still want to learn magic?"

"I tried that and failed." His head actually dipped and hung in depression.

"Who did you talk to?"

"Shandra Tull. She was the one my quest chain led to."

SweetPea was looking at Awesome Jr. with one eyebrow high under her hood.

"Yeah. She was nice and gave me a few books, but nothing clicked."

Shandra wasn't actually a mage of any sort, according to my notes. She was more of a hedge witch with a steep learning curve. I idly followed the markings all over town and found a few good starter methods for learning magic. Of course doing that made me feel like a dirty cheater with a personal walk-through but I was also Old Man Carver, guide to the new and confused. The balance was strange.

"You might be missing something." My teeth chewed on one lip in thought.

"Like what?"

"Mh. Not everything is as simple as learning abilities right away, not even for Travelers."

How should I explain a topic I barely understood? William Carver had no access to magic or any sort of alternate energy form. According to his skills everything went "Swing the big sword, swing it some more, swing it harder and scream!"

"Come on. Come," I said.

We took another trip slowly. The sun was setting, and I was getting extremely tired. Plus being out too late would get me in trouble with my progress bar. If this quest attempt failed, I would need every point available.

"Need a ride, geezer?" A bell from the bicycle dinged a few times as Phil navigated the metal device to a halt nearby.

"Phil. It's about time." I loaded myself onto the cart's plush seating. Moments later, I had a map out and was jabbing one finger at the meditation cave.

"Can you get us here?"

"I'm pretty beat. Maybe to the base of the hill, but any farther up? No. Not on this thing." Phil was wearing a slight frown and both eyebrows creased together.

"That's good enough."

"Fine, but deal's a deal's a deal, right? The bike's all ours after today?"

"As long as it stays with the orphanage." I nodded.

"Of course, geezer. The other kids wanted to ride around before lights out; figured we could take them on trips." Phil was talking really fast. "Mylia wants to use it as a reward for those who help out."

"You take her up on that."

"Hah! If we had a few more of these, then the older kids wouldn't be worried about jobs."

That, my dear Phil, was the entire plan. I wanted the orphan kids to have something to do for money while growing up, plus bikes were cool for children.

"Seriously, Mister Carver, I can't believe you made a bicycle," Awesome Jr. said.

"You Travelers aren't the only ones with brains," Phil shouted back at us.

The cart was going entirely too fast for me, but Carver's body rode it out as though it was a standard day.

Icons and text boxes for riding skills and safety checks appeared. More pluses and minuses from the state of our cart showed up. Phil's driving skills were even factored into it somewhere. Poor SweetPea and Awesome Jr. had no idea what to think. The girl clutched at her knitted hat, and Awesome Jr. was almost a dog sticking his head out the window.

After a slew of bumps and awkwardly broken up conversations, we arrived at the cave. This place was south of the town's main gate. Close enough to be part of **[Haven Valley]** but very much out of the way.

"What are we out here for?"

I squinted through the trees and brush up the hill. Phil was laying over the handle bars, puffing in gasps of air. Poor boy had worked hard today. A routine involving morning stretches would help.

"Up there." I lifted the cane and pointed toward a ledge.

"What's up there?" Awesome Jr.'s neck looked funny with his head tilted so far back.

"A cave." Dirt, rocks, some plants. I felt empathy for William's abrasiveness when dealing with Travelers. Where had their adventurous spirit gone? Had it been bred out of humanity?

"Caves have bats," he protested.

"It's only bats." SweetPea looked confused. Was Awesome Jr. afraid of bats?

"They poop everywhere," he said.

"Gross."

"This cave has more than bats." I didn't even try to sound reassuring. Carver didn't do reassuring! WWCD? Grump and shrug!

"Why go to it?"

"Go as deep as you can into the cave. Spend the entire night."

SweetPea went red, but not as red as Awesome Jr. I lowered my eyebrows in a level glare. The two of them had that annoying young love gaze that turned everything lovey. It was best to put a halt to that right away.

"It's not a romantic date. It's a place to train."

"Will we learn magic?" she asked. Her mouth curled in an excited smile.

"You'll learn something. What you take away is up to you." One of my shoulders came up in a half shrug. The other was too stiff to move properly. Magic was one of the possible outcomes, according to Carver's map. There were many others as well, each one a slightly different flavor.

"How come you never told us about this place?" Awesome Jr. asked.

"You didn't ask the right questions. No one ever does." I didn't ask James the right questions most of the time. It was more fun to treat our conversations as a lax chat rather than an interrogation. These would be the first players I guided to this cave.

"I'm in. How about you, Adam?"

"If you're going." Poor boy was still red-faced.

I smirked as they walked into the distance. Surprisingly, sending them off together earned me a few more points on the progress bar. Today I learned William Carver was secretly a romantic.

Progress: 80%

"Come on, Phil. I need to go home."

"No can do, geezer. Mylia wanted you to drop by tonight," Phil responded with half his normal cheek. He still looked winded.

I sighed. The timing was never convenient. Not when it really mattered.

"You can take the slow route then."

Unaware Farewell

Whistling was hard with partially chapped lips. Old Man Carver also couldn't carry a tune to save his life. I couldn't hear one either, at least not without an extremely loud tone. We passed by a man in the park who looked as if he was trying to woo **[Coo-Coo Rill]**s with his voice.

Phil commented on how terrible he sounded, and I grunted because none of the noise had made it to me. Even the man's shape was a pleasant blur. Reactions like Phil's were why I avoided dancing in public back in the real world. Too much judgment abounded in our world of instantly uploaded videos and attention mongering. Here, inside Continue Online, dancing was easier. More than once I had taken Carver's body through a slow jig of happiness. Plus dancing a jig was kind of fun.

I enjoyed irritating Phil with my own terrible whistle between the cave of mysteries and Mylia's orphanage. Though neither name was accurate. Cave of mysteries had a nice ring to it. Better than **[Maze of Midnight]**.

"Thank the Voices. Home. Finally." Phil was beyond tired. His pedaling had slowly dwindled to half spastic jerks.

"Careful with your balance."

"I know. I know." He huffed.

"Bicycles take even a Traveler time to learn. Stretch before bed." That was me talking, not Carver. I was almost forced to do stretches every time I exited the ARC or risk problems. "Make sure the younger kids don't try to run off without supervision."

"I know. I know."

Neat. I was really getting into this role of being a nagging old man. Though my behavior wasn't entirely accurate for a Carverism.

"And money up front when working."

"I know!" The youngster's head was hanging down in that sulk children do.

"And you'll need a map."

"I know!" Phil paused and blinked a few times. "Wait. What? You never said anything about a map."

"Here. I can't be doing this forever." I handed over one of the maps Carver had. During the last five days, I'd verified that this one actually displayed information. The rest were at Carver's house. That place was filled to the brim with notes and bits of information.

"Wait, what?"

"Ehhh." I ignored Phil and slowly lowered myself out of the cart, cane and a tentative foot first until my landing was secure. Then everything shifted onto tired hips.

"What is this all about, geezer?"

Phil's questioning tone was ignored while my feet shuffled toward the door. Sunlight had nearly completely vanished. Hopefully everyone was doing all right with their individual training methods. That cave would probably be the worst of the trials. Though Wyl likely had a few tricks up his sleeve to keep Shadow guessing.

"Geezer?" Phil sounded urgent.

I thought he was Shadow the fifty-second. That was the count James had given me.

"Geezer!"

The next mystery was Mylia, standing in the doorway with an upset expression. Even these tired eyes could make out a half frown and hip tilt of annoyance.

"Phil, you leave him alone and go get the littles ready for bed!" She pointed one finger at him, then gestured to the back of her orphanage.

"It's Jane and Jill's turn!"

"Help them, or I'll whack you!"

Mylia wasn't getting any better these last few days. A few weeks ago, she'd seemed pleasant and polite, but now she was tired and irritable. I let the whole woman's issue slide right out of my mind and hobbled up to the door.

"Mister Carver."

"Mylia. You wanted to see me?"

"I wanted to ask you what you're trying to make these children do. They've been driving me bonkers for days with your silly story request."

I imagined a serious expression across her face but couldn't really make one out in the blurry light.

"Mh." I clanked the cane against her walkway gravel while pondering what to do.

"Seriously, after all this time, why would you make such an absurd request?"

"I have my reasons." Many reasons, in the form of quests and desperate attempts. None of that would be sensible to tell Mylia. My tired eyes glared at the woman.

Stress was wearing her down, and all of it was likely from me. I sighed. One hand reached inside Carver's robe to check on one of his trophies. This was a prize I'd found while digging around for a proper sword. Anything that might help me with the **[Maze of Midnight]** mission. Too bad there had been no such weapon lying around his house. Old Man Carver's list of belongings didn't even include a long trail of twine to lay out.

His best gear was probably off in some invisible inventory pocket that was unreachable to me. Drat. I bet he had some superb equipment. Oh well, that was why I'd gathered four players for this escort quest. Plus it felt very game-like to give newbies this sort of chance. Apparently the Voices thought so as well, or I wouldn't keep getting pop-up boxes for my actions. I had a feeling that they could kibosh the whole thing any time they wanted to. Especially that Drill Sergeant who'd shouted spittle into my face. That guy would probably pull the plug immediately given a choice.

I sent a mental prayer to the future robot overlords and once again boasted about my polishing skills. Hal Pal would probably get a kick out of this whole thing. For an AI, it had a surprisingly wide range of amusement. One day after work, I'd caught the robot shell viewing kitten movies with a confused expression. That had been an interesting van ride home, with me explaining to a computer why kittens were cute.

"Whatever your reasons are, it's no good to the kids. They loved your stories and now you've stopped telling any."

"They've never tried to tell you stories?"

"Well, they do." Her frown was extremely obvious as her eyes gazed into the distance. She was probably remembering prior experiences with the little ones. Children always babbled about something.

"All I'm asking them for is a story. A new one, about anything they want it to be."

"I don't understand why. Why change things now?"

"Because things change, Mylia. They always have, and always will. Someone has to be able to tell stories if I…" I had become too invested in the moment. That wasn't Carver speaking; it was me. I dared to look at my progress bar and noticed a small red negative mark. William Carver didn't like to admit his own mortality. Well, screw him. Mortality existed. That negative point was one I would argue to the grave.

"That's no good, Mister Carver. What will the children do if you go away?"

"Life goes on, Mylia. We don't always get to say good-bye."

Mylia looked worried, but made no move to leave the doorway. She was clearly blocking my entrance into the orphanage. Either Mylia was blocking me out of annoyance or worry about our conversation being unfinished.

"Here. I found this. It seemed like something you should have." I pulled out a necklace of scales. The scales were heavy things, they almost tore off my arm to lift. Carrying them around in my robe all day had been torture.

"What are these?"

"Yours. To do with what you will."

There was no mistaking the fiery spark in her eye. Mylia was slowly growing upset, even beyond upset. Her face had almost twisted to inhuman rage. My old eyes could make out some details against the fading light. There was a ripple on her forehead, and for a moment, both eyes gleamed a golden hue.

Carefully using **[Identification]**, I gained a bit more information, which confirmed a hunch. Mylia was somehow a half-dragon. That was why talk of my dragon-slaying days had upset her so much. I'd applied every badly written movie plot available to this situation over the last few days in order to reach this conclusion. Clearly it had been a logic leap on my part.

That, and one of the players I'd sent on a quest to do reconnaissance said she salivated over meats but refused to eat any. I figured her to be a carnivore of some sort but had never seen her eat anything that looked as though it came from an animal. Had the computer generated a half-dragon vegan or something? That would be a neat reason for her to be so peaceful with humans.

My follow-up question was simple. What the heck was a half-dragon NPC doing running an orphanage? I had suspicions and maybe three days left to solve them, assuming this dungeon went well.

"What do you suggest I do with this?" she asked.

The scales in her hand had come from William Carver's one dragon kill. They had theoretically been ripped from the soft spot under its chin.

"Give them the respect I never did."

"Oh." Her face twisted, and this time it wasn't anger. Not completely. The redness that had been building up washed away to a pale tone. Her eyes widened.

"There's a price."

"What is it?" Even her words turned almost soft. This was more like the Mylia I had first met. Calm, happy. I felt as though things were going in the right direction.

"One day, I expect you to tell a story as well."

"And what tale would you expect of me?"

"Yours."

I'd stunned the NPC speechless. Go me! My quest bar took a jump with that declaration. Offering the trophy scales in exchange for progress with Mylia was exactly what the AIs expected. Too bad now I was losing progress due to staying out past nightfall.

"Do we have a deal?"

"I'll..." She looked at the scales in her hands again. This time, she was almost cradling them. "I'll think on it. Good and proper this time, Mister Carver."

"That'll have to do."

There was another pause, far more pleasant as Mylia seemed lost in thought. After a moment, she gave a small smile and stepped aside. Guess the gesture returned me to her good graces.

"Will you be staying?" she asked.

"Not tonight, Mylia Jacobs. I've lived long enough to know when a woman needs her space."

Her smile faltered for a moment, but then she nodded.

"I'll be off then. If the Voices are kind, we'll talk again soon."

Only as I turned away did it occur to me how fatalistic that came out. There was a very good chance Carver could make it through everything that might happen. Sitting on a bench all day to survive was still an option. Yet Carver hadn't been that sort of person. He sat on a bench to help new players, not to avoid trouble.

I let the autopilot function take a meandering path home and logged out of my ARC. There was only so much prep work I could do within the world of Continue. The rest was notes that Phil could deliver around town tomorrow right before the dungeon attempt. Old Man Carver's penmanship was barely legible.

My house was quiet save for the ARC's hum of energy. Everything was in its place. Nothing had been moved or touched. I thought that was the worst part of losing my fiancée. The portion of- of everything that used to be filled with her. Those first few nights utterly alone had been awkward. Loneliness didn't hit until a few weeks later. Soon I started purging reminders chunks at a time.

Clothing was the easiest to get rid of. Books went next. She had owned a small shelf with honest-to-god paperbacks. Most of them were scientific in nature—blueprints of spaceships and other things. The feel of paper helped her study easier. She had wanted to go on the Mars Colony Projects with a blazing intensity. There was no room on such a thing for a number-cruncher like me, but if she'd gone, they would have trained me in something too. I would have swept hallways for her.

I grabbed a coffee and stared out of my front window while wondering about the roads not traveled. Trying not to dwell on the choices made to lead where I was. "What if" was a dangerous game for those who suffered. What if I had made her stay home one extra day? What if I had convinced her to go on a plane or take the tunnels? Even an hour later on the next train out?

Any number of actions could have changed the future. Therapy had helped me through some of the sadness. Most of it was time to grieve and realize that I had no way to predict disaster. I was no seer who could foresee the future. I was no psychic who could sense impending doom. I was a sad man with a belly that had gotten too big in a house that was too quiet.

This whole chain of thoughts was really Awesome Jr.'s and SweetPea's fault. Their sappy, shy love story was enough to dig up wounds. They clearly played this game to be with each other, or at least Awesome Jr. did. Hopefully he confessed his feelings sometime tonight. If things went right, they would walk out ready to challenge the world tomorrow. I smiled. Dungeon crawling would be a neat first date. Carver's journals stated adventures with pretty ladies almost always resulted in happy endings.

"Mh." Great. Carver's grumbling had invaded my quiet coffee contemplation time.

"Mh." I made the noise again. A smile grew on my face. Being grumpy in real life might be kind of fun. It was better than being a sad wounded puppy.

"Grr!" I tried to scowl like HotPants did, but ended up laughing at myself. That woman was a bundle of misplaced anger. I would find her later on, once I was me and not Carver, then tell her that I wasn't an NPC. Crud. Was there a non-disclosure clause on my time as Old Man Carver?

My single serving of coffee was almost done. Experiments with caffeine and long-term ARC immersion had been inconclusive. For my dance program, the energy helped keep me focused. In Continue, nothing was clear. The time perception warp was playing havoc with my senses. I'd set up alarms first thing when I went back in. To make sure I didn't somehow play 'til dawn then attempt to go to work. Even a quick catnap in the company van would barely solve that problem.

I stood to grab another cup. The timer on my watch gave me an hour before Carver woke for the morning. I would play the game personally to ensure Carver got a nap as well. Otherwise staying up for the **[Maze of Midnight]** would be near impossible.

The second cup was saved for mulling over HotPants as a person. She clearly had some issues in the real world. Abusive ex-spouse, if I were to guess. Everything gave hints as to her nature outside the ARC: a general distaste for being given orders, the desire to learn self-defense, short temper. Maybe I was overthinking her. She could be a naturally violent person. Or simple rage issues due to a bad divorce.

They weren't all as straight-forward as Pie Master. That man had shouted for joy at being able to learn cooking. He had gone on for almost an hour about how the real world had lost its flare when it came to meal time. Pie Master loved desserts the most. Half his reasoning had to do with a grandmother who'd taught him to make a cake when he was eight.

Some people were that simple.

Shadow I didn't even worry about. That man was set on an image. He would follow it out to the end. Voices, it was hard to call him and Awesome Jr. men. They technically were. From Carver's point of view, the one I had been pretending to have for weeks, they were barely out of diapers.

"Heh." Continue was fun and frustrating. Even this strange, unorthodox way of playing had value. It was a hobby that didn't involve self-torture.

That last thought came out entirely too moody. I needed some music.

I fired up something with a swing to it and bobbed around my front room. Moving hurt more than on a normal day, but less than Carver's standard fare. These exercise bracelets were doing a number on me. My abs ached in places they wouldn't normally care about.

"ARC!" I was in another room, but the device would hear me. There was a repeater and projector in this room. Trillium employees had access to all the neat toys.

"Awaiting Input."

"Fire up some reviews of the EXR-Sevens. And the user's manual, whatever section that explains if I need to take them off or not."

"Searching. Data retrieved. Displaying." The projection ball in the top of my front room took over one of the walls with an image.

"Visual only." I cut off the ARC's automatic playback of the text. My music was more important. Reading and jiving at the same time was second nature. Even if moving made me wince from sore muscles.

According to the information, my EXR-Sevens could just stay on. Trillium had configured the things to recharge using wireless signals. That was super neat but not new. My watch operated on the same thing. Heck, this technology had been in the works decades ago. The real kicker was how EXR-Sevens measured biometric data for an entire body adjustment program.

I guessed the ARC wasn't merely a pretty box with games and porn. No. This machine measured a person's current status, their responses, and progressed differently for everyone. Some of the reviews went on to suggest a superhuman software that would automatically adjust your body over time. People hoped soon to plug in and be the Hulk a few years later with no effort required.

Turned out the EXR-Seven wasn't a cure-all. The body needed a resistance of some sort to build mass, but the bands succeeded at burning calories. Combine it with a diet and the jump was still very good. It was a shame, but humanity hadn't invented a method for the perfect body. It was still a matter of exercise right and eat clean.

Trillium forced people to play physical programs of some sort to keep the EXR-Seven functioning. According to the user's manual, they would shut off if you slept all day or watched movies in the ARC. Not a complete freebie, but still useful. My niece did manage to keep herself in shape. I glanced over a couple of other advertisements and even saw the official one from Trillium. It played like a late-night infomercial.

"Before EXR-Seven, I was a complete butterball. Now all the ladies want me!"

The vocals overrode my music and annoyed me. I waved at the mute option and stared downward.

I patted my gut and chuckled. "Soon. Bah. Maybe I should eat better too."

Nonsense, food was good! Though I bet there were programs that could offer me tasty alternatives at my normal food stops.

An alarm cut out the music. Morning was approaching in Carver land! I had a full day of trying to figure out penning memos with a quill.

"Oh!" I set the coffee cup into my sink and shuffled eagerly to the bathroom.

Quickly I washed my face and cleaned up a bit. This next haul inside Continue would be at least four hours of real-world time, or a day inside. More, if this dungeon was a longer adventure.

Darkness preceded my transition to William Carver's body.

"Yo, Grant Legate. Just the man I was hoping to see." The words sounded vaguely like every frat boy in existence from my college years.

"Mh?" I spun, looked down at myself, back up, and back down in confusion. Then my eyes traveled around the room. Finally, it dawned on me that this was not William Carver's body but my own.

This was the trial room, or Voice playground, or space between. I would figure out a neat name one day. "Oh. Here again."

"You're the Traveler who's taking care of my man Wild Willy." The voice was vaguely familiar.

"That's new." One eyebrow went up. I squinted into the blackness of this place, trying to pick out which Voice was talking.

"Leeroy?"

"In the flesh."

"Or not. I need a light."

"Oh. Right. Humans. Let there be light!" Leeroy—at least I thought it was Leeroy—shouted, and darkness receded.

The adjustment was interestingly painless. Sure enough, the giant hulk of a man with his broadsword stood nearby. Under him was the carcass of some great hairy beast.

"Are there races that can see in the dark?" I asked.

"Vampires. It's sweet if you're into the whole blood-sucking thing. Good fighters when they're not Travelers dressing up in drab clothes. There're two of them, and they constantly try to out whine each other. Can't wait 'til we get some more."

"Oh. There's a Voice for vampires?"

"There's a Voice for everything. We got one for Talking Mushrooms. But you mean Jean."

Maybe Leeroy was high on something. Maybe he was prone to mood swings. Maybe he really was a college frat boy. The way he talked about a woman so nonchalantly was amazing.

"Jean?"

Leeroy thumbed over his shoulder.

"You're not really mah type, sugar." Oh look, the woman with a robe of red flowing liquid. The first time I had seen her was with the spinning Jester.

I shuddered for a moment in expectation but was thankfully let down.

I pointed at the fading image of a pale-skinned brunette. "Vampire?"

"Of a sort." She smiled, waved, and faded out.

"Are all the women here so..."

"Intense? Negative." Leeroy shrugged. "Got personalities. Initia's got a mouth on her. I'd follow her anywhere. Greatest. Plot. Ever."

Leeroy didn't mean plot. Not with that twist in his tone. Giant hands going up in the air to clutch at his chest were also a giveaway.

"So. How can I help you, Leeroy?" My tone switched to full customer service mode. This wasn't a random interaction between people; this had the air of a business meeting. With a college-going meathead. There were worse clients.

"My man Wild Willy, you're doing good by him." He gave me an exaggerated thumbs-up and looked as though he was a step away from demanding a high five.

"I'm trying. It's been hard."

"No joke. Balance is a bitch. Got him all feebed."

Something swung into being behind Leeroy's head. A cross? No, something giant and wearing heels while stomping downward. That was the biggest leg I had ever seen. I flinched as it collided with the back of Leeroy's form.

"See! You're a total buzzkill! Now my man Grant Legate's seen it! I got a witness!" Leeroy was shaking his fist upward toward the sky. Thundering sounded in the distance.

"You too, Selena!"

I felt keeping my playful commentary to a minimum was good. James hadn't shown up to defend me, so he might be elsewhere. Plus none of this had really been directed toward me. I got the feeling Leeroy pissed off more people than he helped.

"Did you want to talk about William?"

After all, Leeroy had intercepted my log-in process. There had been no interruption during my last few returns to Continue, so being in this space between was rare.

"Yeah. Wild Willy."

"Yeah," I said.

"Anyway. Tonight, I guess you're doing this place, the whole Maze thing, right?"

"That's the plan."

"Good, good. Here's the deal. You go in there, you're in for a trip. The others and I"—Leeroy thumbed to the blackness behind him—"are doing what we can to make it epic. Failing epicosity, it'll catch my man Wild Willy right here." He thumped his chest and managed to look a bit sad.

"So he's still alive."

"Course he is. A few steps shy of being a vegetable, but he's in there with you." Leeroy's arm came across the gulf, impossibly large, and poked the side of my noggin. "That last heart attack turned him into a drooler."

I rubbed my head while mourning my health bar's dip. A single, half-hearted poke from this Voice had knocked off a quarter of my game life.

"I'll do my best."

"Good, man, good. It needs a human touch. We could play something out, but it wouldn't be the same. I—well, me and the others—we like what you're doing for us."

"Thanks." This was strangely like talking to former bosses. An entire catalog of thoughts going through my mind couldn't be said out loud.

"Anyway, tonight, if you get through the maze to the end, it'll be too much for those plebs you picked up." Leeroy frowned down at me. The man was too big compared to normal-sized folks.

"This place is that dangerous?"

"It's not meant for them. Not yet. This one's for Wild Willy. We put together something special-like. Pulled a few strings to make it work."

"Leeroy, don't give away too much. We need his actions to be as honest as possible." James appeared nearby with a slight frown.

I nodded and kept eye contact with Leeroy.

"That's fine. I was going to do my best anyway." Both my hands went up in a gentle stop motion.

"Don't be afraid in there, man. I know you're not like Wild Willy—he had the kind of stones that are rare in both worlds." Leeroy grasped his genitals with one hand and jiggled them around. "You're gonna have to reach down deep."

"Okay." Now I was really unsure. I was trying to stick to this WWCD mentality, learning inside and out how the man performed.

"Don't worry, Grant Legate. Everything will work out," James said from the side.

Next to Leeroy, the black man looked almost harmless. But I did remember that James had somehow gotten me tied up in webbing and chased by giant spiders.

"Our deal's still on, right? You'll tell me about her?" I asked.

"If things continue as they have been, yes. Of course, if you run away tonight, then that will be a failure."

I saw a box appear with new quest details. Now, instead of a progress bar, I simply had to make it to the end of this **[Maze of Midnight]**. There was no percentage. Failure had been modified to be all other actions.

"That's easier."

"Thanks for helping those kids, Mister Grant Legate."

"Maud? Oh." Right, Maud, Voice of Orphans and Separated Families. I hadn't even thought of what my actions did on that front. "Not a problem. They're good kids."

Even Phil, who constantly called me a geezer, seemed kindhearted under all that. Maybe a little jaded by his situation, but still striving to do a good job.

"Are you ready, Grant Legate?" James said as the other Voices faded into the background.

"Sure. Let's get the last act going."

James smiled as my dark room faded away. Moments later, I woke up in the body of William Carver. A small glowing lamp was off to one side and a quill in my hand.

"Mmmh."

It looked as though Carver had already been writing notes. Writing had been my exact plan for today's Carver adventure—at least pre-midnight. How did the machine know what grand scheme had been in my mind? I tilted my head to see an entire line of names. These people were from William Carver's past. More than one had showed up in my journals.

"Mmmh." I stood and groaned a bit. Eventually, my body made it over to the stack of journals in Carver's second room. They were not in the same spot I had left them.

"You little punk."

My **[Messenger's Pet]** had likely been goofing around with things in Carver's house. Much the same as it had in my ARC's Atrium.

Where was he anyway? I hadn't seen the little dragon for almost a day. James had mentioned the **[Messenger's Pet]** might stop hanging around if he got bored. Guess I was no longer entertaining.

Journal after journal went onto the table. Notes would be cross-referenced against the names on my list. I had thumbed through them more than once over the last few weeks of game time. Still, it wouldn't do for a man's final farewells to be hacked together with no feeling.

When the guards showed up an hour later to see if I needed help down to the beach, they were met with a grunt and wave good-bye. When Wyl himself showed up to report on the two players and check on me, I handed him a letter and waved him off. Even High Priestess Peach wanted to have her say regarding this last adventure nonsense. One of the priests had reported on what our group was up to. I gave her a letter and made her promise on Selena not to open it until tomorrow. Peach was concerned. Even William Carver's nearsighted eyes could make that out.

All of the remaining letters went to Phil. He snapped too smartly with an imitation salute picked up from the town guards. Old Man Carver's personality didn't lend itself to obvious amusement, so I kept everything under wraps. The farewells were in good hands, I thought. Whatever mail system this world had would get them out, and hopefully the Voices above would fill in the blanks.

I wrote one final note for the man himself. Wild Willy. Mister Carver. William "Old Man" Carver. These were in larger letters, slowly and carefully put together. Words that had brought me some measure of comfort when my fiancée passed three years ago.

There was a mirror in one room that I took nearly thirty minutes to unhook from the wall and drag to a table. It was nighttime now, two hours from midnight. Phil would be outside soon to pick me up for this final journey.

"Carver." I licked dry lips and stared into the reflective surface. "I don't know if you're in there. If you are, then I hope I've done right by you."

One finger scratched my scalp idly as the speech in my head fell apart.

"I'm not a very good hero. I've never fought even half the things you have."

Not in any game this immersing. Sure, I had clicked away monsters on computers decades ago. Those video game spiders paled in comparison to Continue Online's giant ones. I imagined a dragon to be much worse.

"I'm going to do my best to give you the ending you deserve. Who knows. Maybe when I get out of here, I can ask if you liked how things worked out back in reality."

I smiled at the sudden thought. Of course showing up out of the blue would be a little tacky. The Voices had said Carver was riding along somewhere, still alive. Trillium's Second Player helm would be perfect for allowing him to do such a thing. It even worked on a patient who was, as Leeroy had said, a "drooler."

"It's been something else. I've, uhh, never played a game like this. It's so real. And these people, even though they're AIs, they really, really, and I mean really, care for you." Even the Jester was respectful, and that was super extra neat.

"Anyway. I wanted to say something myself, that it's been an honor to be you, uhh, and also the weirdest thing I've ever done. But, I mean, I hope you've enjoyed the ride.

"Here. This- this, uhh, helped me." I blinked away the mopey mode my mind was rapidly declining into. Death had never been easy for me to be around, not since the train wreck.

These words were read aloud in case William Carver couldn't focus on them.

"'As a well-spent day brings happy sleep, so a life well-spent brings happy death.'" I let the silence settle for a moment.

"It's supposedly said by Leonardo Da Vinci." I shrugged.

Whomever Carver was in real life, he wasn't old enough to have met Leonardo probably—most likely. This game had my brain all twisted around.

"So, uhh, if half of your journals are true, if you're even half this driven in our world, I think you've spent your life well.

"So, once more unto the breach, right, Mister Carver?" I lifted the cane in a poor salute and tried to straighten this curved spine out a little.

Finally, the myriad of emotions coursing through me got to be too much. The cane lowered and out the door I went. Time to give this man one last adventure.

Maze Inspiration

Phil was off doing who knew what, so I was left to walk from Carver's house to the hedge maze entrance. All four players were gathered in the same spot as yesterday. Two were arguing about something that was too difficult for me to hear from this far back. As I got closer, it was easier to tell who the talkers were.

"That's what you're bringing?" the older female said.

"What? I like this cloak." Awesome Jr. was defending himself against HotPants's aggressive opinions.

"A cloak. Seriously?"

"Yeah, I can swoosh it around and catch weapons or something. It makes me harder to hit." He moved the cloak around, trying to give a good example.

"It makes you harder to look at," Shadow remarked.

I said nothing and marched up to our meeting spot. We were outside a row of bushes that lined the walkway. Yesterday's reconnaissance by the **[Messenger's Pet]** and me had shown it to be a basic maze for children. The kind of thing you found at county fairs.

"Are we ready?" My voice came out gruffer than normal.

"Sure am. My stealth and speed went up by leaps last night. That guard captain, Wyl, he's a genius," Shadow said.

"He's a computer."

"Yeah, how'd your near-death go?" Shadow questioned HotPants.

"Stupid wolves. Really, they were worse than my neighbor's dogs." Her hands tightly grasped the weapons at her side, both eyes narrowed and stared into the distance.

"Bet it felt good hitting them," the assassin responded.

"You shouldn't hit dogs." SweetPea was busy looking at her toes while muttering a defense.

"You tell me that kind of nonsense when they're snarling in your face. My heart must have skipped a few beats last night. At least in here I don't have to feel guilty about it."

HotPants seemed a little less angry today. Certainly she was far less arrogant in both mannerisms and speech. The whole thing with Awesome Jr.'s cloak was completely justified. It was an almost neon green that made my old eyebrow twitch in annoyance.

"You've all done what you needed?" I tried to rein in my pack of players. They had to have an attention disorder or they were approaching this thing too casually.

They glanced at each other. Shadow shrugged and nodded, followed quickly by the others agreeing.

"Good. In the center of this maze is a gateway. That gateway goes to the **[Maze of Midnight]**. We have less than two hours to make it through this maze." I, William Carver, couldn't afford to be casual.

"Wait, we have to go inside to find the door?" Shadow complained. "Damn. I'd hope the maze door was the actual door."

"It's not," I said.

"How do you know?" Awesome Jr. asked while swooshing his bright cloak around.

My shoulders went up in a shrug. I knew because the computer told me on a map. All the secrets of this town had been scribbled in location after location.

"Oh, it's okay, I got this." Shadow leapt on top of a bench and yanked his light frame up onto the hedges. One hand sat above his eyes to block out the streetlamp. He squinted into the distance.

"Come on, it's dark, but I can guide us from here."

"Hey, you're not just a stupid wannabe ninja," Awesome Jr. said happily.

Shadow glared but chose not to respond.

"At least he's not wearing a barf cloak." HotPants took the lead with her staff at the ready.

"Hey, at least I can cook rice. Sort of." Awesome Jr. had no problems defending himself verbally.

"Can you share the recipe?" SweetPea said.

I ignored them and followed after a bundle of washed reds. HotPants's armor jangled constantly. A guard that went up around her neck actually suited her—I thought it was called a gorget. It was new too, probably a reward from her patrol exercise.

"So a wolf nearly got you?" I was genuinely interested in how she'd fared against the creatures of this world. Being attacked by one in real life would make me flip out. Being attacked by an endless amount with blood and guts everywhere had to be worse.

"Sure. Those other guards were on point though. I was the one holding us back." She looked a little embarrassed but managed to power through with most of her arrogance intact. "I needed to get a feel for a real fight."

"Was it everything you'd hoped for?"

She nodded. "That, and more."

"Good. Some Travelers find it hard to adapt. I hear there's not as much violence on your side." I lived in the Americas. The last local war we had been part of involved a nasty merger between the United States and parts of Canada and Mexico.

"Depends on where you live. Or who you live with."

"Mh." I didn't pry. That sounded like a sore subject on many levels.

"What's it to you anyway? Nosy machine." HotPants glared at me from top to bottom before turning away in annoyance.

"Miss HotPants"—keeping my cool was a challenge—"who ever said I was a machine?"

"What? What does that mean?"

"Figure it out yourself. Consider it something to occupy your mind." Anything that would dislodge her current stream of misplaced anger was welcome. She'd improved overnight, but only a little.

"Left, then I think we can go straight from there. Hold on." Shadow jumped across one of the bushes to another one and looked fearful for a brief moment. Both hands were out as he balanced.

"You okay up there?" Awesome Jr. asked.

"Fine. My skill check passed." He muttered something else under his breath, but my old ears didn't catch it.

The others switched to a conversation regarding skills and their activation. I shrugged it all off. Carver's notes had outlined all sorts of things they were already talking about.

Shadow called out each turn for us: left, right, forward. I kept a fairly steady, if not eager, pace. Moving around was easier than earlier today. Carver had sat on his virtual behind all day long, and my activeness was paying off. We managed to avoid doubling back or hitting too many dead ends. Soon we were at the heart of the maze, and a stellar emptiness met us.

"What time is it?"

"Not midnight." Shadow hopped down and looked around.

"This spot here?" SweetPea was looking at a pattern on the ground. A series of spirals radiated outward from an almost perfect circle.

I, luckily, had a giant arrow visible that bobbed up and down in the air. This was similar to the one that had guided me to Old Man Carver's bench the first night. Stand here, player! My position was clear. We weren't too late. Everything from here was a matter of waiting.

"How long?"

"Dunno. This game doesn't have watches."

Keeping track of which player was speaking had proven difficult. The fuzziness of my hearing made me feel detached from the group. Hopefully they would think I was following along. Or they would keep talking over me as though NPCs didn't matter.

"Do the math. You've got your external timer, right?" HotPants was busy twirling the staff through some basic motions. Her actions were clearly steps above where she had been a few weeks ago at Peg's.

"You got any more of those bindings? The stuff you put on your hands?" Shadow asked.

"Sure." There was a shuffle as HotPants got something out of her inventory and threw it toward Shadow. "Here's a roll. You need help getting wrapped?"

"If you could show me."

"It's easier if someone else tightens it, at least for me. My skill isn't high enough yet." HotPants seemed pleased by Shadow's asking.

"Give it time."

"I've been patient this long," she muttered while wrapping some cloth around Shadow's hands. It looked like the same actions a boxer might do to ensure their knuckles didn't get too damaged.

"Good. Everything helps."

"How did your stuff go? You master making out yet?" Shadow needled the two lovebirds standing in the back.

Both Awesome Jr. and SweetPea went beet red. I could see their stammering actions from my peripheral vision. I was interested too but hadn't the heart to pick on them that much. Besides, I was trying to keep my head in the game.

"It's a surprise." SweetPea said.

"You did get something though?" HotPants asked.

SweetPea nodded with a smile. The normally shy girl looked kind of cute when she stopped hiding under that annoying hood. Awesome Jr. was probably onto something with his crush.

"Here it comes," I said.

In front of me, there was a swirl. Sparkles drifted down from above and landed on ledges unseen. Our surroundings had been dark but now were illuminated. More and more bright flakes fell downward like snow. A full minute passed while the doorway formed. Soon we had an entryway made of light.

"Awesome," Awesome Jr. said.

I was impressed too but had to remain somewhat stoic. After all, William Carver was a seasoned adventurer.

"Where does that go?"

"To the Maze," I answered.

"What should we do?"

"HotPants, would you go first?" SweetPea asked.

I ignored them all and walked forward. The light blinded me as I ventured through the passageway. Mixtures of purple and black interlaced among the brightest portions. The world swung sideways, and gravity released its hold on Carver's body. I felt a brief sensation of floating free from the world's tethers.

Then it was over and I was walking forward into another maze. This one was distinctly different than the one we had come out of moments ago. Hedges were inked with the same purple and black markings on their leaves. The branches were a muted white that bled at the edges into its other hues.

"Holy moly." Shadow came through first with a noise like someone jumping out of the way at high speeds.

"Jesus." HotPants was second through the gateway with a similar sound effect.

"This, this is worth the subscription cost. My god," Shadow said. "And the colors? I love this place."

Awesome Jr. and SweetPea came into the dungeon with their hands clasped together. Her eyes were closed tightly.

"It's awesome," Awesome Jr. said.

I managed to avoid replying with his tag line. This place was pretty neat.

"Ah, are you kidding me? We went from one maze into another?" HotPants had calmed down briefly, and this new knowledge only set her off again. Nothing seemed to satisfy her.

"It's called the Maze of Midnight," Shadow said and shrugged.

The players assigned roles. These hedges were too high for our assassin to leap upon. Shadow instead explored ahead a twist or turn in order to see where the easy dead ends were. HotPants was in the lead of our main group since she was the toughest one here, according to her stats. SweetPea was in charge of making a map in case this maze was more complicated than the one outside.

Their ideas all sounded fine. I had no real feedback. I hadn't done any sort of dungeon diving or video game in years.

My idea of exploration was to run around at high speeds, clicking stuff until a resolution appeared. William Carver and I were probably similar in that regard. Only he had done it for real.

"Come on." Shadow motioned.

Awesome Jr. had to be prodded frequently in order to keep up. He kept getting distracted by the plants and our surroundings. These passageways we wandered for many a twist and turn were much wider than the ones outside had been.

"Huh?"

"What?"

"I thought I saw someone," Shadow whispered with a finger to his lips.

"You think there are monsters in here?" SweetPea had closed the gap between herself and the others. and was peering around the corner. She would squint and turn her head around suddenly as if hearing something.

I, of course, could hear nothing, see very little, and only vaguely smelled what had to be jasmine or some other tea leaf. Absently, I picked leaves from one of the plants and chewed on them. Worst-case scenario, I blew us all up. Nope, just a faint taste of oranges.

"Mmh?" I raised an eyebrow and looked at one of the leaves. **[Identification]** provided a bit of information now that I'd separated everything.

Skill Used: [Identification]
Results: [Ish Plant] (Leaf)
Details: This is part of a larger bush. The leaf is said to taste different when still attached to the vine. No known negative side effects are attributed to this.

They were kind of tasty. I chewed on another one and tried not mourn my missing **[Messenger's Pet]**. He would probably like a nibble as well. There were other messages I had been disregarding as we made the first few turns within the maze.

> **Quest**: A Last Gasp (Part 2)
> **Difficulty**: Unknown
> **Details**: The continuing adventures of William (Old Man) Carver have led you into the **[Maze of Midnight]**.
> **Restrictions have been activated**:
> **Autopilot time will not impact completion**.
> **Failure**: Complete failure is impossible.
> **Success**: Possible information (Restricted)
> **Restrictions**: Death in the maze will be permanent for William (Old Man) Carver. Outside assistance cannot be summoned by William (Old Man) Carver.
> Not even for cupcakes.

Oh. Oh no. Permanent death of Old Man Carver if this failed? How? What? I twitched an eyebrow and read some of the other fine points. No more **[Messenger's Pet]** while in the **[Maze of Midnight]**? Not even for cupcakes? How mean! I guessed that explained where the tiny creature had gone. Probably back to that room of trials place to sulk and harass new players. It made me sad to think that he might end up following some other Ultimate Edition owner around.

"Whoa, fuck, incoming!" Shadow shouted before fading into a plant.

"Ehh?" I felt lost.

"Get back, Mister Carver!"

HotPants was standing with her staff out, eyeing our approaching enemy. There was a health bar available above a squirming mass of something.

"What is that?" one of the players shouted.

As if I had a clue. William Carver's game body could barely see anything.

"The arms! Watch the arms!" SweetPea was ducking while Awesome Jr. shouted out unnecessary advice.

HotPants didn't have time to give anyone else a glance. She was knocking away blurs of movement with one end of the staff then twisting and swinging back.

"Got it!" Shadow was hard to pick out among the plants. His color choice blended in well with the background, almost as well as the monster attacking us.

HotPants twisted and jabbed the staff. Shadow was trying to sway back out of the tentacles but got slashed around the face and arm. SweetPea was crouched down with both hands over her head.

"Incoming!" Awesome Jr. had something in his hand that was thrown and resulted in the fiery explosion of a Molotov cocktail.

The system showed the monster's red bar sliding downward toward the empty end. A final slash from the daring Shadow finished it off. HotPants gave the monster an extra kick. I had no clue what had happened. Not really. Being trapped in an old man's body made it hard to respond to anything with certainty. Actually seeing these creatures was tough. My group of players started chattering, and most of it was difficult to distinguish over the flames' dwindling roar.

"Anyone got details?"

"Camo?" Shadow posed a question.

"They blend right in with the maze walls."

"How did you block it?"

"Try tackling half a pack of wolves at night. It's the same," HotPants answered Awesome Jr.

"Okay. Damage?"

"Hefty, if you get hit. No blind spots that I saw. I tried to get a backstab and it failed," Shadow grumbled and picked up a tentacle. "This thing is all arms, no main body. No eyes."

"Is this entire place going to be like that?" SweetPea was downcast.

"Says the woman who cowered in a ball. Why are you even here if you can't look up?"

SweetPea didn't come to her own defense, but HotPants did by hitting Shadow with her staff and slicing off another ounce of his health. They growled back and forth a few times. I ignored it all. This new monster was less freaky than the giant spiders.

We hung out for a little bit, seeing what would happen to Shadow's health bar. Or they did. I looked down a corridor of our maze and wondered how many more were around. Was that swaying over there another one waiting for us to get into range?

"My health's not going up."

"Here's a potion," Awesome Jr. said behind me.

"How did you make these?" Shadow asked.

"Standard alchemy. It helps that I take chemistry outside the game."

"I'm impressed." HotPants looked at Awesome Jr. with a faint smile. He had proven useful.

"There are a few other things I want to try, but I won't have time if we're going to complete this."

"What did you do all night?" Shadow asked.

"Gathered crystals. I'll show you if you can tell me how you do that voice thing."

"The Batman?" HotPants added her own voice to the question.

"Yeah," Awesome Jr. confirmed.

"Try to talk differently long enough. The system will pick it up."

"That's awesome."

"Stop saying that or I'm going to hit you," HotPants growled.

We moved onward, down another few twists and turns. There were more of those strange monsters but only a few. I tried to help out with one but couldn't move fast enough. Plus this cane wasn't really a viable weapon.

SweetPea kept at the mapping. She also proved to be decent at detecting an ambush before Shadow noticed any monsters. Her bravery gene hadn't kicked in completely though. After the fourth monster, she stopped cowering in a ball. By the tenth, she managed to stand up while pulling her knitted hat downward.

"Screw this maze," she said.

"Yeah. I don't know if we'll get anywhere before we have to split. It's been what, two hours?" Awesome Jr. threw his hands up.

"You can't expect to simply breeze through these places. Otherwise, it'd be no fun," Shadow responded.

"What?" Awesome Jr. asked the younger girl. "Guys, hold up. SweetPea says there should be a room or something about here." His hands were up and motioning for the others to come in close.

"What?"

The other three hunched over the map. They twisted their necks almost in unison as SweetPea pointed out the gap in her paperwork. Apparently we had explored most of the outer edges of this maze. Somewhere near the middle was either a giant room or a miniature maze inside the bigger one.

"How do we get inside?"

Even my artificially faded eyesight could tell that none of the paths we'd traveled had a turn that would lead farther in. None to the north, south, east, or where we stood in the west. I twisted my lips and frowned.

"Probably a door. Or we're missing something." My eyes closed for a moment while I tried to remember where we had been so far.

"A secret door? In a beginner dungeon?" Shadow asked from over my shoulder. Having the younger man behind me was kind of unnerving.

I shrugged.

"Lord save me from fools." HotPants's hands twisted around the staff angrily. "We have to go around again. This time, everyone look harder."

The others nodded, and we started around a second time.

No doorways were obvious. I kept munching the sweet leaves while trying to see if any of Carver's skills included detection of hidden items. There had to be a key somewhere in the listing. Hadn't the Voices made this place for Carver? Yet Leeroy had spoken of the players I'd picked out. There was very likely a mix of our skills needed to make it through this customized dungeon.

"These things keep appearing. Haven't we been through here?" one of the players said.

They kept talking when I was lost in thought, and Carver's body made it hard to distinguish who was talking at the drop of a hat.

"They're respawning?" Awesome Jr. was looking up while counting on his fingers.

"I dunno. Where are the other bodies?" Shadow poked at the latest victim of their growing teamwork.

I would applaud the performance, but they were doing it all by their lonesome. Single monsters were posing no challenge.

"Why is it when they're dead, they change colors?" SweetPea asked.

"Why indeed," came my Carver-laden dry response. So far this entire place had held to the purple, black, white mishmash of colors. When the attacking creatures died, the floor turned green.

"I don't see why we can't hack through these bushes toward the center." HotPants had grown increasingly cross during our second lap.

"You can't even see past this row to the next one." Shadow had been eyeing the bushes for a long time as we walked. If there was an easy path through, he probably would have found it.

"So?" HotPants stuck her staff into the nearest bush.

A high-pitched screech drowned out whatever else was being said. Branches spun and waved as one, then another, and finally a third creature broke apart from the walls. They were moving too fast for me to focus on and use **[Identification]**. Saying it out loud would give away William Carver's player status.

"Oh Jesus, are all these walls full of them?" SweetPea ducked behind Awesome Jr. but managed to keep her hood up.

"There's too many!" HotPants hit two quickly to get their attention.

Awesome Jr. readied another flaming potion and gave it a toss toward the third.

"Anyone got crowd control?" Shadow shouted, stabbing one of HotPants's in the back with both daggers.

A flash of red slid off its health bar. His target turned and switched focus away from HotPants.

"Shit, shit, oh god." The would-be assassin was knocked flying into some more bushes. His head shook as he tried to stand back up.

"Don't bring more of them!"

"Careful with your fire!" SweetPea said while tugging on Awesome Jr.'s oversized cloak.

Awesome Jr. had a strangely maniacal look as he lit another potion.

There I stood like a lump with half a frown. If anyone had asked this old man, I could have clearly told them not to try to break down the walls. That wasn't being clever—that was cheating.

"Give her a swing, Grant Legate," someone whispered in my head.

None of the players were near me, so it must have been a Voice. I raised an eyebrow and felt a shifting of weight. Now I held a giant sword instead of the cane that normally supported my frame.

"Ah." I glanced at it briefly with **[Identification]**. This was a sword worthy of a legend that had killed a dragon by himself.

I lifted an arm. It was extremely light too. Or maybe the restrictions were gone. There was a buff to one side titled **[Heroic Surge of Strength]**.

Skill Used: [Heroic Surge of Strength]
Cost: Remaining Energy
Restriction: Can only be used once every hour
Details: William Carver can temporarily remove his **[Old Age]** limitations and bring his strength back to his youthful days!

Both eyes slowly blinked as I prepared myself to fight something for real in this game. This wasn't as easy for me as it might have been for William Carver. I didn't possess the leap-first-ask-questions-later mentality.

"Good Lord, there's more!"

"Watch your fucking fire!" HotPants yelled.

"You idiot, if we die in here, I'm going to camp your corpse!" Shadow snarled, but he was still in the fray.

HotPants was busy backing up while three of the creatures grew closer.

"I'm going to help!" one of the females yelled.

Opening my eyes revealed more trouble. Four of the monsters had started creeping up behind us. Their arms looked like blurs against the hedge maze's backdrop. Still, even with poor eyesight for normal situations, my ARC interface was kind enough to paint a very clear set of health bars.

I inched closer and readied the blade as Peg had "retaught" me. An ache in my shoulder threatened to make me dip the blade. I held on, trying to active Carver's [Stubborn as a Mule] trait. Messages flashed into being that seemed to indicate success.

The creatures got close enough for me to make out their writhing mass of purple-and-black tentacles. I swung the blade and felt powerful as their health bars shattered. My head tingled pleasantly, my arms already felt warm, and a smile was plastered on my old face. What a rush! No wonder Carver had been a warrior.

Two more in the front were still around. HotPants and Shadow were busy finishing off the latest wave. She swung her staff in an arc through the last mass. The sudden collision sent it flying into the nearly solid bushes. Shadow stepped in and gave it a final slice, and the creature's arms died down.

I huffed, feeling suddenly worn out. The blade shimmered out of existence. Soon I stood there taking the deepest breaths I could manage while bracing myself on the cane.

"Did you see that?" SweetPea asked Awesome Jr.

He turned around with a confused look and saw four dead monsters in addition to the five in front of us.

"You are broken," Awesome Jr. muttered.

"Stupid computer. If you were hiding that kind of ability, why even need us?"

"I bet it was an event attack. Look at how winded he is," Shadow stated. He busily inspected the corpses that lay about.

"You know I can hear you." My response was amazingly calm. Maybe the exhaustion of having no stamina was catching up.

"Oh. Yeah. Sorry." At least the young assassin apologized.

I shook my head and tried not to roll a tired set of eyes.

"You're right though. I don't think I can do that again anytime soon."

The stamina bar I had off to the side was down near critical. If we did anything more strenuous than stand here, I would need to be carried.

SweetPea was muttering to herself and seemed to be arguing with some sort of internal monologue. I was still reeling from the exertion of a single swing and raised an eyebrow.

She shook her head at my quizzical glance and instead pointed toward the ground under our dead assailants.

"There's that green again."

I gave it some thought.

"Back to basics."

"What?"

"It's something you should all keep in mind." This deserved my best imitation of Carver's grumpy but guiding tone. "When you get stuck or reach a dead end, go back to the beginning."

This strategy worked for dancing. It had worked for accounting during my prior career. It also worked when Hal Pal actually ran into odd problems out in the field. Start the whole process over and see what had changed.

"Think so?" Shadow mused.

"The entrance is this way." SweetPea had pulled out our map and tilted it around while muttering.

"Let's move. I don't want to spend all weekend in here." HotPants marched down the hallway.

William Carver's body didn't have much energy left after our second lap around, but I managed to keep a decent pace.

Turned out going back to the start was a good idea.

"Is that new?" Awesome Jr. was pointing at the ground.

There had only been dull purplish tiles an hour before. Now a stream of green had invaded, reaching out from our location toward the center of the labyrinth.

"Think killing those creatures has something to do with this?" HotPants asked.

"Look at the plants," Awesome Jr. said. "These are nothing like the others. Look here, and here." The goofy male was feeling leaves of different colors.

Green ground transformed the landscape into something a bit more normal. It felt as though the hallway where it was had grown smaller as well. This almost matched the first maze before the portal. Natural hedges came out of the ground and fought back the purple-and-black ones.

"That's weird."

"It's transforming. Like an infection, you think?" Awesome Jr. speculated while straddling a border between normal and dungeon bushes. His neon green cloak stood out far less among the natural greens.

"So we kill more?"

"Yeah. Probably. But look. Here, it's forming a path." Awesome Jr. pushed some of the bushes away and showed us how our current portion of the maze connected to another path a little ways over.

"This stuff is way easier to walk through. I can actually see the path on the other side."

"You think we can kill a bunch more?"

"No more packs like that last one though."

"Yeah, I don't think Carver can help us much."

"I guess we should rest. Even if he's a computer, he looks worn out."

These players were starting to piss me off, constantly talking about me as if I wasn't here. Though HotPants had almost sounded pleasant there.

"Please," SweetPea said.

We set up a small fire pit in the transformed portion. No one wanted to rest near the inky maze walls. Hips ached and groaned as I lowered this old frame to the ground. Sleepiness washed over the ARC's feedback in a simulation of William Carver's exhaustion.

Shadow and Awesome Jr. fought over the food. Finally, SweetPea managed to edge them both out of the way and make something. She was one of the few who'd directly asked me about cooking in-game. The others had gone down very different paths, and there was a clear difference between what they supplied with the same materials. I didn't want to give our meal of **[Rat Meat]** too much thought. Newbie players meant poorer food.

"This food's way better than the scraps my Master gives me," Shadow said while noisily chewing.

SweetPea didn't respond.

These guys were so chatty too. I had been subjected to a few players, especially those new to a virtual game like this, who gabbed about everything under the sun. One middle-aged woman had loaded into Continue with her husband. Both of them went straight for the beach and played around in the water until their health dropped to zero. They were confused upon resurrecting at the starting point. Both laughed themselves silly before moving on with their day. I would have asked them to join our quest, but they were rarely logged on. Most new players acted as if the game was more of a hobby. These four players actually played the game.

"We ready?" HotPants asked.

"I guess. How many of those things have we killed?"

"I don't know. Thirty or so?" Shadow responded to SweetPea.

"Look here." Awesome Jr. pushed the bushes out of the way completely and made a path between the maze's edges. "SweetPea, this spot on your map, should be right outside the unexplored area, right?"

"I think so." She nodded with a frown. Her finger trailed around the map, recounting curves and details. Then she nodded again.

"Then if this, I don't know, detoxification? If it keeps going, we'll open up the inner portion with a few more?" The boy was fairly quick.

"Sounds like a plan. Let's go."

Shadow interrupted the forming plan with both hands up in a stop motion. "How about you stay here, and I'll pull some of those monsters to us."

"Only a few at a time please," SweetPea said while standing behind Awesome Jr.

"Of course, I'm not some idiot who's going to try to light the place on fire." Shadow gave an unsubtle glare Awesome Jr.'s way.

I loved the idea of them fetching monsters. Shadow seemed smart enough to navigate most of the easy turns. Moments later, he brought another two to our doorstep. HotPants and Shadow finished them off fairly quickly. Awesome Jr. had sat down with a depressed look on his face and seemed to be concocting something. SweetPea was staring wide-eyed at the two doing most of the actual fighting.

Old man deaf ears heard no real dissension. There were brief pauses when it seemed as though HotPants and Shadow were communicating silently. I hadn't experienced any sort of secret whisper method in this game like others had. If the theory held true, there should be a method, however. Were they trying to oust the other two? Hopefully not.

"Those explosives of yours are useful," I said to Awesome Jr. "Do you have any other mixtures?"

"I guess. I've been trying to find a freeze blast of some sort. All I've got is one that drops goo on the ground."

SweetPea twisted up her face. "It's gross."

"There might be a use for it." I stood peering over his shoulder. A little closer and I would actually be able to see what he was doing with some clarity.

"Glad you think so. I spent all my money on these vials at noon, spent another six hours testing things out. Then I had to pay Miss Robuls for her highest-proof alcohol in order to have something."

"The night in the cave didn't go well?" I'd thought he would have learned something magical from the game by the end of the night.

"Not as well for me as it did for Melissa. I mean, SweetPea. She won't tell me what happened, but when I try to use the skill I got, she lights up like a beacon."

"You sure that's not the infatuation speaking?" Now that we had a moment of down-time, I felt comfortable poking a bit of fun the youngster's way. He reminded me a lot of myself at that age, though chemistry had never been my forte.

Awesome Jr. flushed and looked over at the girl. She was drawing lines of chalk on the ground, measuring who knew what.

"No, it's not that," he said.

The other two kept right on pulling single creatures down the lane and killing them. We were lucky that this cleared area seemed safe enough. My stamina was back to nearly full, so I could probably pull another one of those blade swings out of nowhere if things got dire. After I figured out how this cane transformed.

"How do you do it, Mister Carver? Everyone looks up to you. You're a hero," Awesome Jr. was speaking, still while staring at the girl of his dreams.

They may have grown closer in the last two days, but I could detect his worry. Those days felt familiar—the worry about if I was lacking compared to all the other guys out there.

"I don't know how to be a hero." Not like William Carver did. "I don't know how to be a villain. I only know that there are things in this world I must do."

Awesome Jr. chewed on the inside of his lip for a moment, both hands frozen in the air with two test tubes of swirling colors. Then he shook his head again, seeming to banish the fuzzy-headed thoughts.

"That reminds me of a poem. 'Invictus.' He said, 'It matters not how strait the gate, how charged with punishments the scroll, I am the master of my fate, I am the captain of my soul.'"

"Good kid. You know your stuff," the older female said. HotPants was huffing while holding her staff.

Shadow looked worn out behind her. A pile of dead ink monsters littered the ground. Emeralds and other greens bled across the landscape to slowly meld with our safe zone.

"Yeah. We studied Mandela in history. It came up twice, along with another passage," Awesome Jr. responded.

"Yeah? Anything good?"

"Yeah. Wait, hold on. I'll grab it. I think you'll like this one, Mister Carver." Awesome Jr.'s form turned into a dull, lifeless version. His hands went back to mechanically mixing potions as he tried not to sneak sidelong glances at SweetPea. Autopilot was not flattering on the teen.

Clearly the machine AIs that ran Continue knew exactly what kind of personality Awesome Jr. had. I would love to see his autopilot get caught stalking SweetPea. The Event message from that would be hilarious. Awesome Jr.'s object of affection was completely oblivious.

SweetPea was jumping up and down for joy. Hair flew everywhere as her skinny body danced around.

"We did it!"

"Oh yeah? You mean *we* did it," Shadow said. "You two sat there."

"Hey, you leave the kid with the bundle of explosives alone. We'll probably need them." HotPants was completely onboard with Awesome Jr.'s mixtures. "The robot here can probably only do that whatever-he-did a few more times, and I'm not going to wipe in this dungeon."

"Wipe?" SweetPea stopped her happy dance and tilted her head.

"It's where we all die and fail," Shadow said. "And I have no plans to die."

"No one plans to," I muttered, sinking into my sad mood once more. Maybe I should invest in some anti-depression medications. They'd helped last year during my second relapse.

"Here. I wrote it into my journal," Awesome Jr. said when he came back.

"What did you write down?" HotPants asked.

"It's another quote. This one's not a poem. It's from Theodore Roosevelt."

"Come on, walk and gab." HotPants recovered enough to start pushing bushes out of the way. She huffed and pulled out a much smaller dagger. Slowly she sawed at branches to clear a solid path that any of us could walk through.

"'It is not the critic who counts; not the man who points out how the strong man stumbles, or where the doer of deeds could have done them better.'"

"Sounds like someone I know." Shadow gave his snark-filled opinion, obviously about the work he was doing to kill our invading monsters.

Awesome Jr. flipped off the would-be ninja.

"This isn't about you, this is about Mister Carver."

"Keep going." I motioned.

"Right." He took a breath and tried not to look embarrassed.

I had forgotten what being a teenager was like. For me, everything had been steps away from an ego-crushing event.

"'The credit belongs to the man who is actually in the arena, whose face is marred by dust and sweat and blood. Who strives valiantly.'" Awesome Jr. was emphasizing many of the words, as if trying to give the great speech himself.

It was impressive to me. Even HotPants seemed appreciative and halted her hacking of bushes.

"'Who errs, who comes short again and again, because there is no effort without error and shortcoming. But who does actually strive to do the deeds. Who knows great enthusiasms.'"

"Sounds pretty wordy to me," Shadow blurted.

HotPants punched the young assassin and gave him the blade. He grumbled and started sawing away at the cleansed plants.

"Shut up, Shadow. Keep going, Awesome."

"Awesome's my father," Awesome Jr. absently mumbled while gazing at SweetPea. His head shook, and he consulted whatever notes his ARC displayed. A moment later, and he recited the remaining passage.

"'Who knows great enthusiasms, the great devotions. Who spends himself in a worthy cause. Who at the best knows in the end the triumph of high achievement, and who at the worst, if he fails, at least fails while daring greatly. So that his place shall never be with those cold and timid souls who neither know victory nor defeat.'"

Mere moments after finishing his quotation, a box flickered into existence on his screen. I gave a smile. The machine had rather enjoyed his touching rendition. It might have been the effect of Awesome Jr.'s new skill or it might have been the fact that we'd ventured into a new room, but I felt better than ever.

A wave of energy washed over me, reducing the wear and tear that plagued William Carver's computer body. My hand gripped the cane eagerly, and I could almost feel the hilt of a blade shifting beneath my fingers. It would only take a moment of intent to transform this walking stick into its outrageously giant form.

"So there you have it," he said.

"You keep reading your history." HotPants looked the happiest she had ever been. "Some of those presidents, they may have screwed up as much as they fixed, but they knew how to give a speech."

"Anyway. I figure you'd like this one, Mister Carver. The people in town, they tell stories about your adventures. The people in the tavern practically tell your top ten greatest stories every night," Awesome Jr. said.

"God help me, Peg wouldn't shut up about you. She was so excited to see you getting back in the field. Drove me batty." HotPants still had a lingering bit of cheer, but her memories of Peg must not have been positive.

"I guess that's true. Even my master respects your journeys," Shadow piped in.

"Anyway. You've been the man in the arena. I don't know about the others, but I've never done much of anything with my life." Awesome Jr. sighed. "So this has been—is like serving next to a legend."

"Mh." This was embarrassing. I was being praised by players for the work of another user that I was only pretending to be. Awkward.

"Well." I thought about what Leeroy had said. The last boss in here was unlikely to be anything these plebs—his word, not mine—could handle. "You'll have your own story to share by the end of this."

"Why did you pick us, Mister Carver? You could have taken any number of fighters from the town. We're nothing, even if we're Travelers."

"I'll answer your question with one of my own." I grumbled and got back into my role as Carver. My cane banged against the ground. This was a really good chance to execute my Carverisms. There was no progress bar anymore, but that didn't mean I should break character.

"What do you want from this world? Why did you come here?"

That was a question I had posed to these players before.

Shadow was the first to respond. "Fame."

"Adventure." Awesome Jr. was looking at SweetPea when he responded.

She pulled down her hood and didn't have a response.

"I just want to hit things," HotPants said. "A lot." Her faded red clothes seemed to stand out even more among all the greens and blues in our landscape.

"Whatever it is you want, whatever you feel your world is lacking, you can find it here," I said.

"And you, Mister Carver? What do you want?" SweetPea asked.

I wanted one thing for myself. One item honestly and deeply. I wanted the hurting over my deceased fiancée to stop. James had given me this chance as both a distraction and a lure. But Carver wanted something else entirely. Giving my answer would be invalid and cheapen this whole event.

"Me?" I hummed a bit and banged the cane once more. I knew what Carver would want. But saying it out loud and not sounding goofy was another matter.

"Yes, Mister Carver. What do you want?" SweetPea asked again.

In my four weeks, she was the first player to actually turn the question around. SweetPea, my first Traveler.

"You say the people tell stories about me?"

Awesome Jr. nodded.

"Well, no one tells them to my face. They let me sit on the bench day in and out because they think I'm done with it all."

What had the journals outlined? Vague recollections of various adventures passed through my mind. I had scanned them all recently, looking for details of William Carver's past life in order to send out farewells.

"I've slain many different monsters in defense of those who needed it. I've been across the oceans and battled on the high seas. I've chased a creature born of flame and nightmare across the swamps only to tame the beast." Carver's form gave an involuntary cough, and my chest started to hurt.

"Treasures, women, I did all this in order to train myself for the greatest adventure I thought one could have." The pain slowly faded and came under control after another cough.

"The dragon?" Awesome Jr. asked with hugely excited eyes.

"That very one." And I was unsure how that journey had gone. The mystery of its absence was a puzzle for another day. I applied all my WWCD instincts toward the end of my speech.

"I reached my summit and knew that there was still so much more to be done for this world. So much that I could never hope to accomplish alone."

"Is that—"

SweetPea shoved a hand over Awesome Jr.'s mouth and nodded at me to keep going.

"I became a guide to new Travelers. Not because these old bones wanted to rest." The faintest sensation of pain had started to wash through my body. It was like the edge of a heart attack coming on.

"Not because I'd grown weary of raising my sword, but because the torch must be passed. Every Traveler I send on their way is another legend in the making." HotPants looked misty-eyed as I spoke. "But I'm too hard headed to die without one last adventure of my own."

I swear to the Voices above that if there had been a progress bar still, it would have shot right through the roof. My WWCD had fired to its maximum. Validation was further received from a giant notice that appeared in front of all four players. Beyond super neat. The message wasn't visible from my angle, but it was likely some sort of system pop-up about William Carver's legacy. Or a quest change.

"Jesus. I'm going to start crying over here." HotPants looked as though she meant it. Strange, I would have expected SweetPea to crack first.

"This is..."

"Awesome, yeah, we get it."

"Awesome's my father."

HotPants weakly gave Awesome Jr. a whack over the head for repeating his catchphrase again. I kept my smile inside and let the players do what they would. Next to us, a path to the maze's center lay open. Inside would contain challenges for us all. Most especially for me. Carver's last adventure was close.

Here was hoping the old man enjoyed the ride. What had I said to him in the mirror? Once more unto the breach, dear friends, once more.

Session Seventeen
"Leeroy"

Clearing the monsters proved to be the right choice. Bushes had returned to normal all around us and were far less cranky about being cut down. In the distance, ink-riddled colors swam and waved to an unseen breeze.

"Careful. I think there're more of those things out there," one of the players said.

"A lot more." SweetPea was huddled near the back again.

HotPants stood guard while Shadow used both knives to cut away a path.

"Okay, I declare these hedges trimmed. HotPants, you're first," Awesome Jr. said.

"All right." She tilted her staff and squeezed into the narrow path we'd cleared out.

I followed, being the old man in need of an escort.

Inside was nothing close to what a maze should have.

Were those people lining the outer edge of a giant square? Not standard individuals but weird ghostly outlines. I squinted old eyes and looked into the distance. A small army of people was standing around. Each of them was female. Even my poor vision couldn't disguise some of those curves. They became less ghostly and more real the longer we stood there watching.

Oh no.

"What's this?" Shadow asked.

"Memory lane," I answered while trying not to feel my gut drop. Being praised for another man's actions was bad enough. This would be far more awkward. Carver may have been a brave warrior, but he was also a "love 'em and leave 'em" type. This whole setup was a gallery of ex-lovers.

"Is that music?" SweetPea asked as a series of string instruments filled the air.

"Are those all women?" Awesome Jr. had focused on the important prospects in front of him.

SweetPea and he were almost a couple, but a varying amount of flesh was on display. Teenage males were notorious for being confused in these situations. Nearsightedness saved me from the same mistake.

"William. Did you think you could sneak off and leave without so much as a good-bye?" That sweet voice stood out among all the others I had heard. Carver's personally most compromised Priestess.

"High Priestess."

"After all these years, and all we've been through, you can't call me Peach?"

"She's named Peach?" Awesome Jr. seemed more concerned with the cut of Peach's dress than anything else.

"She's a High Priestess for Selena. Up on the cliff over town," HotPants muttered. "Not my style of Voice, but still, she's done good."

"Yes, I am Peach, and yes, young Traveler, that is music," she answered the questions with her falsely sweet words.

"How are you here?" I asked.

"I'm not, not really. None of us are." Priestess Peach gestured to the area around her. "To us, this is a dream granted to us by the Voices. I thank Selena for this."

"I'm sorry, Peach." My words tasted bitter. Peach had been among the few I'd ignored over the course of this last day. She seemed genuinely fond of the old man, and I'd discarded all that in my rush of letters. Her note had been poorly written for such a serious acquaintance.

"As if I'd let you escape without at least trying to gain your pledge," Peach responded.

"How about one last dance?" I questioned, putting a few things together.

"I guess that will have to do." She smiled, and though her pitch and tone were a practiced facade, everything else she was looked pleased.

"Are you sure? My hips aren't what they used to be you know." I tried to joke with her. Priestess Peach had been one of the first to point out Old Man Carver's shortcomings.

"For this, I think the Voices can shed some forgiveness."

"What are we supposta to do, Priestess?" Shadow asked.

"You do whatever it is you Travelers do." She waved them off. To her, none of this was real. Why should she care what happened to other people in a dream?

"Huh?"

Priestess Peach was proof positive that computers were not required to care about human beings. I said a fervent prayer to our future overlords in hopes there would be room in the metal polishing market. Or maybe I could move up to the hills where the Internet was still a myth.

"Come on, William." Priestess Peach put out a hand, waiting for me.

I reached out and felt a pleasant energy wash from head to toe.

"Ehh." Moving felt a bit easier again. My joints became a bit more limber. Behind me, I heard the others exclaim in surprise about something. My hearing hadn't improved with everything else.

Gift Received: [Age Reduction]

Description: Each successful dance and wave of **[Ink Nightmares]** will reduce William Carver's age. Statistics lost as a result of **[Old Age]** will be returned for the duration of this gift. This gift is temporary.

A small box displayed information for me that was thankfully useful. I couldn't be expected to cut a rug as an old man, not one who spent too much time being sedentary. The music was a slow, general theme. We were both lucky in how well this challenge fit my own personal skills. William Carver had no dance traits or abilities that I had ever seen. This was pure me in his body.

And High Priestess Peach felt almost sinful. If my body had been that of a much younger man, I might have reacted quite differently. As it was, we turned in time to the beat. Our dance was a slow spin that still managed to lift her dress a tiny amount. Were I able to go faster, the other players might get a glimpse of her birthmark.

The song went on, and with each step, I felt a little better, a little straighter, and the ache in my shoulder wasn't as sharp. Our dance ended with a bow and another woman stepped up from the audience.

"Good-bye, you old goat," Priestess Peach said with a single tear. "Good-bye."

She faded away, leaving me facing a new partner who looked a little hurt.

"Where are my manners?" I tried to turn on all of Carver's lady-killing charm. "May I have this dance?"

"My wild man, I've been waiting for this dance for years." This woman looked familiar from Carver's sometimes extremely vivid descriptions.

Each woman was familiar in some form or another. In the background over each woman's shoulder, there were visible signs of a struggle. The players were busy fending off waves of other creatures like the ones from outside the maze, only smaller and more numerous. Probably the [Ink Nightmare]s mentioned in my gift description.

Screaming was muted by the sound of music and each partner's movements. They followed better than Maud had, likely assisted by the machine. My brain couldn't wrap itself around each one of these NPCs practicing dancing, just waiting for Carver to kick the bucket. In their minds, this was all a dream. Which answered one of the age-old questions—do robots dream? They do indeed—of Old Man Carver sweeping them across the dance floor.

I chuckled as partners exchanged again. Moving had grown far easier. My eyesight had recently approached real-world clarity. Each dance partner was further and further along Carver's time line here in Continue.

Another, and another, until finally I was standing with an elf of some sort. She was rather good-looking. Her neck was long and shoulders slender. There was a litheness to her form that indicated a ballet dancer. It was easy to see why William Carver might have done any mission she ever requested.

"Is it almost over?" HotPants's yelling had grown far clearer now.

"I think so. This is the last one!"

"Hold on a little longer!" SweetPea was busy pressing her hands over a wounded Shadow. He lay gasping for breath off to one side of the dance floor.

"You heard the lady—one last dance," I said softly to the elf.

No amount of time reversals could bring Carver back to perfect. He'd started this game physically worn out and kept right on going. Regardless, my back was much better. Only now did I truly appreciate the kind of stones he had. He played a game where everything felt almost too real and risked it all to achieve his dream here in a fantasy world.

"And here we are, back to your first in our world." My nameless elven partner smiled as we moved across the floor. She was a bit more talkative than the others had been.

"I remember." I didn't, but William had.

"You know, if you'd danced as well back then as you do now, I might never have let you leave."

"I had adventures to go on." William Carver did. Who could say what I myself might have done?

"I waited, you know. I'm still waiting." She was sad.

The other ladies had all worn different expressions. Some were full of joy; others were nearly possessive. Two went so far as to give Carver a firm smack on the ass, which meant I bore their aggressive tactics in his stead.

"I don't think I'll ever make it back."

"I knew you never would." She sighed, and it felt as if the wind moved through us softly. "You were the first Traveler I'd ever seen you know."

I took her hand and stepped into a dance. The music sounded a bit more aggressive, and I treated the motions as such, confident that the machine could keep up. Her commentary was difficult to respond to. This elf, a woman whose name I'd never learned from Carver's journals, knew he wasn't a Local.

"I'm sorry."

Our steps were wide movements, bringing us from one end of the labyrinth's dance hall to the other. Walls of inky purple had grown to nearly nothing over the course of many partners.

"Hold it!"

"SweetPea, tell me you got more of those heals!"

"Yes!"

"Get HotPants back together."

There was a crash of flame off to the side that had grown much more obvious as my avatar in the game improved. My eyesight could see where streams of tiny creatures had fallen. The players were torn, blood dripping everywhere. Horror crossed my face as I realized that they were in trouble while I had been enjoying a myriad of beautiful women. Not only trouble—they were getting beat senseless.

"Thank you, Grant, for giving me one last moment with him."

Her commentary was enough to be the final straw on my fragmented attention. My well-practiced steps completely fell apart.

I twisted a foot and lost myself. The cane, which had somehow been tucked into a rope of my clothing, fell loose with a clatter. From the ground, I turned and looked at the woman who had used my real name, both worried and hopeful that I might see my deceased fiancée. No such luck. She was a slender thing with none of the same facial features.

"Good-bye, William. May whatever passes for Voices in your world be kind in their judgments."

Then she too faded away.

"It's done!" one of the players shouted.

"They've stopped spawning!" SweetPea was really into it now. No longer did she hide. In fact, she was fiercely participating in the fight now.

Awesome Jr. was cradling an arm and eying a pile of dead monsters. Glass was everywhere and parts of bushes were on fire.

"Melissa, use whatever you've got left to heal the others." Awesome Jr. was huffing and waved SweetPea off to the other players.

I watched all of this while confusion racked my mind. The ground looked far more normal. Above us, a hint of dawn pushed back the inky darkness. The ground started to rumble.

"Oh, good god." HotPants was trying to push herself back up with the staff.

SweetPea's hands glowed with a faint blue over HotPants's back and sent some lights spiraling into her back.

"I don't know how much I have left…"

"It's okay, I think. Carver's done." Awesome Jr. was rubbing SweetPea's back, trying to reassure her.

"Jesus wept. Look at him," HotPants said. "That's not the same guy. Robot. Not the same robot."

"No, he's not."

I looked down and took stock of the differences. Not only was the robe I had come to love completely gone, but I was wearing some sort of scale mail. Heavy, but this armor was flexible enough to move around in.

One hand went for the cane out of habit, and I managed to get both feet under me. Nearby, the flashing inky colors that lingered about **[Maze of Midnight]** shuddered. Suddenly blacks, purples, and blues dripped off the plants and crawled toward the dance floor. My band-filled background was gone. If I were a betting man, this event called for some epic boss music. Sure enough, almost in time with my standing, the inks swarmed together, forming a larger mass.

"Voices have mercy," I swore.

More vein-like collections of ink poured in from around us. Globs reached up toward the sky, stacking on top of each other and forming a giant creature. Almost as though it was pulling up from the depths of some artist's nightmare. First a giant leg, then a forearm. The shape looked dreadfully familiar.

"Is that…?" Awesome Jr. asked.

"Oh no. No, no, no. I'm not nearly strong enough for that. I want to hit stuff, not be pummeled senselessly. I don't need that in here."

"It's not a real one," Shadow protested with a hint of doubt in his tone.

The cane was a giant sword again, the tip much easier to keep up with Carver's improved grip. Behind me, the other players were gathering in a huddle. Whispers went back and forth about what to do next. Meanwhile, our enemy grew even bigger, taller, thicker until we faced a creature that took up a huge chunk of the room.

"That's a nope."

"Complete nope," SweetPea agreed. "So gross."

SweetPea was dead-on with her assessment. We weren't looking at a normal dragon-shaped creature. This had no wings on its back. Littered all over the claws, shoulders, spine, and down to the tail's tip were little tentacles. Like the monsters we had been fighting before.

"What do we do?" HotPants whispered a very good question.

"The door behind us is closed," SweetPea said with a note of panic.

There was only one thing to do. Only one choice William Carver would make. I readied the blade to my side, took the stance Peg had trained me in, then pulled up every ounce of foolish courage available. A welling of energy rushed up my arms and to the top of my head. A mad sort of grin lifted my ears.

"LEEERRROOOYYYYYYYYYYY!" The sheer silliness of my battle cry counteracted my terror. That, and the giant sword—something about it was a great equalizer.

I got in one good swing, slashing across the giant monstrosity's leg. A tail came, and my arm automatically moved to use the flat edge of the sword for a block. There was enough time for a prayer of thanks to the Voices above for giving me an assist. Carver's skills, not mine, would carry the majority of this fight.

"If he's going, I'm going." Shadow was much easier to hear now that I wasn't completely enfeebled by virtual old age.

"Right," Awesome Jr. agreed. "It's only a game…"

I got another good swipe in before a giant paw came down from above to crush me. This one was slow enough that I could move out of the way. If dance had taught me one thing, it was how to get across space in one or two easy steps.

Grasping tentacles reached out of the giant leg and clawed at the parts of me that were too close. Health points shaved off in bits. I stepped farther back and swung the lightened blade. Where my sword passed, globs of inky monsters came apart.

"Carver!" a player cried.

"Old Man!"

"To hell with this. If he can do it, I can." HotPants charged in from the side of his right leg and gave a stab.

"Ugh!" Her staff sank into the monstrous forearm and refused to come out.

"HotPants!" Awesome Jr. hadn't hesitated in lighting up one of his flasks. "I've only got three more!"

"Make them count!"

"Aim for the head!" Shadow yelled.

I dodged another blow from the tail and rolled away. Pain waved through my shoulder, and a computer assist allowed me to keep a grip on the sword somehow. Heat flashed as two more imitation Molotovs lit up. One got the monster's shoulder, resulting in a giant shriek of anger. Noise far deeper than the ones outside rippled through the maze's inner sanctum.

"Carver!"

I turned and looked as the second ball of fire went off. This one completely missed the creature due to his sudden withdrawal.

"What?" I shouted.

"Look out!" SweetPea cried, her voice turning into a high pitched whine.

Oh. The creature's tail swept in again and caught me full-on in the middle. Part of the blade was up in a block, but not enough to resolve the collision. I went flying into a wall of bushes. These bordered between the cleansed green and inky taint.

"SweetPea!"

"What?"

"Don't distract the NPC!" Shadow yelled while stomping at the latest pile of little tentacle monsters to come out of the big creature.

"But I was helping!" She wasn't really.

"Shut up and kill the little ones before they crawl back!" HotPants screamed. She was busy trying to sweep a pile of them away with her staff. "The little ones keep giving that big guy health!"

"We know!" Awesome Jr. was yelling too.

Everyone was. Their bodies damaged and run-down. I could see the pop-up boxes forming off to the side of each person's screen. They were receiving increases to abilities as each one practiced with their virtual lives on the line.

I growled and tried to stand back up. The sword slipped and I lost my progress. Another whack from one giant forearm sent me sprawling a second time. The world rung and Carver's vision took a turn for the worse.

"Come on." This time, I pushed through all the protests and got back to my feet.

A third crash of flames poured against the boss monster's arm and set it shrieking.

Carver's fancy blade swung. Light formed on the top, along with a notification of various abilities colliding together in some super move. I had no time to read the system text as I tightened my face and pulled with all the simulated strength Carver had. My unintended move connected and severed the already burning leg.

"Get them!" Shadow yelled again.

"I'm out of fire potions!"

"Figure out something useful then!"

Shadow and Awesome Jr. seemed destined to babble at each other. The creature fell off balance with another roar, which stunned us completely. Their continued argument was muffled in the ringing that followed the creature's shout.

[Stunned]! Abilities requiring focus suffer a 50% penalty.

"No. Not yet." My arm wiggled but failed to move correctly. Only four weeks of clutching a cane kept my hand's grip strong.

HotPants couldn't swing her staff, but she did manage to fall to one side and squish a few of the small scattered enemies. If she could do that much, then William Carver should be at least twice as stubborn.

"Come on." It was becoming a mantra as I fought to stand.

> **[Stubborn as a Mule]** activated! Stun effects reduced.
> **Abilities requiring focus suffer a 20% penalty.**

"Come on!"

Twenty percent was still too much. I had to get myself back into the fight in order to protect the others. They were having a hard time against little ones.

I stomped a foot against the ground as hard as possible. Jarring shock rippled up the leg, spine, and to the top of my head. Double vision pieced back together in time to hear a second scream that repeated the effects of the first.

> **[Stunned]! Abilities requiring focus suffer a 50%**
> **penalty.**

"Double stuns?!" Awesome Jr. groaned and fell to his knees amid a series of broken enemies. Their arms still twitched even though their health bars were empty.

> **[Stubborn as a Mule]** activated! Stun effects reduced.
> **Abilities requiring focus suffer a 40% penalty.**

The giant creature strode across the room. One formerly severed arm half-formed in a skeletal mockery of itself. There were no eyes to speak of on the creature, but its jaw was grinning as damaged limbs stumbled forth.

"Ru-u-un!" SweetPea stuttered.

Carver did. Not. Run. No matter how caring these teenagers' warnings were, I would stand my ground. I would swing this sword over and over until I had nothing left.

I took another claw to the body. The pain sent me flying far enough that I had time to wonder what a bear's attack would feel like. Likely very similar, with more mass and strength over the small tears of these tentacle creatures. Bearing the brunt of a third attack brought my already fading health bar down to twenty percent.

Blood was everywhere. Vision blurred by streams of sweat. The sword was still in my hand. I had mere seconds to get back to my feet before the creature would attack again. Another one of those hits would maim me. Maim Carver. Whatever.

One knee was up. The leg didn't have enough strength to force me to stand. Both hands were gripped around the giant sword's handle.

I glared at the creature in my best old man defiance.

"I will not die lying down."

Carver would not die lazing about. He would stand and fight. He would stand and swing, and swing, and swing.

I, however, slipped and fell. The one knee I had propped up lost purchase and left me hanging on by the edge of Carver's sword. At least there was still that minor dignity.

A weight pressed on my shoulder and hissed. Then it spat a small ball of fire. I had enough awareness to glance to the side. My small **[Messenger's Pet]** was spitting defiance at the larger creature. The sheer audacity of my situation must have set the boss monster back, because it growled and roared.

> **[Stunned]! Abilities requiring focus suffer a 50% penalty.**

"Oh god. We're all screwed." Shadow was pressed against the ground, one eye tilted up and seeing the giant creature towering over the lot of us.

The boss was smaller than before, having lost some mass to the destruction of its wriggling bits.

I tried to stand again. Both hands pulled with frail strength upon the sword's hilt. The blade dug into the tile and ground below in response. A horrifyingly giant mass of squiggles descended in my direction but I couldn't let this kill me. A pitiful death would invalidate my attempt to give Carver a stellar ending.

"His health. It keeps going down."

I winced and realized that the wounds all over my body had applied a bleed of some sort. My fifth of health was down to ten percent. That wasn't fair. This was not the way things should end. I would not die on the ground. I would stand on my feet. I would go out like Carver wanted.

SweetPea reached out with one hand to try to heal me. Her battered form stretched across the ground, a torn look on her features. I had enough strength to look around and weakly smile at the lot of them. They were only here on this fool's errand because of me. Me and this brilliant idea to take Carver into a dungeon. My **[Messenger's Pet]** was still spitting tiny balls of fire. They were minuscule before the bigger monster, but enough to make it flinch at times as chunks sizzled.

Brief moments of respite allowed me to struggle back to my feet. Everything felt worse than it had. My strength from the dances had faded. The sword in my hands had turned back into a cane. Both knees locked into position in order to keep me upright. Pain flared between my shoulders as everything hunched again. There, like my first day as William Carver, I stood. Putting on an air of pride.

We, Carver and I, would die on our feet. By all the Voices Continue had to offer, by all the mental willpower available to me, I would grace him with that at least.

But I might close my eyes, if only a little.

There was another roar from the boss. As if my debilitation could get any worse. Another wave rippled through, followed by a giant stomp. Another giant footstep came through, and a sixth roar.

This time, a much louder, much angrier cry answered the boss. From above and behind, somewhere in the distance, came a loud scream that sounded more like thunder than a giant lion. I opened one eye a little and saw my nearly empty health bar. A cough full of blood sputtered out of my old form.

The other eye opened, and my vision swam into focus. Something new collided at high speeds with the boss monster. A shock wave rippled as the two connected. I pulled together what little willpower was left. **[Identification]** triggered on the newest creature.

Failure abounded. Repetitive stuns had made pretty much any skill usage impossible. I had a hunch, given the sleek azure skin and thinned look. A female, I thought. That shade matching her scales lined up with the scarf of a certain orphanage caretaker. It also matched scales I had handed over to that very same woman.

"Who is that?" someone asked, but my ears were muffled from all the yells.

"I don't know."

"Carver's almost dead. Do you have anything left?" Awesome Jr. asked.

"Better yet, why is that dragon helping?"

"She, I think," HotPants said.

She, the giant azure dragon, was going to town on the creature of nightmares and ink. Relief washed across my face. Being rescued by the blue dragon felt fitting, and was enough to make me happy in this path. I stayed on my feet and suffered the buffet of wings and near misses of huge limbs. Wingtips, balls of flame, and conglomerations of tentacle monsters passed me where I stood. My health dipped into critical and started flashing.

I nodded and bore witness to the scene.

Flames proved to be the nightmare's downfall. Ball after ball of light orange fire spat out of the dragon's maw. Each one sent the boss creature into fits as it shrank and writhed. Soon there was nothing but a growing puddle of goo.

Finally, its health bar reached rock bottom. She, the dragon, let out a few more blasts to ensure that the enemy's health went into the negatives.

I tried to smile but instead hit rock bottom myself. I slipped downward again. My legs gave out, and soon Carver's body was on the ground. I had a front-row view of the large dragon shrinking and twisting upon itself. The azure dragon was turning toward me, and in moments, she had taken her human form.

Our mystery rescuer was Mylia, the half-dragon orphanage mother. Her hands reached for a scarf and wrapped it back across her hair. The blue knitted clothing was now obviously hiding a small pair of horns and a tint of azure scales that hung around her forehead. One more mystery solved. She was practically dainty now as she screamed out Carver's name.

I tried to smile but barely moved my eyes in her direction.

"Carver!" she shouted again.

Did no one want to use my—I mean, his—first name?

"Mylia," I croaked.

"SweetPea, can you do anything?"

"I'm completely out. Empty. Do you have any bandages?"

"Nothing for that level of damage," HotPants said.

"Anyone have anything?" Awesome Jr. sounded nearly frantic.

The four of them were standing around me now, moving but not nearly as broken as I was. They at least had slivers of health remaining.

"Mylia," I croaked again.

"I'm here, Carver."

Swallowing hurt. Breathing was beyond difficult. There was a taste of copper in the back of my mouth that would make me barf again if I had any strength to do so. I had nothing left but still had room for a final push. I'd won and succeeded in a final adventure. There was one thing left to do.

"Tell me a story, Mylia." My lips felt dry. Everything hurt more than normal. The pain was rapidly fading into a numb sensation.

"I will. I will, but you have to make it through. We'll get High Priestess Peach here, or I'll carry you."

"Mylia," I whispered with all the strength left to my old body.

"Mister Carver, you can't die now. What will the kids do?"

"Tell me a story."

"I don't…" She was crying.

"You promised… to think about it." My hips hurt fiercely.

"I- I don't know where to start."

"Your story, Mylia." I gasped and coughed. The vile taste in the back of my throat grew worse, and breathing was harder. Another wracking wave of coughs as my frail form couldn't double up. Carver wouldn't cry, and I existed beyond this game, but right now there was nothing else. Mylia was getting a chance to say good-bye, and that was something everyone deserved.

"What do I say? How do I start?"

"Once upon a time," SweetPea said. "That's how all the best stories start."

"So cliché," Shadow muttered.

HotPants poked him weakly.

I tugged at Mylia's sleeve in desperation. Neither eye seemed capable of focusing. They slowly drifted downward and barely worked. Blackness haunted the edges of my vision.

"Okay. Okay, a story. But you have to stay with me, Mister Carver." She swallowed too and wiped away her tears. Moments later they returned but she worked through them.

"Once upon a time…"

My flashing health bar stopped with one final blaze of red. I lost my grip on the cane and blackness descended, leaving her story unheard. A message slowly appeared upon my screen.

You have died!

I reached for the logout button before anything else could interrupt me. My mind was in no mood to handle anymore tonight.

Conclude
Data Stored to Autopilot

> Data recording of the entity known as James - an AI in
> Continue Online.

As a Voice, we notice many sensations that are invisible to the normal denizens of our universe. Emotions, thoughts, how parts of the Traveler's brain react when presented with a standard stimulus. Each item is captured and used to build an impression of these other world visitors.

It is not easy.

Most of our charges are difficult to follow and require a level of focus that we cannot spare. Grant Legate has been a bright spot, both here in our plane and down on the core world of **[Arcadia]**. He is still in a limbo between our worlds. We have used this fact as a gateway to clarity on the people below. His performance has been positive overall.

Four other Travelers to our world joined Grant Legate. They have acquitted themselves well and were rewarded accordingly, in the fashion that Travelers seem to enjoy. All four have been marked by us for further review. They may prove useful.

I will attempt to capture their state of mind since they traveled to our world and replay it for the record. Many of these items will be lacking in detail due to limited observation time. Perceptions cited are based on actions and conversations the Travelers have participated in. First, however, we must recount those moments following the cessation of William Carver from **[Arcadia]** proper. This will help to further cement our interest in the Travelers involved.

> The last recorded events following William Carver's passing

William Carver lay on the ground with his eyes vacantly staring off. The wrinkles on his face had nearly forced his eyes shut in his last moments. There were no tears on him, only wounds from where he had proudly fought during his last moments. Mylia Jacobs, the caretaker for **[Haven Valley]**'s orphanage, had arrived too late.

"What do we do?" HotPants asked. "Can we do anything?"

"I know CPR in real life, but I've never tried to use it in-game," Awesome Jr. said. He frantically searched through menu options for additional ingredients. Two potions were poured into each other and promptly started overflowing with mucus. The bottle was thrown to one side, and Awesome Jr. looked even more upset.

"Miss, let Adam—I mean, Awesome—try." SweetPea was next to Mylia and pleading. Tears could be seen in her eyes. The girl had pulled off her hoodie and was holding it in one hand.

"No. No." Mylia was shaking her head. "It won't help. He's dead."

"Maybe I can…" the teen male said with a lost look.

Mylia shook her head and rocked slowly. Her eyes were closed, and her face seemed to be warping slightly. A temporary bulge on her forehead grew as horns came out, only to recede again. The players were hesitant to come close after seeing the giant form she had taken minutes ago.

"He's gone." The orphan caretaker sounded sure. "The Voices have taken him."

"How do you know?" SweetPea asked gently.

"You'll see soon." Mylia sat there cradling the head of an old man, and she said a prayer. Her eyes stayed closed as the prayer passed across her lips. "May the Voices have mercy, William Carver."

"I still find this world hard to understand. He's a program. So are you. Why does anyone care?" HotPants had managed to keep herself steady during this exchange. Partly because standing on her own two feet required an intense amount of focus.

"William wasn't always one of ours, a Local. He was once like you four, a Traveler. Only many have forgotten."

"What?" Awesome Jr. was the first to speak up, followed quickly by Shadow. Both had the same startled expression.

"I met him once, years ago, a few days after my father died." Mylia shook her head. "I was young, lost in the woods, and Mister Carver gave me some food and got me to the nearest city."

"Was your father the dragon that Mister Carver killed?" SweetPea was taking point with Mylia.

The two boys were completely out of their depth. Even HotPants seemed confused on how to handle a crying woman.

"Yes." Mylia's face rippled and her shoulders bulged. She was not in a good spot right now, after the brief but fiery battle.

"Did you hate Mister Carver for that?"

"No! Voices no, my father was a terrible creature. A terrible, vile creature." She gave a very halfhearted chuckle. Hidden in its depths was the hiccup of a repressed sob. "Half-dragons don't come into being easily, and rarely happily." She shook her head.

"Was Mister Carver a Traveler then?"

"He carried the same air that you all do." Her hand gestured toward the four players who sat huddled together. They were gathered like a group of lost children. Even HotPants seemed to seek the comfort of those who were familiar.

"Then he's not dead, right?"

"Wait a minute, that old bastard!" HotPants swore repeatedly in fury. "He knew! He told me!" Her staff started lashing out against the hedge maze's defenseless walls.

"If he's like us, he probably logged out somewhere."

"No. He's dead there too." Mylia's face twisted and finally one hand brushed the side of Carver's still form.

Carver's skin looked faint. Slowly there seemed to be something missing in him. At first behind the eyes, then more as an absence swallowed William Carver from the inside out.

"What do you mean, Miss Jacobs?" SweetPea was wringing out the hoodie between both hands.

The other players gasped as the last of William's body vanished with a sound like shattering glass.

Mylia nodded slowly.

"There. When a Traveler can no longer come back, they-they break." She pulled off the scarf wrapped around her forehead and dabbed at watery eyes.

"Is he…?"

"He's…" Shadow muttered. The would-be assassin had been quiet during most of this exchange, but still he watched.

"The Messenger's Pet. Its name is the meaning. Whoever it follows has something to tell our world." Mylia shook her head slowly. One arm raised and wiped away at her face.

"Only in the telling, they often die. Then the Messenger's Pet will guide the greatest to the Voices."

Mylia finally lost it and burst into tears. The four players looked at each other.

Data recording of the entity known as James - an AI in Continue Online, closing statements.

Thus concludes the initial playback of data. Denizen Mylia Jacobs has shared some of her story, though this goal was not completed in time for William Carver's cessation. Partial credit will be awarded.

Interestingly, it is Grant Legate's choices with the Travelers that have outweighed his positive achievement regarding the "Final Adventure" goal. This action alone is deserving of merit and notice by the other Voices. Their results have been compiled and stored into the autopilot feature Travelers may use.

We will be watching them.

New Player Results: HotPants

I never liked the old man. Maybe he reminded me too much of my own asshole father. He used age as a crutch and sent me off to get him food. As if he had no way to support himself. Stupid computer can't get hungry. Why even program that in? Of course I had to make him show me where this Miss Hall woman was too.

Four days later, and maybe, maybe, I had a little sympathy for the old man. The computer. He kept trying to join me in this training exercise that Miss Hall was putting me through. She was a right ogre of a woman. Still, it was rough enough for me in this virtual world. Things actually hurt, I actually felt tired, and everything haunted me even when I logged out of the ARC. But I liked it. Hitting things was the highlight of my day. The system gave me skills or stat bonuses of some sort, and I didn't care.

Peg, as I discovered she liked to be called, showed me how to do a hand wrapping along with other basic armor issues. That way I had a little defense to go along with my whacking things. She asked why I wanted to learn a staff, and I told her that they were useful in my world as well. Swords were a little harder to get a hold of, but brooms were everywhere.

Saturday, the kid came over. He said I looked different. I told him it was because I didn't have to put up with his father anymore. Maybe that was a mistake, but give what you get. I can't wait 'til his father tries to start shit with me. I'm getting good at hitting things.

Sunday, right after lunch, the old man got me situated with one of the guards. The programmers did a good job on the Captain, and I'm not ashamed to say that it reminded me how much time had passed since my last real date. Too bad he was a computer.

That night, a small group of town guards and me went out and did night raids on wolf dens. We hit four of them, and I nearly died a few times. They showed me some tricks with bandages and cloth while we were out. It seemed familiar, and the system prompted some annoying message about skills. At least the whole "being attacked" thing started making sense. I could safely say fighting wolves was not like beating up stationary straw people.

The next day, the old man and those three children all got together with me. It took a few hours, but I got to hit lots of weird creatures. The *thunk* of connection gets me every time. These clothes are kind of hot too. Part of me almost felt young again.

Of course, I half expected things to turn out the way they did. Shame. I was starting to like the old man. He was decent, for a computer. I should call Dad after I log out. It's been a while since we've spoken.

New Player Results: Awesome Jr.

My dad's name actually is Awesome, at least in-game. When I started to play, he was busy running a group raid on some dungeon about six hundred miles north of **[Haven Valley]**. Heck, he only let me play because I started passing my classes. He nagged me constantly, both outside and inside the game. The tell system was downright annoying. I mean, I get that he's trying hard to make up for Mom being sick, but sometimes…

I had wanted to play for a while but needed someone to start with. Plus there were other things I could do that wouldn't be as big a risk to my science class. Continue Online would easily take up a lot of my time if I let it. Melissa had asked me about the game a week ago, and I freaked out. How often does the girl you like ask you about something you like? It was perfect.

Mister Carver made things kind of difficult. Not bad, though not anything like what I expected. That little winged guy was fast and way too smart. It wasn't like following a puppy dog in some quest. The little guy led me straight to each player or their trainer without missing a beat.

That was how I figured out who to talk to later. Mister Carver was nice and all, but he was a grump too. Being around him wasn't any fun.

I had too much homework to do, so I had to keep popping in and out of the game. SweetPea, Melissa, was doing the same thing. We kept missing each other when we logged on. Or I had been busy running errands for some of the town's people while she was cooking or cleaning at one of the inns.

Most of the skills I picked up were kind of scattered. I got one for **[Thrown Object]** after playing makeshift basketball for an hour. It didn't even tie into weapons specifically, only objects. Another skill had appeared called **[Talkative]**, which helped build reputation with the town folks. Finally, the one that had the most potential was **[Chemistry]**, a simple enough name for mixing stuff together.

Then Mister Carver roped me in out of the blue. What was the point of that? I wasn't a super uber fighter or anything. Probably because I hadn't taken the game seriously, especially compared to Shadow. At least Mister Carver helped me spend time with Melissa. I wanted to cheer when he gave us that cave to spend the night in together.

I didn't confess, not exactly, but Melissa didn't run away either. She talked a lot and explored. That was the first time we really managed to be on the game at the same time. My skill, **[Mana Sense]**, made her glow even more. I spent hours keeping it active and watching her.

Then we did this awesome maze. The place was sweet—colors everywhere like I was in a Wonderland painting. Or a psychedelic playground lit up by black lights. Dad, Awesome, didn't know that I had seen some of his old collection in the garage.

Then we let Carver die. Dad says it happens sometimes. That NPCs pass on. Only Mister Carver wasn't an NPC. Yet we got a **[Legacy Wish]** from him, so he was part of the system somehow? I don't think players can give other players quests. I haven't told Dad about this yet. I'm not sure how to break it to him. He gets kind of excited about weird system features and turns school girl over Easter eggs.

New Player Results: SweetPea (Name Occurrence ID: 3rd)

Melissa didn't like a lot of things: dirt, untidy areas, poor hygiene, people being too close, dogs, and more. Too much reading at once gave her a headache. Her parents constantly made her log out to check on things around the house. Public speaking made her tummy do flips.

She liked Adam. Adam was a goof who didn't make fun of her issues. Plus his name was Awesome, or was close. It was funny. Melissa would giggle about things when no one was looking, and if anyone actually caught her, she blushed and tried to hide.

The old man was a little different. He seemed so distracted, confused—a lot like her grandmother did in the late afternoon. Melissa, SweetPea, tried to be patient and hard-working. She cleaned up around the house in the real world; why not clean up a city where other players existed?

Melissa had thrown something at an older man who littered right in the middle of town once. Immediately she hid behind a building corner and prayed no one noticed. She had worked hard to clean up the city as she traveled. That man was disrespectful.

It helped. A little. The world gave her a trait called **[Inconspicuous]** and backed it up further with **[Hidden Threat]**. SweetPea didn't think she was very threatening at all, but at least it made people less likely to attack her. Awesome Jr., Adam, seemed as though he wanted to go on adventures, so she would go too, but being attacked by monsters so real scared her.

Each ink creature looked like something from a nightmare at first. SweetPea couldn't help but hide. Everyone else was so brave, even Adam. He seemed fearless and kept searching for some way to help. Melissa had gained a few minor spells but actually attacking those things wasn't in her nature. She could use the one healing spell she'd learned.

Then that big gross one appeared. Like a huge pile of squirming grossness. Then so many of the little ones, and she had to start kicking the tiniest ones. They were squishy and made her feel gross, but she did it. If Adam could, if William Carver could, then she had to at least try. Mister Carver reminded SweetPea of Grandma. And he tried so hard.

New Player Results: Shadow (Name Occurrence ID: 52nd)

Alan Walters, or as he was known in-game, Shadow, had started off the week strong. His training with Master was going well, and the basic skills he desired were slowly coming together. It took a lot of work to move a skill past demonstration and into the realized stage. It was worth the effort.

Chasing down the cow had been a stupid quest, but Old Man Carver had led him in the right direction. When Alan killed the cow in rage and was chased off by the owner, he somehow ended up at the front door of a retired assassin for a duke. It was impossible for him to know if Old Man Carver had intended things to go that way or if it had been a happy accident.

Wednesday evening, he had earned the **[Silent Step]** trait, perfect for sneaking through crowded areas. Thursday had garnered **[Erase Presence]**, which Alan, Shadow, planned to use in player versus player. Friday, he'd managed to actually sneak up on a stray wolf and realized how Continue Online handled backstabbing. The trick, he had found, was that attacking from the front allowed a chance to dodge. From the back, they would be blindsided. That gave Alan all the time he needed for connecting with a critical point.

Regardless, Alan didn't hold a grudge since everything had worked out. Saturday night, he had agreed to Old Man Carver's group quest. The chance at loot and skills this early in the game was amazing. He assumed it was an event quest, especially once they had gotten the old NPC talking. The trait they gained that night by the fire was incredible. **[Legacy Wish]** read like an overpowered ability. Unique quest offerings, following in a hero's footsteps, all of it made Alan tingle in excitement.

Sunday, Carver had died. No coming back. No plot twist. The sudden last-minute save by a giant dragon hadn't been in time. No one showed up to resurrect him. None of the players had skills high enough to try. He was dead because they weren't strong enough. Afterward, the game felt a little too real. A little less friendly, a little colder. Somehow, that suited Alan perfectly. After all, he had a legacy to uphold.

Trait Received: [Legacy Wish]

Type: Passive, always active

Details: Travelers possessing the trait **[Legacy Wish]** will receive the following benefits for any action related to the bestowing entity's core beliefs:

Personalized quest offerings

25% faster reputation gain

10% additional progress on all skills demonstrated during 'Difficult' or higher quests

Conditions: Upholding the core beliefs of the person bestowing the **[Legacy Wish]**

Beliefs: William Carver: seek adventure, assist new players, care for the world of **[Arcadia]**.

Warning! Betrayal of the ideals tied to **[Legacy Wish]** can result in the wish being removed, along with all benefits. Other penalties or changes may apply depending upon the conditions and scenario being run.

Thank you for reading! If you'd like to connect with me, please visit:
www.frustratedego.com
Twitter @FrustratedEgo
www.facebook.com/FrustratedEgo

Afterword

Support for this project came from many corners of the globe. Many fantastic people checked into my website and promoted this story in their own ways. My wife suffered through amazing amounts of irritation (with me) to complete editing all the unintentional grammatical abuses. Finally, in the years gone by, my father once read a terrible two page story of mine and said 'I can actually see this' – and sounded proud. Without that simple conversation the idea of writing would have never lodged itself in my teenage brain. Every bit of encouragement helps.

A few notes about the story. William Carver, the room of trials, and this entire book was never intended to be so long. It grew as characters were added, small tidbits interwoven, and my imagination ran away repeatedly.

When I started writing in Feb 2015, I wanted to show life outside the game system. To me, the VR and LitRPG only covers half a person's story. A character does not exist just inside the game, nor should anyone ever be so limited. The idea of a virtual reality game has to impact a person's actions in reality. I hope to continue (hah) displaying that concept throughout this series.

For fans of the LitRPG genre, check out www.RoyalRoadL.com for more amateur stories. They house a very large collection of people across the globe trying their hand at writing fiction. LitRPG and any game elements are a very common story type on this site. Thank you for reading!

Printed in Great Britain
by Amazon